WRECKER

WOLVES OF IRON VALOR MC BOOK 3

DEX HAVEN

UNDER A TEXAS SKY PRESS

Copyright © 2025 Dex Haven

All rights reserved.

This book is independently published by the author. No part of this book may be copied, reproduced, stored in a retrieval system, or transmitted by any form or by any means, including electronic, mechanical, photocopying, recording, or otherwise, without prior written permission from the author, except for brief quotations used in reviews or critical discussions. It also may not be used for training AI programs.

This is a work of fiction. Names, characters, places, and incidents are either products of the author's imagination or used in a fictitious manner. Any resemblance to actual persons, living or dead, or actual events is purely coincidental.

The author acknowledges any trademarked status and trademark owners referenced within this book. The use of these trademarks is not intended to convey sponsorship or endorsement by the trademark owners.

For inquiries or permissions, please contact:

mailto: dex@dexhavenauthor.com

Website: DexHavenAuthor.com

DEDICATION

Mean Man

At the end of the day, it's the laughter that's my favorite.

PREFACE
A NOTE TO READERS

In the worlds I build, it's always the women who win.

Not because the monsters are soft or because the odds are ever in anyone's favor. Sometimes, the darkness comes for them. But there's a point—a turning, a clever twist in the shadows where the women realize how much they love the darkness. They don't mind when the monster doesn't ask permission. Where the love comes laced with danger, pain, or a hunger bigger than the two of them put together. You read about women who make the wrong choice and never regret it. You read about the men—who take what they want, and in taking, turn the woman into someone new. You see yourself in those pages, even if you don't tell anyone.

There are people who will say you shouldn't like this. That you should be ashamed of what you want. That wanting to be ruined, or devoured, or loved so hard it bruises is a sickness. You and I know better. Shame is for people who take life too seriously. For the rest of us, the dark is where we finally get to take off the mask and breathe.

In these pages sometimes, the women do the saving. Sometimes, they burn the world down and build something better from the bones.

Keep reading, darling. Keep wanting. There's no darkness that can hold you for long.

If you are a person who is triggered, please trust your instincts before reading. A list of trigger warnings may be found on my website: www.dexhavenauthor.com

Contents

Trigger Warnings   X

1. Chapter 1   1
Parker

2. Chapter 2   10
Wrecker

3. Chapter 3   19
Parker

4. Chapter 4   27
Wrecker

5. Chapter 5   34
Parker

6. Chapter 6   41
Parker

7. Chapter 7   50
Wrecker

8. Chapter 8   59
Parker

9. Chapter 9   71
Wrecker

10. Chapter 10
     Parker   80

11. Chapter 11
     Parker   90

12. Chapter 12
     Wrecker   100

13. Chapter 13
     Silas Drake   109

14. Chapter 14
     Parker   118

15. Chapter 15
     Wrecker   129

16. Chapter 16
     Silas Drake   141

17. Chapter 17
     Parker   149

18. Chapter 18
     Wrecker   161

19. Chapter 19
     Parker   173

20. Chapter 20
     Wrecker   183

21. Chapter 21
     Parker   194

22. Chapter 22
     Wrecker   204

23. Chapter 23
     Silas Drake   214

24. Chapter 24
    Parker   224

25. Chapter 25
    Wrecker   234

26. Chapter 26
    Parker   246

27. Chapter 27
    Wrecker   258

28. Chapter 28
    Parker   270

29. Chapter 29
    Wrecker   285

Epilogue   297
Big Papa

Thanks for Reading   310

Also by Dex   312

My Thanks   313

Trigger Warnings

All of my books contain graphic intimacy, and likely some kind of violence (sometimes sexual)—but always with a triumph-centered resolution. Guaranteed HEA. I don't believe in giving away the journey before it begins, but I believe in honoring your peace. If you know certain topics are hard for you, I encourage you to trust your instincts and read with care.

That being said, I thought it was important to note that there are a couple of scenes in Wrecker that include stalker themes, dubious consent, abduction, graphic violence, graphic intimacy, and BDSM themes. If this is painful or triggering for you in any context, I do not recommend you continue.

A complete list of warnings can be found on my website: www.dexhavenauthor.com

CHAPTER 1

PARKER

My life had somehow turned into a colossal shitshow, starring my twin.

"You're not even listening, Parker." He beat a track through my living room, all the way from the front window to the edge of my coffee table and back again. His boots trailed dirt across my new rug, but I gritted my teeth and didn't say anything. "I'm trying to explain how bad it is."

"You said they'll kill you." I clicked my tongue and let my gaze slide from Axel's pointy jaw to the barely touched cup of coffee in his hand. "You've said it ten times tonight."

He huffed and set the mug down too hard. Liquid slopped over the rim, spattering the tabletop with oily crescents. I twitched, but didn't bother cleaning it up. "You're being a bitch. You know that?"

I did. I was. I reached down and picked up the tiny bundle of fur that was resting on top of my feet. My little rescued doggie with a face only a mother could love. His tongue hung slightly beyond his under-bite, those blue eyes begging for the bowl of cereal I'd abandoned on the same coffee table.

"What do you think, Rocket? Am I being a bitch?" One ear flopped up.

"Rocket disagrees. He wants to know how *I'm* the asshole when *you* got me into this mess with the Greenbriar freak-show?"

He spun around, arms out. "I can't believe you got a fucking dog, Parker! Now? You have people who might actually come after you! They said—fuck, Parker, I don't know what they said, I was drunk—just that they needed someone with skills. Like hacker skills or something. I told 'em I knew someone, okay? That's all."

A pause, heavy with the implication that "knew someone" was something I should be proud of.

I scratched behind Rocket's ears and waited. Axel could never outlast silence; I'd weaponized it since we were kids.

Finally: "I'm dead if you don't do this. You know Silas. He'll make it hurt."

"Cry me a river." My voice came out flat, but inside, something hot and sour burned holes through my guts. "You act like *I'm* not dead if I *do*. Anyway, I found this little guy lying next to a dumpster, Axel. Just because nobody gives two shits about me doesn't mean I should treat other living things the same way! Besides, he fucking makes me happy!"

Axel collapsed into the armchair like someone had un-plugged him. He pressed his palm to his forehead and sat there, quiet for once, soaking in my bright house with all the resentment of a man allergic to nice things.

He started up again after a minute. "You don't get it. You think you're so fucking smart, with your fancy computer job, but you don't get the world at all. Everything is a trade. *You* just pay up with numbers and code instead of cash or blood."

There it was, the old twin spite. I shook my head. "That's bullshit. I fucking work for what I get." I was getting agitated, causing Rocket to squirm.

"It's okay, buddy. He's just jealous."

He leaned forward. "Really? You think I'm jealous of *you*? You really think Iron Valor would give a shit if you died? You were always the tag-along. Only reason they ever acknowledged you was out of pity after Mom and Dad croaked."

That one hit. Maybe it was true. At least I was still living my life. It might be a small life, but it was on my terms. At least, it had been until now.

I looked down, running my fingers through fur. The first time I'd ever been caught hacking I was seventeen, cocky, wanting to get a boy to notice me. I'd hacked into our high school's grading system and changed his AP history grade. Wrecker had been called in for IT support, and he found me in the back corner of the library where I was still at it. I wanted to see what other parts of the server I could get into. I'll never forget seeing his shadow fall over me as I sat in the carrel in the corner. He was impressed with my work, and that's what saved me. He just told my parents I needed some direction. They died the following week.

I never told Axel about that. He'd just have been pissed I'd gotten away with it.

He still sat there, waiting. I gave him nothing.

Axel's next words crawled up my spine like centipedes. "Just do the job. You're almost done, right?"

"Almost." I let the lie hang between us, let it thicken the air. In truth, I'd finished two days ago. I'd written the exploit, siphoned off the funds, cracked Iron Valor's accounts wide open and left them bleeding credits into an offshore shell that would take even Silas's best forensics team months to follow. And then, because I had no sense of self-preservation, I'd written a backdoor that let Iron Valor trace it all back to me and from me to Greenbriar. Iron Valor was my pack, even if they'd never forgive me for this betrayal.

He ran his hands through his hair, and for a moment, the desperation on his face made him look twelve years old again. "You said you'd help me, Parker."

"You're my brother." I shrugged. "That's what family does. Even if the family sucks."

He snorted. "You always did think you were the only good one."

I stood, holding Rocket closer to my chest.

"I've spent every hour of the last week crawling through code laced with traps designed by *Iron Valor's enforcer*. You think they won't trace it back to me? You think Wrecker won't burn this whole place down with you inside if he figures out what I'm doing? You want me to move faster?" I said, voice sharp. "Fine. But don't pretend I'm doing this for you. I'm doing it so I don't have to watch them carve you up and feed you to their dogs while you scream my name."

Rocket sneezed.

I looked down at his absurdly cute face. "You're right. That was dramatic."

"This isn't a joke, Parker."

"No. But *you* are."

He opened his mouth, but the look in my eyes must have been enough. He shut it again.

I walked him to the door, the whole way thinking how easy it would be to shove him down the steps and make it look like an accident. But I didn't. I just held the door open pointedly and waited.

He hovered at the threshold. "They're gonna know, you know. Iron Valor. They'll know it was you."

I stopped. "You sound like you're hoping they take me out. You're a real piece of work, you know that?"

He hesitated, looked like he might try to say something soft, brotherly, a last-ditch appeal to our shared blood. But I didn't give him the chance. I slammed the door so hard it rattled in its frame. I felt the impact all the way through my bones. I knew that no matter what, I'd still save his ass when it came right down to it.

The silence after Axel left was deafening. It sat on my chest, dense as smog, and I almost welcomed it.

I put Rocket in his little bed next to the couch. For three seconds, I imagined myself as a cartoon of a happy person: queen of her own place, no one to answer to, no idiotic brother in tow. The illusion held for exactly as long as it took to cross to the kitchen and pour a finger of whiskey into a Waterford highball glass. Me in a pair of yoga pants, and a hoodie with the words 'FUN GIRLS READ SMUT' in hot pink emblazoned on the front, my short brunette hair with a riot of wild pink highlights slightly shaved over my left ear; I was nothing if not classy.

I knocked back the alcohol and shivered as the fire burned its way down. Outside, the sky was a sickly navy of early winter. The neighbors' Christmas lights twinkled in the distance. I should have gotten a tree and pretended I had a reason to celebrate the season.

I didn't want to think about Greenbriar, or Axel, or what the hell I was going to do when Iron Valor found out about the hack. But I *did* think about the other thing. The thing from the other night. The man in the mask.

I picked Rocket up and slowly slipped onto the couch, this time with a large glass of wine in my other hand. "Hey little guy, you've got a Class-A nut job for a mom, you know that?" He answered by licking my face. He was so cute.

I replayed every detail in my mind.

"Let me tell you why," I murmured, scratching behind the floppy ears of my little wheels-off rescue sprawled across my lap. His tail thumped twice against the couch cushion. "So there I was, coming home late from Amarillo—coding disaster, brain fried, you know the vibe. And immediately, I smell..." I paused as he twisted to gnaw on my thumb, inkblot paws batting the air. "Oak. Citrus. Like fancy cologne, but... wilder. Like if a Christmas tree punched a tiger."

Rocket sneezed, shook his head, and stared up at me with clear blue eyes. "Yeah, exactly. Weird, right?" I kept my voice breezy, though my fingers tightened in his fur. "I did the usual checks—closet, couch, bathroom—nada. Security panel green. But something just felt off, you know? Of course, you don't know. You were living next to a dumpster a couple of days ago. Just, trust me on this.." His nose bumped my wrist, demanding pets. "So I started checking things. Sock under the bed, check; dresser neat and undisturbed, check!"

I scooped him closer, burying my face in his puppy-smell of grass and kibble. "Checked everything after; jewelry, safe, fridge. I think he even checked out the family pic magnet." Rocket nibbled my sleeve. "He had to have seen the stalker romance book on the table, too. How's that for irony? I was about to give up. Everything looked...normal. So I thought, backyard."

Rocket yawned, a tiny squeak escaping him. "Don't judge," I muttered, kissing the tuft between his ears. "I turned on the deck light. And there he was, big as a dump truck, Rock. Black clothes, mask. And he just waved. Like we were old pals." The puppy cocked his head, ears askew. "And get this—I froze. Like a dumbass first girl to get the axe in a slasher movie. Heart flatlined. But also..." I grimaced.

Rocket rolled onto his back, belly up, tongue lolling. "Ugh, fine." I gave him tummy rubs. "Yes, masked massive cryptids watching me from my window are a major turn-on for me. Always have been. That's why I read so many dark romances, and listen to so many creepy podcasts." He pawed the air, blissfully clueless. "Can I help it if I'd love for a strong stranger to come in and take away all my choices for once? I'd like to have someone else in charge of what happens to me sometimes. Your owner is completely broken, buddy." And damned if a tear didn't escape my eye.

He wriggled free, skidding off the couch to chase a dust mote. "Yeah, run, buddy. Smart move." I watched him pounce, tail helicoptering. "Worst part? Once I calmed down, I recognized his scent. Wolf. Male. Familiar. And my wolf..." I trailed off, staring at the ceiling. "Didn't hate it."

Rocket trotted back, a squeaky toy clamped in his jaws. "Point is," I sighed, plucking the slobbery duck from his mouth, "I'm my own brand of disaster. Fangirl of toxic book boyfriends, weak for giant creeps in knit masks..." His head tilted. "But hey, you're cuter than him."

He barked once—sharp, decisive—and flopped onto my feet.

"Yeah, yeah. Cuddles fix everything," I muttered, flicking a glance at the fridge magnet. He'd looked at it. At my family. Rocket snored softly, paws twitching in a dream. I wished I could conk out immediately like that.

And somewhere in the night, I realized I wasn't scared so much as fascinated. I knew I had no real reason to be frightened. I was a wolf, after all.

I left the puppy sleeping on the floor and went back to my office nook. I had to look at my camera logs once more just to be sure I hadn't missed anything. There had to be some kind of proof that he'd been here.

I pulled up my home network's logs, running the usual scripts to check for anomalies. I found dozens. Whoever he was, he'd been inside my router, inside my goddamn baby cams, not just snooping but erasing. A proper professional job—no logs, no traces, not even a misaligned timestamp. I should have been angry. Instead, I felt a sick, grudging respect.

I scrolled through video footage, hoping for a glitch, a shadow, anything. The loops were perfect. There was no sign of the man in black, not even in the hours I was home and awake. All I saw was myself pacing and searching.

That should have been the end of it. Shut the laptop, pour another drink, move on. But I couldn't.

Every time I tried to close the feeds, I felt that mask lurking at the edge of my vision. The white circles for eyes, the slit mouth. The way he'd raised his hand in greeting, as if he'd known I was watching, as if he knew exactly what it would do to me.

I told myself it was just a threat display. Standard shifter intimidation tactic. But the more I replayed it, the less I believed that.

I was still at the desk when the desire hit. It wasn't sudden, like a knife; it seeped in, slow and venomous, starting as a spark in my belly and then spreading, rotting away the rest of my good intentions. I'd always been a control freak, always kept my sex life in neat boxes. I liked toys and solo missions because they did what I wanted, when I wanted, and there were never any messy expectations.

But the image of him—impossible, unreal—set something inside me on fire.

I tried to ignore it. I even made it to my feet, crossed my house to the kitchen and started another cup of coffee. But every step was heavier, and by the time I called Rocket and reached my bedroom, I was already undoing my hoodie, peeling it off like it was soaked in sweat.

I sat on the edge of the bed and stared at the far wall. My hands shook as I slid my leggings down, careful not to let the fabric snag on my skin. Even in the stillness, the memory of the masked stranger pressed against me, hot and electric, as real as the bed beneath me. Rocket lay in his plush bed in the corner of the room, snoring away.

I grabbed the new vibrator from the drawer—a last-minute present to myself, still in its little pouch. It was charged and ready. The buzz was soft, almost shy. I laughed at myself, a dry, broken sound.

I leaned back, legs spread, and let the toy rest against my underwear. At first, I pretended I was just taking the edge off. But the fantasy came in hard: he was on the deck, watching. He slipped inside, moving with that bear grace, leaning over me, mask in place.

I pictured his hands, big enough to palm my face. The smell of him, oaky and alive, flooded my senses until I could barely breathe. In my head, he wasn't gentle. He pressed me down, held my wrists, made me open for him.

I moaned, surprised at how loud it was in the empty room. I didn't care. I pushed the toy under my underwear, wetness slicking the silicone. I imagined him kneeling over me, one hand gripping my thigh, the other teasing me until I begged.

I went faster, pulse staccato in my neck. My other hand snaked up under my sports bra, pinching my nipple hard, the way I never let anyone else do. The pressure built fast and mean.

Right as I came, I bit my lip to keep from screaming. The orgasm was sharp, blinding, but faded quickly, leaving a raw ache in its place.

After, I lay there, panting; the toy buzzing quietly in my fist. The mask was still there in my mind's eye, but now it was smiling for a different reason.

I tossed the vibrator onto the bed and rolled to my side, arms wrapped around my chest. I wanted to cry, or maybe just sleep forever. A tear escaped, and I quickly wiped it away. There was nothing left to do. My life was a disaster: my twin betrayed me, my stalker kink had become a reality, and I had no hope of a future. And the packs would come for me sooner or later. But for tonight, I'd found peace where I could. And I'd survived another day.

CHAPTER 2

WRECKER

At seven sharp I slid into the war room—second floor, right off the kitchen, because Bronc liked to keep his enemies and his caffeine close. The walls were hung with yellowed maps and an old Texas flag, cracked along the blue field from a century of neglect. The table in the center was a plank of oak, maybe the only original thing left in the compound, its surface carved with a thousand knife scratches and at least two bullet holes.

Bronc was already there, elbows on the wood, palms steepled. Arsenal and Doc flanked him, both in full leathers, neither looking like they'd slept. Gunner, the new enforcer, loitered near the window, his hands jammed in his pockets, eyes fixed on the horizon. Big Papa was there, carrying peace with him, a black coffee steaming in his huge mitt, the other hand flipping through a Bible as if there'd be an answer in the margins.

No one talked. Even the house had gone quiet, the overnight crowd either gone or passed out in a corner.

Bronc nodded at me. "Wrecker," he said, "you got something?"

I slid into the chair opposite him; the vinyl creaking under my weight. I let the silence build, then set the thumb drive on the table and nudged it across.

"They got the best to fuck us over, that's for sure," I said. "They're bouncing signals off a dozen nodes, some I didn't even know existed. Took a minute to get a bead, and when I did..." I thumbed the drive. "I don't understand why, but the one doing it used to be one of us—Parker Reid."

Arsenal's eyebrows flicked up, but he didn't say a word.

Doc scratched his jaw. "Axel's little sister?"

"Twin," I said. "She's got a degree in comp sci, apparently used to run black hat ops for Amarillo State back when she was a sophomore. After their parents died, she went on to Texas Tech and then went off-grid for a while. She'd been working legit corporate jobs and doing corporate contracted IT for the past year. That's where the money is." I shrugged. "She's good. Not as good as me, but close enough to make it interesting."

Bronc leaned forward. His eyes had that cold, glassy edge they got before a fight. "Why now?"

I shook my head. "Doesn't make sense. She's not hurting for money—her house is paid off, she freelances for three Fortune 500 companies. But she's been poking at our perimeter for a few weeks. Not subtle, either. Almost like she wants us to catch her."

Big Papa set his cup down, careful not to spill. "Maybe she's trying to send a message."

"Maybe," I said. "It's possible she's wanting us to find her breadcrumbs."

Bronc nodded, absorbing, gears turning behind the eyes. "Who else knows about this?"

I snorted. "Just us and whoever hired her to do it. I covered the tracks, salted the logs. If you want to keep it in the family, we can."

Doc looked up, eyes sharp. "What do we do about her?"

I shrugged again. "She's working for the people who are fucking us over. The end game is finding out who and why. Ghosting her might be the best way to do that."

Arsenal grunted. "I say we bring her in. See what she wants."

Bronc shot him a look. "And if she's tight-lipped? Won't talk?"

Arsenal smiled, all teeth and old wounds. "Then we make her."

A silence fell, thick as oil. The only sound was the ticking of the wall clock, the second hand stuttering on the twelve.

Bronc turned to me. "You sure it's her?"

"Yeah," I said. "IP addresses don't lie, Bronc."

He nodded once, then again, like he was getting ready to kill a man he used to call a brother. "We do this clean. No heat, no blowback. Set it up, Wrecker. Do whatever you have to do to find out who the hell she's working for. Any means necessary. I'm fucking tired of this shit."

Gunner shifted by the window. "What about Skeeter?" he asked. "He's growing old in that cell."

Bronc waved it off. "I'm about ready to deal with that little prick as well."

I raised a hand. "It's clearly time. Let's knock off that easy problem."

He smiled, but it was the kind of smile that meant nothing. "By all means, let's."

Meeting adjourned.

The rest filed out, one by one. Only Bronc lingered, tapping a finger on the table.

He waited until we were alone, then leaned in. "What does your gut tell you, Eli?"

I shook my head. "She's not doing it for cash. This is too dirty. She doesn't need the money to be involved in something this underhanded. Plus, this doesn't fucking seem like something she'd do. She comes home every month for the Moon Run. Then she all of a sudden, wants to betray us? Something smells. If they have a hold on her, it's personal."

He grunted. "Axel?"

"Maybe. Or maybe she started hating us for some reason. Can't think of a reason why. We were fucking aces to those two."

He laughed, a low, humorless laugh. "Shit, if she's in the 'hates Iron Valor' camp, she needs to take a fucking number."

We shared a genuine, if not an ironic laugh at that.

"Whatever the reason, I'm gonna find it."

We gathered at Skeeter's cell at the Iron Valor jailhouse late in the afternoon. He'd been locked up for about three weeks now. We'd planned on making this situation short and sweet, but then Menace had to go fight and die, then get not so dead, then get himself crowned king of the Midwest. That took some time to shake out. But here we were, finally confronting Skeeter about just who the fuck he was working for.

Skeeter totally looked the worse for wear. He was scared, and he fucking well should be. He'd been stealing from our Alpha for fucking months. He'd tell us why, or he'd pay for it with his life. The cot in the corner of the cell was filthy, and on it he sat, looking old and defeated.

"J'come to finish me off? See you brought all your men. Too afraid to face me alone?" He sneered at Bronc.

Bronc just shook his head. "If you wanna just run your mouth while you can, don't guess I'll stop you. I'm holding all the cards here, old man."

He clearly wanted the opportunity. "You motherfuckers," he wheezed, spitting onto the floor. "You got no idea what you're up against."

I'd joined him in his cell and let him finish, then put my hands on his shoulders. "I do, Skeet. I know exactly what I'm up against. I've been up against it since I was old enough to walk." I leaned in, voice low. "You know what I *don't* know? Why you'd choose to go against a pack you spent your entire life with?"

His head jerked, a twitch of pride or pain, impossible to tell. "What's it matter? You're all dead, anyway. No one beats who I'm working with."

Gunner stepped up, jaw set, arms crossed. "You might wanna think about our track record you dumb fuck. Iron Valor hasn't ever been beaten."

"This ain't like before," Skeeter said, and grinned, blood leaking from the crack in his lip.

I paced in front of him slow, deliberate. The air was cold and stank of oil and fear. The chill of the Texas panhandle winter was just settling in, but what I felt was the wet chill of something bad about to happen.

"Let's play a game," I said. "You tell me who paid you, and I let you walk out of here with all your fingers."

He snorted, a wet, ugly sound. "Fuck you, Wrecker."

I didn't argue. I just backhanded him, hard enough to ring his ears. He spat teeth and blood onto the floor. "Fuck you," he said again.

Arsenal grunted, but kept his place. Gunner flinched, but he was new. He'd learn.

"Listen," I said, dropping to a knee, so we were eye to eye. "I don't have time for this. You're not gonna talk, not because you're brave, but because you're a coward and you know what your puppet master will do if you roll on them." I let that sink in. "But I'm here to tell you that whatever they got planned, I can do worse."

He looked away, jaw clamped.

Skeeter's lip curled, his voice sharp as a blade in the thick silence of the pack jail. "You call this leadership?" He jabbed a finger toward Bronc, who stood motionless near the cell entrance, his jaw taut. "Kidnappings, an outsider becoming Luna, infighting—all of it's on you. Liam Senior would've spit at the sight of what you've done. We needed a real Alpha after he died. Someone who'd earned their scars, not some pup playing at power." His gaze swept the room, daring others to meet it. "Should've been me stepping up. At least I wouldn't let one of our daughters get snatched, then not be worth squat when she came back until she couldn't even stand to live in her own body anymore."

"Enough." The growl ripped from my throat, low and thunderous, my body a wall blotting out the light in the room as I stepped forward. The air turned rancid with the reek of challenge, my fur prickling beneath human skin, ready to burst.

Skeeter's sneer flashed, all teeth and stupidity. "Or what? You'll lick his boots harder? Face it—Bronc's a failure. Always has been. His old man knew it too. Why else would he waste time salvaging strays instead of—"

The world sharpened, then dissolved into red.

I was a storm. A snarl shredded my lips as I lunged, claws slicing free. Skeeter's smirk died in a gurgle as I pinned him to the wall, stone splintering under his skull. "You don't speak his name," I hissed, vision bleeding gold, fangs grazing his pulsing throat. "Liam Senior saved me. Gave me a pack. A brother." My claws dug deeper, blood blooming hot beneath them. "Bronc's worth ten of you. And I'll peel the skin from your bones before I let you spit on that."

Bronc's voice lashed behind me. "Wrecker! Stand down—now!"

But the past howled louder—dank foster rooms, empty bellies, the beast gnawing at my ribs. Liam's calloused hand on my shoulder. Bronc's grin as we wrestled in the pines. Family.

Skeeter choked, fear sour on his breath. "He's—he's not even your blood—!"

"He's everything." My fist snapped sideways, crushing his jaw mid-sneer. The pack swarmed, howling, but I was feral, untouchable—a whirlwind of teeth and rage.

It took three of them to haul me back, Bronc's roar finally cleaving through the chaos. "Enough! Enough."

I stumbled, lungs heaving, Skeeter's blood slick on my knuckles. Bronc's stare hit me like ice—Alpha, brother, anchor.

I bared crimson-stained teeth at my team. "Anyone else got something to say about Bronc?"

The silence tasted like victory.

I nodded at Gunner. "Lesson one, Gunner. Don't beat your informants almost to death. Unless they really piss you off."

Gunner nodded, face tight.

Skeeter was barely conscious, head rolling, blood pattering onto the floor.

I turned to Gunner. "That's how you know when to stop," I said. "When they stop making sense, or when they can't remember their own name."

Gunner stared at Skeeter, then at me. "Should we... call a medic?"

"He's not worth it," I said. "He's a warning to anyone else who wants to play both sides."

Arsenal dragged Skeeter's limp body, let it drop in the corner. Gunner stood uncertain until I clapped him on the shoulder.

"You did fine," I said. "Next time, don't let the punk get in your head."

He nodded, swallowing whatever rookie bullshit was still stuck in his throat.

I looked down at Skeeter, blood pooling under his cheek. "You had your shot, asshole," I said, mostly for myself. "Now it's someone else's turn."

I wiped my hands on my jeans and walked out, the echo of my boots bouncing off the tin walls.

Outside, the dawn was gray and empty. Hands still shaking, I closed my eyes against the first light of morning.

Bronc looked at me sideways. "Guess he's a dead end? So to speak."

"Parker's the answer." Just saying her name twisted my gut. "I'll get every bit of information we need out of her." I told him as I made my way to my bike.

He shook his head. "Something tells me that's not all you're gonna get out of that girl."

I shrugged. "I'm taking everything I can get from her." I told him as I put on my helmet and slammed down the kick starter on my bike and pulled out into the street.

The door slammed behind me as I kicked off my boots, the silence of my own damn house a relief after the bullshit with Skeeter. Only been here a few months, but already I couldn't stomach the thought of crawling back to the pack house. Too old for that circus—the constant scent of strangers, the hollow laughter, the parade of women who'd never stick around long enough to learn my last name. Not that I'd give it to 'em.

But lately... fuck. Watching Menace and Bronc get all moony-eyed over their mates had dug under my skin like a splinter. Didn't help that Parker's face kept flickering in my head, sharp as a blade. That woman was trouble wrapped in spandex. I'd planted cameras in her house and was quickly becoming obsessed with watching her. I felt like some kind of psycho, but fuck if I cared.

I grabbed a beer from the fridge, the hum of the security feed already pulling me to the screen. Before I could rewind to watch her morning, I saw her on her back deck playing fetch with what had to be the ugliest dog I'd ever seen. Goddamn if watching her laugh didn't do something to me.

I'd rewound to her morning—Axel slinking into her place, all smarmy charm. Her twin. My jaw locked as I watched him toy with her. That slimy bastard spinning lies about debts, about owing him. Parker's fists clenched, her voice cracking raw, and something hot and vicious coiled in my gut. Axel sold her out. Dragged her into Greenbriar's mess. Of course it was them. Those pricks had been wanting revenge since Menace killed their Alpha years ago.

The fact that she knew doing this was going to get herself killed made me want to punish her in the most painful way. She was willing to sacrifice herself for her good-for-nothing brother. And he sat there as if she owed him. She's got to know there is no way for this to end in her favor.

I skipped the feed to later in the evening. Parker downed two glasses of whiskey, her throat working like she could burn the day away. Then she stumbled into her bedroom, yanked that new vibrator from her drawer—the one I'd wanted to see in her hands—and fuck, my blood went molten watching her. Hips arching, teeth biting into her lip to stifle the sounds. Should've looked away. Didn't.

But then she went still. Tears streaked her cheeks, silent and awful, and I nearly cracked the screen, gripping it. You don't cry after an orgasm. Not like that. Not like the world's caved in. That hollow look in her eyes—it punched me harder than any alpha's fist.

Now at least I knew she wasn't a true traitor. Axel's visit proved that. I should've been furious. Instead, I had to think of a way to keep her safe not just from Greenbriar but from Iron Valor also.

CHAPTER 3

PARKER

I woke to something warm and insistent licking my cheek. In a better life, maybe it'd have been a lover's mouth instead of Rocket's sandpaper tongue. But his scrunch-faced grin was its own kind of salvation.

"Breakfast?"

He launched into a tornado of joy, paws skidding on hardwood. For a heartbeat, I forgot the vise tightening my chest. Forgot the clock already ticking in my skull.

By noon, dread had settled into my bones. My monitors glared like triple suns, bleaching the room. The system taunted me—a labyrinth I'd designed myself, now twisted into snarled knots. Every path I tried unspooled into traps, walls slamming shut the moment I brushed them. Wrecker's fingerprints were everywhere: phantom tripwires, bridges crumbling mid-step. My code had been elegant. His was vindictive.

ERROR: Transaction Flagged.

The alert burned crimson. Eighth time. Ninth. Tenth. Each failure carved deeper, until I tasted copper where I'd chewed raw my cheek. This wasn't coding—it was surgery with a chainsaw, hacking blindly at the tumor of my own miscalculations.

Rocket whined, pressing his muzzle to my knee. I choked back acid laughter. Thirty-six hours since Greenbriar's last "reminder." Two days before, they'd come for more than threats. Before Rocket's sad eyes met strangers at the shelter.

I tried brute-forcing the maze's heart. Smashed through proxies like tissue walls, only to find Wrecker waiting—a ghost in the machine. His countermeasures bled through the code, liquid mercury slipping through grasping fingers. My hands shook as I triggered the killswitch protocol, hovering over the key that would burn it all.

Who protects him when I'm gone?

The phone buzzed—Greenbriar's silent scream. I drank merlot straight from the bottle, the bite weaker than my shame. Rocket slept curled against my shin while I mapped exit routes on trembling fingers. Every dead end glowed neon: Failure. Fraud. Fool.

Deep in the monitors' cold light, I saw Wrecker's triumph—smug and effortless—while I unraveled stitch by stitch. My breath fogged the screen as I slumped forward. Not smarter. Just hungrier. And hunger, it turned out, couldn't outwit annihilation.

When Rocket licked the salt from my wrists, I didn't push him away.

"Fuck," I muttered, jabbing the Enter key so hard it left a crescent in my fingertip. Rocket popped his head up at me from his bed across the room. The system clock glared: 3:08 PM. I'd been at this since 9:00AM, fueled by cold coffee and unchewed antacids. I could still taste blood from where I'd bitten the inside of my cheek.

I was losing. I didn't know how to lose.

I typed out a new script, each keystroke sharper than the last. I recited each line aloud under my breath, like a spell, sweat crawling along my scalp despite the chill in my little house. The script built and compiled. I launched it, then shut my eyes tight, bracing for the result.

My chest caved in. I stared at the message for a long time, refusing to blink, as if I could will it into something different.

"Not happening," I whispered. "No fucking way."

I snapped the mouse across the screen and brought up the secondary shell, one that even my employers didn't know about. I opened up the command line and typed in a suicide protocol—erase everything, burn the logs, salt the earth. If I couldn't have the win, I'd scorch it behind me. That was the rule.

But as I hovered over the Y/N confirmation, my vision blurred and my hands finally shook, violently, as if the muscle memory was betraying me too.

The phone buzzed. Not a call—just a silent notification. I didn't need to check to know it was another reminder from Greenbriar. Deadline. Payment. Or else. I ignored it.

I tried the sequence again. I made a tiny change, a single character, an off-by-one error so minuscule it was almost invisible. Maybe the difference would get me through. I exhaled through my nose and ran it.

ERROR: Transaction Flagged. Duplicate Routing Detected. Contact Security.

This time, I didn't scream or punch the table. Instead, I let the air leave me, slow and empty, as if my lungs were made for sighing and nothing else. I glanced around the house—the dead plants on the windowsill. I felt bad about those. Guess I'd be joining them soon.

I was supposed to be smarter than everyone else. That was my thing. Now all I could think about was how cold my sweat had gone, how quiet the house was except for the soft tick of the wall clock, and how I'd run out of ideas. My poor pup. Who would take care of him?

I dragged myself up from the chair and stumbled to the kitchen. I made a sandwich in total silence, hands moving like they were remote-controlled. Deli turkey, a slick of mustard, cheese. I crammed the sandwich into my mouth and chewed without tasting. My hand found the corkscrew on the counter and tore it through the cork on another bottle of merlot, dark as an old bruise. I poured Rocket his dinner. It's not his fault my life was fucked.

"I'm so sorry, little guy. I thought I was doing you a favor by picking you up from that dumpster. I didn't realize my own life was going to turn into its own dumpster fire. You deserved better than me." I picked him up and cried into his fur. I gave myself a three-minute pity party. Then I stood back up to get back at it.

Back at the desk, I poured a glass full to the rim, sipped, then drank it down in three quick swallows. My throat burned, but it barely touched the fatigue eating through my skull.

I stared at the error message, daring it to change, but it never did. I tried to imagine Wrecker's face the moment he'd realized it was me behind the breach. Did he even blink? Or did he just keep typing, faster, relentlessly, until there was nothing left for me to do but give up?

I rolled my head side to side, joints popping. The clock read 5:14 now, and outside the windows the sky had gone that blank, pale gray that meant another day had been thrown in the trash. I finished my sandwich in two more bites and chased it with another glass. My stomach rolled, but I kept swallowing.

I tried again. And again. Each time, the same digital slap to the face.

I wanted to cry some more. Instead, I got up and let Rocket out one last time. When he came back in, I turned off every light in the house, one by one. I left the monitors burning blue, the only thing lighting the room as dusk caved in. I stood for a long time in the center of the living room, staring at nothing, letting the waves of failure crash and break and recede.

When I finally slumped back into my chair, I just stared at my hands, watching the tremors work their way from the pinky up to the knuckles. I'd always believed that if you worked hard enough, you could win any game. But sometimes you just lose, and the only thing left was to face it.

The glass was empty, so I filled it back up. My phone buzzed again, and again, and I shut it off without looking.

The darkness pressed in on all sides. I let it and drank and waited for the next wave.

I peeled myself from the desk and grabbed the half-empty wine bottle around the neck, fingers numb and clumsy. The living room was twilight dark, only the faint spill from the monitors guiding me to the hall. Each step sounded too loud, like the house was listening for weakness.

The bathroom light was surgical, an interrogation bulb that showed every flaw in my face. I set the bottle on the counter and stared at myself: twenty-five, blue-black circles nesting under both eyes, cheekbones sharp from skipped meals, skin pale enough to see capillaries spidering just below the surface. I looked like the kind of woman who didn't know how to sleep, or maybe just never got the chance.

I took a quick shower, shaved all the areas that hadn't been lasered, washed, and conditioned my hair. I felt a little better when I'd dried off. The mirror insisted I was older than yesterday, older than ever, and a hell of a lot more tired.

Even though my hair was cut in long layers on top, it was pretty short overall, so it was easy to towel dry. I brushed my teeth mechanically, slow strokes, the taste of old coffee and metallic fear refusing to budge. I spat, watched the foam slide down the drain, then caught myself in the mirror again. I put some lip balm on my lips to help with how cracked they were. That was about as good as it got.

I poured another glass of wine and watched it swirl and settle. The first gulp was huge, a mouthful that left me light-headed and buzzing. I wiped my mouth with the back of my hand, then topped off the glass again.

My hands moved with a certain efficiency as I dropped the towel. My thighs looked unfamiliar, marked with faint bruises I didn't remember getting. I pulled an old, oversized t-shirt from the hook behind the door and yanked it on. It hung past my hips, swallowing the curves that were desperately hanging on. I took the wine and my phone, then padded the few steps to my bed.

I tucked Rocket into his bed in the corner closest to the headboard. He was snoring in minutes. My bed was still unmade from last night. I crawled in, tucked the comforter under my chin, and propped my phone on my chest. I scrolled through reels, half-watching the endless parade of smiling faces, prank videos, girls with perfect eyeliner showing me ten ways to fake confidence. The light from the screen was too bright, but I didn't look away.

Every few minutes, the anxiety punched through: images of men in leather jackets, of Bronc's pale stare, of Iron Valor's brand burned into my skin. I imagined their faces when they found out it was me. I pictured what Wrecker would do if he ever caught me. Maybe he'd just walk away. Maybe he'd tear out my throat. I tried to guess which would hurt more. He'd been a mentor to me when I was young. Of course, I had a massive crush on him. A lonely seventeen-year-old girl and an older man who was more beautiful than he had a right to be. But he spent time with me when he could. We'd meet in the library on the public computers. He taught me about code and how magical it was. It was a language all unto itself. And here I was betraying him with it. Fuck. I was the worst kind of person.

I scrolled faster, thumb cramping, desperate for anything that would drown out the noise in my head. I drained the rest of the wine, felt it punch through my gut and leave a heavy warmth behind.

At some point, the phone slipped from my hand. I lay there, eyes closed, the room tilting and spinning in the afterglow. My last conscious thought was that maybe I'd wake up and it would all be a bad dream, maybe the hack would have worked, maybe I'd be the one with the last laugh after all. Maybe I'd be dead.

But even as I drifted off, I knew it wasn't true. The blue light flickered on my closed lids, a warning beacon.

I slept, but I didn't rest.

I woke to the sound of a growl—not a dog's, not even a wolf's, but something low and wet, dredged up from the pit of a nightmare. My body shot upright before my brain caught up, lungs stuttering on an inhale. Darkness packed the bedroom, so dense it ate the light from the alarm clock, turning it into a useless blur.

My heart hammered against my ribs, begging to be let out. I blinked hard, scanning the room. Nothing at the window, nothing at the door, just the stench of cheap wine and old terror crowding the air. I waited for the noise again, breath tight in my throat.

Silence. Then a whisper of movement, a scrape of cloth on carpet. The hair along my arms lifted, and my inner wolf went rigid, alert and drooling at the end of a chain.

I slid a hand under the pillow, fingers curling around the heavy flashlight I kept there. I waited. Maybe I'd imagined it. Maybe the neighbor's mutt was at it again, or a raccoon rooting through the trash outside. I convinced myself of this for exactly two heartbeats before the darkness beside my bed moved.

It moved.

I clutched the flashlight harder, then forced myself to speak, voice thin and reedy. "Who's there? Rocket, you okay?"

Nothing. Then, a man's silhouette—huge, broad-shouldered, the kind of bulk that filled the doorway even without setting foot inside. He stepped forward, and as he moved, a glint of white teeth and two holes for eyes resolved out of the black. A mask: white eyes, skull grin. I recognized it instantly. I'd seen it before, in the sick little fantasy that haunted me every night since the incident on the deck.

He stood at the foot of my bed, arms relaxed, head cocked, like he was watching a lab rat try to chew through the bars.

The wolf in me yipped, confused: fight or fuck, it couldn't decide.

He stepped closer, boots silent on the wood. I flung the flashlight; a desperate, stupid move. He caught it out of the air with one hand, twisted it until the plastic casing shattered, then tossed the pieces onto the carpet.

I tried to scream. Nothing came out but a squeak, a rabbit sound.

He leaned over me; the mask filling my vision, teeth stretched wide. He ran a gloved finger down my cheek, slow and careful, then wrapped his whole hand around my throat. He squeezed, not hard, just enough to let me know that I was his now, that he owned the next few minutes or hours or days.

His voice was dark, buzzing through the mask. "Your dog is fine. He's in the guest room with a juicy bone. Are you frightened, little bird?"

I nodded my head.

He pressed my back into the mattress, hand tightening just a fraction. "Good," he said. "You should be."

He let go of my throat and ripped my shirt over my head. Then, pushed me back down. Cold air slapped my skin, and I realized with a bolt of humiliation that I'd slept naked under the shirt, nothing between me and the world but a thin layer of cotton and my own stupidity.

He looked me over, a slow inspection, and even though the mask hid his eyes, I could feel them roving up and down my body.

"Look at you," he said, voice like rough silk. "So perfect."

He traced a finger from the hollow of my throat to my belly button, then lower. The sensation was electric, all nerves and panic. I lay perfectly still, breathing fast, not sure if I wanted to run or pull him closer.

"Spread your legs for me, Wren." His words were simple, but the command in them was absolute.

CHAPTER 4

WRECKER

She looked at me, teeth bared. "Get off me."

"No," I said, and meant it as I tightened my hand around her throat. "You're not in charge here, little bird."

She tried to move my hand, then opened her mouth to shout. I pushed her back and clamped my palm over her lips, pinning her head to the pillow. My knee came up onto the bed, my weight pressing her down.

"Shhhh," I said, and the sound filled the room like a blade in the dark. "You're in no position to be chirping at me, Wren. You want to keep that mouth open? I can fill it with something." She shook her head violently. "Then keep it shut for me. Can you do that?"

She glared daggers. But she nodded, slow, and when I took my hand away, she stayed quiet.

Smart girl.

She looked up at me, lips pressed tight, but there was a challenge in her eyes that tasted like defiance. I wanted to rip it out of her, see what would happen if she stopped pretending to be strong and just let herself break.

I gripped both of her wrists in my left hand and raised her arms over her head as I leaned over her, running my gloved hand down her side, slow and deliberate. She squirmed, but didn't say a word. I could see the flush rising up her neck, a red line drawing itself over her collarbone.

"Look at you," I said, voice low and mean. "Just a little bird, caught by the big bad wolf. You like this, don't you?"

She shook her head, but the heat in her face said otherwise.

I traced her hip, then dipped my fingers between her legs. She was soaked. I pressed down, slowly at first, then harder. She bit her lip, hard enough I thought she might draw blood. I kept going until she started to shake, her knees trying to close, but my hand was too strong.

"Want to know why I'm here, Wren?" I said, leaning in until my mouth was just above her ear. "Because you're stupid enough to think you can outsmart me. You want to win. But the thing is, little bird, you can't. You're not as good as me."

She gasped, and the sound shot through me like whiskey in an empty gut.

I raised my gloved fingers to her face. "Look at this. I know your deepest, darkest secrets. The ones that you thought nobody knew. I know how much you want to let go. To let a stranger take control of you." I put my fingers in my mouth. "You taste as delicious as I expected. Open your mouth. Finish cleaning my fingers, Wren."

Her eyes went as big as saucers as she clamped her lips down tight.

"You've already earned punishment. Don't make it worse for yourself, little bird."

She swallowed hard, and slowly I saw her pink tongue reach out between her lips to my fingers. She lightly licked and then sucked my fingers until they were clean. I could have come in my jeans at the sight.

I let go of her wrists, sat on the side of her bed, then rolled her over onto my lap. "Now there is the matter of your punishment. You know what this is for Parker." I brought my palm down on her bare ass. Once, then twice, until the skin turned hot and red. She yelped.

"Count," I said. "Loud enough for me to hear."

She hesitated, then: "Slap. One!" Then she cried out, "I don't understand!"

"You do!"

I hit her again.

"Two! I don't!"

"You're a smart girl. It'll come to you."

Again and again, until she was sobbing and half-collapsed over my knees. I gave her 10 hard slaps. I stroked her hair, gentle now, and murmured: "You're playing dangerous games little bird."

She was shaking, the tears hot against my thigh, but when I slid my hand between her legs again, she arched into it. I fingered her slow, steady, until she bucked and came with a moan that was almost a wail.

I turned her face to me with my left hand as she still lay over my lap. I licked her wetness off my glove, watching her face as I did.

"Next time," I said, "it'll be my tongue diving into your tiny, dripping cunt, Wren. You think about that when you're alone in this bed."

She squeezed her eyes shut, like she wanted to disappear. Skin glowing, breath coming in sharp, ragged bursts.

I pulled her up, sat her on my lap, and brushed the hair out of her eyes.

I reached for the glass of water on the nightstand and held it to her lips. She drank slowly, still dazed.

"You did well, little bird," I said. "Took it like a fucking champion."

She glared at me, but she leaned into my chest. There was no fight left. I held her for about half an hour until she was dozing off. I tucked her back under the covers, gentle for the first time all night. She curled up, silent. Within a minute, she was asleep, body still trembling with aftershocks.

I stood, went to the guest room and picked up that silly dog who licked me all over my face. "Take it easy there, pal. I'm taking you back to your mom." I slipped him back into his bed with the bone I'd brought for him. He curled around it and promptly dozed off.

I watched Parker for a long time, then slipped out as quietly as I had come in.

Outside, the night was still waiting.

I grinned behind the mask, and let myself disappear into it.

The next day was Saturday, and the clubhouse buzzed with bodies—Juliet, Ms. Pearl, Bronc's sharp-tongued sister Maddie, and a handful of women who kept glancing my way like I'd hung the goddamn moon. Their laughter prickled my skin; their perfume cloying. My wolf snarled low, restless beneath my ribs. *Not her*, it growled. *None of them smell like her.* Parker's absence clawed at me even here, even now.

Since we were all here, it was a good time to debrief. Bronc gathered us all together, then called the meeting to order, slamming a fist on the table. "Toy run's on Christmas day. We need routes finalized, gifts sorted."

His voice was gravel, but my focus fractured. Two women lingered near the door, whispering, their eyes darting to me. One flicked her hair, smiling like she'd practiced it. My jaw tightened. Sad thing was, I couldn't remember if I'd ever slept with her or not. I'm not proud of it, but I'd had a run at more than my fair share of women around here.

Doc leaned over. "You got a fan club workin' at the back of the room, looks like."

"Hell if I even know their names. That's the fucked up part of it." I laughed. "You'd think they'd have more pride than that, since I clearly never gave them a second go at it."

He just shook his head. "You'll never be accused of being a gentleman, Wrecker."

"Hey, I guaran-fucking-tee I never made one promise to any of 'em. If they expected something more, that was a delusion they created in their own minds."

Bronc gave us both the stink eye. "Anything you two sons of bitches wanna share with the class?"

"Not anything you'd have any interest in hearing. Uh, sir." I added with a grin.

He shook his head with a chuckle. "Then shut the fuck up and pay attention, how 'bout?"

I gave him a mock salute.

When the details drained into arguments over wrapping paper and pickup trucks, I jerked my chin toward the back office. Bronc nodded, and the team followed—Arsenal scowling, Ghost silent as smoke. I shut the door hard.

After everyone was seated around the table, I started right in. "First off, I stopped the flow of any funds leaving Iron Valor coffers going anywhere we don't expressly want. I know the who and why now as well. Parker Reid *is* our hack. There is no question."

Every face had looks of hurt and anger all over them.

"Now, as far as getting to the why. Her slimeball, piece of shit, twin brother Axel dragged her into this. Sold her out, more like," I said bluntly. I opened my laptop and pulled up the video from the camera I had put in her house. The screen on the wall suddenly had the feed. The video glared out at them.

Axel's face appeared big as life: "I'm dead if you don't do this. You know Silas. He'll make it hurt."

Then Parker's reply: "Cry me a river. You act like *I'm* not dead if I do. Do you think when Wrecker figures out that I'm the one who did this, he's not gonna burn this whole thing down and me with it? I'm just doing this so Silas doesn't cut you up into tiny pieces and feed you to his dogs while you scream my name."

Axel's laugh came through the speaker. "Iron Valor doesn't give a damn about you. They never did."

Arsenal lunged forward, palms slamming the desk. "And that excuses her selling us out? Burn her. Now." His rage hung thick, but my own flared hotter.

"You think I don't want to tear someone apart?" I snarled, stepping into his space. My wolf surged, teeth bared. "She was scared. Stupid, loyal, and scared." The admission burned my throat. I'd replayed that video a hundred times—the tremor in her voice, the way she'd flinched when Axel spat Greenbriar's name. "She should've come to Bronc. Should've trusted us. But fear makes a fool of everyone. She did leave a backdoor open for me to get through. She *wanted* us to find this. She's one of the best hackers I've ever come across. If she'd wanted to keep me out, she could have. I'd have gotten in eventually, but not this quickly. So you need to fucking back off."

Bronc's hand clamped my shoulder, yanking me back. "Enough." His glare silenced Arsenal first, then pinned me. "You're soft for her, Wrecker. Fine. Use it. Get close, play nice. If she's tangled with Silas and Greenbriar, we get to them through her."

The order landed like a blade. Arsenal scoffed. Doc, Gunner, and Big Papa stood. I felt their support. But Bronc's stare held me. "Do you have a handle on this, Eli?"

"Did *you* have a handle on Juliet?"

He shook his head. "That's fair."

"Bottom line, brother, do you trust me?" I held his eyes.

"With my life." He told me, his confidence clear.

"I swear, I won't let you or this pack down."

"You need help, you tell me."

I nodded, the weight of Parker's secrets and my own damn weakness digging deeper. My wolf whined, torn between her betrayal and the need to keep her safe.

CHAPTER 5

PARKER

I awoke to the now familiar feel of fur and doggie kisses. "I got you, buddy. Just gimme a sec." I could not get my eyes open. I felt like I was coming up through black water. There was an ache deep in my hips, blooming down both thighs, hot and sweet and humiliating. A weight was suddenly dropped on my chest. "What the hell?" I caught the smell first. My eyes were trying to focus on the remnant in my hand. "A bone?" The reason for the ache in my hips came back in a rush. *A nice juicy bone.* I sat straight up and threw the bone across the room. "Shit, shit, shit!" Twenty seconds Rocket dropped the bone back in my lap, standing up against the side of my bed.

I peeked through my hands, which now held my face. His silly ear stuck straight up as he waited with anticipation for me to throw the bone again. "Did the big bad man give you this bone last night, buddy?" The tilt of his head was so precious it was almost enough to make me not want to die from the memory of the stranger's hand striking my ass over and over. I flopped back down onto my pillow. "Ugh! What did I *do*, Rocket?" My arms and shoulders were sore, as if I'd spent all night wrestling with a demon. And maybe I had.

I forced myself upright again. A cold, neutral light filtered in, falling over the chaos of the bed. My comforter was half-off;

one corner of the fitted sheet jerked loose. I was naked, which wasn't unusual, but the state of the room made it different. I took inventory: no blood, no bruises worth the name, but there were finger imprints along my right side where someone had gripped me tight enough to leave a map.

The man in the mask—the one I'd seen at the window, then imagined stalking my sleep—had crossed the final boundary. Had touched me, held me, left me shaken but not broken. I looked down at my little pup, who was probably wondering why I wasn't getting dressed to get his breakfast. "Why am I not more freaked out, Rocket?" I dragged myself out of bed and started to get dressed. I should have been terrified. Instead, I found myself humming with a new and terrible electricity. My wolf was almost purring. What was that about?

He had made me come, not with the slow tenderness of a lover, but with the deliberate efficiency of a musician tuning a guitar. It had worked. Even now, the ghost of his leather-covered hands hovered over my skin, turning every inch of me into an antenna. I traced my ribs with one hand and shivered, remembering the pressure of his grip.

My ass was tender. He'd fucking wailed on it. Punishment. For what? He said I was smart enough to figure it out. No sign of him now, except for that damn bone. That and the glass of water he'd pressed to my lips after. Even the water tasted different, as if the glass remembered him better than I did.

I should have called someone. I should have been angry, or afraid, or at the very least ashamed. But I wasn't. What I felt was closer to relief, a slow uncoiling of something that had been knotted inside me for years.

I padded to the bathroom and flicked on the light. My reflection looked back, not as a victim, but as someone who had gotten exactly what she asked for. My face was flushed, the marks on my neck already fading to yellow. I smiled, then grimaced, then smiled again. It was all very confusing.

I threw on a pair of joggers, a sports bra and sweatshirt. My socked feet skidded along the hardwood as I made my way to the kitchen. Rocket waited patiently by his bowl. Such a good boy. "Who's a good boy? You are? Yes, you are. Such a good, good, boy." I showered him with praise as I filled his food bowl. My hands shook as I made coffee, but not from fear. From anticipation, maybe. Or just the thrill of knowing there was someone out there who wanted me badly enough to take what he wanted. And to give me what I needed.

While the coffee brewed, I powered up my laptop. I had to see if I could fix this mess. The screen flickered, then spat out a series of system alerts I hadn't seen before. For a second, I thought the hack had gone nuclear, but it was just an update request from the network diagnostic tool I'd left running overnight.

I powered my phone back on. So many missed calls. I was the walking dead. It immediately rang. Fuck. Axel.

"Hello, brother dear."

"WHAT THE FUCK, PARKER?"

I had to hold the phone away from my ear. He was shouting so loudly.

"Axel, calm down. What's up?"

"Silas Drake is gonna kill you."

That got my attention, because Silas Drake could very well do that. My life was shit anyway. I looked down at Rocket. My heart hurt. I really didn't want to leave my new little dog. But I might not have a choice.

"Axel, I'm working on the code right now. This isn't as easy as making a pivot table in Excel you know."

"No, Parker, I don't know. All I know is you ignored five calls from Silas yesterday. You're lucky he didn't just send someone to your house yesterday to end you."

"Well, if he'd ended me yesterday, he'd never get Iron Valor money, cuz I'm the only person who can do it, if it can even be done."

"Well, guess what, sis? You've got a meeting with Silas in two hours. You have to come to him."

"Fuck Axel. I don't want to come to Greenbriar pack territory."

"Well, then you should have answered your fucking phone yesterday. You'd better have answers for Silas when you come."

"Fine. I'll be there."

I hung up the phone and logged in, checked the dummy account I'd created to siphon funds from Iron Valor's mainline. Shit! Last night's transfer had gone through! No sign of interruption, no alerts from the receiving shell. I allowed myself a slow exhale, then checked the backup script. Everything looked tight.

But then I looked closer. There was a discrepancy in the timestamp—a ten-minute gap that shouldn't have been possible. I checked the raw logs. In that window, the server should have pushed a confirmation ping, but the packet never appeared. Instead, there was a double-entry—a packet that arrived from my end, then bounced back as if the server was faking its own output.

I ran it again, this time with a different credential. The anomaly was still there. Not a bug, not a hardware fault. A counter-hack.

I stared at the monitor, my heart stuttering in my chest. If Wrecker had found me, really found me, it would be a miracle if he didn't send someone to my house to drag me out by the roots of my hair. Unless he has already set that plan into motion.

"Rocket, I'm doomed." A tear ran down my cheek as I picked up my little goofy dog, his bottom teeth protruding a little more than the top, his tongue hanging out. "I'm sorry buddy. I wanted to make your life better. Looks like I won't be around to make that happen." I had to figure out what I'd do with him. It might be a mistake, but I'd send an email to the Iron Valor Luna. I'll just ask her to take him and make sure he gets a good home in the event that she hears of anything happening to me. I'd heard she was someone you could trust. I set him down so I could find the words to type.

I flinched, expecting to see the black mask in the kitchen window, or behind me in the living room. But the only thing there was the pale morning light and the chill that wouldn't leave my bones.

I leaned back in my chair, rubbed my wrists where the marks he'd left were brightest. I thought about last night, about the way he had taken me—no, not taken, that wasn't right—about the way I had given in. It was unlike anything I had ever let myself imagine. I was a control freak, a rule maker, a girl who could get herself off with two fingers and a cheap toy in under three minutes. But last night, I'd let go. I'd let *him* decide what happened, and the world hadn't ended. In fact, it had gotten better.

I tried to focus on the work, but my thoughts kept looping back to the man in the mask. The way he'd spoken, the way he'd touched me. I'd never met anyone who could make me feel in danger and safe at the same time. I prided myself on being a giant when it came to intellect and independence. I liked being in control of my situation. But not last night. I'd put myself in a stranger's hands. And the unrestrained freedom that came with that was enlightening. No one had ever managed that trick, no matter their size. It went against every instinct I had.

The coffee finished brewing. I poured a cup and then added a splash of cream. I saw from the dirty tan color that I hadn't added enough, but I drank it anyway. My hands were steadier now. I needed to figure out what I was going to tell Silas. He would want to know the progress of the hack, and he wouldn't want to hear about setbacks. He'd want results. He wasn't exactly patient.

I went into the bedroom closet and stared at my clothes. I had to be careful about what I wore. Nothing seemed right. I didn't want to look too good. I didn't want to look weak either. I pulled out a plain black hoodie, one size too big, and a pair of dark jeans. A pink tee and an older pair of Docs completed my nondescript look. If I went too far, Silas would know I was deliberately trying to look off-putting. He was no fool.

My hair was no problem. It's my favorite thing about myself, if I'm honest. Full and wavy, with just a little bit of product in my palms, a quick fluff and my locks swept to the side in short and long chunks, pink highlights mixed in with the natural brunette color. I'd risked having my stylist take the razor and shave the left side of my head with a guard, so it's pretty close over that ear. Looking at myself, I laughed at the lie I told the world. The one that said I'm edgy. Quirky is closer to the truth.

I sat on the edge of the bed, staring at my feet. Rocket trotted over to me as if he wanted to comfort me. To tell me there was one living being on the earth who cared if I lived or died. I picked him up and nuzzled him under my chin. I'd let my memory drift to last night, reliving every detail. The sting of my jeans rubbing against my ass made it unforgettable. Then the way he held me so gently after. Has anyone cared for me like that ever? Not since my mom and dad. Not that I can remember.

I checked my phone. No more calls from Silas or Axel. I had about fifteen minutes before I needed to be on the road. My stomach twisted with dread. I put the phone down, then picked it back up and stared at it. For a second, I wanted to text the masked man. To say thank you, or fuck you, or just to see if he'd respond. But I had no number, no name, nothing except the memory of his voice in my ear.

"You're not in charge here," he'd said. But he was wrong. I was always in charge, or I had been up until last night.

"Ok Rocket, enough cuddling." I put him on my bed and headed to the bathroom and brushed my teeth, avoiding my reflection. I grabbed my bag, threw in my laptop, grabbed my Sig P238 from my desk drawer and put it in its special pocket then zipped it shut.

I let Rocket out the backdoor so he could take care of his business one last time before I headed out. At the door, I paused and looked at my little dog not knowing if I'd ever see him again. He must have sensed my emotions as he ran and jumped into my arms. "Hey buddy, I'll be back as quick as I can, okay? I'm gonna try my damnedest to come back to you. I promise." I set him down and quickly wiped the tear that had escaped my eye. I went through the routine of locking doors and setting the alarms and heading out. The cold waited outside, but I didn't care. I was ready for it. I could handle anything.

CHAPTER 6

PARKER

The drive to Tulia from Plainview cut through pastureland so flat the wind could shear the paint right off a car. I pressed the pedal harder, trying to outpace the sick feeling in my stomach, knuckles bleaching out on the steering wheel. Every mile marker was a countdown to something worse. The dashboard clock said 8:14 a.m., which meant I had exactly forty-six minutes to deliver a decent excuse to a pack of sociopaths and pray they let me keep all my teeth. I kept the heater on low even though the temperature outside read in the high teens. I liked the cold, the way it made the inside of my head go numb and hollow.

The outskirts of Greenbriar territory looked abandoned, half the buildings shuttered with plywood or missing windows altogether. In the daylight, you'd mistake it for one of those fake towns the government built for bomb tests. At night, it looked exactly like what it was: a graveyard for the unlucky, the dumb, or the doomed. I was a little bit of all three.

It stood to reason that Greenbriar hid their wealth. They didn't want to bring attention to the fact that they made the kind of money they did on all of their enterprises. The fact that they were likely worth close to a million dollars or more would surprise every pack in the country. They wouldn't reveal their wealth until they wanted to use it for some nefarious purpose I'm sure.

I braked at the turnoff for the pack territory entrance, the front gate a welded latticework of razor wire and repurposed Harley parts, more art than architecture. There was no sign, but the security cameras were newer than anything within twenty miles. I flashed my headlights three times and waited for the metal gates to part. They did, slowly, like a mouth opening for a very small snack.

I parked in the visitor slot, doors angled away from the main building—two stories, no windows except for slits you could barely fit a crowbar through, much less a body. I almost turned back, but then I thought about Axel. About what Silas would do to him if I flaked, and about what he'd do to me also. I killed the engine and forced myself to sit there a full minute, rehearsing the speech I'd patched together on the drive. The bank's fail-safes are evolving. I'm in, but they may be on to me. I'm searching for a different approach. Iron Valor will bleed out, I'd make sure. I just needed another week. I repeated it until it was as real as the frost building up along the bottom edge of the windshield.

Inside, the air reeked of hot metal, sweat, and the kind of mildew you get from never once opening a window. The secretary was a guy in a Greenbriar crewneck, missing two fingers on his left hand and all the joy on his face. He grunted when I said my name, then thumbed a button under his desk. For a pack that I knew had amassed over a million dollars in ill-gotten gains, this place was a dump. Maybe it was made to look that way, so pack members wouldn't want to know where their fair share was.

"Silas is waiting," he said, and didn't look up again.

The inner office was all cinderblock and fluorescent lights, the hum of the ballast louder than the heater running at full tilt. Silas sat behind a large metal desk, hands steepled, his shaved skull glinting under the blue-white glare. He might have been handsome at one time, but years of hate and hard living had destroyed anything attractive about him. He wore a black t-shirt, sleeves straining against muscled biceps that showed off his heavily tattooed arms—lines and angles that coiled down his veined forearms. His barrel chest showed from under the V-neck of his shirt, tattoos disappearing into the solid, tar-black beard that ate half his face. His eyes were so dark they barely registered as having pupils.

He didn't stand. He didn't need to.

"Sit," he said, pointing to the lone wooden chair in front of his desk. The word had the finality of a coffin lid.

I took the chair across from him and scooted it up to close the distance. The desk between us was neat but had spots of what could have been motor oil or blood, but I put my hands on it anyway, palms flat, nails bitten to nothing. I put on the best air of confidence I could muster. Never let 'em see you sweat and all that.

"I don't like it when people don't take my calls, little girl." His voice was like sandpaper.

The term "little girl" was not said in a manner that was playful. He was dressing me down. Putting me in my place. I grit my teeth.

"No sir. I would imagine you don't. I apologize." I was trying to sound contrite and not like the smart ass I felt like being. "I was just in the zone trying to work out the code needed to get your job done as efficiently and quickly as you require." I swallowed hard, hoping he would buy that. The real reason was I hated his fucking ass and would rather have my nose hairs plucked than have to hear it.

He relaxed a fraction. "I appreciate your commitment to excellence. Your reputation said you were the wolf for this job. I trust you won't let me down."

"I'm doing my best."

"So, you got something for me?" Silas asked, one eyebrow ticking up.

I met his eyes. "The bank's got new protocols. Some kind of anomaly sensor. They flagged the first two transfers as internal errors, but now they're watching the servers every night. I'm having to write new code every time. It's slow, but it's working. Iron Valor has to be feeling it by now."

He laced his fingers, and the tattoo on his right hand—a wolf's eye, inked into the webbing between thumb and forefinger—seemed to stare straight through me.

"How slow?"

I swallowed, then lied: "I can try to move ten grand tonight. I cannot guarantee that it will go through. I can try for more if I risk exposure, but—"

"You're not here to tell me about risk, little girl. You're here to solve problems. I understood you were the person who could *do* this." His jaw tightened.

"I *can*," I said, and hated how fast the words came. "But with new protocols, security is adapting more quickly than in the past. If I push harder, they'll see me."

He grunted, a sound that might have been a laugh if you were generous. He took a pen from the desk, spun it around his knuckles like a magician, then pointed it at me.

"I've got men to handle exposure," he said. "What I need is someone who doesn't cry wolf the second shit gets real."

I kept my face still. "I'm not crying anything. I'm telling you what's happening."

He stood. It wasn't a big movement, but it put him over me, a wall of flesh and ink and hard-earned rage. "You're telling me you can't do it?"

"No, I'm telling you, if you want this done to get the maximum amount of money from those accounts, you have to give me more time."

He leaned in, hands on either side of the desk, eyes inches from mine. His beard was so thick it caught the light like velvet, every hair a threat. "You want more time, you better make it count.

Because if this thing tanks, Axel's not the only one who's going to pay for it."

I stared at him. His breath smelled of coffee and cinnamon. His hands were so big that his fingers seemed to cover half the desk's width. His fingernails were painted black.

My heart hammered in my chest, but my voice held steady. "It won't tank. I just need a few more days."

He was so close I could see the pockmarks of old acne scars on his scalp. He smiled, but it wasn't sincere. "That's more like it."

Then, just as suddenly, he backed off, dropping into his chair. The metal shrieked under his weight.

I fished in my hoodie pocket for the note I'd written out, the new protocol for the next phase of the job. I slid it across the desk, watching as he flicked it open and scanned it. He grunted again, less annoyed this time. "In case you were curious, that's the new protocol I'm running."

He flipped the note back at me, then said: "What about Skeeter? You hear from him?"

I shook my head, honestly this time. "Not in a while. He went dark after that last run."

Silas's face didn't change, but the air in the room did. He tapped the pen on the desk, the click loud as a pistol shot.

"Find him," he said. "He's not smart enough to run, but if Iron Valor finally made him, I need to know."

"I'll do what I can to track him," I said, because saying no wasn't an option.

He studied me for a long second, then did something I wasn't ready for. He smiled. His teeth were so white they looked almost fake.

"You're good at your job," he said, his voice softening. "But I need you to remember who you work for."

He slid his hand across the desk and let it rest on my forearm. The grip was gentle, but the heat of it radiated up to my shoulder.

He dragged his index finger up my sleeve, all the way to my bicep, then back down.

"I don't want to lose you, little girl," he said. "You're too valuable."

The way he said it, I couldn't tell if it was a threat or something worse.

He let go and sat back. The silence stretched, and the only sound was the fluorescent ballast humming overhead.

"You can go," he said.

I nodded and stood, my legs a little unsteady. He watched me the whole time, eyes half-lidded, like a predator bored with the chase. At the door I paused, but he didn't say anything else.

I made it all the way back to the car before I let myself breathe again. When I closed the door, I had to sit there for a couple of minutes just to keep from throwing up. My wolf was frantic, smashing itself against the inside of my chest, desperate for open air.

I started the car, cranked the heat, and stared out through the windshield as the ice defrosted. The gate was still open. I could see the security camera still watching me.

I took a long, slow breath, then put the car in drive.

He said I was valuable. I believed him.

But I also believed what he'd said would happen if something went wrong.

I felt like crying, but I wouldn't. What good would it do? I was still alive, and that was all that mattered.

It was past noon by the time I hit the Plainview city limits. I knew I should just go home, lock the doors, grab Rocket and crawl under a blanket with a bottle of whatever, but something in me was buzzing—hungry, unsettled. My stomach still rolled since I left Silas's office, but it wasn't fear now; it was something closer to anticipation.

My groceries had dwindled down to nothing, and my wine stock was gone as well. And there is no way I could make it without liquid courage, so I stopped at the small local grocery store close to my house. I felt it before I saw it: a shadow, tall and wide, moving behind the rack of magazines near the window. I didn't turn my head, just kept walking, but every step I took was mirrored by another, silent and steady. When I bent down to pick up a bottle, I caught the reflection in the glass: a man, big as a barn door, standing perfectly still, watching me.

My pulse stuttered, then quickened—not with fear, but with a kind of slow, excited calm. I wasn't alone in this store. I wasn't alone anywhere, not anymore. I paid for the groceries, barely registering the exchange, and kept my eyes fixed on the reflection in the cooler door as I left. The man was gone, replaced by my own pale, wide-eyed face, breath fogging the glass.

Outside, the wind had picked up, tearing down the length of the parking lot and making the empty flagpole clatter like bones. I loaded my stuff into the trunk, one eye on the side of the building where the man had vanished. Nothing. Just the parking lot and local people loading groceries into their cars.

I got in the car, shut the door, and for a long time just sat there, hands locked around the steering wheel. I didn't want to leave. I wanted the man to come back, to fill up the space with his silence and his impossible size. I wanted him to make the next move. What the fuck had my life become? I used to be relatively normal. I had a job, a couple of acquaintances. I did regular things, went out to dinner, went out to bars, and now? I sat in a damn parking lot looking for a stalker that I hoped would visit my house while I waited for another madman to kill me. Fucking movie of the week material there.

When my secret masked stranger didn't appear, I started my car, pulled onto the main road, and aimed myself toward home.

The sunlight played at the edges of the trees, sliding past like the walls of a moving coffin. At the turnoff for my street, I slowed, rolling past the neighbor's empty horse field, the wind flattening the brown grass in waves.

That was when I saw him again. Just a flicker in the rearview, but enough—a shadow on a motorcycle, crossing the empty road behind me, moving with the precision of someone who'd mapped every inch of this land before I was born. I slammed on the brakes, heart skidding with the tires, and watched the mirror. Nothing. Just the afterimage of him, burned into the glass.

I sat there, engine idling, until my breathing steadied. I checked the rearview again. The world was as empty as before. I was losing my ever-loving mind.

I pulled into my driveway, killed the engine, and waited. For a minute, maybe more. I waited for the man to show himself—maybe on the porch, maybe by the side of the house, maybe right up against the glass where I could see the outline of him, huge and calm and waiting for me to open the door.

But there was nothing. Just the afternoon sun, and the cold, and the familiar beat of my own pulse in my ears.

I grabbed the bags, walked up the steps to the porch, and paused with the keys in my hand. The front door was locked, just like I'd left it. The world was quiet. My wolf was pacing behind my ribs, just beneath the surface of my skin, desperate for something to run from or toward. I could hear Rocket barking inside the house.

I let myself in and was greeted by my little ray of sunshine doing endless circles. I locked the door behind me and quickly set the bags on the counter. My little man needed my attention and I'm sure needed to pee, so I took him to the backyard.

"There you go, sweetie. Go potty." He took off across the yard, looking for just the right spot to do his business. I couldn't help but scan the perimeter of the yard, sniffing the air for that oak and citrus scent that had already faded from the stranger's visit last night. Nothing. How fucked up was it that I was disappointed that my stalker hadn't been to my house while I was gone? Rocket ran back up to the deck. Such a good boy. We came back into the silent house. Every shadow in its right place but I couldn't shake the feeling that the man was already inside, waiting for me to find him. My imagination was really doing a number on me.

"Rocket, did your new friend come and see you today?" I asked him as I did a lap of the house. He followed right on my heels as I checked each room. Living room, clear. Kitchen, empty. Office nook, untouched. Bedroom, cold and still. "Looks like you were on your own today." His head just tilted left and right. I picked him up and gave him a squeeze. "You are just the sweetest thing."

I wandered back to the kitchen, and as I unloaded my groceries; I heard the loud roar of a motorcycle going past my house. I ran to the front window just in time to see the back of a giant of a man riding a huge black Harley wearing an Iron Valor cut disappearing into the horizon. Fucking Wrecker Leonard.

"Well Rocket. I'm toast."

CHAPTER 7

WRECKER

I called the meeting after dark, right after the last customer wheeled his oil-soaked Harley off the lot and the garage settled into its usual after-hours hush. Bronc was already in the war room, the blue light from his phone making his face look younger than it was, or maybe just more haunted. Papa was seated in his usual spot. Arsenal and Doc came in together, Doc with a stack of folders, Arsenal with a handful of sunflower seeds he cracked with his molars and spat into the trash. Gunner drifted in last, still green enough to hover near the door, back to the wall. No one said a word until I shut the door and hit the blackout switch, killing the lights.

Bronc broke the quiet. "Whatever it is, Eli, you got fifteen minutes before Juliet gets here for dinner." His voice was casual, but the way he stacked his hands on the table said he was expecting a war.

I took the end chair. "Don't need that long." My hands were too big for the little thumb drive, but I managed to slot it into the war room laptop and patch it to the wall monitor.

The main screen filled with a low-res video feed. At first, nothing but audio: Parker's voice, brittle and fast, pacing on some problem. Then Silas, the cockroach, his words oiled and smug. There wasn't much video—just a shot of the inside of Parker's jacket and some glimpses from her watch as she sat in front of Silas's desk. But the mics were good. You heard every word.

"You want more time, you better make it count." That was Silas, already three drinks in, putting on his big bad wolf routine. "Because if this thing tanks, Axel's not the only one who's going to pay for it."

On the video, Parker said: "It won't tank. I just need a few more days." You could see her hands shaking. The camera showed every tremor, like a little earthquake.

Bronc leaned forward, not blinking. Arsenal spit a shell at the trash and missed. "That Silas?" he said, as if he already knew the answer.

I nodded.

Doc made a note. "So it's what you thought." He thumbed through the first folder, his lips moving in silent calculation.

The video kept going. Silas, all threats and pressure, Parker crumbling then holding, then a sound: skin on skin. Not a slap, not exactly—just a grab, a grip. The sort of thing that leaves bruises if you let it. The table tensed. Even Gunner made a fist.

I killed the video. The room sucked up the silence like a punch to the gut.

"He's got her by the fucking throat," I said. "She's the one moving the money for him."

Arsenal was first to react. "She was fucking pack. Born here. Raised here. Her twin too."

"Their entire life." I said.

Doc frowned, eyes going cold. "She was never a joiner, but I didn't take her for a traitor."

"She's not," I said, and realized too late how it sounded. "It wasn't her choice. She's doing it because Silas is holding Axel over a fire."

Bronc raised a brow. "You sure of that?"

"Dead sure. Listened to every minute." I flexed my hands, remembered the sound Silas made when he touched her, the way Parker seemed to hold her breath. "He told her if she didn't get it right, Axel wasn't the only one who'd pay."

Arsenal was grinning, not with happiness, but with anticipation. "So we burn Greenbriar. Make an example."

Gunner piped up, "She's still former pack, though."

Doc shook his head. "Not if she's running ops against us. That's not just pack business. That's war."

I stood, too restless to stay seated. "She's being forced. We're not talking about some glory-hound. She's desperate. And smart. Smart enough to have given us a way in. To show us the way."

Bronc laced his fingers and stared me down. "You got a plan?"

I exhaled, slow. "We flip her. Get her to plant something in Silas's office. Let her run the siphon for another week while we get our ducks in a row. Then we hit him when he's looking the other way."

Doc scratched his chin. "She doesn't know she's made?"

"Think she suspects. She's about to find out for sure."

Arsenal looked skeptical. "You sure you're not too close to this, Wrecker?"

That got under my skin. I was going to protect her if I had to fight every man in this room. "You questioning me, Arsenal?"

He put his hands in the air, then glanced at Bronc. "Nah man. Just a question. I got it, not too close."

That was a lie. I'd watched her for hours now, counting her breaths, watching her with that damn dog, memorizing the way she moved. I'd watched her sleep, watched her cry, watched her make herself come and then cry again. I felt like a ghost in her house. Like I'd always been there.

Bronc didn't buy the lie. "You're obsessed. Is this a liability?"

Now *that,* sure as *shit,* pissed me off. He'd let Juliet in when he didn't even know who she truly *was,* and he's gonna question me?

"I think we all need to take a step back and fucking trust each other. I remember a couple of other women who we put our trust in before we had a good handle on whether or not they could be fully depended on. We put our faith in the members of this team to know what they were doing." I was staring straight at Bronc.

Bronc put his head down.

"Fuck. He's not wrong. Either we trust each other, or we ain't shit as a team. We start questioning each other's judgement then our ability to operate as a team is gone."

I stared at the wall behind him, the place where we used to hang the heads of coyotes that raided the compound. "I'm telling you, she's more afraid of Silas than she is of us. She's got no one. Except the ugliest fucking dog you ever saw she just rescued from some dumpster or some shit." That got a laugh. "But I heard her yelling at Axel, telling him he dragged her into this mess and ruined her life. That he took her away from the only family she had left. Us."

Papa shook his head. "Poor kid. Sounds like she needs *saving* as much as anything."

Arsenal's tone had changed. "So, what do we do?"

I took a breath. "Look, I'm not gonna lie. The reason I know all of this is that since I tracked that IP address, I've had her under surveillance. She's alone 100 percent of the time. Just her, that dog, and her computer doing computer nerd things and reading books. Honestly, I think she wrote the code, so I'd find it. It's her asshole brother that's dragged her down in this. When he barged into her house yesterday, he told her what she's gotta do. Like he bore no responsibility."

I ran my hand through my hair. "What I really need y'all doing is to help me find out what all Greenbriar is involved in. They apparently are running casinos, fight houses, and who knows what all, and *who* all are backing them."

Bronc waited, let the silence hang. "Shit. Sounds like an entire enterprise."

I rubbed my hand down my face. "I'm afraid it is. We thought they were crippled. We haven't been paying close enough attention to what they could be up to. Sounds like they've been up to a lot more than we bargained for. I'm thinking they could be banking thousands, hell, maybe hundreds of thousands of dollars."

Bronc looked at me, shaking his head. "Well, ain't that just a real shit sundae with a fucking cherry on top?"

"We need to know what's happening with them, and she's our best chance to find out." As bad as I hated the idea.

"What if she refuses?" That was Gunner's question.

I smiled, mean and humorless. "She'll want this over. I don't see her backing down. Greenbriar wants a war. We'll give them one."

Doc tapped his pen on the table. "You're going to have to get close."

I nodded again. "I plan on it."

Bronc sighed with resolution. "You got my blessing, Wrecker. But if it gets out of hand, you're pulling the plug yourself."

"Roger that."

The meeting broke up. Doc left first, then Arsenal. Gunner hung back, looking like he wanted to say something but didn't. I stayed, packing up the laptop and pocketing the drive. Bronc waited until the room cleared, then fixed me with that blue-eyed stare he'd inherited from his old man.

"You sure about this?" he asked.

"No," I said. "But I don't see another way."

He exhaled, rubbed his face. "If she's in over her head, you get her out. If she's playing us, I want her dead."

"I'm telling you now, that's a hard goddamn no. She's my fucking mate, Bronc."

"Of course she is. Eli, why can't any fucking thing ever be easy?"

I grinned. "Where's the fun in that?"

He stood, stretched his back until it popped, then clapped me on the shoulder. "You need to talk to Juliet?"

"I'll let you know. Parker might need to."

"Ahh hell. Juliet loves a stray."

I grinned as I left the war room and stepped out into the cold. The sky over the compound was the color of old ash, the lights of the city barely making a dent in the dark. I felt the wolf within me pacing, restless, ready to run.

I mounted my bike and gunned the engine, the sound splitting the night in two.

I was going to see Parker.

And this time, I wasn't just going to watch.

I took the long way to Parker's house, looped the block twice before cutting the engine. The street slept hard, no porch lights, not even a possum made rounds in the ditch. I left the bike hidden behind a utility shed and went the last stretch on foot. The night felt colder here—maybe because I wasn't on pack land. I was a ghost with bad intentions. Or good, depended on your perspective.

I checked the feed from her security cams on my phone. House was dead quiet, all sensors on, every window blacked out. She'd been home for hours, judging from the wine bottle on the counter and the empty sandwich plate she'd left in the sink. I'd watched her earlier, hunched over her laptop in her office nook, eyes burning holes in the code. She'd tried to firewall me out, but every time she closed a door, I just walked through a new one. The effort made her drink faster, and it made me want her more.

Now after midnight, she'd abandoned the war and retreated to her room. I could see the heat signature of her body curled in a tight comma on the bed. Even asleep, she was bracing for impact. That little ball of fur was curled up in his bed. I brought him another bone. Luckily, he liked me. Didn't make a peep the first night I'd entered the house. Maybe it was my wolf he liked.

I let myself in through the back door. No gloves, no mask, just a black T-shirt and old jeans, boots off before I crossed the threshold. I moved slow, careful of the floorboards, feeling for the spots she'd missed dusting. She was pretty meticulous, but she'd been preoccupied with staying alive. The house was pretty, but nothing ornate. There was nothing frilly or overly decorative except for her coffee mugs. They were floral with nice decorative handles. It was like that was the one area she allowed herself to be expressly feminine. Even though everything about her screamed female.

I left the lights off. The dark was comforting. I could see just fine. Wolf thing. I heard the patter of little dog nails where the rugs ended. "Hey little guy," I whispered. "Looking for a treat?" He danced around his tongue hanging out. I had to stop myself from laughing. I picked him up and carried him to the guest room with a meaty bone, perfectly content.

In the hallway, I paused. Her breathing was audible, slow and deep. The wolf in me wanted to charge in and take what it was owed, but the man in me wanted to savor the approach. I let the man win, for once.

The bedroom door was ajar. Her silhouette was visible against the faint rectangle of streetlight leaking through a slit in the curtains. She slept on her side, one hand under her face, the other curled against her chest. Her hair was a wild halo on the pillow, streaked with pink and sticking up in places she'd been sweating. I stood there for a minute and just watched.

I went to the foot of the bed and peeled the blanket back. Her bare legs tucked up, knees to stomach, the rest of her clothed in one of those too-large band T-shirts she wore to remind herself she used to have fun. There was a bruise on her shin, yellow-green and healing. I reached out and pressed the edge of it, just to see if she'd wake.

She didn't, but she made a noise—a little half-sigh that vibrated all the way up my spine. I moved to the side of the bed and ran my hand up her calf, over the knee, up her thigh to the curve of her ass. The skin was soft, too soft for someone who acted so hard. I squeezed until I felt her shift, and then did it again, harder.

She woke slowly. First, the twitch of her foot, then the subtle tensing of her shoulders. She didn't roll over. She just made a sound, something between a question and a moan.

I put my other hand on the small of her back and held her there. She shuddered, then tried to kick her foot free. I let her, but only because it was cute.

She froze.

I crouched a little. Her eyes were open now, wild and almost electric blue, staring at me like she'd known I'd show up eventually, but still didn't believe it. I put my finger to my lips. She nodded, barely, and I felt the tension wind even tighter in her body.

I kept my voice low. "Don't scream," I said.

I reached up and took her by the hair, pulling her head off the pillow. She didn't fight it. In fact, she seemed almost grateful for the violence of it. I leaned in close enough that her breath bounced off my face.

"You know who I am?" I whispered.

She nodded again.

"Say it."

She licked her lips. "Wrecker."

I smiled. "Good girl."

She bit her bottom lip hard and let out a shaky exhale. "Are you here to kill me?"

I shook my head. "Not today, little bird."

I leaned over, put my hands on either side of her face, and kissed her. She didn't resist. She opened her mouth and let me in, tongue meeting mine, the kiss hot and desperate.

"So perfect. I'm going to need you to do everything that I say. Do you understand?"

She just looked at me.

"Do you understand?"

I could see she was struggling with this, which amazed me when she let me take what I wanted when I was masked. That was it. She wanted me to be completely in control.

"Nevermind, Wren. You'll do as I say, or you'll be punished."

CHAPTER 8

PARKER

I heard the sheets shift before I really woke. Sometimes I surfaced from sleep the way a diver breaches, desperate for breath and light, but this was more like a slow, doomed float upward through syrup. All the hairs on my arms stood up, and my heart was already jackhammering before my brain spat out a single word. Danger.

I tried to move, but my body would not obey at first. Not from fear—just the kind of sleep paralysis that comes when you live your whole life bracing for disaster, and disaster finally knocks. I was propped on my side, knees drawn up, one hand in a fist against my chin like a boxer who went twelve rounds and forgot to stand down. The room was black except for the thin line from the slit in the window curtain, which cut a pale halo over the far wall and left everything else in negative.

Not a dream. Not some pre-dawn hallucination. There was a hand on my leg and another at the small of my back. I kicked my foot free. He could have continued to hold it, I was sure. On my back now, I saw the silhouette, the impossible breadth of his shoulder as he crouched next to the bed. It was the masked stranger. Only there was no mask now, but the darkness clung to his features, leaving only the glint of his eyes and the carved stone of his jaw.

It took exactly one pulse of my heart for my brain to slot the pieces together. Wrecker. The same man I'd seen through the window. The same one whose laughter rattled in the phone wires at Iron Valor MC, whose hands I'd imagined clamped around my throat, whose entire existence had loomed just outside my field of view since I was old enough to know what a monster was.

Except monsters don't stand in your bedroom and watch you sleep. Or maybe that's exactly what they do.

He didn't speak at first. He stood over me so close I could smell the wild animal in him: oak, iron, the ghost of a fire somewhere, a trace of oranges. I opened my mouth, but before I could make a sound, he put his finger over his lips.

I made a noise, low and questioning. He grinned, just a flash of teeth, then leaned in so close I could count the little flecks of steel in his eyes.

"Don't scream," he said, voice so low it vibrated in the back of my skull.

I didn't scream. I was never going to scream.

He watched me a long time, as if waiting for some internal clock to run down. Then, without another word, he took his finger from his mouth and grabbed a handful of my hair to pull my head from the pillow. The sting should have made me angry, but it made me feel alive. Maybe I was just thrilled to feel something—anything.

He leaned in; his breath was on my face. "You know who I am?" His gravel voice was deep and low.

I nodded.

"Say it." It was a command I didn't dare disobey.

"Wrecker." I barely squeaked the word.

Then he smiled, and I swear if gods walked the earth, one was holding my face in his hands. "Good girl."

My stomach clenched at the endearment. I hated that I was that starved for praise, but I wanted to bathe in it. I also knew it could be just a tease before he ended me.

"Are you here to kill me?"

"Not today, little bird." Again with that smile. And not *today*. But I could fuck this up and sign my death warrant.

Then he tightened his grip on either side of my head and kissed me.

The last time I'd been kissed like that—well, I'd never been kissed like that. It was not gentle. It was not tender. It was a fucking full-body invasion. His lips and tongue and teeth, each a separate implement of violence and worship. I was so shocked I forgot to do anything, and then my body, in its infinite wisdom, simply yielded. I didn't fight, didn't lean away. I opened my mouth and let him inside, and the world telescoped to just that: the dark, the heat, the slow deliberate ruin of my resistance.

He kissed as if he meant to leave a bruise.

I didn't know how long it lasted. A minute, a year. When he pulled back, I was shaking—not from fear, but from something so old and so deep that I wanted to crawl under the bed and hide from it.

He looked at me, waiting. I waited too. I could hear my own breathing, wild and wet. My heart, deranged in my chest.

He told me I was perfect and that I would do everything that he told me to do. When he asked me if I understood, I just stared at him blankly.

"Do you understand?" he asked, voice a rasp.

I didn't. I stared him down, blinking, and let my jaw clench tight around the only words I had. No. Not yet.

He ran one finger down my jaw, trailing over my throat. I thought he might choke me. Part of me wished for it. Instead, he just watched the way my pulse beat under his touch, and let his hand rest there, a slow squeeze, as if he could set my heartbeat to any rhythm he wanted.

"I'm not here to hurt you, Wren," he said. "Tonight I'm here to meet your needs." He was trailing small kisses up my neck. "To fulfill the fantasies that consume your waking dreams. You're going to surrender your control to me, or I am just going to take it. Either way. Then tomorrow, we are going to discuss why you have put yourself in the middle of a deadly game of cat and mouse between Iron Valor and Greenbriar, and you are going to tell me everything you're guilty of."

I froze.

"That's right. I know all about it. Everything but the details, which you will provide. But the first command I'm giving you is to clear your mind, little bird. Don't worry about your little dog. He is happily gnawing on another juicy bone. Next, you need to realize the position you are in. You have no power here. Not in your life, not in this room, not under me. I am going to use your body in every way you can imagine. Going to make you come over and over again until you beg me to stop. And then, I'm going to make you come again. I would ask you if we are clear on this, but you wouldn't answer, because you don't want to answer. You want to feel what true surrender feels like. And I'm going to show you, Wren."

He called me Wren. My stomach flipped and then went cold. I wanted to know why.

"Can I ask you why you are calling me Wren?"

"Sure. Because you are my little bird, flitting around chirping wishing someone would see you. But you're like a thousand other birds just like you, all making the same noise. So you try to chirp louder, doing stupid fucking shit that will get you killed. And I'm not just talking about what you're wrapped up in *now*, hacker. If you're not careful, you'll wind up just another dead little bird on the side of the road. But lucky for you, you have a big, bad monster who has a Wren-sized cage who's gonna keep an eye on you and maybe, just maybe, keep you alive. But for now, I'm about to fuck your feathers off."

He pulled off the oversized t-shirt that I slept in, and that left me completely bare to him. Then he kissed me again, harder this time, and let his hand trace down the side of my neck, over the bones of my shoulder and straight to the softest part of my breast. I was hypersensitive, every cell on high alert, each brush of his knuckle a spark in dry brush. His fingers found my nipple, pinched and twisted, rolling it between calloused pads until it throbbed with pain, then heat, then an ache that traveled straight down to my cunt. I wanted to say something—a smart remark, a threat, anything to keep my head above water—but his mouth devoured mine and left me breathless.

He kept at it, working my breasts like a mechanic tuning a precision engine. At first just one hand, then two—one palming the fullness, the other tweaking and tormenting the nipple until it stood like a warning light. When he wanted a change of pace, he used his teeth. Nipped, then bit down hard enough that I yelped. He kissed the mark, tongue cool and sweet, before moving to the other side and starting over.

All the while, his thigh was pressed between mine, a pressure point I couldn't ignore. I ground down against it and hated myself for the desperation. He laughed into my neck, as if he'd been waiting for me to make the first move.

"Fucking knew you'd be like this," he muttered, breath tickling my ear. "Tough little bird. Always needing to be broken in."

He slid down, using his body weight to pin me. My arms were above my head, limp and useless, but he made sure they stayed there by grabbing both wrists and holding them with one hand. The other hand drifted down my stomach, splayed out wide, his thumb tracing lazy circles just under my navel. I tried to pull free, but the grip was absolute. I was helpless, and the realization sent a jolt of molten electricity straight through me.

He used his other hand to part my thighs. His fingers were gentle at first, just petting the outside of my mound, but the touch was invasive—a searchlight, a customs inspection, nothing shy about it. He spread me open with two fingers, pressed his thumb right onto my clit, and held it there, firm but not moving.

"Wet already?" he said, sounding genuinely pleased. "I haven't even gotten started."

He was right. I was soaked, embarrassingly so, the kind of arousal that made a mess of the sheets and stuck to your thighs in the morning. He toyed with my slit, slow and clinical, like he was seeing how far he could stretch me before I broke. When he was satisfied, he slid one finger inside, all the way up to the knuckle.

I moaned, couldn't help it. He pumped in and out, slow at first, then faster. The heel of his palm ground into my clit at the bottom of every thrust. I was writhing now, body trying to squirm away, but he just shifted his weight and kept going, adding another finger, then a third. It hurt, but not in a way I wanted to stop. I clenched around him, and he laughed again, a sound that made me want to both spit in his face and beg for more.

"Good girl," he said, voice so low it vibrated inside my chest. "You're gonna come for me, right here."

I didn't want to. I didn't want to give him the satisfaction. But my body had other plans. I could feel it building, a pressure cooker of want and humiliation, and I tried to fight it but the more I resisted, the stronger it got. He must have sensed the shift, because he let go of my wrists and reached up to grab my jaw, forcing me to look him in the eye as he fucked me with his fingers.

"You're mine now," he said. "Say it."

I shook my head, just barely. "No," I whispered.

He squeezed my jaw hard enough to hurt. "Say it."

"Fuck you," I managed.

He grinned and then pushed me harder. His thumb worked my clit now, fast and mean, while his fingers filled me up. I bucked under him, couldn't help it. The pressure inside me snapped, and I came—loud, eyes rolling back, mouth open in a silent scream. It was a full-body orgasm, the kind that leaves you trembling and weak, that makes your toes curl and your lungs seize up.

He didn't stop. He kept working me through the aftershocks until I was oversensitive and kicking at him to make it stop. Only then did he pull his hand free and wipe it on the bedsheet.

I lay there, dazed and half-blind, trying to catch my breath. He rolled me onto my stomach, slow and deliberate, and used his gigantic hands to massage the muscles up and down my spine. He found the knots and pressed them out, kneaded the flesh until it hurt, then soothed it with long strokes.

I would have fallen asleep right there, but then I felt his hand drift lower, down to the curve of my ass. He squeezed, then spread the cheeks apart, exposing my hole. I tensed, a ripple of panic surging through me.

He noticed of course. "You're so fucking tight," he said, almost reverent. He ran a finger over the pucker, just barely touching, then pressed down until I thought I'd break in half. I clenched, tried to shut him out, but he just chuckled and spanked me—once, twice, three times, each hit ringing out like a gunshot in the quiet room.

"That's not how this works," he said, voice in my ear. "You want to clench? I'll give you something to clench around."

He spat on his finger and pushed it against the hole, forcing it in slow, one knuckle at a time. I gasped, shocked at the stretch, at the way it made me feel both violated and alive. He worked it in and out, shallow at first, then deeper, until I couldn't tell where the pain stopped and the pleasure began.

He used his other hand to reach under and finger my pussy at the same time. I was crying now, not from pain, but from the intensity of it, from the sheer, unfiltered reality of what he was doing to me.

He leaned down, mouth hot against my ear. "You know what I want, Wren? I want to fuck you so hard you can't walk straight tomorrow. I want you to remember who owns you every time you sit down. You think you can handle that?"

I shook my head, sobbing now. "No, I can't, please—"

He bit the back of my neck, hard and drove his finger deeper. "Yes, you can. You're gonna take it. Because that's what you were made for."

He kept it up, alternating between the two holes, until I was a mess of sweat and tears and shame. When he finally pulled his hands away, I felt empty and desperate, like I'd lost something important.

He flipped me onto my back again, took my face in his hands, and kissed me, slow and deep, like we had all the time in the world.

"You did so good," he said. "Proud of you."

I was still crying, but I smiled, just a little.

He stroked my hair, wiped the tears from my cheeks, then lay down next to me, pulling me into the curve of his body. I let myself melt into him, into the warmth and safety and promise of something bigger than myself.

I didn't speak. I didn't need to.

He let me linger in the afterglow, let me believe for a few seconds that I'd survived the worst of it, that I could catch my breath and maybe start putting myself back together. But then he shifted, rolled off the bed, and stood at the edge, looming in the dark like something engineered for violence.

I watched as he peeled off his shirt, exposing a body that was all muscle and scars, every inch of him mapped by old wounds and newer tattoos. My eyes caught on the Force Recon emblem inked over his deltoid, then the line of script running down his ribs, then the pale lines of claw marks that looked more animal than human. He unbuckled his belt, letting the metal clatter against the floor, and shucked his jeans with a casual efficiency that made my pulse skip. He wore nothing underneath. Of course he didn't.

I stared. I couldn't help it. His cock was... fuck. I had words for everything, but not this. Big, obviously, but that wasn't the half of it—thick, heavy, veined, with a head that looked engineered for maximum intimidation. My breath caught, and my wolf, so recently subdued, went wild with a mixture of panic and anticipation. He stroked it once, slowly, and I felt my insides clench with both terror and want.

He caught me staring, grinned like a bastard, then crawled back onto the bed. The mattress dipped beneath his weight. He flipped me back onto my stomach and positioned himself behind me, hands splayed across my lower back, pressing me down into the sheets.

"You see this, little bird?" he said, voice all grit and honey. "You think you can take it?"

I looked at him over my shoulder and shook my head, honestly. "I don't know."

"You will." He stroked himself, then lined up the head with my opening. I was still wet, still leaking, but the stretch when he pushed in was like nothing I'd ever felt. Not pain, exactly, but a sweet, tearing pressure that went all the way up my spine. He went slowly at first, just the tip, then backed out and pushed in again, a little deeper each time.

I whined, a sound I hadn't meant to make. He moaned, guttural, like the noise came from somewhere deep within. "Fuck, Parker, you're so tight," he groaned. "I'm gonna ruin you."

He meant it. He bottomed out finally, and held there, grinding his hips into my ass. I could feel the pulse of his cock inside me, hot and insistent, and the sensation was overwhelming. He wrapped a hand around my throat, not squeezing, just holding, as if reminding me whose air I was breathing.

He started to move, slow at first, then faster. Each thrust rocked the bed, the headboard knocking a staccato rhythm against the wall. He kept up a steady stream of dirty talk, never letting me forget what I was, what he was doing to me.

"You like this, don't you? Being fucked like a little toy? Letting me take whatever I want? You're so wet, I could drown in you. You were made for me, you know that?"

I whimpered, tried to answer, but all that came out was another needy sound. He laughed, then bent forward, putting his mouth right next to my ear.

"You're not getting my knot," he said, voice barely more than a growl. "Not tonight. You know why?"

I shook my head, helpless.

He fucked me harder, the slap of his hips against my ass echoing through the room. "Because only my mate gets that. And I don't have one."

The words hit me like a punch. My wolf keened, an invisible agony that twisted in my gut. I wanted it. I wanted it so bad I could taste the need in the back of my throat. I'd never believed in mates, never let myself hope for anything so animal and absolute, but now the denial felt like a punishment worse than anything he'd done to my body.

He reached around and found my clit, rubbing it in hard, ruthless circles that made my toes curl and my vision blur. I felt the orgasm building again, bigger than before, a tidal wave that swept away all thought.

He bit down on my shoulder, not hard enough to break skin, but enough to bruise. "You gonna come for me, Wren? You gonna let me have it?"

I nodded, sobbing now. "Please, please—"

He sped up, fucking me with the kind of abandon that bordered on violence, and when I came, it was with a shudder that left me limp and shattered. I clawed at the sheets, at his hand, at anything I could reach. He kept going, kept talking, kept reminding me that I was his, that he could do whatever he wanted.

He pulled out at the last second, jerking himself off onto my back. I felt the hot splash, the proof of his victory, and it should have made me feel cheap, ruined. But instead, I felt a dark, twisted pride. I'd taken everything he had to give, and I was still here.

He lay next to me, chest heaving, sweat slicking his skin. He reached over, wiped the tears from my cheeks, then kissed me, soft and lingering, as if apologizing for what he'd just done. There was no need to apologize. It wasn't just my body that had wanted it. My heart had too. I wanted him. All of him.

"You did good," he said, voice gentler now. "You did so fucking good."

I nodded, still crying, but not from pain.

He grabbed a towel from beside the bed and wiped his cum off my back. Then he pulled me into his arms, cradled me like something precious. I let myself rest there, let myself be small and safe.

But deep inside, I wanted more.

He didn't say anything for a long time. He just held me, our bodies slick with sweat and spit and come, the sheets tangled under us like the aftermath of a bar brawl. The air was thick with the smell of us, sharp and sweet, and I breathed it in like it was the last clean air on earth.

Wrecker rolled me onto my side, tucked my back against his chest, and wrapped one arm around my ribs. He bent his head and pressed soft kisses to my shoulder, my neck, the line of my jaw. Each one landed with a sting of salt, and it took me a minute to realize I was still crying. Not loud, not even sobbing—just a silent, unstoppable leak that wet the pillow and glued the hair to my face.

He kissed away the tears, slow and patient. At first, I thought he'd tease me for it, call me a baby or a drama queen. But he just kept kissing, working his way from my temple to my lips, then back again.

Finally, he spoke, voice barely above a rumble. "Talk to me, Wren."

I shook my head. "I don't want to."

"Too fucking bad," he said, but there was no anger in it. "You don't get to run off inside your head and leave me out here."

I tried to laugh. It came out a foreign sound. "You're not exactly on my couch taking confessions either, you know."

He wiped my cheek with his thumb, more gentle than I'd ever imagined he could be. "I'm here. Right now. Not going anywhere."

I closed my eyes, letting the words settle. "I don't know why I'm crying," I lied. "Maybe just... it's been a day."

He grunted, unconvinced, but let it go. "You need anything?"

I shook my head again. But he was already moving, untangling himself from the sheets and crossing the room with that predatory, too-quiet stride. I watched as he ducked into the bathroom, rummaged around, and came back with a warm, wet washcloth. He knelt by the bed and started cleaning me up—between my thighs, over my belly, then my back where he'd left his mark. He did it with a kind of reverence, as if he was cataloging the places he'd broken me so he could fix them again.

When he finished, he tossed the cloth into the laundry basket and climbed back in. He grabbed the glass of water from my nightstand, held it to my lips, and watched while I drank. I was still shaking, but he didn't mention it. He just pulled me close, draped his arm over my body, and pressed his nose into my hair. The weight of him was absolute. Immovable. I felt small, and for once it wasn't a curse.

I didn't want to sleep. I wanted to stay awake and memorize every second, every breath, every heartbeat. But exhaustion hit me like a tranquilizer dart, and I could feel myself sliding under.

Right before I let go, I heard his voice, soft and dangerous, right by my ear. "Someday," he whispered, "I'm putting my mark right here. Where everyone can see."

The thought sent a bolt of pain through my chest, but I didn't say anything. I just curled into the hollow of his body, let the wolf in me whimper and keen, and waited for morning.

I dreamed of nothing, and woke to his arms still around me, the scent of oak and citrus thick in the air, and the echo of his words branded on my skin.

CHAPTER 9

WRECKER

I woke with a sheet wrapped around my ankles and the scent of her hair clogging my lungs. Pre-dawn in this house was a hollow thing—nothing but the ghosts of bad coffee and a woman's perfume baked into the drywall. I watched the shadows on her ceiling as they crawled from gray to black, then rolled out of bed without waking her. I went to the guest room and let the pup out so he could relieve himself outside. He acted like he was thrilled to see me. It made me feel a weird joy inside. Which is a little insane. I'm a wolf, for God's sake.

"Come on, you little shit. I'll let you out." He danced along beside me to the backdoor. I walked out onto the deck and watched as he ran around the yard and peed, and then made about a dozen circles before pooping. Everything the little guy did was funny. It's no wonder she loved him. I was suddenly happy she had him.

I headed to the kitchen and started the coffee. No lights. Just the wet thump of my feet on cold hardwood. I opened the fridge. It wasn't as bad as I'd guessed. Cartons of eggs, a shrink-wrapped ribeye, a carton of milk and some creamer. Lunch meat, of course, and some fresh veggies. I pulled out the eggs and the meat. Maybe she was turning over a new leaf and had decided to eat more than plain meat and bread sammies. I found her pans, steel and unscarred, lined up like surgical tools. Not what I expected. She must've bought them for show because she sure as shit never used them.

I cracked five eggs into a bowl. Shells hit the trash can with a click like tiny bones. The skillet went on the front burner. Then I trimmed the steak, fast and precise, and tossed the trimmings into the dog's bowl. He devoured them in milliseconds. The steak hit the hot pan with a sizzle. The smell was savage. I smiled. A quick sear on both sides and then into the preheated oven. Fuck, I was starved from all the activity from last night.

I heard the shower running in the bathroom. Pipes vibrated in the walls. I pictured her standing there, steam curling over her skin, that pink-and-brunette mess of hair gone flat and dripping. The sound turned something in my chest molten.

I threw some butter into another pan and tossed in the eggs. I threw in a little cheese I'd found in a crisper drawer and some salt and pepper. When they were fluffy, I dumped them out into a bowl. She had bread, of course, from all the damn sandwiches she eats, so I buttered a few slices and threw them in the skillet for pan toast.

I'd gotten the steaks out of the oven and let them rest until she wandered into the room ten minutes later. She'd barely made any noise when she'd entered, but I caught her scent immediately—lavender and lemon. I turned and goddamn if she wasn't the most beautiful thing I'd ever seen, skin scrubbed pink and wearing black yoga pants and a tank that clung to her ribs like a desperate thing, formed around her round tits like a promise. The quarter-zip she wore was some eye-bleeding shade of pink.

"Have a seat." I nodded to the table that sat in her breakfast nook.

She stood next to it. "Do I need to feed Rocket?"

"He just had a pretty good helping of ribeye trimmings. I think he'll be fine." I told her.

She looked irritated.

"Did I do something wrong?" I asked her as I fixed her plate of food and poured her coffee.

"Well, I really don't allow him to have table scraps. I found him living by a dumpster, so I try to keep his food regulated. You know, giving him the best dog food on a schedule so I can see if anything upsets his tummy or whatever."

This woman. She was sunshine and goodness through and through, and she'd mixed up with the devil himself.

"I apologize." I told her as I set her plate and coffee with cream on the table. Leaning down, I kissed her. It wasn't a simple good-morning kiss. I wanted to remind her that I owned her. My mouth consumed hers—and she opened for me. No resistance. I decided then and there that I'd never tire of her kisses. They felt right. Like they belonged to me, and only me. When I let her go, she was breathless, and so adorable.

"Now, sit."

She sat down and started moving her food around her plate, eyes flickering over my face. "So, what do we need to talk about first?"

The question hung between us, sharp and bright as a new blade. I let it bleed for a while.

"Right now?" I said. "I want you to eat. You're too thin."

She bristled, but shoved a forkful of eggs in her mouth. "You're an asshole," she said around the bite.

I waited, watching her chew. There was a satisfaction in it I couldn't explain.

I watched her sip the coffee, saw the bruises on her wrists where I'd held her the night before.

"Yeah. I've been told that before," I said. "Well, your little foray to the dark side has caused you to become my problem now."

She set the mug down hard. "I'm nobody's problem. Least of all yours."

"See, Wren, that's where you're wrong," I said, voice dropping to a growl. "You made yourself my fucking problem the second you started stealing from us."

She sucked in a breath, eyes going wide. "You think I wanted this?"

"What you wanted has no bearing on the situation, little bird," I said. "What matters is what happens next."

She looked away, jaw clenched so tight the muscle ticked in her cheek.

"I'm going to fix this for you," I said. "And you're going to help me."

She snorted, a rough little sound. "I don't know how that can be done."

"Well, then you've got a fuck ton more than Silas Drake to worry about little bird."

"How long have you been watching me?" Her leg was shaking up and down.

There was no reason to lie to her at this point. "Not as long as you'd think. And no, I haven't stalked any other women. Only you. The one that belongs to me."

She finished her eggs in silence. I watched every bite, every swallow. She ate her food like a man who was eating his last meal before his execution. Except she had her faithful ugly little dog right by her side. It was as if he sensed her distress. He kept his head on her feet the entire time.

When she was done, I pushed my plate away and got up. I walked to where she sat and turned her chair toward me. I leaned in close and rested my hands on the arms of the chair, caging her in. Her little pup decided it was time to find his bed.

"You're going to do what I say," I said, low and even. "You're going to tell me everything you know about Greenbriar. About Silas Drake. About how you got in this mess."

She looked up at me, eyes burning. "Look, I want to trust you. Fuck knows I want a way out. I left breadcrumbs for you, you know? I was praying you'd figure things out. But I'm still afraid I'm gonna end up paying in the end."

I smiled finally. "You don't have to trust me. You just have to do everything I say."

She didn't move, didn't blink. I waited. I could have waited forever.

When she finally spoke, her voice was a whisper. "You're just as bad as him, you know."

I shook my head. "No, Parker. I'm much, much worse."

I leaned in, took her face in my hands, and kissed her. Hard, deep, unforgiving. When I pulled away, her lips were bruised and her breath was coming fast.

"Now clean the table. We have work to do."

She stared at me, stunned, then nodded.

I watched the way her body moved, the way her wolf hovered just under her skin, ready to bolt or bite or both.

She didn't slam the dishes into the sink. She simply washed them and set them in the dish drainer. Dishwashing was as methodical as everything else she did. It was as though she lost herself in the task's monotony. I sat at the table watching her, picking steak from my teeth. My brain wouldn't quiet. There was no logic to what I felt—the mate bond. This girl had been around me for years before she'd disappeared when she'd graduated from junior college. I'd always watched her with fascination. Now I knew why. Now she was my problem. Now she was in the crosshairs.

She came back over to me fifteen minutes later, drying her hands on a dish towel. If she were trying to look innocent, she failed miserably. She had the kind of face that refused to behave.

I waited until she was close enough to smell the fabric softener clinging to her sleeve before I started in.

"Why Silas Drake?" I asked.

She stopped dead. "Is that a trick question?"

I stood. "How does a bottom-feeder like him get claws into you?"

She crossed her arms. "He bought out Axel's marker. Simple as that. Axel gambled at his establishments and couldn't pay. Next thing I know I'm getting threats from Greenbriar. They wanted a hacker, not an accountant. They wanted me."

"Bullshit," I spat. "Greenbriar doesn't pull stunts like this. Not with Iron Valor. Unless..." I leaned in, dropping my voice. "Unless they thought you'd fold easily."

She glared, but didn't deny it.

"That's not fair, Wrecker. I'm not easy. Axel is the only family I have left in the world. Someone tells you the person you shared a womb with is going to die if you don't do what they say, you ask what they want you to do. I thought I could just fucking slow them down or something. Buy time. Not..." She shook her head, angry with herself. "Not destroy everything."

"Guess you're not as smart as you thought, then," I said.

"Guess not," she said, soft.

I paced the length of the kitchen. The floor creaked under my weight. She watched me, arms still crossed, but the fight had gone out of her.

"What does Silas want?" I asked.

Her fingers tightened on her biceps. "He wants Iron Valor off the map. He wants to see Bronc dead. And he wants you in pieces, floating in the fucking river."

"Nice to know I'm popular," I said.

She gave a sad little snort.

I slammed a fist on the counter. The whole house jumped. "You don't get it, do you? We're not the only ones with something to lose. You think Greenbriar will let you go once they're done?"

She met my eyes, and for the first time, I saw fear.

"No," she said. "I know how it ends."

I nodded. "Good. Then you know why we do things my way now."

She went quiet, chewing on the inside of her cheek.

"I need everything," I said. "Every password, every server address, every contact you have inside Greenbriar. And Parker, you're gonna have to plant a bug inside."

She hesitated. "How? They'll know..."

"You have the benefit of Silas's ego. He thinks he's smarter than us. I'm going to help you make it look like what you're doing is working. He's going to think he's winning. Don't get me wrong. This is going to be dangerous for you. I'm going to keep you alive though."

I took her hands in mine. "I have to know who else he's working with. He knows he can't bring us down alone. You'll need to arrange another meeting to let him know you fixed the transfer problem. I'll give you the tech you'll plant in his office." I told her. Then I reminded her, "You're alive because I let you be. That ends if you cross me again."

She swallowed hard. "Fine. But you need to get Axel out, too. Or there's no deal."

I considered it. "If you help me burn Greenbriar to the ground, I'll get your brother out. But you fuck up once—"

"I won't," she said, and for once, I believed her. I believed she was going to do her damnedest to make this work. The thought of anything happening to her sent my wolf into a fit. We had to be sure she'd be safe.

I grabbed a notepad and pen from the coffee table and slid them to her.

"I don't have stuff committed to memory. Come over to my office nook." She headed over and opened her laptop.

I watched. Every time her eyes flicked up to mine, it was like she was measuring out the weight of her own grave.

"Why didn't you just come to Bronc?" I asked again, not expecting a real answer.

She paused after getting logged in. "Because I didn't want to owe anybody. Not even him."

That stung in its own way. "We all owe somebody," I said. "That's how packs work. That's how families work."

She didn't reply, just grabbed the legal pad and started writing.

"I haven't been inside any of the Greenbriar systems in weeks. It's possible that some or all of these passwords have changed. If they have, at least you have a jumping-off point." She continued to write.

I poured two more cups of coffee. We drank in silence, the only sound the scratch of her pen and the tick of the fridge. I watched the sun finish clawing up the wall. Watched the way the light caught her face and made her look older than she was, more tired. Like the world had already chewed her up and was just waiting for the right time to spit her out.

"Silas is a coward," I said. "He won't come at us directly."

She nodded. "He'll use proxies. Always does."

"He's already got eyes on you. Probably has a tail out back right now."

"I don't think he's gone that far yet," she said, voice flat. "But fuck him if he does."

"That's my girl."

She finished the notepad, tore the sheet, and handed it to me. Her hands were still trembling.

I folded the paper and tucked it in my pocket. "You need a safehouse?"

She almost laughed. "If he thinks I've gone into hiding, I'm as good as dead. You think you can keep me safe?"

I thought about the pack house. The vault in the basement. I thought about what Bronc would say, and then what I'd do, anyway.

"Yeah," I said. "I do."

She let out a breath. "What now?"

"Now you go to work. Act normal. I'll handle the rest."

She blinked. "You're just going to leave?"

I nodded. "I'll be watching, Wren. But if you need me, you know how to find me." I hated that I was 30 minutes out. But I needed to be in my tech room with my equipment.

She watched me, those electric blue eyes, trying to read the part of me that wasn't there. "Why are you doing this? Why not just burn me and move in on Greenbriar?" she asked.

I looked at her, really looked, and saw the truth in it. "Because you're mine," I said, "and I protect what's mine. And when we take out Greenbriar, we're taking it all the way out. We have to be thorough, know all the moving parts."

She didn't answer. Didn't need to.

I walked to the door, pulled on my boots, and left.

Outside, the air was sharp as a razor. I stood on the porch, let the cold bite my face, and listened to the wind cutting across the fields.

The house behind me was silent, but I could feel her there. Waiting.

I was done pretending.

From now on, every move would be war.

And I was ready for it.

CHAPTER 10

PARKER

It was like a bad dream that circled back and circled back, chewing its own tail until only the nerves were left. I was in Wrecker's living room, sitting on a large cushioned sectional. My leg bounced up and down like I was giving pony rides to toddlers. I wish I had brought Rocket with me. I was always more relaxed with that dog around.

A stone fireplace dominated the wall in front of me with a gigantic TV mounted above the mantle. I looked over my shoulder toward the dining area. Wrecker was in the closed-off kitchen to the right, making coffee. A tall sofa table sat behind the long part of the sectional where I was sitting, and I noticed several framed photos there. My curiosity got the better of me, so I ventured around to look at who Eli Leonard would find important enough to memorialize in photos.

I leaned down and saw that most of the photos were candid shots. There was a professional family portrait that made me smile. It looked only a few years old. Thinking of Wrecker putting on a suit for his mother and going to a studio for posed photos is such a 'good son' thing to do. The portrait was of his mother, father, Wrecker, and his two younger sisters. If I remembered correctly, they were about 8 or so years younger than me. Beautiful and blonde. They had none of Wrecker's dark features. The others were military photos. Shots of him in the desert in full military gear with big guns and amazingly bigger smiles. Photos of him and Bronc when they were kids also filled a couple of frames. Seeing him happy made my insides twist.

I was a little worried I'd see pictures of him with other women. He had quite a reputation with the women around here. All the Iron Valor officers did, except Bronc. They're all known for having had lots of women in their beds or flown off to the vampire king's club where supposedly they all had a penchant for domination. Clearly, Wrecker had shown me that side of himself. And I soaked up every bit of that dominance with my own need to submit. Happily, though, the photos were simply a reflection of his family and friends, and they made me feel closer to him, somehow.

A large bookshelf took up the bulk of the adjacent wall. I was surprised to see several fantasy series by Sanderson and other of my favorite authors. He also had a good number of classic novels as well. I don't know why I was shocked to learn that he was apparently well read. Genius-level people tended to be. His tastes ran parallel to mine if you discounted the smut I loved so much. I giggled to myself at the thought.

Thanks to my stream of consciousness, thinking of my smutty books reminded me of when everything broke loose: Wrecker's mouth on mine, his hand clamped at the nape of my neck, the world going white-hot and then blank, like someone tripped a kill switch behind my eyes. But even now, after a night of sleep and a morning of black coffee, the memory still burned in my muscles, so real it made my skin ache.

Standing in front of the bookshelf, I shut my eyes. It didn't help.

Instead, I saw Wrecker's eyes—gray as unlit metal—and heard his voice, the way it buzzed through me: "You're mine now. Say it." I hadn't said it. I didn't know if I ever would. But something in me had already bent, and I felt that break echoing down every nerve.

I tried to focus on something practical, the way I always did when reality threatened to drag me under. Like, what would I do if I could leave? Where would I run? Who would I even call? But every time, my mind doubled back to the same fucked-up equation: If Wrecker wanted me dead, I'd be dead. If Wrecker wanted to use me, I'd be used up, and there would be nothing left to salvage.

But why would I want to run? If I could be anything in the world, I would want to be Wrecker's. That is the only thing that makes sense. It's the only thing that computes inside my soul even if at this moment it was more physical than emotional. Wrecker was my mate.

The word stuck in my throat. It sounded like the punchline of a joke nobody dared to tell. Wrecker. My mate. The man who'd spent his whole adult life barely noticing me, who'd treated me with a kind of detached disregard that only made me want him more. Who had now, in a masked encounter and in another single night, stripped me down to a raw wire and then left me to short-circuit by myself.

I clenched my hands into fists, pressing my knuckles white.

It wasn't just Wrecker I had to worry about. There was Silas, lurking out in the world like a slow-acting poison. There was Axel, whose debts had started this avalanche. There was Iron Valor, who would never forgive me for what I'd done, even if I was technically a hostage now. I tried to catalog my fuck-ups, to assign blame in neat little packets, but the truth was: this was always going to be the end of my story. Alone, cornered, desperate.

I thought of my parents, and my stomach flipped. I tried to reroute. I tried to remember something less painful.

Instead, a memory surfaced: me having just turned eighteen, huddled in front of my old desktop, watching the live feed from the front porch camera. Wrecker, in a T-shirt and jeans, had knocked on the door, arms full of groceries. His hair was buzzed short then, military-style, and there was a line of blood on his cheek. I watched the way his eyes flicked left and right before he set the bags down, checked the lock, and then walked off into the night. He never came in, never said hello. He just made sure Axel and I had what we needed, then vanished again.

I remembered sitting there, watching the grainy video on repeat, trying to decode the message in his body language. Was he worried about us? Was he angry? Did he even know who we were, or was he just running errands for Bronc?

At the time, I told myself I hated him. I told myself that if he ever tried to talk to me, I'd tell him to fuck off. But he never tried, so I never had to. I just watched him, the most beautiful man I'd ever seen. He came and went several times, always just out of reach.

Now I understood. The mate bond had always been there, dormant and malignant, like a tumor nobody saw until it metastasized. My wolf must have recognized him first, which was why I'd spent the next seven years trying to recreate him in every man I dated. None of them came close, obviously. None of them could have.

He appeared from the kitchen entryway, and my heart shot up into my throat. I quickly walked from the bookshelf to the dining table.

Wrecker filled the doorway, all six foot four of him, and for a second I thought I might faint. Not from fear. From want, which was so much worse.

He wore a black T-shirt and jeans, his hair longer than he had always worn it, falling in a careless, perfect mess over his brow. His arms looked like they could break cinder blocks for fun. He carried a mug of coffee in each hand, and when he set one in front of me, his eyes never left my face.

I couldn't look away.

He stared down at me, silent, as if he were searching for something under my skin.

"Drink," he said. His voice was low, a command, but there was something else in it—a tremor, or maybe just the echo of what had happened between us.

I took the mug with both hands, because otherwise I'd have spilled it. The heat radiated up my fingers, and I tried to focus on that instead of the way my pulse thrashed at my neck.

"Thank you." At least I could still be polite.

He sat across from me. The table creaked under his weight.

For a long minute, he didn't speak. I drank the coffee in tiny sips, the taste acrid and perfect, and tried to pretend this was a normal afternoon in a normal house.

But nothing about this was normal. Not the way my wolf whimpered every time Wrecker moved. Not the way I kept glancing at his mouth, remembering the feel of his teeth at my throat. Not the way my body still ached from what he'd done to me the night before.

He spoke first. "You're not as good at hiding things as you think."

I bristled, automatic. "Says the guy who breaks into houses and roots through people's phones for a living."

He smiled, barely. "It's different. I don't try to hide what I am."

I stared at him, letting the words slide around in my head. What was he exactly? Not a monster. Not a hero. Just a man who'd decided I was his problem to solve, or maybe his toy to break.

I set the mug down, careful not to let it rattle. "So, what's the plan now?" My voice sounded strange to me.

He looked at me hard. "Plan is, you do what I say. You do exactly what I tell you, no improvising, no hero shit. You follow every instruction to the letter."

I nodded, though my wolf squirmed at the thought.

He leaned forward, elbows on the table. "And you don't talk to anyone. Not Bronc, not your brother, not Silas. Not unless I give you permission, Parker."

The last word snapped in the air like a commandment.

I tried to muster a retort, but nothing came. I was too busy cataloging the changes in him: the way he watched my every move, the way his hands flexed on the table, the way his voice softened when he used my real name.

"Okay," I said finally. "Fine."

He watched me a second longer, then sat back. "You're going to be bait," he said matter-of-factly. "You're going to feed Silas exactly what I want him to know. You're going to make him think he's winning. And then, when the time is right, we burn him to the ground."

I swallowed. "What about Axel?"

"We'll get him out, too. But you have to trust me."

I didn't say anything.

He let the silence stretch, then finally got up, the chair screaming against the floor. "You should eat," he said. "You'll need the energy. Sit tight."

I stared at the mug for a while after he left.

It was only after I heard his footsteps fade into the kitchen that I let myself breathe again, full and deep. My wolf settled just a little, comforted by the certainty of him.

For the first time in months, I felt something like hope. It was small, and mean, and dangerous. But it was enough. I could do this.

I finished the coffee in three burning gulps. Then I waited for Wrecker to feed me.

Whatever happened next, I was ready for it.

Wrecker's den wasn't a den. It was a war room. Four gigantic monitors, minimum, and every surface wired with gadgets I'd only ever read about in whitepapers or darknet auction sites. The air was cold and metallic, a faint static haze that clung to your skin and left your hair standing on end. The main display glared a rolling blue, washing out our faces and making us look like the ghosts of smarter people.

He took the rolling chair and gave me a stool. My feet didn't even touch the floor, but the vantage was perfect. I could see all four screens at once: left was his custom shell, running a string of fake transaction logs; right was a network dashboard, spikes and dips dancing in real time; the other two monitors were split between packet sniffers and live feeds from at least a dozen remote nodes, probably his own cameras scattered across Dairyville and half the state.

He cracked his knuckles, then pulled up a code editor and gestured at me. "You ever play with remote ATM protocols?" he asked, like it was small talk.

"I did a summer gig for Western Bank during college. Wrote a hook for their PIN brute. Why?" I tried to sound casual, but truth be told, this was fucking exciting to me.

He grinned like he was showing off. "I've piggybacked their mainframe before, but whoever was doing this for Silas prior, maybe it was him, was running a deadman's script that auto-wipes his burner accounts every twenty-four. He thinks he's smart. He's not."

I leaned in, fingers itching for a keyboard. "Show me."

He nodded and spun the monitor around. The code was familiar, but twisted—Wrecker had written his own proto-col stack, a bastard child of C and Bash and something that looked homegrown. I could follow the logic, even as it wound through obfuscated jumps and dummy variables that would have thrown most white hats off the scent. Made me salivate.

He pointed to a highlighted section. "Your transfer payload gets wrapped here—see, it runs a checksum, then double-stamps the timestamp. You'd expect to see the confirmation ping on the return route. But if we reroute the payload to a cold wallet first, then pass a zero-balance packet to the log, you'll never catch the lag."

My brain caught up fast. "So you're bottlenecking his own account against itself, so should he try to check his own balance, it'll look clean—but in reality, the actual funds have already been moved?"

"Correct. And the best part? The confirmation string on his end gets spoofed by this—" he snapped open a side window and pulled up a fake UI that looked identical to the bank's, but ran on a local host. "If you can access his dashboard even once, you can side load the Trojan and keep eyes on every transaction he does."

I couldn't help it. I smiled, sharp and real. "That's fucking beautiful."

He shrugged. "You're the one who wrote the original logic. I just patched the holes you left on purpose."

My heart did a weird little skip at that. I covered it by pretending to study the code. "So, what do you want me to do?"

He looked away, jaw tight. "You're gonna have to load the Trojan on his laptop and set up some surveillance around his place."

I tensed, but knew there was no other option. "I can do it. He's given me access to his laptop before. But surveillance? Silas isn't stupid enough to let outsiders wander around his HQ. If he catches me poking around, it's over."

He grinned again, bigger this time. "That's where the fun comes in." He opened a drawer and set down a tiny plastic case—inside, six motes of something gray and shiny, smaller than the head of a nail. "Micro-cams. They ride static charge, so they stick to any surface you touch. The battery life is shit, but the audio is good for a ten-foot radius."

I picked one up, pinched it between thumb and forefinger. "These are illegal as hell."

He nodded. "They'll run a continuous loop, and the data gets dumped to a relay station I've got rigged to an ice cream truck two blocks from Greenbriar's club. You just have to drop them. I'll handle the rest."

I tested one against the desk. It stuck, invisible unless you knew where to look. "Is it video or audio?"

"Both, but audio's the gold. Silas is a crazy fuck. Talks to himself when he thinks nobody's listening."

I raised an eyebrow. "You ever think about using your powers for good?"

He gave me a shit-eating grin. "Oh baby, I am."

We kept working, cross-checking logs and mapping out the path I'd need to walk in Greenbriar's den. The longer we worked, the more I felt myself slotting back into place, like a bone that finally set after months of wrong healing. Working next to Wrecker felt natural. He was the only one on earth who saw the code in my head and didn't treat me like a freak.

The silence was loaded. I picked up the micro-cam, just to have something to do. "What if Silas finds this?" I asked, rolling it across my knuckles. "Won't he trace it back?"

"I doubt he'd even realize what it is. Anyway, they're one-use only, and the firmware bricks itself after upload. If they got their grubby paws on it, it would likely be destroyed by their hands." He reached out and took the cam from my hand, slow and deliberate. His fingers brushed mine, and my wolf yowled like a banshee, a shiver running down my spine.

He held my gaze, then placed the cam back in the case. "We're going to take down Greenbriar. All of it. I want you to be the one to lead the charge."

I tried to swallow, but my mouth was dry. "Why?"

He didn't answer right away. He just looked at me, his eyes so clear and pale it made my teeth hurt. "Because you're the only one smart enough to finish what you started. And because I know what it's like to have the world pick you apart piece by piece until there's nothing left but bones."

His words set something off inside me—some strange, bitter pride, or maybe just the old ache of being the one nobody noticed until they needed something. I nodded once and locked the tech case shut.

"So I go in, plant these, load the Trojan, and act normal," I said, pushing my stool back.

"Normal as you get," he said, mouth twisting.

I picked up the case, stood, and squared my shoulders. "What happens if I get caught?"

He didn't blink. "If you get caught, I come for you. And nothing on this earth will stop me."

The hair on my arms stood up. I could feel the wolf in me preen, half terror, half something closer to adoration.

"Okay," I said, voice flat.

He stood, and for a second, we were only inches apart. I could smell the wild in him—oak and fire and something more than I wanted to name. His jaw worked, like he was chewing on something sharp.

"Don't let him touch you," he said. "Not Silas. Not anyone at Greenbriar. If they do, they'll regret it."

I nodded again, this time slower. The world seemed smaller, the air denser.

"Wren?"

"Yeah?"

"Don't fuck this up."

"I won't."

CHAPTER 11

PARKER

Wrecker didn't tell me where we were going. He just appeared in the hall as I was stowing the micro-cam kit in my bag and jerked his head. "Downstairs. Now."

I trailed him, my heart beating a little faster than I wanted to admit. The main floor of the house was immaculate, but the air changed at the top of the basement steps—cooler, spiced with the tang of old leather and a faint wisp of citrus. He unlocked the stairwell with a heavy key, opened it, and gestured for me to lead the way.

The steps were finished concrete; the walls lined with bare pine planks stained almost black. At the bottom was a steel fire door, which he keyed open and held for me.

The room beyond was not what I expected. No cinderblocks, no low-slung pipes. Instead: a single, high-ceilinged space, painted deep charcoal, lit by a bank of recessed LEDs set to a dying-sunset orange. Against the left wall, a long shelf over a row of hooks held things I recognized only from the darkest corners of the internet and the even darker corners of my own reading habits: floggers, paddles, cuffs, crops, ropes of every width and weave, and a row of beautifully sinister wooden canes mounted like museum artifacts. Against the opposite wall stood a pair of St. Andrew's crosses—one steel, one padded black leather, each fitted with shackles at every joint. In the middle of the room was a heavy padded bench, arched like a gymnast's pommel horse. It had lower padded ridges with hanging straps for arms and legs to rest.

And near the far end of the room, suspended from the ceiling by chains so thick I could have hung my own body from them, was a swing.

I stopped dead. My first thought was, *is this for me?* And then, before I could stop myself, my wolf keened so loud a small whimper escaped my throat.

Wrecker was behind me in an instant. He put one hand between my shoulders and walked me forward, the pressure gentle but non-negotiable. "This," he said, "is the only place in the house where the rules don't matter. If you want to run, you run. If you want to fight, you fight. If you want to cry, you cry. But you don't get to hide. Not here."

I took two steps forward. The smell hit me—a combination of polished steel, oiled wood, and the sweet, dark undertone of submission. It made my head spin.

He circled around to face me. "You ever done this before?" he asked, voice flat.

I shook my head.

He grinned, but there was no mockery in it. "Good. Means you won't have any bad habits for me to break."

The words made me shiver. My mouth went dry.

"Last chance. Head up those stairs if you don't want this."

I looked over my shoulder at the door to the stairway and then back into his steely eyes. I never wanted anyone or anything more in my life. I stood taller as I faced him.

"I want this. But I want you to understand that my submission only extends to the bedroom. I want and need you to be the one in charge of my body, my pleasure, and my pain. Everywhere else, we're on equal footing. Understood?"

"I will always want to keep you safe. That might look like trying to control aspects outside of the bedroom. But yes. I understand and agree. Now. Take off your clothes," he said.

I hesitated just for a moment.

"Now."

I stripped. Hoodie, tee, shoes, joggers. I folded them and set them on the nearest bench, careful to keep my hands steady. I kept my bra and panties on, unsure what the protocol was, but he made a tsk sound and hooked a finger under the band of my sports bra, snapping it. "All of it."

I removed them quickly and stood there, skin prickling in the cool air. I wasn't embarrassed of my body. I knew I'd lost weight, as he had so rudely pointed out. But since I was so short, I had soft curves that I was proud of. And I was fit. Being a wolf made our genetics predisposed to physical fitness if we gave the slightest bit of work at it.

He circled me, just once. "Good. Now over here."

He guided me to the bench and put a hand on the back of my neck, pressing me down until my chest and belly rested on the padded leather, which made me ass high. The bench was warm, the surface faintly tacky with whatever he'd used to disinfect it. My thighs straddled it as my short legs caused my feet to rest on the lower supports.

He leaned over, so close I could feel the heat coming off him. "You want a safe word?"

The question caught me off-guard. I'd read about them, sure. I'd imagined using one, but never thought I'd have to make the decision for real.

"Yeah," I said, voice tight. "How does that work, exactly?"

He didn't hesitate with his instruction. "Many people prefer the traffic light system. Green for good, yellow for mildly uncomfortable but want to keep going, and red for stop. You give me your stop word, and I stop what I'm doing and we do not go back to it, so be certain."

Being the extreme book nerd that I was, I settled on different words. "Okay, I've chosen my own words."

"Of course you have. Let me have them. And be sure they are not words you could accidentally say, because I will take them to heart and follow them."

"Dumbledore, for everything is good. Snape, for I'm unsure if I like what you're doing. And Voldemort, for stop, I don't like this."

He patted my head. "Little bird, just when I thought you couldn't surprise me, you come up with something like that," he chuckled. "Those are good. I doubt you'd accidentally say any of those words."

I watched as he walked to the wall of implements. He'd removed his shirt and was only wearing a pair of low-slung jeans. His body was a fucking masterpiece. He turned and walked back after choosing a flogger from the rack. He held it up so I could see—long tails of suede, soft and flexible, nothing harsh.

"First time, so we start light."

He walked over to me and lowered the bench. He pulled me back a bit, so I was no longer straddling the bench, but bent over at the hips, my feet on the floor. With no more warning than the slow sound of his breathing, he laid the first stroke across my ass. It stung, but more than that, it woke up every inch of skin. I gripped the sides of the bench with both hands.

He worked methodically, covering the tops of my thighs, then the curve of my hips, then the arch of my lower back. The sound was less a crack than a heavy sigh, the tails biting and then fading to warmth.

After a few rounds, I realized I was clenching my jaw so hard I thought I might chip a tooth. He noticed too.

"Relax," he said, and ran his hand down my spine, then over my ass, the touch more soothing than sexual. "This isn't punishment, Wren. It's calibration. I need to know what you can take."

He kept going, the rhythm changing, sometimes slow, sometimes two quick strikes in succession. At first, I tried to count the strokes, but I lost track after ten or twelve. The pain blurred into heat, the heat into something I couldn't name. My eyes started to water. Not from pain, but from the tension that had nowhere else to go.

He stopped, and for a moment, the only sound was the hiss of the air vents and my own ragged breathing.

He set the flogger aside and cupped my ass with both hands, kneading the muscle like he was testing the dough of a loaf he was about to bake. "You're shaking," he said, almost curious.

"Am I?" I asked, but my voice gave me away.

He stroked the backs of my thighs, his fingers tracing the patterns he'd left. "Are you wet?"

I blushed so hard I felt the heat at my hairline.

"Let's find out," he said, and slipped his hand between my legs. His fingers found the slick, and he hummed low in his throat, a sound of approval.

I thought he'd take me right then, but instead, he stood, wiped his hand on a towel, and walked to the far end of the room. He fiddled with the chain on the swing, adjusting something in the rig, then turned and beckoned.

"Here." He pointed at the ground in front of him.

I stood, my skin alive with pins and needles, and walked to him. Heavy straps dangled from the ceiling, each one anchored by a quick-release carabiner. The swing was made of two wide strips of thick, padded leather; one to support my shoulders and one for my ass. There were two loops for my legs to fit through up to my thighs. Two arm supports swung freely.

He turned me gently and helped me up. "Just lean back. Feet through these loops." He guided my legs apart, slipped each thigh into a support. With my shoulders cradled by the top padded strap and my ass resting on the bottom, the feeling was strange. My body weight was supported at my lower back and under my knees, arms held out and up by the angled cuffs. It felt less like bondage than like a surrender to gravity.

He adjusted the swing so my hips were level with his waist. He bent over, his face level with my cunt, and inhaled deeply, like he was breathing in the best air in the world.

He licked me once, flat and slow. The swing rocked just slightly under the motion.

I gasped, then caught myself. "Oh, that's—"

He looked up, face serious. "Good?"

He licked me again, slower this time, then circled my clit with his tongue. The swing's micro-movements amplified every sensation. He hooked his hands under my knees, holding me open, and went to work.

My head fell back at the sensation.

"Look at you. My little bird, your cunt is so perfect for my mouth. I could eat you all day."

I was already sensitive from the flogging, every touch was almost too much. He didn't let up. He alternated between sucking, flicking, and tracing slow spirals. When I tried to squirm away, the swing just rocked me back into him.

"You can't fly away, Wren. There's nowhere for you to go, anyway."

There was nowhere else I wanted to be. He added two fingers, fucking me in slow, deliberate strokes, then curling them to press against that spot inside that nobody else had ever found. My brain scrambled. My body went hot and cold and hot again. I knew I was dripping as I floated, weightless.

He pressed his tongue hard against my clit and fucked me with his hand, his fingers relentless in and out of me, and when the orgasm hit, it ripped through me like a tidal wave. The chains of the swing jerked when my stomach contracted. I cried out, loud and raw, and the echo bounced off the walls.

He didn't stop. He kept going, dragging the aftershocks out until I was shivering, my legs jelly and my hands numb from clutching the straps.

When he finally let go, he stood and wiped his mouth, a satisfied gleam in his eyes. "That's one," he said.

I heard the zipper of his jeans as he removed them. I hung there in the swing, my clit pulsing with the beats of my heart. I remembered the stretch of his cock, and I tingled in anticipation of feeling it again. He lifted my hips, my upper back supported by the padded strap. Then he lined himself up and slid into me in one long, slow thrust. The angle was perfect—he hit every nerve ending at once, and the fullness was so much I almost blacked out.

He grabbed the swing's side chains, using them to pull me onto his cock again and again, each time harder, each time deeper. The swing creaked, and my breath came in little animal pants.

"God, you feel fucking fantastic. You were made for me."

He fucked me for what felt like hours. At one point, I came again, this time so fast and so bright I couldn't see for a few seconds. He kept going, relentless, until finally, with a growl, he came inside me, his hands tight on my hips.

He stayed inside for a moment, then pulled out and spun me. He kissed me gently, cradling my head against his chest.

"Breathe, little bird," he said, and stroked my hair.

I did. Slowly, the world stitched itself back together.

He unstrapped me and carried me to the bed that sat in the corner of the room. Gently, he laid me down and caressed my face. "You handled everything so amazingly for your first time, Wren. Are you okay?"

I saw the look of concern on his face. "That was everything I didn't know I needed."

He tipped my chin up and kissed me, slow and deep. I tasted myself on his tongue, the flavor sharp and dark, and something in me purred at the knowledge. He tasted like sex and coffee and a kind of dangerous, elemental joy I'd never felt before. The world went soft at the edges.

He sat with his back against the headboard and pulled me up my back against his chest. He stroked my hair with one hand, the other drawing slow circles on my thigh. I breathed in the scent of him and let the silence fill me up.

When he spoke, it was so soft I almost missed it.

"I didn't like you for a long time, you know."

I twisted, looking up at him. "What?"

He shrugged, face blank. "Not you. The idea of you. The possibility." He worked his jaw, looking anywhere but in my eyes. "You were this... thing that haunted me. I'd see you running around the compound after your parents died, after you'd graduated from high school and were attending junior college. You were too small and too reckless, and I'd think *she's going to get herself killed.*"

I felt the laugh before I heard it. "You weren't wrong," I said.

He ran a finger along my jaw, the touch gentle, almost reverent. "But then I started watching you. Not in a creepy way—"

I snorted. "That's a lie."

He grinned, then sobered. "I saw you grow up. Saw how you took care of your asshole brother. Saw how you never gave up, even when you were alone. And I thought maybe you were stronger than I knew. Maybe you were just built different."

I tried to reply, but my throat went tight.

He leaned down, brushed his lips against my forehead. "I want to claim you, Parker. Want to give you my mark, my knot. But I... I just can't. Not yet."

I rolled onto my side, facing him, and let my hand rest on his chest, right over his heart. "You don't owe me anything."

He looked at me, really looked, and I saw the wolf come up behind his eyes—hungry, wild, and finally, finally, mine.

"Fuck Wren. It's not about owing you. Don't you feel it? You're my mate," he said, voice rough as broken glass. "You're mine. I know it as much as I know anything."

My heart stuttered, then restarted at double-time.

"Tell me you've felt it," he said, barely above a whisper.

I nodded, unable to trust my voice.

"Say it," he said, his breath fanning over my lips.

"I know it's true, and I understand." I said. "I want it. I want your mark. I also understand that it's too soon to make such a big move. We've only been back in each other's lives for a few days, really. It doesn't matter that we've known each other forever. And I'm starting with a deficit the size of Texas. I know I have to earn your trust. I hate it has to be like this. That I *made* it like this. But I swear I'll make you proud of me. Prove myself to you and Bronc and the pack."

The weight of the day pressed against my ribs, but Wrecker's hands—rough and steady—anchored me. His thumb brushed the curve of my cheekbone, tracing the tears I hadn't realized I'd shed.

"You're not alone in this," he said, voice roughened by emotion, yet softer than I'd ever heard it. "Not anymore. Every step you take, I'm taking it with you. Greenbriar's days are numbered, Parker. We'll burn their pack to the ground, together." His palm settled over my racing heart, as if he could imprint the promise straight into my pulse. "But when the ash settles... we can start to build something better. Something ours."

A shuddering breath escaped me. His words weren't just vows—they were a lifeline. "And after?" I whispered, the question trembling between us.

Wrecker's smile was a slow, dangerous thing, edged with tenderness. "After?" He leaned in, his lips grazing my temple, lingering like a sealed oath. "There'll be time. Time for me to claim you properly. To make sure the whole damned world knows you're mine."

The truth of it thrummed in my veins, fierce and sure. For the first time, the future didn't feel like a shadow—it felt like a dawn waiting to break. I pressed my forehead to his, our breaths mingling. "Together," I echoed.

"Now." He got up and held out his hand for me. "I think you have a puppy dog who'd probably like to be fed."

I grabbed his hand and pulled myself out of bed. "Fuck! I'm a terrible dog mom! I should have brought him with me, but I didn't know I'd be here so long!"

"Hey, calm down, Wren. It's not as late as you think. It's not even 5:00."

That was a relief. That was usually when he ate. Dinner would only be a little late.

I raced up the stairs and grabbed my bag then headed for the door. I gave him a kiss as I headed for my car. "Thank for today, Eli. It was amazing."

"Call me as soon as you get home."

Wow, I guess someone gave two shits about me, after all.

CHAPTER 12

WRECKER

The war room at Iron Valor's clubhouse always stank of old sweat and machine oil, even after Juliet went on one of her cleaning frenzies. It was after hours, the kind of night that crept in through the cinderblock, making the skin between your fingers go numb. The battered conference table had been in service since before I patched in. It was held together by more blood than screws. Bronc stood at the head, sleeves rolled up, a legal pad under his elbow and a marker in his hand. He hadn't shaved in a few days, and the stubble made him look more tired than tough.

We were down to business. Arsenal and Doc flanked the Alpha, both running on fumes and black coffee. Gunner was missing, but he'd been on patrol for two days straight, so he'd turn up at some point. I took my seat at the far end, fingers drumming the lacquered pine. Papa sat in his usual spot nursing a cup of coffee. The lights flickered overhead, a strobe that turned every movement into a threat.

"First order," Bronc said, voice gravel. "Toy run goes Christmas Day. Route's clear except for the Dairyville bypass. Arsenal, you got the east side?"

Arsenal grunted affirmative, eyes never leaving the tactical display mapped on the far wall. The black pinhead showed every street in our territory. The bypass blinked yellow. "I'll run the advance with Papa," he said. "Two units, unmarked. If Greenbriar shows, we'll cut 'em at the rail crossing."

Doc's knuckles rapped the tabletop in that dry, precise way he had. "Medical's tight. I restocked the kits myself. Juliet's team is running the warming tent, but there's some kind of norovirus at the elementary, so I doubled gloves and brought in bleach wipes. No cross-contamination this year."

"We got toy collection going strong." Big Papa's face lit up. He loved this shit. "We are full to overflowing. More toys this year than ever."

Bronc scratched at his beard. "Basement of the compound gonna accommodate?"

Papa was all smiles. "We'll have to take a closer look. Every underprivileged kid in Dairyville is gonna have toys out their wazzoos this year."

We all laughed at that. It was nice that something good was happening in our world for once.

Bronc nodded, made a note. "Good. Check the Civic Center for staging if necessary. Let's play it by ear. I'd prefer to keep it in the compound with all the nonsense going on, but we'll roll with the punches. Talk to Ms. Pearl and Juliet to help coordinate."

His eyes turned to me. "Speaking of nonsense. Wrecker, what's happening with the Greenbriar problem?"

That was my cue. I stood. Every other eye at the table followed, some out of habit, some out of suspicion.

"Greenbriar thinks they've got it made," I said. "They're going to get more than they bargained for. I've got Parker set up to get micro-cameras and mics all over their compound."

Arsenal's lip curled. "You trust her?"

I didn't blink. "I wouldn't have brought her in and given her the equipment if I didn't."

He didn't buy it. "You sure she's not still running a side op for her brother?"

I could feel my hands clench. "There's nothing in it for her to be doing anything for her brother. He fucking sold her out. She only wants to be sure he comes out of this alive, like any good sister would. I told her we'd pull him out when the time came. He'll be dealt with then."

The room went cold for a second, then Big Papa cleared his throat, low and gentle. "If it's a trap, we got a contingency?"

"Have y'all heard a goddamn word I've said?" I was on a razor's edge. "I built the program she's running. If she didn't have it, she'd be dead. Silas would end her. Without Iron Valor, she's dead. What trap do you think she's running?"

"She's a fucking traitor," Arsenal snarled. "I say she takes one step outa line, we end her."

My wolf surged up, hotter than blood. I was across the table before I knew it. Arsenal rose to meet me, all wiry anger and sharpened teeth. We'd fought before. He had scars on his back to prove it.

Bronc's voice dropped two octaves, that rare Alpha edge slicing through both of us. "Enough."

We froze. I could feel the veins in my neck pulsing, the animal in me howling for release. But Bronc had command. Always did.

"Sit down," he growled, to both of us.

We did. My hands shook. Arsenal wiped a fleck of spit from his chin.

Bronc eyed us like we were wayward kids, then cleared his throat. "Here's what you all need to know, so we don't kill each other before the real enemy does."

He waited for silence. You could hear the pipes ticking in the wall.

"Parker's not just some wayward pack member," he said. "She's Wrecker's mate."

The words hit like a car crash. Arsenal's jaw popped. Doc's pen rolled off the legal pad and clattered to the floor. Even Big Papa leaned forward, one elbow on the table, a slow smile cracking his scarred face.

I wanted to tear Bronc's throat out. This was my secret, my business. Not for the table.

"We respect mate bonds. Period."

He continued. "This is not up for debate. If anyone has a problem with it, you talk to *me*." He let his eyes settle on Papa, then Arsenal, then Doc, then me. "Otherwise, we follow the plan."

Big Papa's voice was the first to break the spell. "Mates are a gift," he said, his preacher's cadence cutting through the tension. "Even when they come wrapped in trouble. Even an ugly bastard like me has hopes that someday..." His voice filled with longing, trailed off.

There was a pause, then the table relaxed. Just a little. Arsenal flexed his hands, Doc scribbled something on his pad, and the world didn't end. Not right then, anyway.

Bronc finished the briefing, the rest of it a blur. The routes, the signals, the fallback codes. It all faded into a white-noise hum. I was already thinking about Parker, about the enemy territory she was walking into, about the way she'd smiled when I showed her how to activate the micro-cams.

When the meeting broke, Bronc caught my arm, squeezed once.

"She'll be fine," he said, low. "If not, I'll burn Greenbriar myself."

I nodded. "If she doesn't come back, there won't be enough left for you to burn."

He laughed, the old scars around his mouth going white. "That's my wolf."

Arsenal passed me on the way out, gave me a look like he wanted to say something. Maybe sorry, maybe fuck you. Hard to tell with him.

Big Papa lingered by the door, massive arms hanging casually by his sides. "You got your work cut out, brother," he said. "But you don't have to carry it alone."

I grunted, but it wasn't a dismissal. The youngest of us had a way of getting through the armor. Always did. He was the definition of a good man.

I left the war room, the cold following me out. The compound was dead quiet; the moon scraping the ground. I felt the wolf in my chest, pacing, ready to fight. Ready to kill. It was definitely time to let him out to run.

But mostly, I thought about the woman who'd turned my world upside down, headed into the heart of the enemy.

If anything happened to her, I'd end the world for it.

Dusk hit the plain like a bullet, and the wind carried the day's cold straight through the skin. I parked my truck in Parker's driveway and sat for several minutes. Her porch light was on, just a 40-watt bulb, but it burned through the blackout curtains in her front room like a warning flare.

I finally made my way to the door, knocked twice, and didn't wait for an answer. Inside, her house smelled like dryer sheets and lavender. I hadn't made it two steps before a little bundle of fur came tearing down the hall and right into my arms. She was running behind him, trying to pull a turtleneck sweater over her head. The hem was bunched at her chin, arms stuck overhead like a prisoner mid-surrender. I watched her wiggle free; pink and brunette bunches of hair fluffing out as if freed from prison as the neckline finally made it over her head.

I tucked the dog under my arm like a football, and he squirmed as I walked up to her to pull on the collar of her top so I could see the love bites I'd left on her shoulder and collarbone.

My wolf growled under my ribs with satisfaction. The bruises had faded, and while they weren't claiming bites; they were mine. The turtleneck was high enough to hide the marks. She checked herself in the mirror.

"Let's just hope he doesn't notice any of these little bruises or hickies," I said, my voice rougher than I meant.

She looked up at me, slightly panicked. "Shit. Do you think he'll notice them?"

I dropped Rocket onto the sofa and drank in her scent. "I doubt he'll be able to see them if you keep your hoodie zipped." I told her as I nuzzled her neck. I was careful to keep my body off of hers. "I don't want to put my scent anywhere on you."

She stopped, then let her hands fall. "Damn it. That's right. I almost forgot. I'd like to have your lips on me. Save it for later?" She gave me a look that told me she was determined to get this done and come back to me.

I stepped into the hall and leaned against the frame. "You ready?" I asked, but what I meant was, Are you scared?

"Yeah. Let's go over it again, just in case I choke."

We moved to the kitchen. She grabbed her bag and pulled out the micro-cams. How should I carry these?

I told her to just drop them in the easy-open case in her inside jacket pocket. She'd told me they'd never searched her. I just hoped that held true.

I picked up a micro-cam, turned it in my hand. "You remember the placement?"

"Five points," she said, voice flat. "One on the bookshelf, one on the edge of the desk, one on the corner of the credenza and his laptop, and one on the thermostat. I'll activate them with a touch. Three seconds, max."

She seemed confident. But getting the Trojan loaded was the most dangerous task. "While you're showing him the dummy accounts that look like the drain on Iron Valor funds are on schedule, you'll need to load the Trojan. It's a risk since you have to do it on his laptop, but as long as you're casual about it and seem to be proud of the work you did, you can sell it."

"I got it." She gave her bravest smile.

I nodded, set the cam back in the tray. "If it goes sideways, you bail. Don't look back."

She gave a dry laugh. "I'm not a hero, Eli. If it gets ugly, I'm gone."

"You say that," I said, "but you like the game too much."

She looked up at me, blue eyes shining. "I like the game, but I like breathing more."

I couldn't argue. I took the burner phone and dialed the test line, held it up to my ear while it rang. On the fourth ring, a recording of Doc's voice answered: "Code green. All clear. Next check at twenty hundred." I killed the call.

"Let's run it again," I said.

She rolled her eyes but did it anyway, picking up each micro-cam and palming it, then miming the touch against the wood of the kitchen table. The movements were delicate, precise. She could have been a surgeon, if she hadn't ended up a hacker.

I caught her wrist when she went for the last cam. My thumb and forefinger circled her bones easy. "You ever think about just running?" I asked.

Her mouth twisted. "All the time. But I suck at hiding, and I'm not good company for myself. If I left, I'd just end up in a place like this, making trouble for a new set of psychos."

I let go of her wrist, but not her gaze. "You're not trouble."

She snorted, but her cheeks went pink. "Liar."

Rocket stood up with his paws on her lap. She talked to that dog like he was a person.

"I'm nothing but trouble, isn't that right, boy? Yes, it is. Yes, it is." She kissed his head. Then she looked up at me; those clear blue eyes were glossy with unshed tears.

"If I don't come back, Eli, please take him. Don't let him wind up back by a dumpster."

I wrapped her in my arms. "You are coming back to him and to me." I kissed her forehead.

We finished the run-through. She pocketed the cams and slid the thumb drive into her sock, the way girls used to hide cigarettes in high school. I checked the clock on the stove. Five minutes until she had to leave.

I leaned against the fridge, watched her stare at the coffee pot like she could will it to brew faster. The silence sat between us, heavy and tight.

"You sure you want to do this?" I asked one more time.

She looked at me, then past me, like she could see the whole mess laid out in advance. "I have to," she said. "There's no other way out."

I walked over, caught her chin in my hand, forced her to look at me. "You're not going to die."

"Promise?" she said, the word almost a joke.

"Promise," I said, and it was as close to a prayer as I'd ever gotten.

She stood, tucked her hair behind her ear on the unshaved side, then zipped up the collar to her chin. "You gonna walk me out?" she asked.

"Yeah," I said. "Can't let you get mugged in your driveway."

She turned and looked at that pup. "You take care of the big guy, okay, Rocket? He needs all the help he can get." I swear that little dog winked at her.

Outside, the air had a winter chill. The sky was black already, clouds edged with orange from the city to the east. We stood on the porch, side by side, the silence familiar. She jangled her car keys, then looked up at me. "If I'm not back by midnight—"

"I'll come for you," I said.

She grinned. "I know. That's what scares me."

She made it to the end of the walk, then turned. "Hey, Eli?"

"Yeah?"

"Keep your eyes on me tonight, okay?"

I nodded. "Hey, Parker?" She stopped before shutting her car door. "Come to my house when you're done. I'll have the dog with me."

She slid into her car, started it, and pulled away with no hesitation. I stood in the yard, hands in my pockets, watching her taillights disappear into the dark.

"I love you, little bird."

The wind cut through the seams in my jacket. I didn't shiver. I didn't blink.

She was driving straight into hell, and I had to trust her to come back in one piece.

If she didn't, I'd tear the world apart to find her.

CHAPTER 13

SILAS DRAKE

The war room in the Greenbriar house looked like a bunker after the bombs: battered wood, paint peeling from too many winters of men pissing and bleeding on the floor, air curdled with sweat and spilled whiskey and the ozone tang of power that didn't belong to the living. I sat at the head of the table, a plank so warped it could have been pried up from the hull of a wrecked ship. The only light came from a caged bulb over my head, swaying on a cord and stroking shadows across the faces of the monsters I'd called family, or worse.

To my right: Vex, thin as a switchblade, face mapped with a scar from eye to jaw. She chain-smoked cheap menthols, but the air already stank of brimstone, so nobody complained. Next to her, Dagger—twice her mass, skull tattooed in blue ink that crawled up his neck and into the hairline like mold. Rook was last in line, hands folded in front of him, glasses perched low on his nose, looking like he'd rather be calculating your mortgage than your murder. They were my lieutenants, my wolves, the only creatures I trusted to watch my back in a room full of predators.

On the other side of the table, the hired guns: three demons and two vampires, all on loan from friends of friends in places where the law was just another dead dog in the street. The demons sat together, shoulder to shoulder: Malvex, who smiled like he knew your browser history; Krag, built like a refrigerator stuffed with explosives; and Rath, the kind of skinny that made you forget he could rip your arm out of its socket with two fingers. Their nails were black, their teeth a little too pointed, and when they blinked, their eyes flashed red like bad brake lights. The vampires, Elias and Marrow, looked like identical pale statues, except Elias wore a tie and Marrow looked like he'd eaten his last meal raw.

We all looked at the map.

I traced the perimeter of Iron Valor's compound with a finger, black nail gliding over the paper. "Three routes in," I said. "Two are watched; one is booby-trapped with motion sensors. But here—" I tapped the far western fence line, where a creek cut through the prairie—"they've got a blind spot. Floods every spring, makes it hard to keep the cameras up."

Dagger grunted, "So we hit 'em from the west?"

"We do," I said, and grinned, letting the split in my lip widen. "But not tonight. Not even soon. We wait until they're all inside, every last one of 'em. Christmas Run, Iron Valor hosts a toy drive for Dairyville's little bastards. They load every available hand into the basement to sort donations. Even Bronc gets sentimental for a hot second. The place is packed, and the only ones above ground are the women and kids."

Vex tapped her cigarette ash into an empty beer can, never breaking eye contact with the map. "You want to murder their brats?"

I laughed. "No. But I want Bronc to see what happens to a man who lets his guard down."

Malvex smiled, tongue flicking over the point of his incisor. "How do you get past the guards? Their Luna is—what's the word?—paranoid."

"She is," I agreed. "But you'd be amazed at what people will overlook with a little financial encouragement. We can buy staff. You ever meet a maid who turned down a ten grand Christmas bonus?" The demons snickered, and even Rook cracked a smile. "And if not, I've got an idea for a distraction. While they are looking one way, we'll go in another."

Dagger's eyes narrowed. "So we plant the bombs in the basement before the party?"

"Exactly," I said. "Vex, you'll go in as a janitorial sub. Use the uniforms I bought from that dry cleaner in Amarillo. Nobody looks at the help, especially when they smell like bleach and regret."

Vex stubbed her cigarette out on her palm and licked the wound, grinning. "I love it when you make me play dress-up, Silas."

"Don't get sentimental. You're planting C-4, not mistletoe."

Rook asked, "How do you want to time the detonations?"

I rolled my shoulders. The old injury flared up. A memory of the time Bronc's right hand shattered my collarbone and left me crawling in the snow like a kicked dog. "We time it for the last hour. By then, the upper levels are packed with children and the Luna's guard is down. We hit the supports, bring the ceiling down, and let them suffocate under their own fucking charity."

Elias, the vampire, interjected—voice soft as a knife sliding through silk. "What about survivors? There are always survivors."

I turned to him. "That's what you and your partner are for. Clean up the mess. You can eat whoever's left."

Marrow stared back, unmoving, the red in his irises eating the light. "And what do you want done with the Alpha?"

"Bring me his head." My wolf surged under my skin, claws digging at my insides. "Alive if you can, but I'm not picky."

Krag, the fridge-shaped demon, rumbled, "And if the Council sniffs this out before we move?"

I snorted. "Council's got its own problems. Varic Otero's playing nice with Iron Valor for now, but he's still pissed about what they did to King Calloway. Council only intervenes if it gets too public. That's why we do it fast and dirty. Keep our names and faces out of it. Iron Valor has amassed many enemies after what Menace did to Calloway and Madison."

Vex leaned forward, one thin hand reaching for the map. "What about the guards in the east tower? They rotate every four hours. Even if you get in, they'll spot the explosives before they go off."

I smiled, all teeth and old pain. "Leave the east tower to me. I'll have it taken out."

Rook looked surprised. "How?"

"Doesn't matter," I said. "Just be ready to move when I call." I let my gaze sweep the table, took a long drag of the cigarette Vex had just lit. The tip flared bright and then went to ash, a little death on the tongue.

Silence soaked the room, thick and nervous. I could feel the wolf inside me pacing, counting the heartbeats of everyone here.

Malvex broke the silence. "Why not just poison the kids? Less collateral. No witnesses."

I stared at him, enjoying the discomfort as I ground the cigarette out on my own wrist. "Because I want Bronc to see the bodies. I want him to hear them scream. I want him to feel what I felt when Menace gutted our Alpha in front of everyone. I want him broken, not dead. Not at first."

Dagger looked at me, hunger in his eyes. "And after?"

"After, we bury them. Burn the compound to the ground. No survivors." The memory of my old Alpha's last gurgling breath rose up like a ghost, and I smiled to let it pass.

Vex slid the map toward herself, studied the fence lines, then looked up. "You ever think about what happens if they see us coming?"

I shrugged. "They won't. They'll be too busy playing nice for the community and the news cameras in the days leading up to the run. And like I said, I have a plan to take his eyes off of the minor details of the run."

Rook folded his hands. "And if it all goes to shit?"

I leaned in, letting them all see the scars on my face, the truth of how much I'd already lost. "If it goes to shit, we tear them apart the old-fashioned way. There's no scenario where Bronc gets out of this alive. That's a promise."

The vampires and demons exchanged looks, silent communication passing like static. I saw what they were thinking: if this failed; we were all dead men. I wanted them scared. I wanted them sharp.

I let the silence fester, then stood and walked to the window, taking all my strength to stifle the limp in my left leg. Outside was nothing but dead trees and darkness. Our world had already ended; and I was determined to yank it back from the dead.

Behind me, chairs scraped. Deals were struck. Blood was owed. I felt the promise of violence hardening in my chest, cold and absolute.

"Dismissed," I said, and listened as the predators slithered out.

The war room emptied, but I stayed behind, staring at the map, fingers tracing the lines again and again until the paper tore under my nails.

This is going to be beautiful, I thought. *The perfect massacre.*

And Greenbriar would be the last ones standing, even if it killed me.

I lingered for a while longer, watching smoke curl from the dented ceiling fan and spiral into the dark. The meeting had gone better than I'd expected. Wolves, vampires, demons—usually you get three minutes of civility before they start measuring dicks and pecking order, but tonight everyone was hungry enough to swallow their pride. Nothing bonds a room like the promise of blood.

I gave it another five minutes, then followed the drag marks on the floor to my office. The room was comprised of stark cinder block walls. You'd think it was a prison cell if not for the furniture and pictures displayed here and there. Our dead alpha didn't go in for much in the way of decor or nice things. I, on the other hand, tried to upgrade things as much as I could without looking like a pussy. There was a fine line with this pack, but bringing up our reputation from trash to a pack to be respected and feared had been a goal of mine. I might be about to blow that to shit with murdering an entire pack. I didn't know how we'd land. But I lived with the motto, *'might makes right.'* Guess I'd see if the rest of the supernatural world believed that as well.

I dropped into my chair, let the pain in my shoulder pulse through me, and watched the camera feed from the perimeter. Everything outside was frozen and motionless. But inside the compound, you could practically taste the anticipation—the way everyone moved a little too quiet, eyes always just a hair too bright. They all knew what was coming. They were just pretending it wouldn't matter.

I thumbed through the reports on Iron Valor my people had been compiling. More promising than I'd hoped: two officers already at each other's throats, their Luna's moods were wild and erratic. The toy drive was shaping up to be the best-attended in years. The perfect setup. I laughed, then coughed, the old scar tissue in my throat buzzing like an electrical burn.

On the next page: the latest from Parker Reid.

Parker wasn't like the others. Most hackers? Pathetic scavengers—cash or fear bought them. But her? She was a blade sharpened on stone, cold and precise. The kind that cuts deeper the harder you grip it. I'd dealt with lone wolves before, snarling things who thought themselves untouchable, but Parker... she wasn't that. No, she circled Iron Valor like a storm that returns each month, predictable only in its inevitability. Full moon runs, shifts, vanishing before dawn. No attachments. None that I could find, anyway. Her brother? A weeping cockroach. Offered her up like a trinket when I came to carve my due from his ribs. Weak blood. How had they shared a womb?

First time I saw her, I almost laughed. Expected some mousy code-rat, hiding behind thrift-store armor. Instead, she walked in like she'd spun her own gravity. Five feet of nerve and hunger, wild dark hair tinged with pink, eyes electric blue. Didn't blink when I let the monster breathe. Just stood there, tasting the danger, wrists loose at her sides—ready, not afraid. "Will this save his life?" She asked, no tremor, no plea. As if her brother's worthlessness was a fact, not a regret. I admired that. Hypocrisy's a stench I can't stomach.

She made my skin itch. Not because she defied me. No, any fool can bark. But because she mirrored the parts of me I'd buried under corpses and ash. Same gnawing void behind the ribs. Same contempt for rules that aren't hers. Wanted to crack her open just to see if she'd bleed ambition instead of red. Wanted to... well. Monsters have appetites.

She'd worked for a few weeks on a plan to siphon over a hundred grand from Iron Valor's accounts without tripping alarms. And that's just the beginning. The bank security gave her friction, firewalls, encryption, singing hymns in binary. But she'd bent it. I'd gotten an email from her telling me as much. Wanted to meet to give me the details about how it'll go down. That girl was an artist when it comes to this shit. Tonight, I'd sit back and watch her create a masterpiece.

Once she triggered the worm in Iron Valor's network, every financial asset they had should be rerouted through a chain of shell companies that all led, eventually, to me. They'd be bled dry as a gutted stag. It wasn't about the money. It was about humiliation. The only thing Bronc cared about more than his pack was his reputation. Stripping him bare would be the real kill shot.

I leaned back, propped my boots on the desk, and let my mind wander. If Parker worked out, if she stayed on the leash, we could take more than Iron Valor. We could bleed the vamps in Kazmir's kingdom, sabotage the demon lord's empire. She could be a weapon, a bomb I could drop wherever I wanted. Or I could just watch the world burn, take her with me, see who survived.

There was a knock at the door.

"Come," I said, and Parker slipped in, hood down, hair wild, shoulders squared. She looked like she'd spent the last six hours in a server room or a bar fight, maybe both.

She closed the door behind her, then took the chair across from me. "Looks like you're set to go," she said, voice even. She nodded at my laptop. "Can I show you?"

I rarely let anyone touch my computer, but she was interested in keeping her brother alive. She wouldn't dare put him in danger by fucking me over.

"By all means." I slid my open laptop over to her and watched her fingers fly across the keyboard. She watched the screen, then turned it back to me so I could see.

"Funds will hit the first offshore at midnight. All they'll see is a denial-of-service, like they've got a worm but no infection."

I nodded. "All the accounts?"

"They have several. This is just the first. It will happen in a sequence. The first tonight. The second tomorrow and the last the next night. They'll be so busy trying to figure out what went wrong on the first, they'll never see the next."

I almost smiled. "Good. You know you're the only reason I haven't killed your brother yet?"

She looked at me, flat. "I know. That's the reason I'm doing this."

That got a real smile out of me. "You value family, Parker. I like that."

She leaned forward, elbows on her knees. "What happens after the transfers? Am I done?"

I watched her. She wasn't nervous, not exactly, but her left hand kept clenching and unclenching, like she was rehearsing a punch she knew would never land.

"No," I said. "You're not done. Not until I say."

She glared, and for a second her wolf surfaced, pupils wide and black. "I've done everything you asked."

"And you'll do more," I said, voice low. "You want your brother alive? You do what I say."

She stood up, hands balled into fists. "Fuck you."

I was on my feet before she knew it; the chair clattering against the wall. I moved faster than she thought I could. I caught her by the throat, my hand inside the turtleneck she wore, and pressed her up against the cinderblock wall, squeezed just hard enough to see her eyes bulge, my mouth close enough to feel her breath. "You're mine," I said. "You have been since the moment I first laid my eyes on you. I was just waiting for you to figure it out."

She clawed at my wrist, but it was a show. I could feel her pulse, could feel the wolf in her wanting to bite and run. "I hate you," she said, voice ragged.

I leaned in close enough to bite the shell of her ear. "You hate yourself more."

She shuddered, then went limp, not submission but something closer to resignation. I loosened my grip, let her slide down the wall. She didn't fall. She didn't cry.

I waited. She caught her breath, put her hand on the bookshelf to balance herself, wiped her mouth, then glared at me with new hate. "If you touch my brother—"

I cut her off. "You'll what? You'll kill me? Try it. You won't be the first."

She laughed, bitter. "I'll do worse."

For a second, I believed her.

I decided it was best at this moment if I let her leave. She had nowhere to go, no one to turn to. She could go back to her lonely little house and stew all by herself and enjoy her last days of freedom. There was nowhere she could run that I wouldn't find her.

"You're dismissed, Parker. Remember, you can run, but you can't hide."

CHAPTER 14

PARKER

I made it as far as the county line before the shakes hit me. By the time I turned off onto the gravel, I couldn't feel my hands. I tried to flex the wheel, but all the strength was gone from my arms, eaten up by the memory of Silas's hands around my throat and the echo of his words in my skull. Every time I blinked, I saw his office, his face, smelled his breath on my cheeks.

The drive to Wrecker's house was muscle memory. I don't remember the turns, just the splinters of old fear that caught on every rut in the road. The sky was dark; not even the moon was brave enough to show its face; the fields wet with frost. I pulled into his side yard at a crawl, headlights barely illuminating the low shape of his truck in the drive. For a second, I just sat there, sweat freezing to the insides of my jacket, the urge to disappear stronger than anything I'd ever felt. But there was nowhere else to go, and I'd already crossed the point of no return a hundred times tonight.

He was on the porch before the engine cut. The porch light haloed his head, making him look less like a man and more like an executioner or an avenging god. He was barefoot, hair sticking up in a wild storm, and he crossed the yard with the kind of stride that made the ground look like it was trying to get out of his way.

I didn't even get the door open. He ripped it wide, reached in, and unbuckled me with one hand. The other arm scooped me up and out before my feet could hit the dirt. My head lolled onto his shoulder. He carried me, not like a lover, not like a child, but like he was rescuing something half-dead from a burning building.

He smelled like Wrecker; oak and steel and that faint, raw bite of oranges. I wanted to say something, anything, but all I could do was shudder in his grip, my face mashed into the black cotton of his shirt. The door slammed behind us, a shotgun blast in the dark.

He set me down on the entryway tile, but didn't let go. His hands—huge, calloused, trembling at the knuckles—clamped on my face his thumbs caressing my cheeks. The warmth was animal, overwhelming, and for a moment I thought I was going to puke from the rush of it.

He spoke first, his voice scraping the roof of his mouth. "I watched the whole fucking thing," he said, and the rage in it made my eyes snap open. "It took everything I had not to drive straight there and kill him with my bare hands."

I shook my head, but the movement wasn't mine. My body was working on a different logic now, something older than words. I tried to form a sentence, but nothing made it out of my mouth except a gasp.

He guided me into the living room where Rocket came flying in from the hallway. He jumped into my lap as the big couch swallowed me whole. "Hey buddy." I whispered. "I'm happy to see you, too." I told him as I laid him beside me. Amazed at how just that silly little guy's presence had started to calm me.

Wrecker knelt in front of me, hands on either side of my jaw, eyes boring into mine. "Are you hurt?" he demanded, but there was a softness buried under the grit. He reached for my neck, fingers pulling down the collar of the turtleneck. He traced the outline of where Silas's meaty hand had squeezed. I flinched, and he snarled, a raw sound meant for killing.

"Answer me, Parker. Did he touch you anywhere else?" The question hung in the air like a blade.

I managed to shake my head again, this time with meaning. "No. Just—" I lifted my hand, showed him the band of bruises already rising on my throat. "He wanted to make a point." My voice was sandpaper, shredded to nothing.

His shoulders slumped, just a fraction, but enough to show the relief flooding through him. He let out a breath and closed his eyes, then pressed his forehead to my knees. We stayed like that, locked together. I leaned over, my forehead on the back of his head. I started to cry for real.

Not big, cinematic tears. Just the slow, stupid kind that ran down your face when you're too tired to fight them. He pulled away and sat up. Gently, he wiped my tears with his thumbs, and I hated how good it felt to be touched by someone who wasn't trying to break me.

I sat shivering while he went to the kitchen and came back with a cup of tea. He handed it to me, then wrapped a throw blanket over me. His eyes never left my face as he sat on the coffee table across from me.

I sipped, then choked, then set the cup down next to him. "I did what you told me to do," I said, my voice a whisper. "I planted the first micro-cam at the entrance. Another in the main hallway, right by the office. I got two on the doorframe of his office—one high as I could, one low. I uploaded the Trojan to Silas's laptop when I showed him the account logs. And I..." My throat closed up. I looked at my hands, the way they shook on the blanket. "I got extra lenses onto his computer monitor and his bookshelf. But I couldn't get one on the credenza. I never had the opportunity to get close to it. I'm sorry."

He made a noise, not quite a word. He sat next to me on the couch and gathered me in his arms. "It's enough," he said. "You did more than anyone could've." His palm landed on the top of my head, heavy and safe. "You did perfect, little bird."

The phrase made something in my chest twist. A tight knot of shame and pride and the bone-deep need to be good for someone, even if it meant bleeding for it.

He picked Rocket up and set him on the floor. "I'm gonna take some time with our girl, Rocket. Go lay in your bed, buddy." The sweet pup went right to his bed and curled up. Amazing.

Then he shifted my legs, so they draped across his lap. He started rubbing my calves, slow and methodical, like he was working the poison out of my muscles with each sweep of his hand.

"Silas believed it?" he asked, voice low.

I nodded, eyes blurring. "He was convinced the money's already on the move. He thinks I'm going to trigger the next worm tomorrow."

Wrecker's jaw ticked, the scar on his chin going white. "Good. Let him think he's winning. We'll burn his world down when he's not looking."

I tried to laugh, but it came out a cough. "He's going to come for me. You know that, right?"

He shrugged, the motion like an avalanche under my thighs. "Let him come. He won't make it past the porch."

"Come on," he said, and I followed him down the hall, feet bare and numb.

The den was lit up with his monitors, each cycling through security feeds, code overlays, and a snarl of encrypted messaging threads.

He booted up his main rig and motioned for me to sit. He didn't look at me, just typed in a string of passwords that would have made a cryptologist cry, then unlocked a drawer and fished out a thumb drive. The drive was marked with a strip of blue tape, a single letter on it: P.

He plugged it in and dragged a file onto the main screen. "This is what Silas is seeing," he said, and the blue light washed over his face, turning his eyes into steel.

The desktop was a perfect mimic of Iron Valor's financial server—every log, every balance, every false note. But as he clicked through, I could see the seams in the forgery, like faint scars under new skin. The real magic was in the subroutines: every attempt to "patch" the worm only embedded it deeper, every security alert routed to a dead drop. It was a digital ouroboros, feeding on itself.

"I've set it up to make it look like we're trying countermeasures but failing," he explained, voice low. "We push back just enough to make Silas think he's got us. But the real payload..." He zoomed into the code, flicked a finger at the monitor. "Here. See it?"

I did. The infection wasn't just a worm. It was a relay. Every byte Silas stole, every message he sent, bounced through our ghost servers first. It was genius, and it made my heart lurch with something ugly and envious.

We watched the feeds together, side by side. The audio stream from Greenbriar's den was live—crackling, full of echo, but every word was crystal clear. I could hear Dagger's laugh, Vex's cursing, even the tick of Marrow's nails on the conference table.

At the head of it all, Silas's voice, slick with victory: "All the accounts will hit at midnight. They'll never see it coming."

Wrecker kept his gaze on the monitor, but his hand landed on my knee, grounding me.

"Don't let him get in your head," he said, thumb tracing a circle through the denim.

I nodded, but my whole body was trembling now, every cell vibrating with adrenaline or memory or both. I wrapped my arms around myself, tried to get small, but it didn't help. The pressure in my chest built until I could taste iron on my tongue.

"He grabbed me here," I said, pointing to my throat. "But it's everywhere, you know? I feel dirty." The last word barely made it out. "Like I'll never get it off."

He froze, then turned away from the screen and knelt in front of me, hands cupping my face. His eyes were so pale they almost looked blue now, the gray leeched out by rage. For a second, I thought he might punch a hole in the wall, but instead he just held me, fingers gentle.

"Let me fix it," he said, voice scraped raw. "Let me make it right."

Before I could answer, he stood, scooped me up, and carried me down the hall to the bathroom attached to his bedroom. It was huge—tile everywhere, cold and white, the kind of place you could clean up after a massacre and no one would ever know. He sat me down on the marble counter, then turned on the water, running the tub full blast. The sound filled the room, deafening, but all I could focus on was him.

He stood me up and peeled off my hoodie, then the turtleneck. Then he knelt and rolled down my jeans. He did it slow, like he was afraid I'd vanish if he moved too fast. His hands lingered on my hips, then my thighs, every touch soft as wind. I watched him, half-expecting him to stop, to reconsider, to realize I was more trouble than I was worth. But he never hesitated.

He undressed himself next, and my breath caught in my chest. I'd seen his body before, and it was just as majestic as I'd remembered. But now, in the bright white light, every scar was a map, every tattoo a history. He was built for violence, but there was a tenderness in the way he folded his clothes, set them aside, then climbed into the steaming water and reached for me.

I followed, skin prickling, heart jackhammering in my ribs.

He pulled me between his legs, my back to his chest, his arms a cage of warmth around me. The water was almost too hot, but I didn't care. I let it scald the memory of Silas from my skin.

He reached for a washcloth and lathered it with soap. The scent was wild: bergamot and sage. It smelled warm. It smelled like home. His hands were careful, reverent. Every time he found a bruise, he lingered, thumb tracing circles until the ache went away.

His soapy hands lingered, rinsing the memory from my skin. At first, the cloth skimmed across the surface—shoulders, arms, ribs—each stroke steady, impersonal, as if he was working on a puzzle instead of a person. But as the water cooled and the bruises faded from blue to red, the way he touched me changed. His thumb trailed the line of my collarbone, then slipped down to the curve of my breast, tracing circles until the nipple stood up in shock. He shifted, legs bracketing mine, and the heat from his body lit up the whole bath.

I pressed my thighs together, but he noticed, always noticed, and reached between them with a wet hand. His fingers were rough and callused, and the contrast to the soft cloth made me gasp.

He washed me slowly, starting at the outside, then working in. I let my knees drift apart; the water sloshing in little waves, and waited for him to do what he wanted. He watched, lips twitching into a crooked smile. He liked watching. He liked making me squirm. He liked knowing that even after everything, I would still give myself to him.

His hands drifted lower, and my breath caught. The first touch was gentle, the second rougher, and by the third I was grinding against his palm. I couldn't help it. I wanted to hate myself for it, but it felt too good. He ran a finger along my slit, then circled my clit, light as air. I moaned, and it echoed off the tiles, a sound I didn't recognize as mine.

He bent forward, pressed his mouth to my ear. "You want it?" The words were hot and thick. "Say it."

I tried, but the air wouldn't come. He pinched my nipple, and the shock of it broke me open. "Please," I whispered, the word small and pathetic.

He smiled for real then. "Good girl."

He lifted me from the tub, water streaming down my skin. The air was cold, but his hands were hotter than before, working over every inch of me with the towel, drying me but also teasing, testing, leaving marks of a different kind.

He slipped a robe over my shoulders and took my hand.

"Let's go." He said as he gave my hand a small tug.

Within just a few minutes, I stood at the edge of Wrecker's playroom, the air thick with the scent of leather and something darker, primal. The dim light cast long shadows across the room, and I felt the weight of his gaze on me, heavy and unrelenting. My heart pounded as he stepped closer, his bare feet silent against the cold tile floor. He wore the towel from when he'd exited the bathtub, his muscles flexing with every deliberate movement, his tattoos twisting like living shadows beneath his skin.

He led me to the padded St. Andrew's Cross.

"Turn around," he commanded, his voice low and filled with promise.

I obeyed without hesitation, my breath hitching as I faced the St. Andrew's Cross. The leather padding felt cool against my palms as I pressed my hands against it. Behind me, I heard the soft clink of chains, and I shivered, anticipation curling low in my belly.

His hands were rough as they gripped my wrists, securing them to the cross with practiced ease. The metal cuffs bit into my skin, but the pain was distant, overshadowed by the electricity sparking between us. He stepped back, and I felt the loss of his warmth like a physical ache.

"You're mine, Parker," he said, his voice a growl that reverberated through me. "Every inch of you. And tonight, I'm going to make sure you forget everything, every other touch but mine."

His words sent a thrill down my spine, and I whimpered, my body already reacting to his dominance. He moved behind me, and I felt the heat of his body as he pressed against my back. His hands trailed down my sides, ghosting over my hips, and I shuddered, my breath coming in shallow gasps.

"I'm going to take care of you tonight, Wren. Spread your legs," he ordered, his voice a growl that sent shivers down my spine.

I obeyed, my legs parting for him, and I felt his hands grip my hips, pulling me back against him. His tongue traced a path up the inside of my thigh, and I gasped, my hands gripping the cross as pleasure shot through me.

"You're so fucking wet for me," he said, his voice thick with desire. "You're dripping, baby. Do you know what that does to me? Knowing how much you love my touch?"

I moaned, my hips rocking against his face as he licked and teased, his tongue tracing circles around my clit before plunging inside me. I cried out, my body bowing as he devoured me, his hands holding me firmly in place.

"Wrecker," I gasped, his name a plea on my lips.

He stood, and I felt two of his large fingers enter my pussy and pump in and out of me at a relentless pace. I could hear the sound of my wetness as they pistoned in and out. My body writhed against his hand. His mouth was at my neck kissing and licking a trail down my spine.

The feeling was incredible.

"I love how your pussy sucks my fingers into your body hungry for me to fuck you anyway it can. You're so tight. God, what you do to me little bird."

He took my face and turned it towards him so he could shove his tongue in my mouth, kissing me with desperation like he wanted to consume me whole.

He stepped away for a moment and then came back with something in his hands. It was an embossed black leather riding crop with a braided handle.

He showed it to me. "See this sweetheart?"

"Yes," I told him.

"I'm going to use this on you now. It will sting, but my intention is not to harm you. You remember your safe words?"

"Yes, sir. Dumbledore if things are good, Snape if I'm concerned, and Voldemort for full stop."

"Such a good girl." He praised me, and it made me feel so good inside.

The first swat carried a shocking sting. I jerked at the feeling. He trailed swats up and down my back and then across my ass. Back and forth, up and down. They hurt until they didn't. I found myself leaning into the crop, my ass reaching for it. Evey so often he'd stop and press his fingers into my pussy, which was dripping wet.

"There's my pain slut, enjoying the sting of my crop." He laughed as he circled my clit with his finger.

"Wrecker, I'm close. Please." I needed to come so bad.

"I love to hear you beg, Wren. To see you squirm under my touch."

He took the handle of the crop and pressed it to my entrance, and I stilled.

"Dumbledore?" he asked.

"Yes," I told him.

He slowly inserted the handle into my pussy, then pumped it in and out. The ridges of the braid felt unbelievably good.

"Oh my god."

"Come for me, Wren."

And I did. I came apart. The sensation was too much. I shuddered and jerked as he continued to pump the crop handle in and out. My moans filled the room.

He undid the cuffs and laid me on the bed in the corner of the room. He hovered over me, weight on his forearms.

"You are the most fucking magnificent creature I have ever laid my eyes on. Are you ready for me?"

I looked down the length of his body as he sat back on his heels. He gripped his enormous cock in his hand. I wanted him more than anything.

"Please," I said.

He lined himself up at my entrance and entered me with a powerful thrust. There was nothing like the feeling of being filled with him. It was the most complete I'd ever felt. I gripped him with my legs as much as I could, gripping him with my heels. He set an unrelenting pace.

"That's right, take all of me, Wren. You squeeze my cock so tight. Nothing has ever felt as good as your pussy wrapped around me. You're mine. Say you're mine."

My eyes never left his face. For once in my life, I truly felt as though I belonged to someone. "Yours, I said. Forever yours."

He reached down and stroked my clit as he pounded into me and I came completely undone; the orgasm taking me by surprise. He followed with a shout and groan filling me completely.

He rolled off, then scooped me into his arms, cradling me against his chest.

"Still feel dirty?" he asked, voice gentler than I'd ever heard.

I shook my head. "No."

He kissed the top of my head, then tucked me under his arm. "Good. Because you're mine. And I take care of what's mine."

We didn't talk about tomorrow, or the war, or Silas. For now, there was only the bed, and the warmth, and the way his heart beat steady under my cheek.

I let myself drift, knowing that when morning came, it would all start again.

But for now, I was clean.

And I was loved.

CHAPTER 15

WRECKER

I watched her sleep.

The bruising on her throat had bloomed, blood pooling beneath the skin in a ring where Silas's grip had closed. She lay on her back, face slack with exhaustion, hair splayed brunette and pink against the pillow. I'd washed her clean, but violence never comes out in the laundry. It stains, seeps, soaks into the marrow. My wolf paced beneath the surface, restless, jaws clicking, hackles up every time she exhaled a dry little whimper.

I didn't sleep. I never slept when there was a job unfinished, and Silas Drake wasn't just unfinished—he was half-cooked, rotting, maggot-bait in a suit. I kept my hand on Parker's thigh, anchoring us both, thumb tracing up and down the soft curve of muscle. If I let go, she'd drift off somewhere I couldn't reach. If I held too tight, I'd shatter what was left of her calm.

The clock on the dresser ticked over 2:22 a.m. I slid out from beneath the covers, careful not to wake her. She stirred, eyelids fluttering like wings in the dark, but didn't break the surface. The room was chilly, still reeking faintly of bath soap and sex, and the coppery tang of her panic from earlier. I dressed in silence, pulling on sweats and a T-shirt. I paused at the mirror. Stared. The scar on my chin was white as a rope, my jaw bristling with three days' stubble. I looked feral. I looked perfect for the task at hand.

I shut the door behind me. Rocket, the ugly little dog, lay curled in a death spiral on his bed. He twitched one ear, then went back to his dreams.

Down the hall, I passed the den. The monitors were all dark. Power cycled to cut the heat signature. The house was silent, the only sound the low hum of the fridge and the haunted creak of old boards. In my office, I flicked on a desk lamp and sat in the chair, elbows on knees. I picked up the burner cell, thumbed Bronc's number, and let it ring.

He picked up on the second buzz. "You up?"

I could hear the background noise—low voices, the clink of glasses, maybe the TV at Pearl's bar. "Always," he said. "Status?"

"She did it. All the devices are in. Trojan's running. Silas bought the whole show, but he put hands on her."

A long, hollow pause. "Is she—?"

"She's alive," I said. "But he meant it as a warning. Said he's not done with her. Won't be until he says so."

Another voice cut in, faint but sharp. "Is that Eli?" Juliet. Bronc's mate. I heard a rustle, then the sound went on speaker.

"Yeah. I figured you'd be there," I said.

She didn't bother with preamble. "How bad was it?"

I told her, flat and spare: bruises, nothing broken. Fear, but no fractures in her pride. The things you learn to look for after enough years seeing what men do to each other and to the women they think they own.

Juliet swore, voice all steel. "That girl deserves better. You know it."

I didn't answer. I ran my finger along the edge of the desk, catching the sharp burr where the finish had chipped. The silence stretched, cold and suffocating.

Bronc broke it. "You sound off, Wrecker. What's the real ask?"

I hesitated. My tongue felt too big in my mouth. "When did you know?" I asked finally. "About Juliet. That it wasn't just the bond, but actual love?"

Another pause. This one, softer. "First time I saw her laugh at my ugly ass. I knew the wolf part, sure. But the man part took longer." He waited. "You having doubts?"

"No." That was a lie, and everyone on the line could taste it.

Juliet's voice went warm, almost gentle. "Are you worried you'll lose her to what Silas will do to her, or worried you'll lose yourself if you claim her?"

I gritted my teeth. The memory of Parker's body, slick and sweet and shivering in my arms, slammed back into me. I'd almost bitten her. I'd almost gone full animal, just to stamp out the stink of Silas's hands on her. If I hadn't held back, I'd have marked her—forever, whether she wanted it or not. "It's not the bite that scares me," I said. "It's the after. Once I do it, that's it. No way to undo it."

Bronc's laugh was a slow roll of thunder. "That's the point, brother. No take-backs. No trial period. You put your mark on her, you're in for the long haul."

Juliet cut in. "You don't have to wait, you know. There's no perfect time, no event horizon. If you want her, you do it now, when she's awake and can say yes."

"She deserves a choice," I said.

"Then ask," Juliet said, voice sudden and sharp. "Don't be a coward. It's better than marking her by accident during a full moon."

I leaned back in the chair, head thumping the wall. The urge to howl was close, so close, but I'd rather die than let anyone hear that sound. "She's every bit as smart as I am," I said. "Maybe too smart for me. She's all about books, and nerd movies, and her dog. She thinks she's broken, but she's not. She's just—" I stopped. Started again. "She's good. Like, *really* good. Her heart, it's got a pureness like I've never seen."

Juliet snorted, but it was affectionate. "I bet she's also a pain in the ass, just like you. Most people with pure hearts are. Maybe that's why it works."

Bronc's voice softened. "What do you want, Eli? Not what the wolf wants. Not what your body wants. What does the rest of you want?"

I thought about Parker, her laughter in my kitchen, the way she poured coffee like it was holy water, her obsession with taking things apart just to see if she could fix them. I thought about her loyalty to her brother, even after he screwed her over. I thought about the first night I saw her in the pack house, years ago, when she was nothing but a spitfire kid with a chip on her shoulder and a hunger to prove herself.

"I want to keep her," I said. "I want to protect her. But I want her to want me, not just the bond."

Juliet let out a sigh, all the air in the room rushing out with it. "If you wait for certainty, you'll wait forever. She's already choosing you, Eli. Let her."

I stared at the phone. The little glowing screen, the line of dead pixels across the top. "Thanks," I said, and meant it.

"We got your six," Bronc said. "But don't wait too long. Silas's got a death wish, and I'd hate to miss the fireworks."

I ended the call. Sat there in the half-light, listening to the blood thrum in my ears.

Maybe Juliet was right. Maybe my wolf knew something the rest of me didn't. Maybe it was time to stop waiting for the perfect moment, and just grab hold before it slipped through my fingers.

I went back to the bedroom. Parker hadn't moved. She'd pulled my pillow to her chest, and her lips moved in a half-smile, like she was dreaming of something sweet. I knelt by the bed, put my head on her hip, and let the silence fill me up.

"I'll wait until you say yes," I whispered, the words barely audible, even to myself. "But when you do, I won't ever let you go."

I stayed there, counting her breaths, until the sky outside shifted from black to orange and blue and the day began again.

The days passed in a blur of static, screens, and the slow decay of willpower.

We watched Silas on the cameras she'd planted, each grainy feed flickering in the darkness of my den. Parker hunched over the monitors, knees tucked to her chest, mug of tan coffee balanced dangerously on the arm of the chair. She only ever seemed at ease when she was surveilling. There were moments when I caught her smiling—sharp, feral grins when Greenbriar's dumbest foot soldiers tripped over a trap, or when Silas launched into one of his classic fits of desk-flipping rage. But mostly, she watched with the same hollow focus of someone waiting for the guillotine blade to fall.

I was there too, glued to the other half of the war: the code. Every hour, I combed the server logs for evidence that the data tap was working, cross-referenced every ping, every shadow in the Greenbriar system. We were getting everything: schedules, blackmail, bribes, the dirt Silas needed to run his empire. He talked to his men like a dictator in a bunker, every word weighted with contempt. But the real work, the plotting, always happened in the locked "war room." No camera. No audio. No sense of what went on behind that door, unless Parker was in the room to plant a bug herself. Which would never happen, not after last time.

Her neck was still ringed with bruises, now a sickly mix of yellow and green. She wore high collars, but I saw her fingers ghost up to the bruising every time Silas's face appeared on-screen. It made my wolf want to kill him, slow and public.

On the third day, I came back from the shop at lunch to find her still staring at the monitors, face bathed in the blue-white glow. She hadn't moved in hours except to refill her coffee. Her eyes were dry and red, like she'd forgotten how to blink.

I crouched next to her chair. "You're starting to look like me," I said, keeping my voice soft. "It's not a good look."

She didn't react at first. Then she turned, pupils huge and bottomless. "I can't stop," she said. "What if I miss something?"

I glanced at the feeds: Silas in his office, Silas at his desk, Silas in the kitchen berating the world's most nervous prospect about the coffee. "He can't hurt you from there," I said, taking her hand. "And if he tries, I'll make it ugly."

She stared at our joined hands like they were a foreign object. "You don't understand. If I let my guard down—"

"You'll break," I finished. "Yeah, I know the drill."

I let her go and stood up, stretching my arms behind my head. "You need a break, Parker. Fresh air, or at least a window that isn't a screen."

She looked at me like I'd suggested skydiving without a parachute.

"Come on," I said. "There's something at the pack house you need to see."

Her first reaction was suspicion. Her second was to grab Rocket from his donut-bed and tuck him under her arm like a talisman. I didn't say anything about it. She wore armor where she could.

The drive out to the compound was silent except for the panting of the dog and the squeak of the truck's shocks. Parker stared out the window the entire time, watching the landscape for threats that weren't there. The sky was a featureless stretch of gray; the air so dry it left dust on your teeth.

As soon as we hit the pack road, I could smell the difference. The air here was full of life: wood smoke, baking bread, the clean metallic bite of wolf. This was home, even if I spent most of my time outside its walls anymore.

There were five cars in front of the clubhouse, all parked at awkward angles, as if the women who'd driven them couldn't be bothered with lines or order. Inside, it was chaos—laughter, shouted insults, the slap of cards on a table. Kids ran up and down the hallway, cute little wolf cubs. It was a scene I'd grown up inside, but now I watched it from the threshold, just another shadow among a hundred moving parts.

Maddie and Juliet were there, along with three other pack women. When we walked in, Rocket barked once and made a beeline for the only other dog in the room—a beefy hound with paws bigger than Parker's hands. The women barely glanced up, but I felt their attention skate across us like radar.

Parker hung back, all nerves. I watched her count the exits, map the room, read every face in a second. Everybody knew her, knew her story.

Juliet came over first, arms folded, mouth curled into a smirk. "Look who decided to crawl out from behind his monitors." She looked me up and down, then glanced at Parker, her gaze softening. "Hey, Parker."

Parker gave a typical practiced smile. "Hi, Juliet."

Maddie waved from the kitchen. "There's food. You look like you haven't eaten in a week." She called out over her shoulder, "Arsenal's on his way back from Amarillo—he said to save him the big cinnamon roll. Hey girl! It's been a damn month of Sundays since you've been around. It's good to see you." Bronc's younger sister Maddie was all personality. You never knew what was going to come out of her mouth. Your best bet was just to buckle up and hang on.

"Hi Mads. Good to see you too."

Juliet herded us toward the table, which was covered in craft supplies and a tangle of wrapping paper. "Toy run's in a few days," she explained. "We're trying to get toys gathered. Pearl's been wearing us out to get these toys wrapped like something she saw on TikTok."

Parker scanned the table, the neat rows of books and puzzles and small plush animals. "Y'all still delivering the presents to the same places?"

Juliet shrugged. "Pretty much. Most go to the children's hospital, some to the foster home, and the rest to the church out on County 9. They handle the rest of the disbursement to needy families. This is just a tiny fraction. Most of the toys, especially the bigger ones, are down in the basement. But I think we're about out of room down there. We're considering moving the operation to the Dairyville Civic Center so we can really spread out."

Parker smiled. She twisted a piece of ribbon in her hands until it snapped.

I let the conversation drift, watching her from across the room. She tried to fold into the background, but Maddie kept pulling her back in, asking for help with scissors or tape, or asking her opinion on which toy was "least likely to traumatize a second grader." It was clear, after ten minutes, that none of them had a clue about what Parker had been involved in, or what she'd endured. To them, she was just a pack member who'd been gone for a while. Another wolf, awkward about being back.

For the first time in days, her shoulders unclenched. She even laughed—a weird little cackle, but laughter all the same. Rocket, meanwhile, got into a wrestling match with the hound, and for once, lost.

Juliet brought me a coffee and leaned on the counter beside me. "She's doing okay," she said. "Better than I thought."

I looked over at Parker. She was showing Maddie how to tie a ribbon without the knot coming undone. Her hands were steady; her face flushed with the heat from the stove.

"She's tougher than she looks," I said.

Juliet nodded. "So are you. You gonna tell her?"

I sipped the coffee. "Tell her what?"

"That you want to mark her. That you're thinking about forever, not just right now."

I shrugged. "I actually told her that the other day. Told her we needed to wait. She thought it was because I didn't trust her."

Juliet snorted. "You're the scariest bastard in four counties, and she didn't run. She's not going anywhere. She understands. That's pretty damn brave, if you ask me."

"It's different," I said. "I meant it when I said it. I know she's my mate. She's mine."

Juliet smiled, but it was sad. "Well, sometimes you have to reach out and take what's yours before it slips away."

She left me with that, and I watched Parker for a long minute, studying the way she moved, the way she fit into the chaos of my life. It didn't matter what had happened before, or what was coming next. She belonged here. Always had.

I left her working with the ladies while I gathered with the guys in the conference room.

As always, Bronc sat at the head, blue eyes sharp enough to slice, his elbows planted wide and steady. Arsenal was already there, the first as always, his knuckles white against the wood and the whites of his eyes catching every movement. Pearl hovered in the doorway, mostly for the excuse to eavesdrop, though everyone knew her word carried farther than most of ours. Gunner, Doc, and Papa all sat in their usual places around the table.

I took the seat Bronc motioned me toward. My hands were steady on the tabletop. I'd practiced the speech a dozen times in my head.

"Update," Bronc said.

I started with the facts. "Parker made the drop. All cams and mics planted, Trojan installed. We're getting continuous feeds except from Silas's war room. He keeps the door locked, rotates his muscle for every meeting."

"Any heat?" Arsenal asked, his voice flat but his foot bouncing under the table.

I hesitated for a second, then told them everything: "Silas grabbed her by the throat. Didn't just threaten. He wanted to prove he owned the leash." I left the details raw—how Parker's voice had gone hoarse, how the bruises looked worse each morning.

Arsenal's reaction was immediate. His hand closed on his coffee cup so hard the styrofoam caved. "Motherfucker."

Pearl gave a low, dangerous hum.

Bronc didn't move. "Was she able to keep her cover?"

"She sold it," I said. "He thinks the funds are already in motion. He wants her to trigger phase two tomorrow morning. We're ready to push the false ledger anytime."

"Damage on our end?" Gunner asked from his side of the table.

"None," I said. "Our accounts are dead-end mirrors. If anything, we're about to learn who else he's working with, and who he plans to cut out of the next buy."

Arsenal hadn't looked up. His jaw was set, his eyes like gun barrels. "You want me to take care of Silas?"

I shook my head. "Not yet. He needs to keep that sense of invulnerability. Parker's the only thing that keeps him off guard."

"She's not bait," Arsenal said, not to me, but to himself. "She's family. That's how we treat our own."

The shift was subtle but seismic. Three days ago, Arsenal would have gutted Parker for the offense of breathing too loud in the same room as club business. Now he was ready to burn down the world for her.

Bronc gave him a look—a nod, slight and approving. "We'll get one shot at this. Doc, you got your end handled?"

Our resident doctor grinned. "Greenbriar's got eyes in a lot of places, but they can't see past their own egos. We'll keep our perimeters covered. One of our cleaning service people was approached. They came to me. We know they want in. We just need to let them get to what they think is the bottom of our accounts, and then we'll strike. Maybe reverse accounts. Drain them. That's what they seem to care so much about these days. The money gives them prestige."

Bronc turned to me. "What's your confidence level, Eli?"

"I'm sure. About the accounting end. But are they going to make a big move? And if so, what? when?"

Pearl, still at the door, cleared her throat. "She's still welcome at the house, Eli. Maddie's got a room made up if she needs it. No questions asked."

I nodded. "She'll be there for the toy run. After that, we see what happens."

The meeting broke up, men filing out with the quiet efficiency of old soldiers. I waited until the room emptied. Arsenal lingered behind, as I knew he would.

He approached me with a look I hadn't seen before: respect, maybe even apology. "I was wrong about her," he said. "I know what it's like, getting used by someone stronger. If he touches her again, I'll take care of him myself."

"I'll handle it," I said. But I let him have the last word.

"He won't leave the room alive."

He left, but not before squeezing my shoulder—a pack gesture, silent but absolute.

Afterward, I walked back to the main pack room. It was still buzzing with activity. The sun was already going down, a hard orange through the cloud cover. I could hear the laughter and yelling from the kitchen before I even stepped onto the porch.

Parker was at the table with Maddie, Pearl, and three little kids. Rocket was asleep in the middle of the floor, belly-up and snoring. Parker's hair was a mess, and her face was flushed. She was teaching a girl how to tie a knot in a piece of string.

When she saw me, her eyes flashed a question: Is it over?

I nodded, and she excused herself from the table.

We stepped outside. The cold was sharp, bracing, real. She hugged her arms to her body, but I could see the tension gone from her posture.

"How'd it go?" she asked.

"Better than I expected. They trust you now."

She gave me a look that was all skepticism.

I laughed. "Arsenal wants to kill Silas. You're in."

She smiled. Not a huge thing, but it felt like the first real one since this started.

"Are you okay?" I asked, voice low.

"I am now," she said. She hesitated. "It's starting to feel like it used to, before my parents..." she trailed off, words unfinished.

"It doesn't have to happen all in one day," I said. "It takes time."

She let out a slow breath. "Maybe I'll get there."

I put my hand on her back, felt the warmth through the flannel shirt. "Of course you will."

She leaned into my touch, just a little. "What about you? You don't seem like the pack house type."

I shrugged. "You'd be surprised. I just moved out about five months ago."

She grinned. "Oooh, I bet all the ladies cried."

"You bet they did!" I picked her up and tickled her stomach. She squirmed until I put her down.

"I'm gonna pee my pants if you do that again!"

"Remind me not to do that again." Damn, it felt good to laugh.

We went back inside, the noise and heat swallowing us up. The night wore on, and when it was time to go, she hugged Maddie and Pearl, and even let one of the kids braid a pink ribbon into her hair.

Driving home, she fell asleep in the passenger seat, with Rocket curled on her lap. I watched the road, hands steady on the wheel, my wolf quiet for the first time in weeks.

Maybe tomorrow might bring war. But tonight, we had peace. And that was enough.

CHAPTER 16

SILAS DRAKE

Even though war rooms aren't built for comfort, we'd taken to meeting in here instead of my office because the vampires and demons showed up when you least expected them. I'd turned on the torches—no they aren't actual torches, but they are a pretty close facsimile. I had a weakness for the classics, and this meeting needed a certain ambiance. I hoped the demons who'd been joining us from time to time stayed away, for their sakes.

I looked down at the table: a map of our holdings, fresh-printed and although it was new, it was already out of date. Stacks of ledgers. Smeared glass tumblers filled with scotch and God knows what sat ready to drink. No one here ever drank for pleasure.

The clock in the hall struck 10 p.m. right on cue.

Dagger arrived first, silent as a mugger. He wore his hair long, in a ropy braid that glistened in the torchlight. He leaned in the doorway and waited, his left eye always scanning, right eye fixed on me. Old habit from a childhood nobody asked about.

Rook next, as huge as a walking casket. He ducked under the lintel, jaw clicking as he worked it. I've seen him rip a man's arm off and then use the bone to open a bottle of beer. Subtle he was not.

Vex was last. Always last, always wearing black, always looking like a violinist at a funeral she planned to crash. A cigarette sat between her fingers; her tall boots clicked across the concrete.

I didn't waste time.

"This is our war council," I said, and all three of them took a seat at the battered table. Dagger, with his knife already out, spun it on one finger. Rook pulled up his sleeves so he could plant his elbows, arms meaty and powerful. Vex reached for the ashtray, then unfolded her hands, as if about to recite the rosary.

I stood and leaned over the table. The first sound from me was a fist. I brought it down so hard on the wood the ledgers jumped. The flicker of torchlight caught the edge of Dagger's blade as he spun it, but I didn't flinch.

"Every inside line's burning up," I said, pacing the war room like a man unmoored. Let them think I was furious. Let them taste the theatrics. "So, turning low-level grunts turned out to be a dead end. Nobody was willing to do our dirty work for us from the inside. If they went to Bronc or his council, the most they could know is that we were looking for a way in. Good. Let them choke on that illusion."

Rook's knuckles whitened against the table. "So, is it time to take the girl out?"

I scoffed. "Parker? If I wanted her corpse, she'd already be rotting. But why kill the architect of their ruin?" The truth simmered beneath my words: Parker's code was humming like a Swiss watch, siphoning Iron Valor's accounts dry night after night. Their coffers bled out quietly, and their panic would taste sweeter than vengeance.

Vex, ever the skeptic, leaned forward. "Maybe she turned rat."

I let myself laugh—cold, sharp—for their benefit. "You think the tooth fairy's taking money from under my pillow? Parker hasn't run. She values her worthless brother's life too much.

That's her weakness. And we're not finished with her. When we're through with Iron Valor and she's left with no one, I'll have her move on to our next target, whoever that may be. We deal in blood, Vex. It's what we do. Trust the plan," I said, softer now.

I paced, slow, using the limp to my advantage. You learned how to weaponize your own wounds after a while. "Iron Valor stole our birthright. We had an up-and-coming pack, one that the Council and the rest of the supernatural world had started to notice. Bronc and Iron Valor stormed in here without so much as a green light and ended it all in a day." My voice was coming out in growls.

"All we did was bring our Alpha's choice of mate to her new territory so she could see for herself how good her life could be. And for *that*, our pack was decimated, left without a voice for years. Then Iron Valor gets a slap on the wrist for *murdering* an Alpha?" We've waited long enough to even the score. There are others who agreed that it was a miscarriage of justice.

"And demons don't fear reprisals do they?"

Rook flexed his hands. The old tattoos on his knuckles—*sinner, suffer*—caught the light's glow. "Maltraz," he said, as if just the name might draw the creature through the wall.

I smiled. "The demon king wants money. We have money. Between our underground fight nights, traveling casinos, and strip clubs, there is more than enough money to burn. Once we've added Iron Valor's hundreds of thousands, no pack in the country will be able to touch our wealth. Money is power. He also wants territory. We have that, too, and we're about to have more, once we end Iron Valor and swallow up their land. Most of all, he wants chaos. I think we can deliver."

Vex looked queasy. "He wants souls."

"Who doesn't?" I said, pouring myself a drink. "The trick is, you only promise them if you're sure you can keep them for yourself."

Dagger finally spoke up. "And if he double-crosses us?"

"He can't," I said. "Not if the contract is sealed right. Besides, he's not stupid. He knows Iron Valor will never play ball with him. He's got no use for honor, but he respects power. Anyway, he plays in the shadows. "

Vex nodded, but it was shaky. "So we invite him in?"

"We send a message," I said. "Tonight." I looked at Dagger. "Do you know the man who can bring the demon king to us?"

He grinned, teeth like headstones.

Dagger wiped his blade and slipped it into the sheath. "Yes, sir, I do. Do we need to worry about Iron Valor finding out?"

I shrugged. "We don't. Maltraz voted against them when Menace and his bitch mate came before the council. There is no love lost between them. I'm sure he'd love to take a shot at Bronc if given a chance."

I stood at the head of the table and raised my glass. The others, dutifully, did the same.

"To escalation," I said. "To the endgame."

They drank.

And somewhere, not in the room, but close enough to feel, the walls listened. Hungry, hopeful, waiting for the next name to be whispered in the dark.

After they left, I stayed a while in the empty war room, listening to the silence. I caught my reflection in the screen of the large TV that was mounted on the wall. I noted the wrinkles and random scars that mapped a lifetime of battles and bitterness. It reminded me that all beauty is temporary.

We were going to lose unless I burned all the rules to hell.

To do this, a bargain had to be struck with the demon king. It required a ritual I knew little about, but I knew of a man who was well versed in darkness.

You never get used to the taste of sulfur.

The old man—who had no name, or maybe had too many to keep track—did the prep. He shuffled into the war room with his kit of relics and powders and started drawing the circle on the flagstones. Salt, bone ash, some kind of oil that made the whole place stink like burned popcorn and dead teeth scattered around. He hummed to himself as he worked, never once glancing up at me or the guards in the doorway. He needed only one look, right at the start, to know who was paying the bills.

I watched the lines take shape, thinking of all the times I'd stood in a different kind of circle, a different kind of war room. We used to do it with guns and hands and threats of violence, back before the world got smarter and everyone decided to play God. Now even the monsters needed lawyers.

The cold set in as the hour approached. First a chill, then a bite, then the kind of subzero air that freezes your sinuses and turns your lungs to glass. Rook started shivering, and Vex looked like she wanted to crawl into her own shadow. Only Dagger kept still, but even he tucked his hands into his pockets.

The last touch: a single drop of blood, mine, onto the center of the circle. The old man handed me the scalpel, and I didn't hesitate. It's only pain.

A gust of wind, though there were no windows in this room, and the air vents never offered such a breeze. The center fluorescent light swung as if paying homage. The darkness in the corner of the room got deeper, more solid, until it resolved itself into a shape.

He presented himself in his more demonic form, not the human form he showed the world. He wore a suit, expensive and perfectly cut. The shirt was white, but not the white of fabric—more like the inside of a bone. His skin was translucent, an iron hue, and the veins underneath pulsed with something that wasn't quite blood. His eyes were black glass, and his mouth, when it opened, was a neat line of human teeth sharpened down to points. The hands were wrong, too: five fingers, but each joint bent a little too far, nails painted with a clear gloss.

He smiled.

"Silas Drake," he said. The voice was rich, deep, but didn't seem to come from his mouth so much as from the center of your skull. "It seems you have need of something from me, and I have need of something from you."

I tried not to show my relief or my disgust. "Yes sir. I believe we have mutually beneficial needs. It seems you already know why I've summoned you, so to speak." I gave a short cough.

"Many things are known. Few are understood." He loved to speak to people he saw as underlings in this bullshit manner.

I resisted the urge to roll my eyes and got straight to the reason we were here. "I need your Clovis compound."

A flicker of interest. "And you offer?"

"The Amarillo cut. Plus, we intend to take Iron Valor. Every drop we take from them, you get a quarter."

Vex made a choking noise, but I ignored her. This was my table, my risk.

The demon king's smile widened. "A quarter is not enough."

"Take it or leave it," I said. "You know the numbers. Nobody else can touch what we're pulling out of that city."

He considered the deal. Not for long. "Half."

I grinned, all teeth. "I don't think I need it that bad."

He leaned forward. The temperature dropped another ten degrees. Dagger's breath came out in clouds.

"Forty percent," he said, eyes like obsidian marbles. "And I will throw in the safe house in Albuquerque. You'll likely need it before this is done."

I made a show of thinking, but we both knew I'd take the deal. "Done," I said. "But I want it signed, sealed, and protected. No back doors. No clever curses. You fuck us, I'll find you. And I won't bring the old man next time."

The lights went out. When they came back on, the demon had grown until his head almost touched the ceiling.

His voice was like thunder, even though his mouth did not move. I wanted to put my hands over my ears. Vex, Dagger, and Rook did.

*"I'm not quite sure who you think you are dealing with, boy. I am the King of Demons. Only one sits higher than I in all of hell. I do not need your deals. Remember, **you** summoned **me**. Any room in which I stand can be considered **my** kingdom and as such all who inhabit it, my subjects. Treat me with the respect that I am due."*

At that point, Vex, Dagger, and Rook hit the floor on their knees. The urge to do the same was overwhelming. Try as I might, I could not remain in my chair. In the blink of an eye, I, too, was on my knees before the demon king.

The room went dark once again. When the lights came back on, Maltraz was back to his normal height.

He looked down at me as I struggled to rise, my bad hip making it difficult. "Now, I assume my integrity will not be questioned again."

Not wanting another humiliation I bowed my head. "No, sir."

He continued, "The contract is sanctified by blood. If you break it, your lineage is forfeit. If I break it, the lineage of Maltraz is forfeit."

"Noted," I said. "Let us continue."

He produced a scroll from thin air; the paper brown and curling at the edges. It unrolled itself, hovering above the table. The writing was in a script I didn't recognize, but my name—my true name—was there at the bottom, waiting for a signature.

He handed me a silver dagger. I took it, sliced my palm open, and pressed it to the line. The blood hissed as it touched the paper, then vanished. Maltraz did the same, and for a moment, the room filled with a scent like flowers and rot at the same time.

The scroll rolled itself up, then disappeared with a soft pop.

"It is done," he said.

"Details," I demanded.

"You may take possession of the Clovis compound at dawn," he replied. "A full inventory will be waiting. All of the properties on the premises will be open to you. Now, forty percent of all Amarillo revenue is payable to me, in quarterly installments, first payment due within thirty days. Miss a payment, and you belong to us."

I nodded. "Noted."

He inclined his head, then began to dissolve. First his face, then his hands, then suit and the shoes and the last glint of his shark-smile. In ten seconds, he was gone, and the room was warmer for it.

The old man gathered up his things, not looking at anyone.

My lieutenants waited until he was gone before they spoke.

"Was that wise?" Vex asked, voice raw.

I wiped my bloody hand on a towel. "Nothing we do is wise. It's just necessary."

Rook licked his lips, as if trying to remember what warmth tasted like. "What now?"

I shrugged. "We prep our people for the move."

Dagger smirked. "Yeah boss. We're running low on time."

He wasn't wrong. I just sold my soul so I could make my biggest move yet. After I made it, Bronc and Iron Valor would come for us. We'd be long gone when they did.

CHAPTER 17

PARKER

I made Wrecker drive my car back to the house, not because I was too tired or too traumatized, but because if Silas Drake had even one of his creeps on lookout, the last thing I wanted was for them to clock the black F-350. My car was an Audi that blended into Plainview's streets like a whore in church, but they'd never expect *him* to be in it. I was glad he could squeeze into the driver's seat.

He didn't say a word the whole drive. His eyes never left the mirrors. Not once did he touch the radio or fidget with the heater. The silence was loaded, radioactive, but safer than trying to fill it with words.

We parked at the very end of my dirt driveway right up to the garage, headlights off before we even made the turn. The porch light was out—just as I'd left it—but Wrecker hesitated anyway, hand hovering over the center console.

"You need me to clear it?" he asked.

I wanted to say, "Don't be ridiculous, it's my own goddamn house," but the truth was I wanted him in there first. I wanted him to walk through every room and tell me it was safe, even though my brain screamed that nothing ever would be again.

"Please," I said as I cuddled Rocket in my lap.

He grinned, savage and beautiful, and slipped out into the night like a shadow. For such a huge man, he moved with a weightless kind of violence, the kind you only saw in panthers on TV or in old reels of MMA fighters just before they knocked someone into a parallel universe.

I counted to a hundred in my head. Got as far as fifty-seven before the porch light flashed on. I almost broke my ankle running up the steps. He waited inside the door. Arms crossed, Rocket almost leaped out of my arms into his. The man had dog-jacked my pup.

"All clear, little bird," Wrecker said. He set Rocket down, and the mutt disappeared to his bed.

I followed him inside, then immediately headed to the ther-mostat to crank up the heat. The wood floor was ice on my sock feet. I dropped my bag, tried to pretend I wasn't still trying to process everything happening in my life right now.

He caught my wrist, gentle, and said, "Shower. Now."

I thought he was kidding. He was not.

"Come on," he said, guiding me toward the bathroom. "You need to get warm. And you'll feel better cleaned up."

The way he said it—*cleaned up*—made my stomach do a flip. I had been working in the clubhouse for hours and had gotten sweaty. He was absolutely right. I *did* want to clean up, but I hated he knew that. Or maybe I loved that he knew that.

He walked me to my bathroom and turned on the shower while I undressed. I was not at all self-conscious standing stark naked before him. Had no compulsion to cover myself or hide myself from him. How could I be when those gun metal eyes looked at me with what could only be described as adoration? We had the benefit of history on our side. Granted, it was a history that seemed superficial, but it was more. And it calmed me because I *knew* this man. I had known him for as long as I could remember. And as long as I'd been aware of what love truly was, I'd loved him.

His callused hand on my back gently guided me into the shower. Moments later, his clothing removed, and I assumed, neatly folded and stacked somewhere, he joined me. The water was scalding, but I didn't care. Steam curled around us, thick and heavy, clinging to my skin like a second layer. His hands were everywhere, rough and demanding, yet somehow tender in their brutality. His eyes dark with hunger, his cock was already hard, begging for my touch. He didn't bother with foreplay—not yet. He just shoved me under the spray, causing the water to rush down my body, a feral urgency driving him that made my knees weak.

"Turn around," he growled, his voice low and gravelly. I felt his wolf on the surface, causing mine to howl against my ribs. I obeyed without hesitation, pressing my palms flat against the stone-tiled wall, my breath hitching as he stepped in behind me. His chest was a furnace against my back, his cock a hot, insistent pressure against my ass. He wasted no time. One hand slid between my legs, fingers parting my folds with a rough, possessive touch that made me gasp.

"Fuck, you're already soaked for me," he muttered, his breath hot against my ear. "You've been thinking about this all day, haven't you, little bird?"

I nodded, my hips rocking back against him, desperate for more. He chuckled, a dark, predatory sound that sent shivers down my spine. "Damn, you are so perfect, always ready for me."

His fingers plunged into me without warning, curling just right to hit that spot that made me see stars. I cried out, my head falling back against his shoulder as he worked me with a ruthless precision that left me trembling. But he wasn't done. His other hand slid down, fingers teasing at my asshole, circling the tight ring of muscle until I was squirming, begging for more.

"Wrecker, please," I whimpered, my voice breaking on the word. "Please." Both of his hands were working in tandem. Two fingers pounding my pussy and one in my ass, back and forth. The sensation was confusing, incredible. But I needed more.

"Please what?" he demanded, his voice a low growl that vibrated through me. "Tell me what you want, Wren."

"I want you," I gasped, my hips bucking against his hand. "I want all of you."

He didn't make me wait. His fingers left me empty for only a moment before he was pressing the head of his cock against my entrance, the thick, rounded head stretching me open in the most delicious way. He pushed in slowly, inch by agonizing inch, until he was buried all the way, his hips flush against my ass. I could feel every ridge, every vein as he filled me completely, and it was almost too much.

"Fuck," he groaned, his hands gripping my hips hard enough to leave bruises. "You're so fucking tight, little bird. You feel like heaven."

He started to move then, slow, deep thrusts that had me clawing at the stone tiles for purchase. His cock dragged against my walls with every stroke, hitting that spot inside me that made my vision blur. His fingers found my clit again, rubbing tight circles that had me moaning his name like a prayer.

"That's it," he growled, his voice rough with need. "I love to hear my name on your lips, Wren. And the way your pussy takes every inch of my cock makes me want to stay here forever. It feels like home."

I took everything he gave me, my body arching back to meet his thrusts, my pussy clenching around him as he fucked me with a relentless intensity that left me breathless. His fingers never stopped moving, never stopped teasing and tormenting until I was teetering on the edge, my orgasm building like a storm inside me.

"Come for me," he commanded. His voice low and insistent, sent a shiver down my spine. "Come all over my cock, little bird."

I did. My orgasm hit me like a freight train, my body convulsing around him as wave after wave of pleasure crashed over me. He didn't stop, didn't give me a moment to recover. He just kept fucking me through it, his thrusts growing harder, faster, until he was slamming into me with a force that had me crying out his name.

"Fuck," he groaned, his hips stuttering as he buried himself deep inside me one last time. I felt him pulse, felt the hot rush of his cum filling me as he came with a low, guttural moan that sent another shiver down my spine.

We stayed like that for a moment, both of us panting and trembling as the water continued to pour down around us. Then he dragged himself from by body, his hands gentle as he turned me to face him. His eyes were dark, intense, and filled with something that made my chest ache.

"You're mine," he said, his voice low and rough. "Mine to protect, mine to claim. And when the time is right, I'm going to mark you so everyone knows it."

I nodded, my heart pounding in my chest as I reached up to cup his face in my hands. "I'm yours," I whispered, my voice trembling with emotion. "Always have been. Always will be."

He kissed me then, deep and possessive, his tongue claiming mine with a ferocity that left me breathless. When he finally pulled away, his eyes were soft, filled with a warmth that made my heart ache.

"I love you," he said, his voice rough with emotion. "More than anything."

"I love you," I whispered back, my voice breaking on the words.

He smiled then, a slow, wicked smile that made my stomach flip. "Good. Now let's get you cleaned up."

He turned me back around, his hands gentle as he washed me with a tenderness that made my chest ache. He took his time, his touch reverent as he ran the soapy cloth over every inch of my skin. When he was done, he dried me off with the same care, his hands lingering on my body as if he couldn't bear to let me go.

Then he led me to the bed, pulling me down beside him and wrapping his arms around me in a way that made me feel safe, protected. We lay there in silence for a while, just listening to the sound of each other's breathing.

"Do you want this?" he asked finally, his voice soft but serious. "The claiming mark? I need to know how you feel about it."

I turned to look at him, my heart pounding in my chest. "I want it," I said, my voice steady despite the butterflies in my stomach. "I want to be yours in every way."

He smiled then, a slow, satisfied smile that made my stomach flip. "Good. Because you're mine, little bird. Forever. I just didn't want to take away your choice in this. I know you're my mate. I've known it for a while now."

"I believe that also. I've always felt a connection to you. It became an unexplainable pull when I saw your face that night in my bedroom. That's why I wasn't afraid of you. Not really. I just felt like I was yours."

"When this is all over, I'm going to claim you. I'd like to do it properly, with a ceremony, if you're up for that."

I couldn't believe what I was hearing. It was so traditional. Almost nobody did claiming ceremonies anymore. I wanted nothing more than to honor him in this way. "Eli," I choked on my tears. "I think that is a beautiful idea. I would love that."

We fell asleep like that, wrapped up in each other, and for the first time in what felt like forever, I felt content. Safe. Loved.

But the peace didn't last.

I woke to sunlight in my eyes, my mouth dry as dust, and the familiar bony elbow of Rocket pressed to my hip through the comforter. For a few sweet, confused seconds, I thought I was home alone and that everything from the last month—the violence, the threats, the collar of bruises—was just a dream.

Then Wrecker came out of the bathroom, towel slung low on his hips, hair wet, and I remembered who and what I was.

He glanced at me, saw I was awake, and said, "Hey beautiful. I think you need to rise and shine. Looks like you're late."

"Hi handsome. Late for what?"

"War," he said, and grinned, the scar on his chin twisting with the rest of his mouth. "Get up, Wren. The bank logs are lighting up."

He wasn't joking. My phone on the nightstand, vibrated with a steady, epileptic pulse. I grabbed it and started scrolling before my feet hit the floor.

Dozens of alerts: pings from three separate accounts, a spike in activity in the Greenbriar ledger. The worm was working, and it looked like Silas must be checking to see how his accounts were growing. We needed to be sure everything looked normal to his eyes.

I crawled out of bed, tripped over Rocket, and headed to my office nook. Wrecker had made coffee—strong enough to kill a horse—and left the pot on the warmer. I poured a cup, burned my tongue, and dove straight into the logs.

I lost three hours that way. The outside world dissolved into screen glare and the low drone of Wrecker's voice as he made phone calls from my living room, always short, always quiet. When he wasn't on the phone, he hovered over my shoulder, watching the code scroll by, eyes flicking up and down my neck like he wanted to bite me just to keep me in one place.

I ignored him. I ignored everything but the lines of code and the chase.

I switched to the camera feeds that Wrecker had given me access to. The hallways were clear. Silas's office was dark. I didn't see anybody around.

"Wrecker," I called. "Do you think it's odd that I'm not seeing any activity on any of the cameras I planted?"

He walked up behind me and frowned. "Not necessarily. They've been spending most of their time in their war room. Check the camera you put on Silas's laptop."

When I switched the feed to that camera, it came up static. "Shit, what does that mean?"

"It means that the only problem with those micro-cams is that they are easily dislodged. He may have tossed his laptop into his bag, and the camera was knocked off and disabled."

"Damn it. So we've lost that access. That sucks ass."

He grinned at me. "It does, but there are several other cameras. Keep your eyes peeled for any little thing. But don't just stay there. You'll drive yourself nuts if you do."

A cold, greasy dread uncurled in my gut. "I just have a weird feeling something is up."

Wrecker didn't answer. Instead, he paced to the front window and looked out, silent and predatory.

He came up behind me, set his hands on my shoulders, and squeezed until my knuckles went white on the keyboard.

"Take a break," he said. "Eat something."

"I'm not hungry."

"You need to keep your head clear." He bent down, mouth at my ear. "I'll make lunch."

I wanted to argue, but the caffeine and the adrenaline were making my vision double. I closed the laptop and slumped in the chair, watching him move around my kitchen with the clumsy precision of a bear pretending to be a chef.

He made eggs. Not just eggs—eggs and thick-cut bacon and toast so buttery it was almost yellow. He plated it for me, then set the plate in front of me and waited until I picked up a fork.

"You'll make someone an outstanding wife," I said, laughing.

"I'm gonna tan your ass as soon as I get you back in my playroom, and 'he who must not be named' won't even be able to help you."

I swallowed hard around my bite of toast. A small grin on my face.

He poured himself a glass of water, downed it in two gulps, then came back to the table and watched me.

"You always eat this fast?" he asked.

"We're wolves. You know how we do?"

He smirked. "You ever miss it?"

"You mean eating with my family? Yeah, I suppose I do." I wiped my mouth with a paper towel. "But I've always eaten alone since they died."

He went quiet. Not the awkward kind, just the kind that said, I understand, and I'll sit here as long as you need.

We finished in silence. Rocket snuffled at my feet, licking my toes.

When I went back to the laptop, the camera feed was still dead. I rerouted through three proxies, then finally got a ping on an external mic I'd planted in the main hallway. It was a live channel, but the only thing I could hear was a low hum. Maybe a vent, maybe a refrigerator.

"I'm getting nothing," I muttered.

"You'll get it," Wrecker said. "You always do."

He'd just hung up the phone. "That was Bronc. They moved the toy drive prep," he said. "There were just too many toys for the basement, so they're at the civic center now. Whole crew will be there for the next few days, packing toys."

I loved that. "So, the clubhouse is empty?"

He nodded. "For the first time in forever."

He looked at me, then at the clock, then back at me. "Bronc's coming by to get me. You wanna come with? Might help you get your mind off things."

I wanted to say yes. But the terror of missing something on the feeds had my insides twisted up like a rope.

"I'll catch up with you later," I said. "I want to keep an eye on the transfers and maybe catch wind of what they're up to."

He studied me for a long second. "Don't go anywhere alone, Parker."

I snorted. "I have a guard dog."

Rocket farted, then rolled onto his back, paws in the air.

Wrecker shook his head. "Some guard dog."

There was a knock at the door. Not the kind that asks permission, but the kind that says, I'm coming in whether you like it or not.

Wrecker tensed, then relaxed when he caught the scent through the door. He opened it and Bronc filled the frame, jacket unzipped, sunglasses pushed up on his forehead.

"Ready?" Bronc asked.

"Hey Bronc!" I hollered at him. I wasn't going to let him step into my house without acknowledging me.

"Hey, kiddo." He looked around Wrecker so he could see my face. The term of endearment took me back.

Wrecker turned. "Give me a second."

He came to the table, leaned down, and kissed my forehead.

"Text me if anything changes," he said. "I mean it."

"I will," I said.

He left with Bronc, and I listened to the sound of their boots on the gravel until it faded.

I lasted all of thirty seconds before the dread came back.

I reopened my laptop, eyes darting between the account logs and the dead camera feed. I tried another dozen tricks to hack the signal, but all I got was static.

"Fuck you, Silas," I hissed at the screen.

Rocket whimpered and licked my ankle.

I checked the locks on every door and window. I closed the blinds, then reopened them just enough to let in a sliver of light.

I paced the kitchen, the living room, the hallway, over and over until I was dizzy.

Every ten minutes I checked the driveway for strange cars. Every fifteen I checked my phone for missed calls, even though the ringer was turned up as high as it could go.

Nothing.

But the silence felt like the air before a tornado, thick and expectant.

By four in the afternoon, I had chewed my nails down to the quick. I reheated my coffee three times, but never finished a cup. Rocket followed me from room to room, whining softly whenever I sat too long in one spot.

When the phone rang with Wrecker's call, I about jumped out of my skin.

"What happened?"

"How'd you know? Nevermind. Have you heard from Maddie?"

"Maddie? No. Haven't seen or talked to her since last night. Why? What's going on?"

Wrecker's deep sigh told me something bad was going on.

"She left Pearl's an hour and a half ago to grab some wrapping paper from the dollar store on her way up to the civic center. She never arrived."

My heart sank. That's it. That's the dread I'd felt.

"Well, y'all need to find her!"

"What the fuck do you think we're trying to do, Parker?"

"I'm sorry. I'm going to go back through this fucking video feed to see if I missed something while I was making my sandwich for dinner or something."

"Okay, let me know if you find anything."

"Of course. Eli, I love you."

But he'd already hung up.

I started rewinding camera footage from this moment back to an hour before I'd made my dinner. I turned the volume all the way up. Suddenly, I heard faint voices. They were just close enough that I could barely make out what they were saying if I listened closely enough.

It sounded something about watching the gate for the girl and grabbing her when she comes out. I kept running it back and re-listening. It didn't make sense. They said they'd drop her back at the gate after two hours to give Bronc and his boys time to come get them. And she'd be back at the clubhouse for the 'big boom.'

"Big boom, big boom." I looked at Rocket. "Why would they take her and bring her back?" He just tilted his head. I grabbed my keys as I jammed my feet into my tennis shoes, heading for the door. "You stay here, boy. I'll be back."

I dialed Wrecker as I headed for my car. I was out the door while Wrecker's phone went to voicemail.

It dawned on me as soon as I put my car in drive. I understood what 'big boom' meant. They were going to blow up the clubhouse, and they wanted Maddie to blow up with it. FUCK! I called Wrecker again. Again, voicemail. "Wrecker, call me! They have Maddie, but they are bringing her back to the Iron Valor gate! They are going to blow up the clubhouse. Don't go near it!" I was trying to drive and look up phone numbers at the same time. I had very few saved in my phone.

I tried Juliet. Voicemail.

Pearl. Voicemail.

Bronc. Voicemail.

"WHY THE FUCK WON'T ANYONE ANSWER THEIR PHONES?"

CHAPTER 18

WRECKER

Bronc's truck hit the brakes hard, the belt biting into my collarbone as we skidded to a halt at the back of the Dairyville Dollar King. I was out before he finished shifting to park. The parking lot was mostly empty, sun bleaching the paint from the few cars left for the evening shift. Maddie's Ford pickup sat by the dumpster, lights off, driver's side window cracked.

I didn't want to approach the vehicle. The wolf in me already knew what it meant: prey taken, trail gone cold.

I checked the driver's seat anyway, hands flat on the door, nose pressed to the glass. The keys dangled from the ignition. Her purse was on the floor. Cupholder: Big Gulp, lipstick smudge, quarter-melted ice. Back seat: Christmas wrapping paper, Target bags, a stuffed unicorn with the tag still on. The door wasn't even locked.

"She wouldn't leave it like this," I said, and the words were a stone in my mouth. Bronc hovered a step behind, scanning the lot, eyes narrowed to slits.

"Anything?" he asked.

"No sign of struggle," I said, forcing calm. "No blood, no glass, no noise. She either went with them or they took her clean."

Bronc's hands were fists. "This is Greenbriar."

It wasn't a question. It was what you said when you found a friend's boots in the yard, but no trace of him anywhere. It was the old, ugly feeling from four years back—Emma's hair, caught in a door hinge; Emma's shoes, found at a truck stop in the panhandle; Emma's scent, fading off the highway like it had never existed at all.

I slammed the door shut and stalked a slow circle around the truck, head low, letting the wolf take over my senses. There: a faint, sour note, unfamiliar. Someone male. Recent. They'd waited until she was alone, then snatched her quick, silent.

Bronc was already calling the war room. His voice was glass: "They have her. It's the same as last time. Get everyone in."

I wanted to punch her truck until the doors fell off.

Instead, I followed him back, heart shaking, fingers burning with the urge to kill.

We drove the back roads to the Iron Valor clubhouse in near silence. My mind replayed the Emma tape on a loop: the way we played it by the book. We took it to the Council, knowing that Greenbriar Alpha fuck had taken her after Bronc told him she wasn't interested in becoming his mate. The fucking Council "investigation" that turned up nothing. Then our own investigation that found sweet Emma bound in silver, half starved to death. She wasn't the same after. And died three months later.

Greenbriar paid with the death of their Alpha that time. Clearly, that hadn't been enough. My wolf rattled my ribs, insistent, a thousand-yard snarl inside my chest.

When we turned onto the compound drive, the entire war council was already waiting: Doc, Gunner, Arsenal, Papa, even Pearl's old sedan at the end of the row. Half a dozen bikes gleamed under the yellow porch lights. The clubhouse itself was dark except for the meeting room, where windows glowed like fever eyes.

We filed in. I'd grabbed my club laptop from my office. The table was crowded: maps, coffee mugs, the shotgun always kept within arm's reach. The air smelled of sweat and gun oil and the faint sweetness of Bronc's aftershave.

Arsenal spoke first. "Confirmed?"

"Confirmed," Bronc said. "Wrecker smelled them."

Papa slid his phone across the table. "Surveillance shows Maddie outside the store at 4:19 p.m., then nothing. No one follows her in. No one follows her out. We checked the tape five times."

Arsenal's jaw flexed. "Someone inside her truck?"

"Didn't see 'em make entry. Maybe they knew the camera angles," Gunner said, voice soft as sandpaper. "Makes sense why her truck wound up where it was. No struggle. Just gone."

"Her purse was on the floorboard, phone still in it." I told them, rubbing my hand down my face.

I looked at the faces around the table. Every one of us had scars from Greenbriar's last game. Everyone of us wanted blood.

Bronc said, "Same plan as before. Small team, surgical entry, in and out. We don't let them see us coming." He looked at me. "You lead. You remember what worked and what didn't."

The war room shifted. My hands stopped shaking. The wolf retreated, replaced by something sharper, colder.

I nodded once.

"Gunner, get ready for your first taste of war. Doc, you're in backup position. Arsenal, I want your eyes on entry and egress. Papa, you run comms. We're all on this. All heading out."

Pearl poked her head in the door, arms crossed, face set in lines of concrete. "Don't let her die, Bronc," she said. "She's not like Emma. She's not strong that way."

"I know," Bronc said. "We're bringing her home, Ma. Head back to the civic center. That's where everyone already is."

We broke to prep.

Thirty minutes: that was all I asked.

In the armory, the lights were cold and blue. I went down the row of guns, checking weights, stocks, ammo. I grabbed the Sig Sauer, loaded the magazine, holstered it on my left side. Backup piece in the boot. Knife on the belt. Kevlar on, black T-shirt over top. I checked the radio and the comms twice, then once more for luck. Gave Parker a call to see if she'd talked to Maddie or seen anything on the cams. She hadn't yet, but was still checking.

The rest of the crew was a symphony of motion. Gunner and Arsenal loaded the bikes with extra mags, hydration packs, blacked-out helmets. Doc was on the phone with his hospital contact, prepping the back end for a wounded return.

I could hear Bronc upstairs talking on the phone to Juliet. His voice was low, but I caught the edge in it: a mix of fear and fury, the kind you only heard in alphas who loved something more than themselves.

Papa found me at the back door, jacket zipped to the throat, helmet under his arm.

"Wrecker," he said.

"Yeah?"

He looked down, thumbed the strap of his helmet. "Let's get her. Don't go full reaper, though. We'll need you here after."

I nodded, not trusting myself to speak.

He squeezed my shoulder. "You can do this."

I wanted to believe him.

Outside, the cold bit straight through the shirt, even with the Kevlar. I pulled on my leather jacket. The bikes lined up under the porch light, black and silent. Gunner handed me a comms set and a tiny packet of salt. "For the shakes," he said. "Never fails."

I took it, pressed the earpiece in place.

Arsenal came out last, carrying a duffel stuffed with C-4, detonators, wire. "Just in case," he said.

We loaded up. The engines rumbled to life, low and angry, the sound of half a dozen heartbeats in unison.

Bronc swung up onto his ride, nodded at me. "You ready?"

I pulled on my helmet, the chin strap digging into the scar there. "Let's ride."

We peeled out of the compound, rubber screaming on gravel. The sky was bruised purple, the moon a clipped thumbnail. Wind clawed at my face, pulled the breath out of my lungs. The road ahead was a ribbon of black, straight as a gun barrel.

We rode tight, no wasted space, no daylight between the wheels. Every minute counted. Every second was another that Maddie was out there, alone.

The cold air sharpened my senses. Every mile marker was a drumbeat, every sign another reminder of the last time we'd done this and how close it had come to being a funeral ride instead of a rescue.

This time, I wasn't going to let anyone die.

This time, my wolf wasn't going to be in the fight.

This time, the man was enough.

Forty miles outside Dairyville, the plains stretched dead and bare, the only sound the wind howling through my helmet and the drone of Bronc's engine just ahead. We cut the line close, staggered formation, the way wolves run in a blizzard—tight, fast, ready to pivot at a single yelp.

My comm crackled. Then her voice: "Wrecker? Wrecker, can you hear me?"

Parker. Her voice was wrong—higher than normal, every syllable flayed open. I nearly wiped out, turning up the volume.

"Parker, talk."

She was already on a roll: "It's a fucking setup, do you hear me? They're not keeping Maddie; they're returning her—they want to bring her back to Iron Valor. They're going to blow the fucking clubhouse, Eli. They're going to blow it up."

The highway blurred. I fought to keep my bike straight, snapped my head to Bronc and gestured: emergency, pull over.

Bronc peeled off, dirt spraying in a rooster tail as we skidded onto the shoulder.

I killed the engine, voice shaking. "Say again, Parker. They're bringing Maddie back where?"

"*To the fucking gate,*" she screamed. "They want to leave her at the gate. But it's not about Maddie; it's about the explosion. 'Big boom.' They said, 'Big boom.' It's a trap."

Bronc was off his bike, helmet in one hand, phone in the other. "She's saying it's a bomb," I yelled to him, voice ragged.

His eyes went flat, glacier blue. "Where's Maddie?"

"Unknown. Parker says she's being dropped at the gate, but I don't trust it. We have to go back now. We have to beat them."

Bronc was already dialing Pearl's number, face gone gray.

My hands shook as I fumbled with the phone, trying to patch Parker through the helmet mic. "Parker, listen. Do not, I repeat, do not go into the clubhouse. If you're on the property, get out. Do you hear me?"

Her breath was static in my ear. "I have to check, Eli. If Maddie's inside—if they fucking locked her in—she'll die. I have to check."

"NO," I said, my voice foreign, thin as paper. "It's too dangerous."

"I have to. If she's down there and I didn't at least try, and something happened to her, I'd never be able to live with myself. Look, I know I'm not some hero, but I'm the only one who's here. If it were me, I'd hope someone cared enough to try to save me." She said—and I hated her for it, loved her for it, both at once.

Bronc barked into the phone. "Juliet, listen. Stay at the civic center. Do not leave. Do not go home for any reason. Be sure Little Wolf. Nobody leaves the Civic Center. Everybody must stay at the Civic Center. Tell me you hear me. Good. I love you." He hung up and kicked the dirt. "We have to go."

We mounted up and spun around, bikes shrieking against the asphalt. The return trip was worse than the first. Every pothole, every turn, every shadow on the road was a timer ticking down.

The phone was still live. I could hear Parker running, breath sawing, her voice echoing off the empty halls. "Eli, I'm in. A few lights are on. I don't see anyone. MADDIE! ARE YOU HERE? Let me check this one hall."

"No, Parker. Get the fuck out."

"I promise I will."

I gripped the throttle until the tendons in my wrist sang. "Parker, please. Don't do this."

She laughed, a brittle, beautiful sound. "Just let me check real fast."

I could hear doors opening and closing.

"I'm running down to the basement real fast."

Come on, little bird. Just hurry.

"I'm almost there. Man, I gotta start doing some cardio."

She was taking too long.

I could hear her in the stairwell, steps pounding.

"Thank goodness. I don't see her. I need to just check the back room. I'm hurrying I promise."

Her breath was coming in pants. I could feel the fear coming off of her in waves. Every mile was a razor blade. My whole body shook. Bronc was white-knuckled beside me, face set in stone. The rest of the pack was a blur in the rearview. Time stuttered, then sped up, then stopped altogether.

Parker's voice again: "Eli?"

"Get out, Parker. Get out right now." I could hear her on the stairs.

Her voice went soft, almost gentle. "Hey, Eli?"

"Yeah?" My heart was a grenade.

"If I don't make it out—"

"Don't say that."

"—just know that I love you, okay? I always did. Tell Rocket he's a good boy. And take care of him, okay? Tell Bronc I said sorry for what happened with Axel. Tell Juliet she makes everything better."

My throat closed. The bike veered, gravel biting into my tires. "Parker, don't. Stop talking and run. Hear me?"

She laughed again, softer this time. "I'm almost to the top of the stairs. And hey, it's okay, Eli. I found you again. That's all I ever needed."

"Little bird, I love you. Please—"

The world blew apart.

A roar. White noise. Then nothing.

The line went dead.

I don't remember dropping the bike. Just the taste of blood in my mouth, the crunch of gravel in my palms as I crawled back to the road.

Forty miles out, and I knew she was gone.

I screamed her name into the wind, and the sky swallowed it whole.

The bike skidded out from under me at sixty. I went down in a roar of gravel and glass, helmet slamming the guardrail, sparks everywhere. Didn't feel it. My body had gone numb the moment Parker's voice cut out.

I tore the helmet off and staggered to my knees. I couldn't fill my lungs with air. The world spun, and I let it, the cold slicing through my jacket, dust caking the blood in my nose. My hands shook so bad I couldn't make a fist.

Bronc was there in a heartbeat, boots gouging the dirt, voice low and mean. "Eli! Look at me." He grabbed my shoulders, fingers like steel. "You don't know she's dead."

I wanted to kill him, tear him apart for lying, but I had nothing left. Just the hollow rattle in my chest, the sound of my own name echoing back to me.

"She's gone," I said, and my voice was a stranger's.

Bronc shook me hard enough to pop something in my neck. "We don't quit until we see a body. She's a fighter. You said so yourself."

I blinked through the tears, tasted iron. "If she was in the house, it's over."

"Not unless you make it over," Bronc snapped. "We go now. We don't stop. We get her back, or we die trying."

The words lit something inside me. Not hope, not yet, but the muscle memory of a thousand drills, the urge to move, to act, to fix what was broken even if it meant burning down the world.

I got up.

We rode hell for leather, engines screaming, the horizon a line of black smoke against the purple sky.

By the time we reached the compound, the fire had eaten the clubhouse. It was a pile of cinder blocks and burned timber. We met two fire trucks, a sheriff's cruiser, and three ambulances. The air was a goddamn furnace, thick with the smell of scorched wood, melted plastic, something sweet and awful under it all.

I jumped off the bike before it stopped rolling and ran to the smoking ruin, heart trying to punch its way out of my chest.

The clubhouse was gone.

Just gone.

Walls folded in on themselves, bricks spattered across the yard, beams twisted and snapped like matchsticks. All the windows were teeth biting at the sky. There was no roof—just open air, black and glittering with falling ash.

People everywhere. The pack had come back from the civic center. There were a few of our own EMTs, and a few lost faces I didn't even recognize. Someone yelled, a kid maybe, but all I could hear was Parker's voice in my ear, that last laugh, soft as a goodbye.

I staggered to the wreckage. The firefighters kept shoving me away, shouting about danger, but I kept coming. Finally, T-Bone, one of our patched-in members, appeared at my side, face streaked with soot, hands already torn up from moving debris.

He grabbed my arm and pointed. "Stairwell survived. Kinda. If she was in there…"

He didn't finish.

I nodded, ran for the jagged hole where the stairs had been. The heat was brutal, singeing the hair off my arms, but I didn't care. I climbed over a collapsed beam, boots slipping, hands raw. Every breath was pain. Every movement threatened to collapse what was left of the structure.

"Parker!" I yelled. "Parker, answer me! Please! Wren!"

Nothing. Just the hiss of burning insulation, the pop of distant embers.

I clawed my way down the first flight, then the second. The lower stairs were intact, sheltered by the concrete wall. That's where the debris was thickest—an avalanche of plaster, glass, furniture, and steel. I started to dig.

My fingers bled, nails ripped off at the quick. I tore at every board, every chunk of drywall, calling her name until my throat was raw.

Someone else joined me—Papa, I think, or maybe Gunner. Together, we pulled away the junk, brick by brick, the dust so thick I couldn't see.

Then I heard it.

A faint, rasping breath.

"Stop," I shouted. "Everyone stop."

Silence.

I pressed my ear to the rubble. There it was—a whisper, barely there.

"Here!" I roared, and the guys swarmed in, hands and shovels and crowbars, anything they could use. We worked like maniacs, moving a wall's worth of garbage in minutes. Sweat blinded me, the world a tunnel of pain and noise.

Then a hand.

Small, pale, streaked black with ash.

I grabbed it, squeezed. "Parker! I'm here. I'm here."

The hand twitched, weak as a baby bird. But it was alive.

The next few minutes were chaos. The paramedics got there fast, cut her out with a saw, dragged her tiny broken body up and into the ambulance. She was unconscious, face pale, lips split and blue. Her clothes were burned away in patches, skin raw and bleeding.

But she was breathing.

She was alive.

I climbed into the back of the ambulance with her, ignored the shouts of protest, held her hand the whole way to the hospital. I didn't care about the blood on my shirt, the reek of smoke, the grit in my teeth. All I cared about was the steady, stubborn pulse in her wrist.

I whispered to her, over and over, "You're alive. You're alive. I'm here."

I don't remember much after that. She was taken to the pack hospital. We were one of the fortunate packs that had actual pack medical doctors. Thanks to Doc we also had a state-of-the-art hospital. Wolves tend to heal faster and need doctors less often than humans, but we do need them occasionally, so having a hospital nearby is another reason Iron Valor pack is envied. The ER was a blur of white lights, shouting, hands tearing at my clothes, patching up my cuts. Bronc showed up, face set, arms folded. He stood by the gurney and watched, as if his will alone could keep her alive.

At some point, they let me see her.

She lay on a hospital bed, bandaged from head to toe. Her face was a mess of bruises, gauze, and tape. She looked like a corpse, but she was warm.

I sat down, took her hand, and waited.

An hour passed. Two.

Then a day went by and she still didn't wake up.

"Please, little bird. Please come back to us. Rocket needs you. I need you."

CHAPTER 19

PARKER

I made it down the stairs in record time. Every step cracked with panic, my left shoe untied and flopping, the phone clamped between chin and shoulder as I ran. I hit the basement floor on a dead sprint. The fluorescent lights hummed, highlighting the furniture and happy activities that had been happening here just hours ago. My voice bounced off the cinderblocks: "Maddie! Are you here? It's Parker! Shout if you hear me!"

No answer. Nothing but the beat of my heart, the imaginary tick of the timer going off in my head, and the gnaw of fear chewing through my stomach lining.

I scanned the rows of low shelves and bins. Gift wrap, toys, box after box of bikes in pieces. I flipped the light switch for the back rooms, praying the power was still on. The bulbs flickered, barely illuminating the hallway. The phone slipped, and I nearly dropped it before Wrecker's voice pierced my ear.

"Parker. Stop. You have to get out. Right now. Do you hear me?"

He sounded like he'd been running—out of breath, out of patience, on the edge of howling. It made my hands shake harder.

"I just need to check the last room!" I yelled, banging through a storage closet. Empty. Just reams of colored paper and a metal cart that must have weighed two hundred pounds.

"She's not in there," Wrecker said. "You have to trust me. Get to the stairwell, Parker. Now."

But what if he was wrong? What if I left Maddie behind, and she never had a chance to see her mother and Bronc again? It would be my fault.

"Gimme a sec," I told him, breathless. "I'll make it out. I promise."

"Wren." That's what he called me when he was being easy with me. "Please."

I ran, every part of me pushing my body forward. Turned the corner. There, the last room. I flung open the door. Only cardboard, plastic, an old air hockey table, half collapsed. I did a sweep anyway.

Nothing. No Maddie. No one at all.

Wrecker's voice was in my head now, not the phone: Get out. Get out.

I bolted back down the corridor, banged my hip on the doorframe, and fumbled the phone. My lungs burned. It felt like gravity had tripled.

Somewhere in my mind, I could hear a clock ticking. Then I realized it was my heart, racing so hard it blurred the rest of the world.

I reached the foot of the stairs. "Eli!" I yelled. "I'm coming up. You better not—" I stopped. I didn't know why. Maybe the floor shifted. Maybe the air pressure changed.

I pressed the phone to my mouth, teeth clicking on the plastic. "Hey. If I don't make it, I need you to know something."

Silence, then static, then, "What?"

I wanted to say so many things. Things like how much I loved him and that he was the best thing that ever happened to me. I hope I told him to take care of Rocket. My sweet, ugly little pup deserved to be loved.

I know I said, "I love you, Eli. I always did."

The explosion didn't sound like anything I'd ever heard. It was too loud for that. It was sound weaponized, turned to air and shrapnel and pain, packed into every nerve ending at once. It sucked the breath out of the world, then spat it back into roaring fire and debris. The stairwell dissolved, and I dissolved with it. Then darkness.

Then silence.

There was a sudden calm. Bright sunlight. But not. Just brightness. A light. And then I saw her.

My mother.

She was standing in the backyard of our old house in Dairyville, wearing a blue sundress I remembered only from photos. The sun behind her turned her hair to flame. She looked younger than I remembered, but also older. She emanated peace. Every good feeling I'd ever known as a child was wrapped up in this beautiful woman.

I ran to her, even though I thought my legs wouldn't work. I crashed into her, clinging to her like I was six years old again. She smelled like sugar cookies and freshly laundered sheets. Her arms wrapped around me, strong and solid. I sobbed. I couldn't believe how badly I had missed her. How much I'd needed her. She felt like home.

"Am I dead?" I asked, snotty and pathetic.

She ran her hand through my wavy hair. "No, sweetheart," she said, her voice the sound of early mornings and rain on the roof. "You're not dead. You're just resting."

I pulled back, searching her face. "I don't understand. I know there was an explosion. I was there. In it. I know you're no longer alive, so how can I be? Did I mess everything up? I screwed up didn't I?"

She smiled, and it was the saddest smile in the world. "No, Parker. You did everything right. I'm proud of you."

I wanted to believe her, but it hurt too much. "I'm scared. I didn't want to die. Don't want to die. I just found my mate. Wrecker. You remember Wrecker? He's my mate, and I love him so much. We've just found each other again and realized. And even though it feels so wonderful here, to be able to rest finally, I don't want to leave him."

She laughed, low and bright, her eyes shining. "Oh, I know, baby. I always knew he was yours." She wiped the tears from my cheeks with her thumb. "He's been lonely too long. You're supposed to be with *him* now, not here. Not yet." She squeezed my shoulders, gentle but immovable.

I looked past her, expecting to see a tunnel or a white light or something. But there was nothing but the soft green of the grass, the lemon tree in bloom, the old rusty swing set I remembered Axel falling from when he was four. I wanted to sit there forever, but I could feel something pulling at my heels, a tether dragging me backward.

The pain started up again, behind my ribs and in my throat.

"I don't know how to get back," I whispered. "I don't know if I can."

She took my face in her hands. "Just listen," she said. "You'll know. And I'll see you again someday my sweet girl."

As she faded from sight, I listened.

At first, there was nothing but the sound of the wind through the lemon tree. Then, underneath it, a hum—low and electric, like an engine or a heartbeat.

Then I heard him.

"Parker!" Wrecker's voice, ragged, desperate. "Little bird, where are you? Wren?"

The hum got louder. I felt the earth shiver. The world started to come apart around the edges.

I fell through the blackness.

Someone was pulling at me—lifting, dragging. The pain was back, worse than before, but it was good pain, genuine pain. I clung to it. I took as many breaths as my lungs would allow.

I heard men yelling. The sound of boots on concrete. Hands scraping at brick and plaster. A crash of something heavy being thrown aside.

"Here!" a voice shouted. "She's here!"

Strong arms closed around my chest, squeezing the breath back into my lungs. I couldn't see. My eyes wouldn't open. But I knew the arms. I knew the shape of the hands. I knew the heartbeat.

"Got you," he whispered into my hair. "I got you, little bird. Don't you fucking die on me. Don't you dare."

I wanted to say his name, but my throat wouldn't work.

Someone pressed a mask to my face. Cold air rushed in, sweet and chemical. A hand brushed the hair off my forehead, slow and trembling.

I drifted in and out; the world flickering like a busted TV.

Each time I woke, Wrecker was there, holding my hand. Sometimes he was crying. Sometimes he was swearing at the ceiling. Sometimes he just stared, unblinking, as if he could hold me to earth by willpower alone.

Once, I tried to smile. My face barely moved, but he noticed.

He bent down, mouth close to my ear. "Stay," he said. "Just stay."

So I did.

I woke to the sound of my own breath—wet, uneven, a hollow little whistle that didn't match the rhythm in my dreams. The ceiling above me was off-white and covered with raised dots, the kind of tile you see in schools and hospitals and nowhere else on earth. There was a tube in my nose and tape all over my face. The air smelled like sanitizer and something sharper, the animal tang of blood.

For a minute, I couldn't remember where I was, or even who I was. Then I heard him.

"Hey, little bird," Wrecker said, voice soft enough not to shatter me. He was sitting in a chair so tiny his knees were nearly to his chin. "Don't move. Doc's right outside."

He looked like he hadn't slept in a week, his stubble gone from designer to derelict, hair sticking out in every direction. His hands were clasped together, knuckles white, forearms streaked with lines that could have been soot or grease or dried blood.

I tried to sit up, but it was like someone had taken a cheese grater to my ribs and then wrapped them in barbed wire.

"Easy," he said, and his hand was on my shoulder before I could even flinch.

Doc strode in, a clipboard in one hand and a scowl on his face. Black-rimmed glasses on, looking like a thrift store Clark Kent. His scrubs looked like they'd come out of the wash ten minutes ago. He put down the clipboard, took out a penlight, and flashed it in my eyes.

"Name?" he said, voice brisk.

"Parker Reid," I croaked.

"Date?"

"Sorry, Wrecker and I are exclusive." I coughed out on a grin. This guy. My brain was fuzzy, but Doc was a guy who didn't smile nearly enough. Clearly, I hadn't changed that.

Wrecker coughed into his hand.

I thought hard. "Sorry, sometimes I joke. December. Probably?"

Doc still didn't smile. "Good enough." He pulled the penlight away and checked my pulse, his touch impersonal but not unkind.

"Where's Rocket?" I whispered.

"Dog's fine," Wrecker said immediately. "He's with Maddie."

"Is she—?"

"She's fine, too. She got hit with some flying debris, nothing serious. Paramedics checked her out. Put her on a diet of grilled cheese. Her words, not mine."

Doc rolled up the blanket, revealing my left arm encased in a brace the color of blue Gatorade. "You took a big hit, Parker. Three broken ribs on your left side, one of which punctured a lung. Broken ulna. some superficial burns, and a lot of cuts. The lung's already sealing up, shifter healing, you know. The area of most concern was the head injury you sustained. You had serious brain swelling that should have ended you. It was there, then it wasn't." You're a goddamn walking miracle. Everything's healing quicker than...He checked the monitor by my bed. "Maybe Menace's angel friend made a stop by the room," he muttered to himself.

I tried to laugh, but it hurt too much. "Guess my luck is changing," I said, and tasted copper at the back of my throat.

Doc handed me a cup with a straw. "Sip. Small sips."

I drank, each swallow burning all the way down.

"You remember what happened?" Doc asked.

"Bomb," I said. "Clubhouse. I went to check for Maddie. I was stupid. Got caught."

Doc's eyes went flat. "You weren't stupid. You were brave." Sounded like a compliment and not just a fact. "Most people wouldn't have made it out. Or wanted to."

I looked down at my hands. They were clean, but the skin was shredded in places, pink and shiny with healing. "I saw my mom," I said. "I was pretty sure I was dead."

Wrecker shifted beside me. "You weren't dead."

"I think maybe I was. Just for a minute."

Doc pressed two fingers to my neck, counting the pulse. "Did she say anything interesting?" he asked, and I almost laughed at how clinical he made it sound.

I nodded, then winced. "She told me to listen."

Doc's lips quirked. "Good advice. Maybe you should try it more often."

Wrecker glared at him, but Doc ignored it.

"How long was I out?" I asked.

"Twenty-four hours. Not the worst I've seen, but I'll want to keep you here for at least another day. Two if you're smart."

I nodded. "I'll be smart."

Doc snorted. "That'll be the day." He finished his checks, made a note on the clipboard, and turned to Wrecker. "No strenuous activity for at least a week. And keep her away from power tools." He left without waiting for a response.

Wrecker scooted his chair closer. He ran his thumb along my jaw, careful not to touch the bruised side. "You scared the shit out of me," he said, voice low.

"Sorry," I said, and meant it.

He didn't say anything for a while. Just looked at me, like he was cataloguing every freckle, every cut, every inch of me.

"I heard you," I said. "In the rubble. I heard you calling for me. That's why I came back when I died."

He shook his head. "You don't have to make everything into a joke, Wren. Sometimes people just get lucky."

"I'm serious. I wanted to stay. Because of you."

He looked away, jaw working. "You're not allowed to die before me," he said finally. "That's the deal."

I tried to smile. "You planning on dying soon?"

His mouth twitched. "Not if I can help it." He reached out and took my hand. "You're not getting rid of me that easy."

I squeezed his fingers, even though it hurt. "I don't want to."

He bent down, brushed his lips across my forehead. "Rest. I'll be here."

He stayed with me throughout the entire night. When I woke up, he was reading a battered paperback, his feet propped on the windowsill. When I asked for water, he was already halfway out of the chair. When I needed to puke, he held the basin and didn't even flinch when some of it got on his arm.

The second day, I heard voices in the hallway. Bronc, low and furious, and Juliet, sharp as a knife. I caught the words "Greenbriar" and "retaliation." I caught my own name twice.

I tried to get out of bed, but the pain was too much. When Wrecker came back, I said, "You need to let me help. I can hack the cameras, I can—"

He cut me off. "No. Not this time. You almost died, Parker. You're sitting this one out."

"You can't just—"

"I can," he said, voice gone dark. "And I am. You're staying here, where you're safe. Bronc can handle the rest."

I wanted to argue, but my throat closed up. Maybe it was the drugs, maybe it was the ache behind my ribs, maybe it was just the sudden, absolute exhaustion.

"Fine," I muttered. "But you better not let him do anything stupid."

He grinned. "I'll do my best."

We watched bad TV for hours. He made fun of every commercial, every plot twist, until I was crying with laughter. He never let go of my hand, even when I dozed off.

Once, in the dead of night, I woke to find him asleep in the chair, mouth open, head back against the wall. He looked peaceful for the first time since we'd found each other again. I watched him breathe, slow and even, and realized I didn't hurt as much as I thought I would.

The next morning, Doc cleared me for solid food. I demanded pancakes. I ate every bite, even though it tasted like cardboard.

I asked about Rocket again.

"Maddie's bringing him by this afternoon," Wrecker said. "She said he's hogging the bed."

I tried to picture it, and it made my heart hurt in a better way.

We didn't talk about the war, or what was coming. We didn't talk about the next move, or how much time we had before Greenbriar tried something worse.

For now, it was enough to breathe.

For now, it was enough to know that he was here, and so was I, and even if the rest of the world was burning, we'd survived this round.

I drifted off again, Wrecker's hand wrapped around mine. The last thing I heard was his voice, soft and true:

"Rest, little bird. I've got you."

CHAPTER 20

WRECKER

I was never one for hospitals. The wolf in me equated them with failure—meat laid out for the scavengers, bodies cold and sterile and too far gone for the pack to heal. Yet here I was, breathing recycled air and bleach, counting the seconds between Parker's rattling inhales. Watching her chest rise, maybe not fall, maybe not again. Machines did the work I couldn't: they buzzed, beeped, spat telemetry in green lines that looked like electrocardiogram mountain ranges. Peaks and valleys. The nurse called it "optimistic" when the valleys didn't bottom out.

Her face was half lost in the sheets, skin gone ghostly with undertones of blue. The worst of it was the right temple, swollen above the brow, purple-black and tight as a drum. Doc had shaved a patch around it for the CT scan, the stubble coarse against behind her ear. Looked like she'd been scalped in a bar fight. At least the bleeding had stopped. I counted the IV bags, tried to guess if any of them were morphine, and if so, if she could even dream through this.

Doc hovered at her left, chart in one hand, reading out the numbers for no one but himself. His voice, usually clinical, ran low and fast. "Pressure's holding, but we're right on the edge. Swelling's the bastard. It's just moving faster than her wolf's healing ability. The broken bones will heal in days. But that damn brain swelling...." He glanced at me, not unkindly. "You can talk to her, Eli. You never know what gets through."

I nodded, but my tongue was a dead snake in my mouth. I'd done enough talking for one lifetime. Instead, I pulled a chair to the bed and put my hand over hers. Warm, but not by much. The monitor on her finger flashed at the contact, as if scolding me for risking contamination.

The wolf in me wanted to fix it. To lick the wound, to push life back into her by sheer will. I could do neither. I could only sit and wait and remember every fucking thing I never said to her.

The evening nurse, a girl with bubblegum scrubs and a face like an angry sparrow, shooed Doc out for his next rounds. He left with a look at me, as if daring me to let go. I didn't.

The sun dipped behind the parking lot pines. The room changed: light went blue, shadows stretched, and the glass took on a mirror shine. I could see myself reflected behind Parker's sleeping face, and I hated the man that stared back. I traced the rise of her knuckles, watched the slow oxygenation of each finger, told myself she'd wake and call me an idiot for staring.

I couldn't take the silence anymore. I pressed my phone flat against my thigh and dialed the only number I'd never wanted to use again.

Menace answered on the third ring, voice hoarse. "Eli?"

"Got a situation," I said. My own voice sounded wrong, used up.

He grunted. "Heard about the explosion. Is she—?"

"Alive, but barely." I glanced at Parker. "Head's bad. Doc says the swelling's not responding. I don't know if she—if she's going to make it."

Menace didn't speak. I could picture him in his home office, boots propped on the battered desk, a bottle of Glenfiddich sweating through the label. The man did nothing by halves.

I pushed on, like tearing out a rotten tooth. "That time after Calloway stabbed you—" I paused. Even the memory was like swallowing ground glass. "We all saw the angel. Savannah said...you'd died."

A long, cold beat. Then, "Yeah, Archon Seraphael." His voice dropped a register. "You're not thinking it's to the point you need that kind of intervention?"

I was. I was so fucking desperate I'd summon a demon if it would put color back in Parker's lips.

"Can you contact him?" I asked. "I know it's insane. But she—I can't lose her. Can't let her go."

Menace's reply was all gravel. "Let me see what I can do. I'll call you back."

I hung up before he could say more. The shame was a stone in my chest, but it was smaller than the fear.

Back in the room, I watched the blue digits on the monitor roll over, then back, like a slot machine stuck on a losing streak. Parker's mouth twitched, then settled. I counted her breaths: nine a minute. I willed it to ten. Twelve. I stroked her hair, now sticky with sweat, and whispered nothing words into the space between us.

Nurses came and went, shadows in the night. One offered to bring me coffee. I shook my head. If I left, she might be gone when I got back.

I took off my jacket, used it to cover her toes, tried not to think of the morgue slab Doc would roll her onto if the numbers didn't turn around. I squeezed her hand, thumb pressed to her wrist, counting not the pulse but the proof that something of her was still in there.

The world shrank to that touch.

I fell into a daze, half-waking, half-dreaming, the hours ticking by with no change in the pattern. At some point, the janitor passed in the hallway, his mop squealing on the tile like a rat in a trap. He never looked in, never made a sound. I envied him his work: clean the mess, move on. Repeat.

Menace texted just before 3:00 a.m.: *Will try at dawn. Hang on, brother.*

I set the phone aside and waited for the light to shift again. I didn't let go.

The night didn't end, just wore out. I'd memorized every second of her heartbeat, the way the color in her face seemed to fade in and out with each nurse's shift. I counted the needle marks on her arms: four on the left, five on the right. IV drip was half-gone by dawn, the liquid silver shrinking with every tick of the clock.

I'd promised Menace I'd wait for daylight, but the sky outside stayed coal-black. I didn't close my eyes, not once.

The first hint of change was Doc's footsteps, heavy on the tile. He came in with a new file, thumbed through the printouts, then looked at me instead of her. "It stopped," he said. "The swelling. It's receded."

I didn't get it at first. I'd lived in crisis mode so long, my brain couldn't process good news. "What do you mean, receded?"

He dropped the scan on the counter, pointed with a capped pen. "See this? Last night, pressure was rising. This morning, it's baseline. No medical reason for it. None." He didn't say miracle. He didn't have to.

I blinked, stared at Parker's forehead, expecting the skin to split, expecting the universe to take it back. But it didn't. Her hand was warmer now. The blue had faded from her lips. I let out a breath and said a silent thank you to whatever bastard angel Menace had roped into this.

Doc checked her vitals, tapped a note into his phone, and left with a nod. "If she makes it through the day, she's out of the woods. You can stay, but don't expect her to wake up soon."

I stayed. I watched the monitors, ignoring the hunger that gnawed at my ribs, the stench of sweat pooling under my shirt. Every few hours, the nurse came to check her, and every time, I flinched like she'd come to tell me it was over.

Sometime around three, the rhythm changed. Parker's eyes flickered under the lids. Her fingers twitched. I leaned in, whispering, "You're not done yet, little bird. You gotta wake up and call me an asshole."

She did eventually. Her eyes cracked open, unfocused at first, pupils blown wide. She croaked, "You smell like you fought a sewer rat and lost."

I laughed, the sound more like a sob. "Missed you, too," I said, and squeezed her hand until I thought I'd break it.

The first hours were a blur of micro-conversations. She answered Doc's questions. Gave a smartass reply. Mentioned seeing her mother. Doc had a snide remark. She asked about Rocket, about Maddie, about the house. She didn't ask if she was dying, and I didn't tell her she almost had. The room felt smaller with her awake, and the machines seemed less hungry for her blood.

On day two, she could sit up with help. She winced with every breath, ribs wrapped in tight bands, her arm in a brace and tape over her temple. I found a brush in the visitor's bathroom and tried to detangle her hair. She made fun of my technique, but let me finish.

Later, when we were alone, she said, "I saw my mother. When I died." The words dropped like a body from a bridge. "I told her I'd found my mate, and it was you. She told me she always knew it was. I told her I had to get back to you."

I pressed my lips to her knuckles and said nothing. My throat had locked up.

She studied the window, the faded sky. "It felt wonderful there, so peaceful, but my pull to you was stronger than wanting to stay there with her. She told me it wasn't my time to be there. And to listen. That's when I heard you calling me."

She went quiet, and I watched the side of her face. The bruises were already fading, the cut on her cheek closing up like an afterthought.

"Why'd you do it?" I asked, when I couldn't stand the silence. "Run in there, knowing what they planned?"

She didn't look at me. "Look, I know I'm no hero. But if Maddie had gone in there, she'd have died, and I was the only one close enough to tell her to get out. She's Bronc's little sister. She never did anything to deserve that."

"And if you had died?"

She shrugged, a tiny motion. "After my part in this? Wouldn't be the worst thing."

I hated her a little, right then. Hated her for being so ready to take the hit. Hated that she'd thought so little of herself.

"That's where you're wrong, Wren. It *would* have been the worst thing. You're not just a random run-of-the-mill woman. You're the woman who picks up sad little ugly starving dogs and gives them a home. You give money to the homeless guy who parks his buggy next to the little grocery store where you buy your groceries every week. You donate to homeless shelters and domestic violence centers because you have a heart for people. You put your life on the line for your brother, knowing it could get you killed. And you have made my life better in every single way that matters. So, if you had died, it sure as fuck would have been the worst thing to *me*."

She swallowed hard, tears streaming down her face.

"I'm glad I didn't stay dead."

I had my own tears falling at the thought as I gently wrapped her in my arms.

"I'm glad you didn't stay dead too. So glad."

When the paperwork cleared, I didn't let her return to her house. She curled up in my bed with Rocket against her belly and slept for a whole day straight.

I set up water, pills, snacks, and the remote within reach. Put the laptop by the bed, just in case she wanted to hack a government server for fun. I didn't leave her side.

Not even once.

We turned my living room into a war room. The kind with rings on the table from fifty years of spilled whiskey, and all the chairs scuffed by people who couldn't sit still. Every surface was covered in something: tactical maps, burner phones, three laptops, and a battered legal pad with my handwriting on every inch. The whiteboard I'd pulled in from the garage was already losing its magnets under the weight of bad news.

Bronc presided over it, arms crossed, beard shot with more silver than last month. Next to him, Arsenal hunched forward, a knuckle pressed to his lips, eyes flicking between the digital feed and the wall. Pearl brought in coffee, poured herself a cup, and sat with her back to the window. Only Gunner seemed relaxed, booted feet up on the ottoman and a Glock tucked into his waistband, safety off. Juliet hovered here and there.

Nobody said much at first. We watched the sunrise through the gap in the curtains, a slant of blood orange over the half-built bones of the new clubhouse. You could hear the hammering even at this hour—construction crews working two shifts, trying to raise the frame before Greenbriar could send a second wave.

When Bronc spoke, it was to the floor. "Advance said they cleared Greenbriar territory last night. Not a single wolf. Not a single soul."

I grunted. "Everything abandoned. Looks less like they ran than just moved. It didn't look rushed. Looked like a relocation."

Pearl frowned, eyes sharp behind reading glasses. "Abandoned, or just hiding?"

Arsenal pointed to the map. "They're not local anymore. They left the perimeter scattered. We tracked three separate convoys, all heading different directions. Our assumption is they met up at a central end location."

Gunner said, "Like trailing fucking smoke."

Bronc's jaw flexed. "We need to hit them before they get organized. This was their big shot, but it's not the last. They know it failed, but I'm sure they think they shook us. I'd bet they want to hit us quick while they think we're scattered and scared."

I sipped cold coffee, wishing it was bourbon. "We don't even have a location. Could be Amarillo, could be Lubbock, could be fucking Mexico. We can't chase ghosts."

Pearl said, "You're not going to like this, but some other packs are starting to talk. Some of the smaller ones are asking if Iron Valor's up for the job. The Council wants answers."

"Council can suck my dick. I'm so goddamn sick of the Council. I have fucking *kings* in my corner. These small packs forget who they're dealing with." Bronc's voice rose to a growl, causing Juliet to stroll to his side. One touch of hers had an immediate effect on him.

She spoke next. "We need to let calmer heads prevail here. We are smarter than Greenbriar. *We* certainly wouldn't have made a move that made us look as incompetent as the one they just made. That's the message that needs to be pressed. They are a desperate renegade pack who clearly attacked a peaceful pack without cause. We've learned from past Council experience that going to them for aid is futile. So I say, we continue as we're going. But we sure as fuck better collect every scrap of evidence as we go. We'll have to prove every claim when we're brought up on charges, as we surely will be."

I had to point out the obvious. "They aren't working alone. Parker knows there are demons and vampires involved as well. To what degree? She's not sure. But she's seen them there."

"This just keeps getting better and better." Bronc's frustration was reaching an all-time high. "We have a few days until the clubhouse is finished. That's when we'll be most exposed. We have to assume Silas knows it."

Pearl took off her glasses, polished them. "What's the plan?"

Bronc looked at me. "Wrecker, you're point on cyber as always. Get every possible feed, every data point, every sniff of a target. No mistakes."

"I got you. Finding them is the first step. They still think the back transfers are occurring. That might be our in. Hopefully, there will be an IP address I can ping. It will be fucking poetic justice if that is the thing that gives them away."

I stood and stretched. "I've gotta head to my computer room so I can access everything. I have a good feeling about this." I didn't notice when the living room got quiet. It was only when Pearl cleared her throat that I looked up.

Parker stood in the doorway. She wore sweatpants and one of my old shirts; the sleeves hanging off her wrists like she was twelve. Her hair was a rat's nest, and the bruises on her face were turning a sickly yellow. But she stood on her own, one hand braced against the frame.

Nobody said anything for a long second. Then Bronc nodded at her, slow and respectful. "You should be in bed."

She ignored him. "You need me."

It wasn't a question. Just a statement of fact delivered from chapped lips that mine wanted so badly to soothe.

Arsenal started to protest, but Gunner cut him off. "She's right. Nobody runs a trace like Parker."

I didn't say anything. Just gestured for her to follow me.

She walked over with a small limp, and we headed to my den. I put my arm around her and helped her into the big chair. Thanks to her shifter healing her left arm was out of the brace but still in a sling. She slipped it off and flexed her fingers as though she wanted to see if her hand still worked. It did. Within seconds, she was knee-deep in phone records, looking for anomalies, making notes on the pad between her knees.

Pearl brought her a cup of coffee. Parker took it without looking up.

Everyone wound up in the room with us. Bronc watched all this, jaw set, a proud father with no words for his kid.

"Got something," she said, not five minutes later. "Three phones. Two dumps prepaid. One keeps pinging the same tower in Farwell."

Arsenal leaned forward. "That's west. Near the border."

"Could be a relay. Or could be they're making a show for us." She looked at Bronc. "You want me to go in?"

He looked at me, then her, then back at me. "You okay with this?"

She didn't wait for my answer. "You need me to do it. And I want to."

Bronc nodded. "Do it."

She got to work, fingers flying. Gunner watched the feed, calling out hits on vehicle plates. Arsenal started running background on every rental property within ten miles of the ping. Pearl paced, her phone glued to her ear, organizing food and perimeter checks for the construction crews.

I watched Parker. She had her jaw set, lips pressed together, a bead of sweat on her brow from the effort. She didn't stop, didn't slow down. It dawned on me then that I was more than in love with her. I respected her. She was perfect, and it was so much more than her beauty—her curves, her softness. I realized her mind was maybe the sexiest thing about her.

After two hours, she had a map of the entire area, a dozen likely addresses with acreage who owned them, and a list of cars tied to Greenbriar proxies. Looked like they'd moved west.

She looked up at me, eyes clear for the first time in days. "You okay?" she asked.

I shrugged. "I am now."

The others finished their tasks and drifted into the kitchen for more coffee. The house was quiet, just the two of us and the hum of the laptops. I put a hand on her shoulder, squeezed, careful of the bruises.

"You don't have to do this, Wren."

She grinned, lopsided. "I want to."

I grinned back. "Fine. But if you pass out, I'm carrying you to bed."

She snorted. "You'd like that, wouldn't you?"

"Maybe." I leaned in, kissed her hair. "Just don't die again. I'm not sure my wolf can take it."

She nodded. "I'll try."

We went back to work.

Outside, the construction never stopped. The world kept spinning, and the war wasn't over. But the house was full of light, and for the first time since the fire, it felt like we could win.

Maybe that's all you ever get.

Just a chance to try again.

CHAPTER 21

PARKER

Wrecker's den was a shoebox full of ghosts. The walls hummed with the tick of cooling electronics, the afterimage of blue light still burning my retinas from hours of screen time. The place was a temple for night creatures—cold pizza boxes as altar offerings, coffee rings like ritual stains, that singular absence of sunlight you only get from blackout curtains bought in the "doomsday prep" aisle.

I'd sat there all morning, tracking the digital footprints of Greenbriar's ghosts, reanimating their every call, every late-night ATM ping, every fake Uber ride and disposable phone. The servers were spitting back results faster than I could read them. By noon, my head was one long error message.

Wrecker checked regularly, bringing me coffee, sandwiches, and anything else he could think of. He replaced the battered gel wrist-rest at my station, and once just stood in the doorway and watched. He didn't say a word, but I felt the weight of his stare, heavy as a hand on the back of my neck. I was half-aware, half-feral, my body still healing from the last round of fun with Silas. The tape across my ribs pulled and itched every time I turned, and my lungs gave a wet little click if I breathed too deep. My left arm was a roadmap of healing fractures and scattered bruises—turning yellow at the edges, but still a horror show in the right light.

Bronc also made several appearances. It felt good to see him, if I'm honest. He was giving off proud dad vibes, oddly enough. Juliet was at his side just looking in to be sure I wasn't being bullied.

By three o'clock, my vision kept jumping a frame ahead. Lines of code split and re-stitched on the monitor. Voices crackled out of nowhere, little hallucinations born from fever or hunger or the morphine crash I'd been riding all week. At some point, I realized I'd been talking to myself for ten straight minutes. When I finally came up for air, my head weighed as much as a cement block. My spine didn't so much ache as vibrate.

I must have fallen asleep in the chair. I woke to the sound of water running.

Wrecker's shadow moved across the hallway. Then he was there—silent as a ghost, big enough to block out half the room. He said nothing, just slid an arm under my knees and scooped me up like I weighed nothing at all. My first instinct was to hiss at him, but he smelled like oranges and oak, and I didn't have the energy to argue.

He carried me into the bathroom, which was already steaming, lavender curling from the air like the memory of a pleasant dream. The large modern tub was just full enough, white foam rising. He set me down on a small vanity chair by the sink, which hadn't been there before. It was new, the tag still swinging from the bottom.

"Special for you," he said, noticing my eyes on it. "Your ass deserves comfort."

I laughed, and it hurt, but in the way a new tattoo hurts—sweet, sharp, a proof of life. "You gonna join me?"

He grinned, the dimple in his left cheek coming out of retirement. "That's the plan, Wren."

He bent to untie my shoes, then peeled off my socks, one slow tug at a time. His hands were always careful, but now they moved with a kind of desperate reverence. Every patch of healing skin made his jaw tighten.

I tried to stand up to undress, but he stopped me with a hand on my shoulder. "Let me do it. Please." His eyes wouldn't meet mine.

He started with the hoodie, sliding it off and folding it on the edge of the counter. Next, the tank top. The bandages underneath were stained, but mostly dry now. He unwound them with surgical precision, fingers trembling just a little at the sight of the bruises beneath.

His thumb traced the edge of the largest one, still a raw smear above my hip.

"I'm fine," I said, voice almost steady. "Wolf healing. It's tons better."

He said nothing, but I watched his mouth work around a word he couldn't say.

He knelt, undid the drawstring of my sweats, and pulled them down. My body had never looked so fragile—scarred, ribbed, held together with hope and bandage wrap. But he didn't flinch, didn't avert his eyes.

He just breathed, deep and slow, then gently lifted me up and into the tub.

The water was a shock, then a balm. Heat flooded every nerve, dissolving the aches. My head lolled back against the porcelain.

He stripped in silence, which should have been erotic, but was instead profoundly sad. Every scar on his body glowed pale in the vapor—military, motorcycle, maybe the kind you don't get in a fight but in a bad dream. He climbed in behind me, knees bracketing my hips, arms wrapping around my waist.

For a long time, neither of us spoke. He washed me, hands slow and steady, running the soapy sponge over every inch of skin as if each mark was a secret to decode. His fingers trembled every time he hit a bruise.

I leaned my head back on his shoulder. "You don't have to be so gentle," I said. "I'm not going to break."

"I almost lost you," he said, voice muffled against my hair. "Forgive me if I'm a little fucked up about it."

The sponge drifted lower across my thighs. He massaged each muscle, working out the knots from hours at the computer, and I let myself melt into it, for once not needing to be in control of my body. The feeling was narcotic.

He ran the handheld nozzle, water as hot as I could stand, over my head, careful to avoid the patch where they'd shaved me for the stitches.

He lathered up my hair, then applied the purple conditioner I liked. He massaged my scalp, slow, with fingers that felt magical, making my brain fizz out at the edges.

"You smell like a spa," he said, nuzzling into my neck. "Is this your secret weapon?"

"That, and coffee. The true lifeblood of the hacker."

He set the bottle down, but kept working the conditioner through my hair. His voice dropped lower. "I have to tell you something."

I tensed. He felt it, and held me tighter.

"When you were out, I called Menace. I asked about that angel—the one that saved his life. Your brain kept swelling. Didn't look like it was going to stop. I asked Menace if he might contact him to see if he might give you a little touch."

I blinked. "Did he do it?"

"Got a message back from Menace saying he spoke with him."

"Did he say anything else?"

Wrecker shrugged, but I could feel the hope trembling in him. "I didn't have a chance to ask. Doc came in and said the swelling was going down. Said you should have died, but you didn't."

"When I saw my mom, I remember being scared because I didn't know how to get back to you. That's when she told me to listen. The only thing that mattered to me was getting back to you."

His hands stilled. The water sloshed, the only sound for a long second.

He pressed his lips to the nape of my neck. "I should have claimed you before all this. If I'd been stronger—"

"Don't be stupid," I said, cutting him off. "You didn't wait. It's not like we started on steady footing."

He let out a shaky laugh. "That's true. You're sure you want me to do it. To mark you? Claim you?"

I twisted around in his arms, ignoring the ache in my ribs. "If you don't, I'll spend the rest of my life tormenting you about it. Is that what you want?"

He grinned, but there was a glassiness in his eyes, a grief I'd never seen before. "No, Wren. That's not what I want."

I tilted my head forward, letting my wet hair fall over his face. "Then do it. whenever. I don't need a ceremony."

He kissed me then, a slow, careful thing. He tasted like love and agony. His hands roamed up my back, one finger tracing the line of my spine. He paused when he got to the place around my right ear.

"What's this?" he said, gently parting the hair.

I reached up, fingers finding the patch where the nurse had shaved a coin-sized circle. The skin underneath was weird—slick, smooth, almost plastic-feeling. I tried to catch my reflection in the faucet, but couldn't see it. I scraped at the patch and it tingled, a faint, static electricity sparking up my arm.

"Look at it," I said, tilting my head for him to see.

He leaned in. "Holy fuck. That's new."

"What is it?"

He didn't answer right away, just stared.

"Hand me a mirror."

He reached over to the vanity and pulled out the drawer. He pulled out a handheld mirror and handed it to me. I held it up and pulled the hair back. Just behind my right ear was a spot. The patch was faint blue, pale as glacial ice. Under the bathroom lights, it almost glowed.

He ran his thumb over it, gentle, reverent. "Looks like a scar. But not. Maybe it's where the angel touched you."

I snorted. "That's stupid."

He grinned, wolfish. "You got a better theory?"

"No," I said, then quieter: "But it doesn't hurt. Not even a little."

He let out a breath. "You're a wonder, you know that?"

I shrugged, which made my ribs protest. "I try."

He finished massaging the conditioner through my hair and rinsed it until the water ran clear. His hands didn't shake this time.

We sat there until the water cooled and my fingers went pruney. He helped me up, wrapped me in a towel, and dried me with the care of someone preparing a relic for display. He carried me back to the bedroom and dressed me in one of his old shirts, which hung down to my knees.

He lay down beside me, drawing the covers over both of us. His arm wrapped around my waist, anchoring me to his body.

I let myself drift, knowing that whatever the blue mark on my skull meant, it didn't matter. I was here. I was loved.

I woke up in a world of static and pressure.

Wrecker's body was a furnace behind me, one arm a steel cable around my ribs, his hand cupped under my breast. His heartbeat pounded through my spine. He was always warm, but this morning he was molten, radiating through the layers of my borrowed t-shirt. There was another pressure, urgent and familiar, pressing against the small of my back. It took my bleary brain a second to realize it was his cock, rock hard and twitching against me, insistent as a metronome.

For a minute, I just lay there, breathing in the scent of him—soap and oranges and that raw, animal note that meant home. My body flushed awake in stages: first a low hum in my chest, then a fluttering in my gut, and finally a pulse of heat between my legs. It had been too long, and my wolf was out of patience. The memory of how he filled me, the burn and bliss of it, hit me all at once. I tried to shift, but he only tightened his grip, pinning me in place.

I turned in his arms his deep breath telling me he was still sleeping soundly. I reached inside his sleep pants and tenderly ran my fingers over his erection, watching his face. His eyebrows furrowed as he gave a small moan that made me even wetter than before. Gently, I traced my fingertips across his balls, then back up the length of his cock, a grin on my face.

"Morning, Wren," as his eyes slowly opened.

"Morning," I managed, as I gripped him a little harder.

His hand reached out and grasped my wrist. Not hard enough to hurt, but hard enough to make his point. "Hmm, a little bird thinks she's in charge of something this morning. She could not be more mistaken."

He wrapped his hand around mine and rocked his hips, eyes never leaving mine. "Fuck, that's a nice way to wake up. You sure you're up for this? We can wait. Let you heal."

I twisted in his grip, finally managing to roll onto my back. He loomed over me, eyes gone storm-gray, wild but worried.

"I'm not fragile," I said, reaching down to grip him again. He was huge in my hand, hot and heavy and already leaking. I stroked him once, twice, just to watch his eyes close.

When he opened them, he was smiling. "You trying to top me?"

I squeezed, hard enough to make his whole body flex. "Maybe."

He growled, deep and hungry. "That's not how this works, little bird."

He pushed the t-shirt up and over my head, baring my skin. He paused at every bruise, every healing cut, tracing them with a thumb. The way he looked at me made me feel less like a victim and more like a miracle.

He spread my legs with a knee, settling between them. The heat of him was torture, so close, but not enough. His mouth went to my collarbone, sucking a line of fire down to my breast. He circled my nipple with his tongue, then bit down, gentle but possessive.

I arched into him, desperate. "Please," I said, not sure if I meant for him to fuck me or just never stop touching me.

He slid his hand down, fingers skimming my ribs, my belly, then lower. He slipped two fingers into my panties, found me already soaked and aching. He circled my clit, feather-light, then slipped inside with maddening patience.

"You're so wet," he murmured, watching my face. "You are a needy little thing aren't you?"

I nodded, unable to trust my voice.

"So am I, baby."

He pulled back, making me whimper, then slid my panties down my legs and tossed them aside. He spread me open, studied me like a work of art, then lowered his mouth to my pussy. The first lick was slow, exploratory. The second was a punch of electricity straight to my core. He worked me with his tongue, alternating soft laps with sharp, insistent flicks. When I bucked against his face, he held me down, growling into my skin.

"Fucking fuck, Wren. You taste like happiness."

I came fast, the pleasure blinding, white noise in my brain. But he didn't stop. He kept eating me, relentless, until I was shaking, begging him to let up.

He finally surfaced, chin slick with me, eyes blazing.

"I love how you taste," he said, voice gone ragged.

He lined himself up at my entrance, the head of his cock nudging my pussy. He hovered, teasing, waiting for me to say something.

I reached for him, wrapped my arms around his neck. "Claim me," I said. "Now."

He didn't hesitate. He thrust into me in one slow, agonizing stroke, filling me until I couldn't breathe. The stretch was brutal, but perfect. He gave me a second to adjust, then started to move—slow at first, then harder, deeper. Every thrust hit the spot inside me that was made just for him.

I wrapped my legs around him, my heels digging into his ass cheeks.

He bent his head to my throat, breathing me in. "You ready to be mine forever?" he asked, voice trembling.

"Yes. Yes, Eli, please—"

He fucked me harder, each stroke building the pressure. When I was right on the edge, he struck—his teeth breaking the skin of my shoulder, pain and pleasure braided together. I screamed, body clamping down on him. I felt the rush of his release, the knot at the base of his cock swelling, locking us together. The euphoria was otherworldly, a tidal wave that erased everything but the feeling of him, inside and out.

He kept biting deeper, drinking in my soul. I felt the mate bond snap into place—a tether, a lifeline, electric and eternal. Every nerve sang with the knowledge that I was his, now and forever.

He pulled back, blood on his lips, eyes black with satisfaction.

"Will you return the claim, little bird?" he whispered, voice a dare.

My own fangs descended, sharp and eager. I dragged him down and bit into his shoulder, tasting the copper of his blood, the raw wildness of his wolf. He shuddered, nearly collapsing on top of me as the bond went both ways, sealing us together in body and mind.

My second orgasm ripped through me, violent and pure. I screamed into his flesh, nails digging bloody crescents into his back.

When the world came back, I was floating. He was still inside me, still pulsing, his knot keeping us locked tight. I licked the wound on his shoulder, then kissed it, dizzy with the taste of him.

He rolled us onto our sides, careful not to break the seal. He stroked my hair, kissing my forehead.

"I love you," he said. "More than my own life."

I clung to him, shaking. "Don't ever let go."

"Never," he promised.

We lay there, tangled and messy, the room bright with morning light. I closed my eyes, the echo of the bond humming through every cell. For the first time in my life, I felt whole.

He cleaned me up with a damp washcloth, tucking me under the covers. I drifted off, his scent all around me, the mark on my shoulder throbbing with a sweet ache.

I dreamed of the lemon tree again. My mother watched from the window, smiling.

This time, I knew I was home.

CHAPTER 22

WRECKER

The new Iron Valor clubhouse rose from the ashy footprint of the old in just days. That's all it took when you had teams of crews from around the state, fueled by Bronc's bottomless bank account. They had worked nonstop around the clock with the kind of determination and drive that only dedicated and skilled wolf packs could muster.

I did my own walk-through the night before the meeting. The windows were mirrored, triple-glazed; the fire doors weighed more than most cars. Bronc went overboard, insisting on vault-style steel for the secure rooms, electromagnetic locks on every corridor. I personally wrote the code for the RFID system, mapped the IR cameras, patched the motion-sensor feeds through three offshore proxies. Above the roofline, silent quadcopters patrolled a preset route, night vision and heat sig trained on the empty prairie. Every few feet, I found a new hiding place for an old pain—brushed my hand along the wall and felt a ghost pulse where the blood could have been. The clubhouse was a fortress, but it wasn't home. Not for me, thankfully.

On move-in day, the place was buzzing with prospects, wives, and kids hauling new furniture and fixtures everywhere. The guys who took up residence all had new bedroom furniture and linens. The women spent time with Juliet, adding dishes to the kitchen and bar area. It was important to her that the place felt like a home and not a bunker. Bronc was fine with it being a bunker. He agreed to compromise and let Juliet have her way.

Bronc called a meeting that morning. Not the usual war council, but the kind where some big players dialed in from their own offices or bunkers to measure their dicks over a Teams call. It was a show. That's how he wanted it. Our guys gathered around the new large conference table with Bronc sitting at the head. Arsenal, Doc, Gunner and Papa all sat quietly to watch the show on the large screens mounted on the walls.

I logged in early, booted the central laptop from the network closet, and locked the door behind me. The connection was solid, audio crisp. The light from the single bulb overhead cut everything into blue and black; the rest of the room faded into the kind of gray that looked like water on asphalt after a rain.

At 0900 sharp, the icons started popping in.

Bronc's video feed was first: clean desk, the old Army flag in the background, beard trimmed down to regulation, eyes flat and pale as glacier melt. The man never looked more dangerous than when he was being polite.

Next was Rafe Mayfield, King of the South. The frame caught him from the chest up, all six-foot-four of him crammed into what looked like a lawyer's home office. He wore a white shirt, the top button open, a crimson and white Alabama tie tossed on the back of the chair. His beard was perfect; his eyes dark enough to look fake on camera. He sipped coffee from a mug that said, "Roll Tide, Y'all." Didn't blink. Didn't smile. Just waited.

Third up: Kazimir Kozlov, vampire king of the East. The screen struggled to color-correct his skin, which was so pale it made printer paper look tan. His hair was black, slicked into a widow's peak. He wore a silk bathrobe over a t-shirt that read, "Fangs Out For Freedom." The background was all glass and nighttime skyline—Philly. There was a woman at his elbow: Lucia, his daughter, her black curls tied up, face a painting of boredom and mischief. She waved at the camera. Her nails were red, the kind that drew blood just by looking.

Last: Menace. Midwest Wolf King, and still our bastard at heart. He showed up from the seat on his big front porch. He wore mirrored aviators and a leather jacket with an Iron Valor patch, his white-blonde hair cropped and styled, with an attitude you only get by living through a thousand bar fights and coming out the other side. He was muted, but his smirk did all the talking.

Bronc gave the intro. "Thank you for coming, gentlemen. And lady," he added, nodding at Lucia.

Rafe gave a two-finger salute, the Southern version of "let's get this over with." Kazimir smirked, canines out for the party, just visible. Menace raised a thumb, then dropped it.

Bronc ran through the formalities. "Two weeks ago, Greenbriar Pack attempted a major hit on Iron Valor. They failed, but not before blowing the clubhouse sky high and nearly killing one of our own. Intel suggests they are not acting alone. Now, their entire pack is MIA. They moved lock, stock, and barrel. Don't know if they're even in Texas. We tracked them in four different directions. This is now an interstate problem, and unless handled, *will* escalate to the Council."

He let that hang.

Rafe spoke first, slow and precise. "Greenbriar is unfortunately a Southern pack. If they have relocated; the Alpha moved without prior notification. This is, of course, against the Council charter rules and would need to be addressed."

Menace: "Midwest is clear. Any movement, I'd know. I got scouts who patrol the entire territory. Nothing's come up yet."

Kazimir ran a tongue over his teeth, eyes on Bronc. "My territory runs twenty-four-hour surveillance on stray shifter activity. As you know, we're careful of what wolves we let mix in vampire clubs. If Greenbriar comes here, I will notice. But I doubt they are that smart." Lucia snorted into her phone. The sound came through as static.

Bronc glanced at me. "Wrecker, you want to run down what we know?"

I did. I leaned into the camera, letting the light hit the scar on my chin just right. Then I proceeded to give them the entire run down on Greenbriar's activities for the past several months, from the theft of funds from the motorcycle shop, escalating to trying to drain bank funds, to the attempted hacking of our networks. I paused for a moment to be sure everyone was keeping up.

"Things escalated when Bronc's sister Maddie went missing. We took a team to Greenbriar to find her. We were only 30 miles out when my mate who was watching and listening to surveillance feeds heard they planned to blow the clubhouse, thinking it would be crowded with pack members prepping our annual toy run. Thankfully, we'd moved that operation offsite. The guys that had nabbed Bronc's sister returned her to the compound, hoping she'd make entry in time to be killed along with everyone else." You could see the anger rising on their faces.

"Parker ran to the compound, thinking Maddie was inside. My little mate has a hero complex, apparently. I was on the line with her when the bomb went off. She was the only one inside at the time."

Kazimir shook his head. "They intended to kill entire pack?"

I didn't flinch. "All that they could."

Rafe spoke up next. "Your mate. She's okay?"

I nodded. "Yes. Once we dug her out of the rubble and got her to the hospital. It was only through what I suspect was divine intervention that she's still alive." I glanced at Menace.

His voice was a steel rasp. "You want me to send a team? I'll drive a tank through their front yard."

Bronc shook his head. "We want to contain. Council gets wind, we're all in the soup. Rafe, so nothing from the Alabama connection?"

Rafe shrugged, a slow roll of muscle under his shirt. "Nothing reported so far. I'll have my men sweep again tonight. They're good. If Greenbriar so much as farts in a Waffle House, I'll know by dawn."

Kazimir cut in, "Why not just let them run? Wolves never last more than a season without territory. They'll die off, no?"

Bronc said, "That's not how this works, Kazimir. They have resources. Apparently they've been running fight clubs, casinos, strip clubs, all over west Texas, all underground. Silas has a mountain of his own cash. He's also playing with what he thinks is my money. He hasn't realized yet it's all fake. No better than Monopoly money. If he's leveraging with that to buy favor with anyone dangerous, that could get him killed. But I'm not comfortable with waiting for his own stupid ass mistakes. I owe him. He's taken it one step too far."

Kazimir laughed, dark and low. "I like the optimism. But if they come at me, I will simply eat them." Lucia put her hand over the mic, but not fast enough.

"He will, too," she said. "With ketchup."

I ran my tongue along my teeth. "We have a couple of other concerns. Parker had seen a couple of raggedy vampires at the Greenbriar compound. Don't know if they were possibly rogue or if that's even possible. Kazimir, that's your territory. And she also flagged something weird in the transfer logs. Most of the money siphoned didn't stay with Silas—just bounced from Greenbriar through a shell, then vanished. The signature looks like a demon mark."

Rafe leaned forward. "Maltraz?"

"Could be. You know him better than we do."

Rafe's eyes went cold. "If he's in play, this is a three-alarm fire. You're sure about the trace?"

I nodded. "I wrote the tracer myself. It's as good as it gets."

He muttered, "I hate that fucking demon. You want to talk about someone who stinks up a Waffle House..."

Bronc cut in. "So, gentlemen, what's the play? We need to get ahead of this. Wrecker will run digital, but we need boots on the ground. Gut tells me it's New Mexico. And we don't have a relationship with Slade Steward. That's a king we've never had reason to deal with. Rafe? You got any feelings one way or another?"

Rafe's eyes flicked left, then right. "He plays things fairly straight. I know he wasn't at the trial, Menace, when you and Savannah were going through it. He had just lost his mate. He was in no shape. Since he's in Arizona, he's not far. I'll make contact later today and get back to you."

Kazimir sipped something from a crystal glass. "I will alert my lieutenants. If they've heard of rogue vampire movement or weird wolf movement, they will shoot first and not bother to ask."

Bronc tried to slow Kazimir down. "Kazimir, if your people could get information out of them first, I'd really appreciate it." He was walking a fine line. But Kazimir loved Juliet, so he'd capitulate to Bronc's wishes.

A simple nod was the vamp's reply.

Menace added, "I've got a new enforcer. He's meaner than I am. I'll send him."

Bronc nodded. "Thank you. We'll run silent for a few days, then meet again."

They signed off, one by one. Kazimir last, his eyes lingering on my face. "Take care of your mate, Wrecker," he said, voice soft. "The world is cruel to women who cross lines." Lucia made a gun with her fingers and winked. Then, the screen went black.

I sat in the blue afterglow of the empty call, the weight of the war settling in around my neck like a collar. Parker was upstairs with Rocket and the other women unpacking things. The pack house felt less like a place for families and more like a tomb, but they'd have it warmed up in no time.

I hung around after the kings logged off, waiting to see if anyone would circle back. I didn't have to wait long.

Kazimir's avatar flickered alive again. His face filled the screen, pixels warping his smile into a jackal's. Lucia had moved on—she was probably chewing up a late-night dance floor or a neck—but he was all presence, no distractions.

He leaned in, voice low. "Is it true what they say? That the mighty Wrecker is now tamed by a tiny woman?"

I rolled my eyes, but he was relentless. "I confess, I did not expect this. But I hear she is very smart. A hacker, yes? A pretty bird who pecks holes in your firewall." He bared his teeth, the joke sharper than it needed to be.

"She's not just smart. She's dangerous," I said. "Ask Silas. Oh, wait—you can't, because he's gone off the grid with his tail between his legs."

Kazimir's laugh was soft. Then he sobered. "We had a... minor incident. One of my men found device at club in Dallas. It was old tech, meant to explode if tampered. Vampire friendly, so not made to harm us. Had a Greenbriar scent and something more. Perhaps demon. We thought it amateur hour. Now I think maybe not so simple."

His eyes never left mine. "Why would they be so careless to leave it at my club? To send message?"

"Fuck," my mind was running scenarios. "They know you're friendly with Iron Valor. Could be they wanted to imply they can be anywhere they want to be. Destroy anything they want to destroy. They knew you'd give us the details. Silas thinks he's untouchable and if Maltraz is ballsy enough to be working with a low-level Alpha..."

Kazimir's eyes lost their glint. "Maltraz is idiot. He plays in shadows. He keeps... how do you say it? Plausible deniability. His minions will take fall for any deal he has with Silas. If your mate is a part of it, they could still come for her. You tell her, if she needs safe house, she comes to me. I have many. No one gets in unless I say."

I could see the honesty reflected in his red orbs. "Noted," I said. "But she's a wolf. She'll never run."

He nodded, like that was the only answer possible. "Be careful, Wrecker. Your enemies now watch you from every shadow. They are powerful." Then he cut the feed.

I watched the cursor blink for a minute, as if it might give up a secret if I stared long enough.

The next ping was Menace. No video, just a call.

"Still breathing?" he asked. The voice was softer, and in it I could hear the ghost of the kid I knew here in Dairyville when Bronc's father first brought me to my adoptive family. Before we lost all of our innocence. Before war made us all ugly.

"Barely," I said. "You?"

He snorted. "Never better. Listen, about Maltraz. He's not just a wild card. He'll play both sides against the middle, and he always leaves a backdoor. If you find him, go for the headshot. Don't talk. Don't hesitate."

"I think he and Silas have some kind of partnership. I just talked to Kazimir. He thinks the same. But he said what you just did. He'll have his minions take the fall. He'll keep his plausible deniability. I cannot wrap my head around why these big players are aligning themselves with such a small fish."

Menace sighed. "They hate Iron Valor, man. Everything we stand for. We've fucked up their shit on too many occasions, and their lives would simply be easier if we were eliminated. The human world would be way too dangerous without supernaturals like us and the others like us standing in the gap."

"No fucking kidding. I just wish it didn't always seem to start and end with us."

Menace made a sound like a growl. "Ain't that the truth? Bronc has had to deal with more than his share of the shit."

"I'm here to try to lighten that load as much as he allows, which ain't much." I said with a strained laugh.

"Dude, I sat where you are for years. Good luck with all that."

I almost thanked him, but that wasn't our way. Instead, I said, "If you hear anything, call me direct. Don't trust the relay."

"Of course not. And Wrecker—if anyone threatens Parker again, I'll come myself. Not as a king, but as her pack."

He ended the call before I could say anything. It felt good. It felt like old times, when your brothers would murder half the world just to keep you from bleeding.

I stared at the dark screen, the afterimage of the kings' faces burned into my brain. I wondered how many of them had killed for love, or if it was all just another game. For a second, I hated them for being so calm about it.

I sat there, thinking about the drones humming over the roof and listening to the ticking of the clock in the hall. The new clubhouse felt like a submarine—hermetically sealed, pressurized against the outside world. But I liked it. You couldn't be betrayed if you never let your guard down.

I heard footsteps behind me. They were Parker's, soft and light. She wore one of my old flannels, the hem nearly to the knees of her leggings, hair wild, like her. Rocket followed at her heels, head on a swivel. The sight of her in my shirt did things to me that had nothing to do with lust and everything to do with need. The bruises on her face had mostly faded to nothing.

She eased up behind my chair, set a hand on my shoulder. "How'd they take it?"

"They want their pound of flesh," I said, leaning back so her fingers dug in. "Kazimir offers safe houses. Rafe offers southern muscle. Menace sends his best. It's a united front."

She smirked. "So, status quo."

"Yep." I set a hand on her knee. "Except now you're in the middle of it, too."

She didn't flinch. "Good. I'd rather be in the middle than in the crosshairs."

I wanted to tell her she was still there. But I didn't. Instead, I pulled her onto my lap, made her straddle me in the leather office chair. She smelled like jasmine and coffee, and her laugh was a knife, sharp and bright.

"You think it's really Maltraz?" she asked, nose brushing my ear.

"If it isn't, it's someone just as bad."

She drummed her fingers on my chest. "Let's burn them down, then. Before they get to us."

Her eyes were clear. No fear. No regret. I loved her for that, more than anything.

We sat that way for a while, her heartbeat steady against mine, and I let the world outside go silent.

It wouldn't last. It never did.

On cue, I heard Bronc coming down the hall.

"Whatever y'all are doing in there, stop it. We still got plans to make." His voice was gruff, but there was a note of humor.

I quickly put my laughing mouth on Parker's, stopping her mocking repeat of his words before he could hear them. I stood and pulled her legs around my waist, my hands under her ass anchoring her to me. My mouth was still attached to hers in a searing kiss. God, I could live with my tongue in her mouth. Everything about her was addicting, and I was hooked.

CHAPTER 23

SILAS DRAKE

The new strip club in Clovis was still wet around the edges, a scabbed wound on an otherwise featureless strip of highway. I'd kept the original neon—tacky, pink as bruised gums, spelling out "Eden's" with the E burned out so it always read as "Den's" after midnight—but the rest was gutted and rebuilt, all dark glass and steel. Inside, the air reeked of broken dreams and bad decisions. It fought a losing war against the ghost of cheap perfume, tequila sweat, and fresh blood from where the new doormen got a little eager.

I was juggling several things at once, so the main room had doubled as my war room and office for a while. Stage lights shone a cycled mix of purple and red lighting over the silver pole on the center of the platform. The concrete floor had a high-gloss epoxy finish, which would make the spills and fluids that would soon cover it easier to clean. The tables and booths were an eclectic mix of this and that, but it worked with the rest of the aesthetic. I wasn't going for high-end, necessarily, just nice enough to keep the clientele coming back for more. The girls were what sold a joint like this, and I intended to pack the place with the roundest, sexiest, and most willing I could wrangle.

I watched the stage from a high-backed chair, something meant for a degenerate CEO or a Bond villain, and ran my finger along the cold rim of a whiskey glass. First round of auditions and already the place felt like mine. The promise of money and notoriety had drawn the usual horde: girls with dead eyes and worse stories, predators looking to be put on salary. I'd told Rook to bring only the ones who could handle real work. I had plans for this particular business. None of them involved a nice night out.

Vex stood to my left, clipboard in hand, her bleach-blonde hair tied off in a scalpel-sharp bun. She wore leather pants and nothing above the waist but a men's undershirt, rolled so tight around her chest it could have doubled as a tourniquet. The way she ticked off each girl's "stats" was both clinical and faintly gleeful, like she'd finally landed a job that let her be herself. I'd have to keep an eye on her, but for now, she was useful.

First up: a bottle-blonde in stripper heels so tall they made her knees wobble. She stepped onto the stage and tried to make eye contact, which was mistake number one. Her name was Cherry, or Cheyenne, or some other C-word; it didn't matter.

"Walk to the pole and back," I said. She did, but even from here I could see the tremor in her calves, the way her knees threatened to pop inward with each step. I looked at Vex. "Two months clean, tops."

Vex snorted, jotting it down. "Could do private rooms, if you want high turnover. She won't last a week."

The girl reached the end of the runway and looked down at us, waiting for her instructions. I held up a finger, savoring the pause. "Take off your top," I said. "Slowly."

She obeyed, but her eyes never left the exits. The breasts were work; the rest was luck and genetics. There was a patch of bruising on her left hip, the kind you get from either a lover or a fall. I preferred not to guess. She tossed the top aside, revealing a tattoo of a pistol over her ribs. I liked the art, hated the skin. I beckoned her down off the stage.

She shuffled over, past the pit, to where we sat. I waited until she was within reach before speaking.

"You're new," I said. "Probably hoping this is just another club, and the worst thing that happens is some asshole grabs your tit." I drained the whiskey. "But this isn't Bumfuck. And I am not some asshole."

She made a noise, not quite a question.

I gestured for her to turn around. She did slowly, revealing the knife-edge of her back. I reached up and gripped her by the wrist, pulling her closer.

"If you want to work here, you will do everything I tell you," I said. "There's a room in the back for customers who want more than a dance. You will not say no. You will not cry. You will not threaten to call the police." I squeezed her wrist harder. "If I catch you skimming, if I catch you lying to me, I will break your fingers one at a time. Do you understand?"

She nodded, just once, but it was enough. I let her go. She stumbled back, mascara threatening to run.

"Now," I said, "pull down your panties. Let's see if you've got anything worth selling."

She hesitated. Vex's pen tapped the paper, then stopped.

"Do it," I said, voice low.

She obeyed, tugging the flimsy string of black cotton down her thighs. The skin underneath was pale, marred by a strip of scarring high on the inside, maybe from a childhood surgery or something less accidental. I stared for a moment, then gestured for her to put them back up.

"Not bad," I said, though I didn't mean it. "Go wait by the bar. If you need to call your sponsor, now's the time."

She pulled her clothes back on with shaking hands and hurried off, eyes locked on the floor.

Vex looked at me, a question in her expression.

"Too soft," I said. "We'll keep her for numbers, but she's not the type I want."

The next girl came in before I finished the thought. Taller, brown hair, straight and sharp. Eyes so dark I couldn't place the color in the light. She wore a cheap dress, but it fit her body like she'd been sewn into it. She walked to the center of the stage and stopped, waiting.

"Name?" I asked.

"Alexis," she said, voice level.

I gestured her down. She took the stairs two at a time, confidence in her stride. This was better. Vex grinned, showing too many teeth.

I looked her over, arms crossed. "What did you do before this?"

"Waitressed. Drove for Lyft. Nothing steady."

I nodded. "Drugs?"

"No."

"Busted for anything?"

She smiled, a flash of wolf, even if she wasn't one. "Not that stuck."

I liked her. I told her to sit on my lap.

She didn't flinch, didn't hesitate. She straddled my knee, her scent—generic store perfume and something rawer—hitting my nose like a slap. I slid a hand up her thigh, watched for a shiver or a twitch. None. Good.

"Turn around," I said, and she did, back to my chest. I bent to her ear and whispered: "If I told you to take three men in the back, you'd do it?"

She didn't move. "If you paid me enough."

"Money's not the only thing," I said. I let my hand rest on her ass, fingers digging in. "I want loyalty. I want silence. I want a girl who won't ask questions about what happens in the VIP rooms."

She nodded, hair brushing my cheek.

"You think you're that girl?"

"I *can* be."

I looked at Vex. "She's better," I said. Vex grunted, made a note.

I let Alexis go and stood up, feeling the rush of adrenaline through my chest. I towered over her, and she didn't shrink.

"Now, take off the dress," I said, gesturing to the back office, where the real interviews happened. She looked at Vex, and then back at me, and in that half-second I saw the calculation, the cold math of survival. She unzipped and let the dress pool at her feet, standing in just a black bra and nothing else.

"Turn," I commanded.

She did, slow and steady, letting me see every angle.

"Good," I said. "Now kneel."

She dropped to her knees on the newly painted concrete.

I circled her, boots echoing in the hollow room. "You will call me sir. You will not question my orders. If a customer asks you for something, you give it. If they want to tie you up, you let them. If you need help, you ask Vex, and she will decide if it's worth my time."

I knelt, bringing myself to her level, and put a hand on the back of her neck.

"Say you understand."

"I understand, sir."

I grinned. The world was full of broken girls, but this one wasn't quite finished. That was the fun part.

I stroked her hair, then grabbed a fistful and pulled her head back. I leaned close and ran my tongue along her jaw, just to watch her skin goosebump.

"Last test," I said, voice soft. "If I fucked you right here, would you come?"

She smiled, not with her mouth but with her eyes. "If you're any good."

Vex cackled behind me. I let go of Alexis's hair and stood.

"Put your dress back on and wait with the others. Don't talk to anyone unless I say so."

She obeyed. I watched the muscle in her calves as she moved. She didn't look back.

I sat back in the chair, ignoring the hard-on pressing against my zipper. Vex wrote a note and tore off the sheet, flicking it into my lap.

Her handwriting was ugly, all block capitals: "THIS ONE WILL DO WHATEVER YOU WANT."

I looked up. "You think she'll last?"

Vex shrugged. "She's got enough wolf in her to survive. But if you want her to do the really sick shit, you'll have to train it in."

"Noted," I said, folding the paper into my pocket.

The rest of the auditions blurred together. Some were barely legal, some too old to care. I picked three more, but none with the promise of the brown-haired one.

I watched them go, then signaled the bartender for another double. The glass was in my hand before I finished the nod.

The world was full of tiny possibilities, but there was only one I wanted to cage. When the time was right, I'd bring her here. I'd chain her to the stage and let her watch as I trained the others. She'd learn. They all learned.

The whiskey burned down my throat, hot and mean. I liked the pain.

I closed my eyes and listened to the hum of the lights. The world spun, and I spun with it, anchored by the promise that soon, very soon, I'd have everything I wanted. All I had to do was wait.

But I was never any good at waiting.

The first time you see a demon, you know it, even before your eyes catch up to the rest of your senses. The air gets thicker, like you're inhaling molasses, and every nerve in your body lights up and says "danger." Demons don't walk into a room. They take it, strip it of oxygen, and leave only enough for themselves. I knew as soon as I felt the prickle on my neck that tonight's appointment had arrived.

The auditions were still cycling onstage when Adramal, Maltraz's right hand, stalked into the club's main room. Two others followed, identically tall and broad-shouldered, with the kind of symmetry you only get in a manufacturing plant or a particularly sick joke of genetics. All wore black suits, matte as coal, tailored to show off the impossible shapes underneath.

Adramal's skin gleamed like wet obsidian, almost blue in the club's lights. His eyes were black on black, with no separation between the iris and pupil—just a well of void with a dot of faint silver at the center. He scanned the room and found me instantly. His lip curled. I'd met a lot of monsters, but few as hungry as him.

I shot a glance at Vex, who had just finished making Alexis demonstrate how to lick a dollar bill off the floor. Vex recognized the cue, abandoned her experiment, and started toward me. I flicked my hand for Dagger and Rook to join us. Dagger was always nearby, shadowing Vex, his braid swinging like a noose. Rook emerged from the back, silent as always. He took up position behind me, arms folded, face an expressionless slab of flesh.

I stood to greet Adramal as he approached, the three of them moving with the antigravity precision of parade generals or sharks. They stopped at my table. The two silent ones flanked him. All three exuded a reek of ozone and sulfur, like a thunderstorm about to break.

Adramal fixed me with his abyssal stare. "You have business for us."

I gestured to the table, which Vex had cleared in anticipation. "Let's sit. The details require focus."

He didn't move, not at first. "We required focus the last time, and your plan fizzled like a spent cigarette."

He meant the bomb. I felt my jaw clench but forced a smile. "Unforeseen circumstances, not incompetence. We have a replacement plan."

Vex and Dagger slid in beside me. Adramal and his bodyguards stood, looming over us.

I gave them the best smile I could muster. "The new plan is three-pronged. Precision, speed, and deniability."

Adramal's mouth moved, almost a smile. "Maltraz has gotten word. Explain it to me."

Vex looked a bit uncomfortable hearing that Maltraz was privy to our plans as she unrolled a cheap paper blueprint, creased and smudged. "We traced the water supply lines for Iron Valor's compound. There are two access tunnels miles from the main gate, guarded by nothing but a dead coyote and rusty locks." She jabbed at a point on the printout. "We are in the process of procuring a deadly toxin that we plan on introducing into their water system. It starts to work upon ingestion."

I cut in. "It's shifter-specific. Engineered to target our breed and nothing else. If anyone outside the compound gets a taste, they just puke and move on. In phase one, we'll introduce it to the outlying water lines. It'll spread through that part of their population in just hours. Upon ingesting even a small amount, it will begin to make them weak. Start breaking down their bodies until they can't get out of bed. Eventually, it shuts down all of their vital organs." I looked Adramal in the face.

Adramal's head dipped, a barely perceptible nod. "Go on."

Dagger, always eager to brag, picked up the thread. "Then, in 24 hours, we'll infect the second line. They'll have no idea how it's spreading since it won't hit everyone at once. By then, people will be on the verge of death. Their Alpha will be showing signs of the illness, and they'll know the end is near for all of them. He'll be helpless to stop it."

Adramal's gaze bored into me, stripping the lies from the truth. "And what of the girl?" he said. "Maltraz says she is the only one that matters to you."

Vex looked down, but not before I caught the spark in her eye. She thought I was weak for Parker. I wasn't weak for her. I just knew a valuable tool when I saw one. The fact that I wanted to sink my cock inside her tight pussy was just a bonus. Maybe it was the fact that she belonged to Iron Valor that made me want to ruin her.

I put my hands flat on the table. "The girl is mine. I'll take her personally. There won't be anyone who'll be able to stop me."

Dagger said, "You really want her that bad? She'll get sick along with the others, anyway." There was acid in his voice. "You have your pick of the club, boss. Why her?"

I looked at him, at the table, at the reflection of the demon's smile in the polished black. "Because taking what used to belong to Iron Valor and making it mine gives me a special satisfaction. Plus, I'll have the antidote. She won't stay sick."

The table went quiet. For a second, all you could hear was the DJ testing the sound system in the empty main room, a pulse of synth and a dying echo.

Adramal spoke, his words slow and gravelly. "We have a vested interest in chaos. But the girl is not to die, not until Maltraz says." He fixed his stare on me. "If you fail again, you answer to him. Directly."

I felt the sweat bead under my collar. "I won't fail."

He nodded, once, then glanced at his companions. "Show them."

The two silent demons lifted small briefcases onto the table. They opened them in perfect sync. Inside: a dozen glass vials, each filled with a clear liquid. Labels in a spiky, runic script.

Adramal: "Maltraz was feeling generous. He decided to give you the most potent toxin for your use. The toxin and antidote. Derived from wild shifter blood."

Vex leaned in, eyes wide. "Is it safe to touch?"

The demon's hand shot out, fast as a bullet, and gripped her wrist. "Not for you." He released her, and Vex cradled her hand, a red mark already forming on her skin.

I watched, savoring the moment. She'd been riding high, but now she was reminded of her place.

Adramal rattled off instructions, precise and unfeeling. "Pour into water main. Walk away. It is undetectable."

The meeting wrapped in five minutes. The demons left, sucking the heat from the room as they went.

The four of us sat in silence. Rook had said nothing the entire time, but I could feel his anger simmering. He didn't like being shown up in front of outsiders, especially not the demon kind.

Vex broke the quiet. "They didn't even blink. You sure this isn't going to come back on us?"

I looked at the vials. "We're just the trigger. They're the bomb. When it goes off, we'll be gone."

I watched them leave. Vex and Dagger, side by side, whispering like wolves at the edge of the pack. Rook hung back, his shadow blotting out the doorway.

He waited until the others were gone, then turned to me. "You keep this up, you're going to get us all killed," he said, voice low.

Back on the club floor, Alexis caught my eye from across the room. She raised her glass, a dare. I liked her more every minute.

But when I looked at her, all I saw was Parker—her hair, her eyes, her neck bared just enough to show where I'd bite her when I finally got my hands on her.

I leaned against the bar, the glass vial burning cold against my ribs, and pictured her chained to my bed. The way she'd fight. The way she'd break. The way she'd beg for mercy, and I'd give her exactly none. Exactly what I'd do to the entire Iron Valor pack. After four long years, victory was at my fingertips.

CHAPTER 24

PARKER

We met in the new war room, a bunker rebuilt in the image of the old: no windows, large wood table, every surface scrubbed of comfort. The fluorescent lights hummed in concert with the buzz in my ears, the sickness a fever sweat inside my skull. Bronc sat at the head of the table, posture rigid enough to splinter, his eyes shining with that blue-cast clarity only terminal patients or drowning men possess. Doc was to his left, a coffee mug braced between both hands as if the ceramic alone could warm him. I sat next to Wrecker, who slumped in his chair as though the years of military discipline had all unspooled at once.

We'd all known it was bad, this plague. At first, it was just a headache, the kind you could blame on hangovers or the west Texas wind. Then the muscle aches, a dull lead that settled in your thighs and calves, made walking to the bathroom a project worthy of debate. Now, it was everything. My ribs throbbed where they had been healed. My skin burned, nerves confused by a dozen signals at once. When I reached out for Wrecker, I could feel his heat from a foot away; his wolf ran feverish and broken, a trapped animal pounding at the cage.

The rest of the pack was the same, or worse. Maddie had missed the meeting. Pearl was home, quarantined and delirious, calling Bronc every hour to update him on her latest symptoms, as if there were a scorecard. Even Gunner—usually indestructible—was curled in the far end of the room, hood up and sunglasses on, breathing through his mouth so he didn't puke.

The screens at the far end flickered, and then the kings came online. Their faces swam in the toxic blue light. Rafe was on high alert, knowing things were bad. Menace was ready to come through the screen. He couldn't get here fast enough. Kazimir was worried about us. Everyone was baffled.

"Let's get this over with," Bronc rasped. His voice had gone gravelly and thin.

The camera panned down. I saw a listless row of lieutenants, all of them hunched, all of them gray.

Rafe led off. "What can we do? What is happening specifically? Doc, tell me you have something."

Doc pinched the bridge of his nose. "We sequenced the bug. It's not natural, not engineered either, not by human hands. There's something in it...almost adaptive. We pump one antiviral, it morphs. Throw antibiotics, it eats them. Wolf healing is nonexistent. I've never seen anything like it."

Kazimir purred, "You're saying this is demonic."

Doc didn't answer, but his eyes said, *Isn't everything lately?*

Menace leaned in. "How are you feeling, Parker?"

"She's sick too," Bronc said, with a flick of his hand. "We all are."

"Parker, can you hear us?" Menace's tone was gentler than I'd expected. "Anything you've found?"

I tried to focus, but my thoughts drifted like leaves in a gutter. "The traces are all dead ends. Whoever did this, if they're talking about it, used commercial VPNs, wiped the logs before we even noticed the breach. Best guess, the attack came in on a water shipment, but it seems like a stretch."

Kazimir bared his teeth, bored already. "What is Maltraz's end game?"

No one answered. We all knew what they wanted. The same thing everyone wanted.

"Power," Rafe said. "If Iron Valor goes down, it leaves the southern territories weaker. Council will get involved."

Bronc tried to steer it back. "We still have a job. We hold the territory. We protect the families. If we go down, we go down fighting. But we need help. We're all about to wind up bedridden. We can't fight like that. They'll sweep in and kill us all."

I looked at Wrecker, searching for any hint of the monster I'd loved.

Menace spoke, "We're packing the jet right now. I'll have a team there in two hours."

Rafe chimed in. "We'll be there in two and a half, fully armed and ready to make a stand against whoever did this. My guess is they're waiting for everyone to simply die. Then they'll come in and dispose of the bodies. No shots fired. They're too chickenshit to fight."

Doc said, "We have three days, maybe four, before this tears through the rest of us."

Menace said, "Need to find an antidote."

Kazimir nodded. "We'll start looking."

The room emptied fast. Nobody wanted to linger. Every second wasted was a chance for us to drop where we stood. Gunner left first, then Arsenal, then Doc, clutching his bag like a rosary. Bronc lingered, staring at the blacked-out screens, the old man in his eyes visible now.

I tried to stand, but my knees buckled. Wrecker caught me, or maybe I caught him. We staggered to the door, our bodies welded together by fever and muscle memory. In the hallway, I smelled vomit. Someone had lost the battle with their stomach and just left it for the janitor.

Outside, the air was cold and sharp, a knife after the stagnant war room. Wrecker led me to the truck, but he could barely work the keys. I took them from him, gentle, and started the engine.

"Are you okay to drive?" I asked. The question was pointless.

He grinned, a ghost of his old self. "You crash, I heal."

I didn't want to say that he might not.

The drive back to our house was silent. Didn't bother with the radio. My skin prickled with every pothole, my head a riot of pain and memory. Wrecker leaned his head against the window, eyes closed, breathing shallow.

I reached over, squeezed his knee. "I'm not losing you," I said, and the words tasted like a lie.

He didn't open his eyes, but he smiled, just for me.

We made it home somehow. Rocket met us at the door, tail between his legs, whimpering in sympathy or terror. I tried to get Wrecker to bed, but he collapsed on the couch, shivering. I pulled a blanket over him, crawled in beside him, and listened to his heart stutter against my back.

When I finally drifted, I dreamed of the lemon tree, the branches heavy with fruit. My mother's voice in the breeze: Just listen.

When I woke, Wrecker was burning up, breath coming in shallow little sips.

I'd never felt so small, or so alone.

The world resolved into fevered fragments: the sweat-stuck sheets, the red digits of the bedside clock, the rasp of Wrecker's breath at my shoulder. Time lost all meaning. Sometimes it was morning; sometimes it was three AM, the only proof being the cold draft off the window and the blue light puddled on the floor. At some point, I stopped trying to track the hours and just counted his heartbeats instead.

His fever never broke. The skin of his forehead was so hot it felt like metal in the sun. I made a game of checking his temperature every hour, though the thermometer always glared back with the same digital outrage: 105.1, then 105.4, then just HI. I wiped him down with towels, rotated Tylenol and ibuprofen like I was running a pharmacy for the dead. Every so often, he'd groan awake, eyes unfocused, and beg for water. His voice came out wrong, not even his. I brought him water, spooned it into his mouth when he couldn't lift his own head. Sometimes he'd seize up, thrashing so hard I worried he'd break the bedframe.

Rocket whimpered at the foot of the bed, licking his own paws raw. Even the damn dog was sick.

The mate bond flickered in and out. Usually it was a hot wire under my ribs, but now it was a radio tuned to a dead station—static and silence, sometimes a pulse of feeling so faint I thought I'd imagined it.

Once, I dreamed I was drowning. I woke to find Wrecker on top of me, shivering, his arms wrapped so tight around my ribs I couldn't breathe. His lips were blue, his face sunken. I pried his hands off and rolled him back, but he just reached for me again, like a child afraid of the dark. I lay down next to him, let him hold me, and closed my eyes. There wasn't enough of me left to keep us both afloat.

The next time I surfaced, the room was strange. The window was open, a sheet flapped in the air. The clock read 2:17 AM, but the house was lit up like a convenience store. I heard a sound from the kitchen—footsteps, heavy and deliberate.

I tried to get up, but my legs wouldn't listen. I rolled onto the floor, crawling, using the dresser for leverage. Every inch sent a bolt of pain through my temples. I got to my feet, nearly blacked out, and staggered to the bedroom door.

Another sound. A voice—male, guttural, not Wrecker's. Words in the hallway, then the hollow ring of boots on tile.

Maybe Menace's team had gotten here. Finally. I relaxed and let sleep take me.

I woke to cold metal biting at my wrists. I tried to sit up, but the chains snapped taut, pinning me to the headboard. My first thought was that I'd been left for dead. Second thought: this wasn't my bed, not Wrecker's, not even Bronc's, but something older. Gray walls, rough and unfinished. Heavy curtains hung over the window, which were closed but leaked light at the edges. The only furniture was a nightstand, a large dresser, and a wing-backed chair.

He was there in the chair, waiting for me. Silas Drake.

He looked completely satisfied with himself. Facial scars less noticeable. His beard was neatly trimmed, bald head freshly shaved. His clothes were black, sharp, expensive. He was not smiling, but there was a hunger in his eyes that was worse than a smile.

He leaned in, elbows on knees. "Hello, my little hacker. Welcome back to the land of the living. I was afraid I'd lost you."

I growled at him and showed my teeth.

He laughed, genuinely amused. "Still got your spirit. Good. You'll need it."

My head throbbed. The fever was gone, but in its place was a deep, icy ache in my bones. I tried to reach for the mate bond, but it was absent, not even a flicker. My heart stuttered, then flatlined into panic.

"What did you do to him?" I rasped.

"To who?" He cocked his head, mocking innocence. "Oh, you mean Wrecker. Or Bronc, or Maddie, or Doc, or anyone else who tried to stand up to me." He grinned. "Nothing personal, Parker. Just business. Anyway, I did nothing. No need. Just let nature take its course."

I scanned the room for a weapon, a key, anything. The chains were thick, bolted to the bed frame. I flexed against them, testing the give. None.

"Why am I alive?" I asked. "Why not just kill me?"

He stood, stretched, paced to the window. Sunlight struck his face, making the scar on his cheek burn white. "Because you're useful. And because I like you. Always have." He walked over and ran a finger down my jaw. I jerked away, but he just laughed.

"You always were a fighter," he said. "I've seen it since I started watching you."

I swallowed my fear. "What do you want?"

He smiled. "What I've always wanted. Power. Control. Revenge." He ticked them off on his fingers. "But most of all, I want to see Iron Valor burned to the ground. You'll help me do it."

"Go to hell," I said.

He leaned in, close enough for me to smell the coffee on his breath. "I've already been. Came back with a souvenir." He fished something out of his pocket and tossed it onto the bed. A vial, stoppered with red wax. Inside, a swirling black fluid, oily and alive.

"The demon's mark," he said, as if reading my mind. "It's beautiful, isn't it? Engineered for wolves, but it doesn't discriminate. Hits everyone the same. Except you."

I looked at him, icy rage rising. "Why me?"

"Because you're clever, and because I want you to watch what you did to your precious pack. I want you to feel it." He set a hand on my knee, squeezed until my bones creaked. "You're immune now. Congratulations."

I thought of Wrecker, burning up in that bed, alone.

I said, "You're lying. If you'd killed him, you'd brag about it."

He grinned, wolfish. "Not dead yet. But by the time anyone gets there to help, they will be. That's how you set a trap, Parker. You starve the animal, and when it's weak, you take its head."

I twisted away, bile in my throat.

He dropped the vial on the dresser, then pulled a small suitcase from under the chair. "You're going to be a good girl now, Parker. You're going to sit here and heal. When I come back, we'll see if you're ready to help." He set the suitcase on the dresser, popped it open so I could see row after row of vials, the antidote for my dying pack.

He closed the case, locked it with a code, and smiled. "Don't bother screaming. No one will hear you."

I said, "Where are we?"

He stopped at the door. "Clovis. New Mexico. Outskirts. Nearest neighbor is three miles. Try not to get frostbite if you make it that far."

He left. I listened to the click of his boots on the stone, then the heavy slam of the iron-banded door. Silence.

I pulled at the chains, hard. The metal bit into my skin, drawing blood. I didn't care. I yanked again, felt the headboard shift, then stop.

I knew the angel Archon Seraphael was real. I heard he had walked right out of the stands and healed Menace on the spot after he had been stabbed and died. I knew that someone—I'm guessing the same angel—had touched me behind my right ear in that hospital. And I knew that I'd seen my mother when I had died. She had told me to listen. So that's what I did.

I closed my eyes and listened. There was nothing at first, then a faint hum—electric, starting at the spot behind my ear where I believed the angel had touched me. It felt alive, running down my neck, through my chest and into my arms.

I whispered, "If you're real, if any of this is real, help me. I need to save them. Please."

The hum grew louder, a vibration under my ribs. I didn't know if it was a prayer, or just madness. Either way, it was all I had.

I opened my eyes and stared at the suitcase on the dresser, the cure for my dying world.

I swore to myself, and to whatever angel or demon might be listening, that I would find a way.

Even if it killed me.

My hands started to glow a faint blue, the color of arctic ice, the color of midnight with a moon.

The cuffs around my wrists grew hot, then molten. I hissed, not from pain, but from the power of it. The sound shook the walls, vibrated the dresser, made the suitcase tremble. The chains fell from my wrist just as I heard footsteps in the hallway. I jumped up and ran to the other side of the heavy door. I hope to hit him with it, maybe surprise him enough to make him fall.

The door crashed open. Silas filled the frame, a pistol in his hand. I slammed the door towards him, hitting him squarely in the back. The sheer weight of it caused a jolt that sent the gun sailing from his hand. It all seemed to happen in slow motion. The gun slid under the bed, and I made a sliding dive for it. There was no way Silas could get his massive frame under that bed. I had the Glock in my hand when that fucker looked under to see if I'd found it. It was like shooting fish in a barrel. I put a bullet right between his ugly eyes.

The two bodyguards at his back ran into the room. I crawled out onto the opposite side of the bed. I had the element of surprise when I stood and shot twice, center mass on both of them.

The suitcase was no longer locked. The code had defaulted to 0000. I grabbed it and made for the hallway. I heard other voices, but I still felt the power of the angel mark guiding me. The corridor was long and lined with stone torches set at regular intervals. It looked like a wine cellar or a crypt. I could smell blood and bleach, could hear the soft thud of footsteps from somewhere behind.

I kept low, suitcase pressed to my chest.

I heard men's voices, thin and furious, but they faded as I ducked through the labyrinth of corridors. I took every left, every down stair, until I reached a heavy wooden door set with a rusted bolt.

I listened: silence.

I slid the bolt free and slipped through.

On the other side was a garage. Three cars, a row of motorcycles, a workbench lined with tools. There was a service door at the far end, but it was chained shut. I saw a side window, half open, and sprinted for it.

I dove through the gap, slicing open my arm on the broken glass.

Outside, the sun had barely risen. No sound. Just fields and the cold, brittle air of winter. My bare feet hardly registered the icy ground as I ran dressed in whatever nightgown that bastard had dressed me in.

A car was parked next to a building by the unmanned entry gate, keys dangling in the ignition. I slid into the driver's seat and turned the key.

Then, I drove.

I kept driving until I was far enough from the house to risk stopping.

I looked up at the sky, at the clouds over the plain. I didn't pray this time. I just whispered, "Thank you," to whoever had heard me.

I checked the bag. Twelve vials, all intact. I patted it, then started moving. The house behind me was alive with movement, but no one followed yet.

I set the car's GPS to Dairyville and headed towards home. I could feel Wrecker now, faint but alive, a distant hum in my bones. I focused on that and drove harder.

CHAPTER 25

WRECKER

Darkness.

Not the cool, forgiving dark of sleep, but a red-black suffocation behind the eyes. I thrashed against it for hours, or maybe days. My mind cut the hours into pieces, fed them back to me in random order. Sometimes I wandered the dead hallways of the old compound, every turn ending in a locked door or an empty room. Sometimes I chased a shape through the ruined corridors—my little bird, always just out of reach, her pink and dark brown hair a flash in the smoky air, her scent burned away by bleach and rot. Always, I woke up more tired than before.

I knew she was gone. The bond between us was a slack wire in my chest, a phone line severed by a careless backhoe. For days, her feelings had been sunlight under my ribs. Now nothing. A cold, empty ache, like a mouth with all the teeth knocked out.

Sometimes, when the fever hit the right pitch, I saw her. Not in dreams, but in the flicker between blinks. She'd stand at the edge of the room, arms crossed, eyebrows drawn together in that look that meant I was being an idiot. Sometimes she just watched. Sometimes she mouthed my name. Sometimes, if I let my heart slow enough, I could almost hear her through the static—*Eli, Eli, where are you?* But there was no voice at the other end. Only silence, thick as blood.

I don't know how long I'd lain in the bed. The sheets were knotted around my legs, slick with sweat and maybe worse. My own smell was unbearable. I'd soaked through the mattress; every inch of me stuck to every other. When I finally tried to stand, my knees collapsed. My face hit the floor and stayed there.

I must have blacked out, because the next thing I knew, the world returned with the sound of a door smashing open and the rattle of voices.

I tried to get up. Couldn't. My limbs twitched but refused to organize themselves. I could feel the blood slick on my cheek, tasted iron pooling in my gums. The air was full of body odor and disinfectant. Something about it made me want to cry.

The bootsteps came closer, hard and insistent. They stopped at my head. I saw the edge of a heavy boot. I'd know the pattern anywhere.

"Eli! Wrecker, fuck, get up!" Menace's voice, sharper than a fresh razor. He hauled me up by the back of the neck and propped me against the wall. My skull thudded against the drywall. I blinked at him through swollen eyelids. He looked pretty as always—white blonde hair cropped short, golden skin. The eyes, though the same hazel, no longer held their unflinching coldness. No, they had a look full of fear.

I tried to speak, but all that came out was a hiss.

He looked up with a helpless sigh. "Fuck." Then helped me slide down the wall until I sat there, barely upright.

He yelled over his shoulder. "Savannah! Do you see her any-where?"

Her voice came back from somewhere in the house, frantic. "No! She's not here!"

He slapped my face, not hard, but enough to get my attention. "Where is she?" he barked. "Where's Parker?"

The name tore a hole in my chest. I looked at him, tried to focus, but my vision split him in two. "Gone," I managed, voice a gravel pit. "She's gone."

He didn't flinch. "What the fuck does that mean? Gone? Gone where, Eli? You don't mean…"

"No, not that. Fuck, at least not then." I coughed a shredded cough through tears. "I heard voices. They must have." My lungs locked up. The rest was just air.

He shook me again, harder. "Try. Try harder."

"I can't feel her," I whispered. I let my head drop to my chest. "She's dead, Bridger. She's dead."

He let me fall over. The room spun sideways; the floor was the only thing that made sense.

A softer voice, behind him. Savannah. "Let me see." She pressed a cold hand to my forehead, then my neck, then my chest. The touch sent a shiver through my bones. She murmured something. I couldn't make out what she was saying. "He's burning up. You shouldn't have left him alone!"

Menace growled, "I only just got in. He locked himself in here and tore up anyone who tried to help."

"Did I hurt anyone?" I asked, though I knew the answer. The taste of blood in my mouth wasn't all my own.

She shook her head, curls trembling. "Just yourself."

I laughed again, or tried to. My jaw clicked out of joint. "I can't do this."

The next minutes were a blur. Savannah and Menace dragged me to the bed. My arms didn't work; they flopped behind me like muscles and tendons had forgotten their jobs. Someone had changed my sheets. I saw the others in a pile on the floor stained with sweat and blood and other fluids. It looked like someone had butchered a pig. Maybe they had.

Savannah brought in a clean, damp rag and pressed it to my mouth. The icy sting made my gums bleed more. "It's the fever," she said, to herself or to Menace. "It's eating his brain. We have to cool him off."

Menace carried me to the bathroom where he'd run a tub of cool water. The first splash was a shock, but then it was like sinking into a lake after a long run. My pulse slowed; the red haze in my vision faded to pink, then blue. I could see the lines in the ceiling tile, the way they made constellations if you stared long enough.

They worked in silence. Savannah used a cup to pour cool water over my head. Menace kept my arms pinned. I tried to fight, once or twice, but there was no strength in my body. My bones felt hollowed out.

After a while, Savannah leaned in and whispered, "You need to hold on. She's not dead. I just know it."

I shook my head; the effort dizzying. "You're wrong. She's gone. I lost her."

Menace was watching me, his face unreadable. "She'll come back," he said. "You just have to be here when she does."

"Easy for you," I spat. "Your mate didn't leave you to die."

"Stop being a whiny fuck. Your mate didn't *leave* you. She was taken. Stop pitying yourself and concentrate on your bond. And I *had* a mate who was taken from me if you forgot. And I did die on *her*, remember?" he was pissed. And he was right. My little bird would never leave me. She'd die with me before she'd do that.

The fever pulled me down again, but this time I dreamed of nothing. Only the hum of the lights, and the sound of my own heartbeat, slowing, slowing, slowing.

When I woke, I was back in my bed, alone.

My mouth was dry as a fistful of sand. The taste of blood had faded to the back of my tongue, replaced by the bitter tang of old medicine. I tried to sit up. My muscles responded, barely. The room was empty except for the shadow of the door.

The mate bond was still dead. I probed it gently, but there was nothing. No Parker. No little bird.

I let out a sound somewhere between a growl and a sob. My chest folded in half. I slammed my fist into the mattress. I screamed her name, over and over, until my voice was a shredded cord and my eyes blurred with tears.

Then Menace was there again, holding me down until the storm passed.

"Stop," he said, when I finally ran out of air. "She's not dead, Eli. You'd know. You'd fucking know."

"Don't tell me what I'd know!" I spat. "You don't feel it. She's gone. There's nothing there. It's—" I broke, couldn't finish.

He sat beside me, boots on the bed. "Let it hurt. But don't let it kill you."

I wiped the blood and snot off my face with the heel of my hand. "Why are you here?"

"Because you're my brother," he said, as if it was the most obvious thing in the world.

Savannah came in, carrying a tray with water and what looked like a sandwich. She set it down, then pressed a cold hand to my cheek. "You need to eat," she said. "If you want to heal."

I turned away. I didn't want to heal.

But when the door closed behind them, I forced down a sip of water, then another. It tasted like nothing, like empty glass. I chewed the bread, forcing my jaw to move. It hurt to swallow, but I did it anyway.

I sat on the bed and stared at the ceiling until the sun changed places in the sky. Then I let myself sleep, not because I wanted to, but because I had nothing left to fight it.

In the dark, I whispered her name over and over, like a prayer.

Wren. Little bird. Parker.

Come back to me.

Hours passed, or maybe it was only minutes. I sweated through the bedding, then the sheets, then whatever thin layer of mattress pad Parker had added to our bed. The shivers came in waves, sometimes rolling up from my feet, sometimes crashing down from the base of my skull. Every so often, the pain would ease just long enough for me to hope I was getting better, and then it would come back twice as bad, as if my body hated me for even entertaining the thought.

Sometimes, I imagined I was dying. Sometimes, I hoped I was.

The only sound was the slow drip of water into a tin pail Menace had set beside the bed. At some point, the darkness behind my eyes lit up with odd flashes of blue, so vivid I tried to bite them with my teeth. It didn't work, but the taste of ice lingered in my mouth. Maybe the fever had burned through the last few working neurons in my head.

Then, without warning, the universe punched me straight through the heart. I arched off the bed, spine locked and buzzing, every hair on my arms standing up. My eyes shot open. I tried to scream but couldn't get air. The world collapsed into a pinpoint and then exploded, white and blue, sharp as a fresh wound.

And she was there.

Not in a dream, not in the memory, but real. The mate bond flared up, strong and wild, pouring every flavor of Parker into my veins at once—her scent, her fury, her hunger for me. I started to sob, ugly and loud. Tears ran out of my eyes and down into my ears. It was the most beautiful pain I'd ever felt.

Menace burst into the room, shotgun in one hand, Savannah hot on his heels. I don't know what I looked like, but the way his face changed, I must have been a vision.

"Wrecker!" Menace shouted, crossing to me in two long strides. "What's happening? Are you dying? You look like you're dying."

I gasped, managed to suck in half a lungful of air. "She's alive," I rasped. "She's alive! I can feel her. She's close. Fucking, fuck, I can feel her."

Savannah pressed a hand to my chest, then a cold compress to my temple. "His fever broke," she said, voice shaky. "But he's not out of the woods. His pulse is all over the map. Nobody has recovered yet."

"Wren," I said, the word a desperate laugh. "I have no fucking idea how, but she's coming back to me. My little bird is coming home." I could barely get the words out. I was still barely hanging on to life by a thread.

Menace set down the shotgun and put a hand on my shoulder. He tried to hide it, but his hand was trembling. "Just keep breathing, Eli. Let her come to you."

I tried. I swear I tried, but every time I blinked, the blue light came back, brighter than before. I focused on it, drew it in, made it my only thought. The pain faded, replaced by the sharp, cold joy of knowing she was alive. I tried to scream her name once, twice, just to make sure the universe understood what it had given back to me.

Footsteps hammered down the hallway. A second later, the door banged open, and she was there, in the flesh. Parker. My mate. My everything.

She looked like hell—hair a mess, face streaked with dirt and blood, one arm bandaged to the elbow—but I swear I saw a blue halo around her head. Her eyes locked on mine, and she ran to the bed, crawling up to straddle my lap.

"Never leaving you again," she whispered, crushing her lips to mine. I tasted salt, blood, tears, and something electric that made my tongue go numb.

I buried my face in her neck and sobbed. I couldn't stop. I didn't want to stop.

As soon as she saw Menace, she jumped off the bed and grabbed a suitcase. Fumbling with the latches, she opened it. "It's the cure," she said. "These are vials of the toxin and vials of the antidote. The sigils tell you which is which. You have to get it to Doc—now. It's the only way to save the pack."

Menace took the suitcase from her and looked at the contents. "You sure you can trust this stuff?"

She held her arms out. "Look at me. I'm perfectly fine. He gave me the antidote before I put a bullet between his eyes. Doc needs it first. He'll know the best method of distribution. The toxin was introduced into the water system. Test it to be sure it's all been flushed."

I'd never seen Menace speechless.

"On it," he said as he ran out, yelling for Doc and Bronc, Savannah at his back.

Parker pressed her forehead to mine. "I thought I'd lost you," she said. "I thought I'd never see you again."

I tried to answer, but the words tangled up behind my teeth. Instead, I hugged her tight, breathing in the strange, beautiful scent of lavender and lemons.

She collapsed back onto the bed beside me, clutching my hand. Her fingers were ice cold, but the grip was strong as ever.

"I think the angel came through for me again," she said, voice raw. "There was no way I was getting out of the room Silas had locked me in. I was literally chained to the bed. There were metal cuffs around my wrists I couldn't break."

I reached up, touched the spot behind her right ear. The blue mark was still glowing, faint but steady. I wanted to ask a thousand questions, but only one mattered.

"How did you get out of those cuffs?"

She got a faraway look in her eyes and told me what happened. "I asked for help. And this is gonna sound wackadoodle, but I felt a tingling from my angel mark. It ran down my arms, and those cuffs heated up, and just like that...they just opened."

"Miraculous."

She nodded, then kissed my knuckles. Then told me how she disarmed Silas and killed him and his bodyguards. My mate was a true badass.

She told me how she remembered her mother had told her 'to listen' and she swore she heard a voice guiding her out of the compound after she snatched up that suitcase and fled. She'd located one of their cars that had the keys in it, and here she was.

We held each other for a long time. I could feel the mate bond pulsing between us, stronger than before, a living thing. Every throb of her heart echoed in my chest.

I pulled her close and whispered, "I love you, little bird."

She smiled, just for me. "I know."

And in that moment, nothing else mattered.

The antidote worked, but not like magic. It was slow, ugly, and left a trail sadly not fast enough to save everyone. I wound up in a ward at the hospital. The worst of us were here. She was beside me, exactly where I knew she'd be, slumped in a vinyl chair the color of old blood. Her head hung forward so her chin nearly touched her chest. The ends of her hair were stained with dried tears, sweat, and mucus from her nose. Her hands were clasped together, white-knuckled, one wrapped around the other as if she could will my heartbeat into not stopping.

I tried to move my hand. It responded; a surprise. I reached out, grazed her knuckles. She flinched, then looked up, the whites of her eyes shot with red but sharp, electric, alive.

"You're back," she croaked. Her voice was a box of nails.

"Looks that way." I tried to smile. My lips split again. "What's the verdict?"

She wiped her nose on her sleeve, uncaring. "Doc says you'll live. Most of the pack, too. Some didn't make it."

I nodded. I could feel the emptiness through the pack. "Who?"

She looked away. "Old ones mostly. Sable, Mr. Alonzo, Gunner's grandma." Her face twisted. "It was my fault."

I squeezed her hand as hard as I could, which was less than a handshake but more than a prayer. "Wasn't you, Wren. This was Silas and whatever demon he rode bareback. You saved us. You brought the antidote." I wanted to say more, but the effort tore the air from my lungs. "If you hadn't, we'd have all died. Greenbriar had been planning something for years."

She shook her head. "Stop. Just stop." The words came out sharp, but her grip didn't loosen. "I just feel responsible. Maybe it wouldn't have been so bad if I'd have stayed gone."

It took all my strength to push myself up. The room spun, slow at first, then steadied. "You want to hear my theory?" I coughed. My own voice was strange to me, like listening to yourself on an old tape. "I think you made the shit start mattering. Before you, I didn't give a fuck about much of anything. Now I want to kill everyone responsible for this, and then I want to come back here and figure out how to live. With you." I let that hang between us, ugly and real.

Her face trembled, and I watched the wall come down and the girl I remembered peek through, just for a second. "You always were a terrible liar, Eli Leonard."

"Never lied to you, Wren. Not once." I forced my fingers to curl around hers, and this time, she let herself believe it.

Doc came in every few hours to check vitals, hang new bags, mutter about "goddamn miracles" and "demonic gene-editing." He'd gotten the first shot of the antidote himself, so his hands only shook a little. He said the others were stable. Some needed more time. A few, like Rocket, were being kept in isolation, so their tiny hearts didn't explode from the shock.

On the third day, the room was quiet. Not dead quiet—just the absence of fear. The antidote had done its job. We'd lost six, maybe more. The pack would be okay. They tried to take us down, but we'd come back stronger.

Bronc was up, but weak, his voice gone to hell. He called a meeting, insisted on it. Doc argued, said it was too soon, but

Bronc's face was set and he would not be moved. So the survivors gathered, limped, dragged, or wheeled in. Even Rocket was there, carried by a nurse in a sling like a baby.

The war room looked like an ICU. Blankets on the chairs, IVs run into arms and legs, oxygen tanks for the worst of us. Bronc presided at the head, face gaunt but alive. Juliet beside him, pale and shaking but with the same iron in her spine as ever.

When I walked in, the room went still.

I pulled Parker with me, not caring who saw.

Bronc's eyes narrowed, then softened. "Sit," he said. "We need to talk."

I did. The chair felt like a punishment, but I'd earned it.

He looked at Parker. "Tell us what happened after they took you."

She took a steadying breath. "I woke up in a room at the Greenbriar compound in Clovis. Apparently, they relocated everything and everyone there. I was chained to a bed. Silas was in the room, and he told me about the toxin and that I had been given the antidote. He said that everyone here would be dead in a few days. He showed me the case that held the vials and that he'd gotten them from Maltraz. He'd left me alone for a while, and I managed to slip the cuffs. I waited for him to come back. Don't know if he was watching me by camera or what, but he came in with his gun drawn. I hit him, and the gun went under the bed. I went under after it. He looked under the bed, and I took the opportunity to put a bullet in his head. Silas is dead. I also managed to kill two of his bodyguards. But I didn't see Vex, Rook, or Dagger. Those are his main officers. They're still out there."

"Holy shit. Thank you Parker. Sounds like you cut off the head of the snake. That leaves the body, and we know that with Greenbriar there is always someone waiting to sew another head right back on it. Maltraz is a different matter altogether. I think, for him, he saw an opportunity. Greenbriar has to be the priority."

No one argued.

"Doc says we're through the worst," Bronc said. "But if we don't answer this, they'll be back. I need ideas."

Gunner groaned, "They might have vampire help too."

Arsenal, from his wheelchair: "I say Greenbriar first. Then we'll deal with the other parasites later."

"Agreed. We don't wait," I said. "We take the fight to them. But we do it smart. Not like last time. Not a head-on charge. We bait the trap, and when they come, we finish it. We wipe out everyone in leadership. And their pack?"

Bronc contemplated. "Damn it. They are likely innocent. Just because you're born into a shitty pack doesn't make you a shitty wolf. Or maybe it does. I don't like the idea of a wholesale massacre. That's not who we are."

I spoke up. "Well, they're in the West King's territory now. Slade Stewart can pick up the pieces."

Bronc's grin was mean. "Shit, that'll endear Iron Valor to another territory. I doubt they've even registered their presence, much less pledged fealty to Stewart. Maybe after we take down Greenbriar leadership, we can see if Rafe can make contact to let Stewart know that a pack in his territory tried to genocide the south's strongest pack. That should get Stewart off his ass to get the remnants handled."

Menace offered to send his healer and her team to help everyone heal faster so we'd be healed and ready to face Greenbriar when they strike.

Bronc agreed. He adjourned the meeting with a wave. The pack filed out, with a plan in place.

CHAPTER 26

PARKER

It took forty minutes to peel the plastic from the new mattress. The box spring had arrived already dinged at one corner, but the driver dropped it on the porch like a ransom demand, and I had to drag it inside myself, sweating and cursing, a blood offering to the gods of moving day. Now the mattress loomed over the room like a cathedral step. The old one still reeked of bleach, ghost stains running the length of the thing, but Doc had insisted, so here I was, wrangling two-hundred-dollar sheets onto a slab of engineered foam.

Wrecker's room, our room now, always looked wrong in daylight. The windows faced north, so even at noon the light skulked in like a thief, pale and watery, just enough to outline the shapes of his things and mine jostling for territory. Motorcycle magazines fought for space with my dog-eared paperbacks. His battered boots stood sentinel in the closet, next to my pile of "nice" shoes that mostly went unworn. The room was painted gray, a compromise between "masculine" and "not quite feminine," but it only made the shadows more solid, a deeper blackness at the corners of the ceiling.

I made the bed, pulling the fitted sheet tight, then folding the top corners under with the precision of a funeral director. The blankets went next, then the comforter and pillows—three for him, two for me. The air was heavy, humid with the tang of latex and lingering Clorox. I opened a window and let the cold in, the wind so strong it shook the glass in the frame.

For a second, I thought about nothing at all. That was rare.

After the Greenbriar escape, after the shot of demon toxin and the blue-white fever, after the hallucinations and the days of bone-deep agony, the world had collapsed down to a small, hard core: the bed, the sheets, the cool air, the sound of the wind. I'd nearly died, or *had* died, more than once, and yet here I was, elbows deep in domestic chores, dreaming about the future.

I'd never thought much about angels or miracles—if I believed in things like that. But the explosion that sent me to my mother, where I saw her, standing by the lemon tree in our backyard—that seemed kind of like a miracle. I felt her brush my hair back and tell me it wasn't my time yet. The circular scar behind my right ear, from where they checked on my brain swelling, still has a faint glow. *That* was definitely something. The doctors said it was nothing; a side effect of head trauma. The truth was, it hummed every time I thought about her, or about the angel Archon, or about the impossible fact that Menace and I had both walked back out of the darkness when we should've stayed dead.

Call it fate or luck, or pure animal stubbornness. Call it what you want. I called it the angel's mark, and when I pressed my hand to it, I felt something alive, like the wings of a moth fluttering just under the skin.

Rocket jolted me from my musings. My ugly little dog, who'd almost kicked it during the worst of the toxin, limped in on three legs with the fourth still bandaged, tongue lolling, eyes wild with joy and confusion. He ran full-tilt into the side of the bed, rebounded, and launched himself up next to me, scattering pillows everywhere.

I sat stunned for a second. I watched him circle, digging and turning, barking at nothing. He looked like hell—fur half-matted, scars running down his flank, the stink of hospital still all over him. He was perfect. I scooped him up, crushed him to my chest, and let the tears come.

"Hey, buddy," I whispered, running my fingers through his matted fur. "You did it. You made it." He licked my nose, then my chin, then howled like a coyote at the ceiling. I laughed until I hiccuped. My body still hurt in a dozen places, but my heart ached in a good way, a clean and tired way.

Rocket squirmed until I let him go. He patrolled the perimeter, sniffed at the closet, then came back and wedged himself against my hip, daring me to move him.

The house was quiet for once. No pounding boots, no raised voices echoed from the hallway. Just the wind outside and the sound of Rocket's breathing, snorty and irregular, like he was still learning how to use his own lungs.

I sat on the edge of the bed, one hand buried in Rocket's fur, and let myself go blank.

I felt him before I saw him. He filled the doorway, casually leaning against the jamb. My beautiful monster. Deadly and magnificent. He said nothing as he crossed the room. He just opened his arms, and I went to him like water poured into a gutter—inevitable, easy, desperate. I jumped into his arms, trusting he was strong enough to hold me. Clung to his neck, legs straddling his waist, nose pressed into the place where his shoulder met his throat. I inhaled him; salt and sweat, oak and citrus scent radiating from his skin. I trembled against him, unable to stop, and he stroked my back in small circles. He turned and sat on the bed.

The first kiss was an accident, a misfire; I meant to say his name, but our lips collided and it broke something between us. His hands tightened on my waist, then he kissed me like he needed to inhale me or else choke. I bit his lip, tasted copper, and he groaned, and the sound pierced through my body.

He twisted us down onto the mattress, the clean cotton wrinkling under our weight. His body was heavy, but not crushing—he bracketed himself over me, forearms locked to keep his weight from hurting me, but I wanted all of it. I wanted every bruise, every scar, every splinter of his presence to crush the part of me that had been hollowed out by Silas, by the drugs, by the blue light that marked me as something not quite human or wolf anymore.

I dug my nails into his back, hard. He hissed, but didn't flinch.

"Don't be gentle," I said, voice already ragged. "I can take it."

He pulled back to look at me, his eyes storm-gray, rimmed with the red of a man who hadn't slept in weeks. "You sure?" he whispered. "You're still healing. I thought—"

"So are you. I'm so fucking tired of being scared. Please."

He shuddered, jaw clenching so tight I could hear his molars grind. "Wren," he said, barely audible, "when you were gone—when I couldn't feel you in the bond—it was like someone ripped out my soul. I would have burned the world to bring you back."

I believed him. I closed my eyes and let that truth settle in the hollow behind my heart, where so much else had been scraped out.

He pressed his mouth to my collarbone, the bite just shy of bruising. He worshiped my skin as if mapping the return of a lost continent: lips to the hollow of my throat, the edge of my shoulder, down the line of my arm to the bandaged wrist. He traced the blue-tinged scar behind my ear with a trembling fingertip, and his breath hitched.

"Does it hurt?" he asked.

"Only when you stop touching me," I whispered.

He smiled, but it was more of a wound than a grin. "God, I missed your mouth."

"Then use it," I said, and pulled his face down to mine.

The second kiss was hungrier, less apologetic. Our teeth clashed, and I tasted blood again. I let him have my mouth, my tongue, my jaw. I let him bruise my lips until they went numb. His hands fisted the hem of my t-shirt and pulled it off in one smooth, violent motion, baring my chest to the light of evening.

His eyes went darker. He cupped my left breast, thumb grazing the nipple, and when I arched into him he growled—an actual, animal sound, low and dangerous. He took my breast into his mouth, sucking and biting until I twisted underneath him. Every touch sent sparks through my body, white-hot, pain-pleasure until I couldn't tell where one ended and the next began.

He worked his way down, kissing every inch as if to prove I was real. When he hit the line of my sweatpants, he paused.

"Let me," he said, voice thick.

I nodded, "please." He hooked his fingers in the waistband and pulled them down, slow, baring my thighs, my scars, my everything. He stared at me for a long moment, eyes flickering over the marks Silas left, the yellowed bruises. I'd put up one hell of a fight, even in my delirium.

He kissed the worst one, gentle, then laid his cheek against my hipbone.

"You're fucking perfect," he said. "I want to kill everyone who ever touched you."

I grasped his hair with my fingers, pulling him up to me. "I don't want to talk about them. Only you."

He got the message. He kissed down my stomach, then further, mouth hot and soft as he licked a line down the inside of my thigh. His tongue found my clit, slow and deliberate, and I arched up, hands clutching the comforter, breath leaving me in a single, shattered moan.

He was patient, but I wasn't. I clamped my thighs around his head, grinding against his mouth, and he let me. He devoured me, not with the practiced precision of a lover but with the ravenous, greedy want of a starving animal. I came once, maybe twice, before I could even process what was happening. It was rapture.

Every spasm was a fresh birth of something that had been dead too long.

He licked me through it, then kissed back up my body, pausing at every rib, every cut, every inch he could claim. I tried to reach for his sweatpants, to tear them down, but my hands were shaking too hard.

He laughed, soft. "Impatient little bird."

"Fuck me," I said, voice raw.

He obliged. He kicked off his pants, and when his cock sprang free, I almost laughed at how desperately I wanted it. I'd been dead, then alive again. And then on the brink of death once again only to be physically taken from him. Now I was alive and fucking starving, not just for sex but for proof of life evidenced by his body inside mine.

He lined himself up, tip brushing my entrance, and paused again.

"Look at me," he said.

I did. His eyes were luminous, glassy with the promise of tears he'd never admit to.

"Never leave me again," he said. "I can't breathe without you."

I reached up, traced the scar on his chin, the one that had appeared after he'd deployed his second time. "I won't. Not ever again." It was a vow.

He pressed in, slow but relentless, filling me until I couldn't tell where I ended and he began. The mate bond flared between us, a live wire under the skin. He moved, hard and deep, fucking me with a force that bordered on violence, but every thrust was a benediction, a prayer answered by the chorus of my own moans.

We fucked like we were the last two people alive. I wrapped my legs around his hips, as far as my legs could reach. He buried his face in my neck, biting hard enough to draw blood. I scratched his back, marking him as mine. Every time he whispered "little bird" or "mine," it shivered up my spine like an electric current.

A blue light lit his face faintly, or maybe it was just in my head, but when I came again it flashed behind my eyelids and for a moment, I thought I saw angels, wings and all.

He came with a howl, knot swelling inside me, and I clenched around him for everything he had. We stayed fused like that for minutes or hours, breathing together, letting the world fall away.

He pulled me into his arms and kissed the top of my head.

"You saved us," he said, voice breaking. "You saved me."

I didn't have words for the ache in my chest, the certainty that I would die a thousand times if it meant coming back to this.

So I just held him, and let the blue mark glow in the dark, a beacon for the living and the lost. I needed to ask Menace about it. To see if he saw it as well or had I tipped over into 'cuckoo for Coco Puffs' land?

We drifted off together, locked tight, the world outside already plotting how to tear us apart. But for now, for this one night, we were whole.

The new war room looked like what I imagined you'd see at the Pentagon. There were large LCD screens on the walls, and everyone's laptops glowed with blue light. Wrecker had all the latest tech networked to where nobody would be able to get past us again. The effect was surgical: you could see every cut, every bruise, every patch of skin gone sickly yellow from the aftermath of demon toxin.

Bronc sat at the head of the table, beard trimmed down to a fresh start, eyes weary, a signal that meant he hadn't slept, not really, since I'd put a bullet in Silas's skull. Juliet was at his right hand, a notepad in front of her and a fist knuckled tight against her mouth. Arsenal and Doc flanked the far side, both looking a little less worse for wear but pale nonetheless but upright. Gunner hunched at the end, hat low over his eyes, a thermos of something steaming cradled in both hands. Papa's chair was pushed back from the table; he watched the room, not the screen, his hands folded in his lap and his expression the definition of "grave."

Wrecker stood behind me. His hand was on my shoulder, thumb stroking the line of my collarbone, and I wanted to lean back and just stay there, let the world dissolve in the haze of his skin against mine. But the energy in the room was a live current, and it kept me upright, alert, wired in.

Menace and his team were still here. He would not leave until the Greenbriar matter was settled. This entire battle started with his sister Emma almost four years ago. It would end with his being part of its conclusion.

On the screen, two side-by-side windows: one map of the region with every town, strip club, and back road flagged in color, the other a spreadsheet I'd built, columns and rows for every known Greenbriar member, their family, every property and phone number ever connected to Silas. The map pulsed with red where the last three Greenbriar packs had been pinged—Clovis, Tulia outskirts, and a nowhere ranch just this side of the New Mexico border.

No one spoke for a long minute. The only sounds were the soft grind of Gunner's teeth and the low hum of the HV/AC system kicking on.

Bronc finally broke the silence, his voice a sandpaper rasp. "We know Silas is down. But we don't know who's in charge, or exactly how many of them are left. Wrecker, Parker—what's your take?"

I swallowed, feeling the weight of every eye in the room, then flicked my finger over the touchpad. "After Silas, their power structure is a hydra. No single heir. Dagger was always the brute, but I'd bet Vex is running logistics now. She's smarter, but she doesn't care about rules. Their communications went dark, then ramped up with dummy traffic to throw us off. If I'm right, they'll want to make a play fast before the Council steps in. Rook is their muscle, but he never had much to say. My money is on Dagger. He's an arrogant prick who is always looking for blood. My guess is they'd want to hit us while they think we're still down- two days, three days tops. They'll definitely be coming out of the Clovis compound. It seemed big, but I ran so fast I didn't really get a look around."

Wrecker squeezed my shoulder, the approval hot as whiskey. "I agree," he said. "They're likely thinking we took heavy losses from the toxin. Even if they know Parker got out with the antidote, which I don't know if they realized that. They probably have no idea how fast it would actually work."

Juliet nodded. "So we let them think we're half-dead. Spread some rumors, keep pack members indoors, make a show of quarantine. Although I am a little worried because we are in a weakened state."

Menace spoke up then. "My healer and her team lands here in 20 minutes as we discussed earlier. Their healing gifts go beyond the traditional. They can definitely help here."

Doc piped in, his voice more like the Doc I remembered: crisp, clinical, but edged with a new kind of determination. "I can vouch for her ability. I saw her work after Meance's unfortunate brush with the Grim Reaper. Of course, he had a little angel help too." Menace glanced at me at the mention of the angel. Doc continued, "We'll issue a public notice that the death toll is higher, and that the Alpha is in critical. Anyone with a mole in our system will buy it."

I gave a small half-wave. "I might be able to get a message to the inside. As much as I hate it, my asshole brother may still be there. I could give him a bullshit call. Tell him I'm scared because I was too late with the antidote. That people were still dying. That it looks like Bronc isn't going to make it, and the entire pack is unraveling. If he's still on their side, which I sadly think he is, he'll have them at our doorstep within hours. We can wipe them all out then. Including Axel." I added in a quiet voice. I felt Wrecker's fingers lightly rubbing my neck and mate mark, trying to send me all the love he could.

Bronc looked to Arsenal, whose only response was a flat stare and a single nod. "They're big enough cowards to try to finish what the toxin started."

"We could stage it," Arsenal said. "Leave the gates with a simple chain and lock. Make it look abandoned, but keep our shooters on standby. The minute they show, we cut them down."

"That's assuming they hit the compound," Gunner drawled, voice gone rougher than sand. "I'd take the kids instead. Pick off the weak and sick, then use them for leverage."

Juliet tensed, but Bronc just set his jaw. "Which means we need two layers. Parker, can you rig the cams to loop? Make them think we're here, even when we're not?"

I nodded. "Already done. The security feed is patched through a relay. We can make it look like there's a full house. But the network is porous. If they send someone physical, they'll figure it out."

Bronc nodded. "First thing is to secure civilians in the bunkers. We've got way more fighters than Greenbriar, always have. And since we have reinforcements from Rafe on standby, we've got more than enough men to handle the number they'll send. The four bunkers are plenty big for those who aren't warriors. We'll work on the quadrants we've always had in wartime. Papa, call quad leaders and have them start the evac. Bunkers should be ready to receive people. After the bombing, I had quad leaders inventory in case we had another emergency."

Wrecker grinned, teeth white in the flickering light. "Then we let them in. Get them in the kill box, then close the door."

Papa finally spoke, his voice low and calm. "This is all assuming Maltraz isn't playing his own game. If the demon wants to make a point, he'll show. He'll want an audience."

Arsenal took a gulp of coffee. "Let him come. I'll put one in his head, just like Parker did Silas."

Everyone else at the table grunted or muttered agreement.

Bronc stood. Even battered, he could fill a room with threat. "Good. We get one shot at this. Tomorrow morning, we go dark. No outgoing comms, no social. Only Parker and Doc are allowed through the firewall. When Menace's healers get here, we'll all get a little touch of magic to juice us up. Then we're underground until further notice."

He swept the room with his eyes. "We were on the brink of losing everything. We still lost more than was acceptable. I won't lose more. I want every able body armed and on the line. If Greenbriar comes, we finish it this time. No more mercy."

Gunner finally lifted his head, eyes shot with red but burning. "They'll come. And we'll meet 'em when they do."

"Fuckin' damn straight we will," Bronc said. He adjourned with a single finger point.

People filed out, most in silence. Only Doc lingered, packing up the medical reports, muttering about "sample runs" and "field tests." Arsenal waited at the door, gun already in hand, scanning the hallway like a soldier in a haunted house.

Wrecker stayed behind with me, his hand still on my shoulder.

I turned then to face him in the ghost-glow of the LCD. He looked at me like he could drink me in through his eyes, raw and wild and still a little afraid.

"You think it'll work?" I asked. My voice sounded smaller here, less like a hacker and more like a girl who had run out of options.

He bent down and kissed the top of my head. "If you're running the show, it will. You're the best of us."

The words caught me off guard. I wanted to deflect, to laugh it off, but instead I just nodded and pressed my cheek into his palm. "I don't want to lose anyone else," I said, not even sure if he heard it.

He did. "We won't," he promised, but there was something in his voice that made it sound like a prayer, not a vow. Then, he handed me my phone. "You wanna make that phone call now?"

"Shit. I think I need to."

CHAPTER 27

WRECKER

I handed Parker her phone. The thing felt heavier than it should in my palm. She took it with her thumb and index finger, delicate, surgical, as if it might detonate on touch. Her lips pressed together in a colorless line. She scrolled to Axel's number, then paused. For one solid heartbeat, I thought she'd change her mind and throw the phone straight through the war room window. She didn't. She called, and the line clicked to life with the sound of her own breathing, doubled by nerves and the phone's shitty compression.

The call went to voicemail the first time, but on the second, he picked up. "Yeah?" Axel's voice: nasal, impatient, even through the speaker. Parker took it off speaker and pressed it close, but I could still hear both sides of the conversation.

"Axel, it's me." Her voice was small, hollowed out with panic and fatigue. "Where the hell are you?"

"Why, you need money or something?" He tried for a laugh, but it came out like a crow choking on wire.

She took a breath that I could hear across the table. "No, I just—" A sob, raw and barely faked. "I came back. I tried to fix everything. It's too late. The antidote wasn't enough. Bronc—he's on a vent. Wrecker's barely alive. They put us all on lockdown. Everyone thinks I'm the one who brought this down."

"Gee, that's rough," he said, with the total lack of empathy of a man checking the weather for a city he'd never visit. "I told you not to go back there. Fucking told you, Parker. Iron Valor will always use you up."

"It's not like you gave me a choice." Her anger was an undercurrent, just enough to make it real for him. "They said you stole from them. That you put me in this position. But I lied for you, Axel. I fucking lied for you, and now—" She coughed, wet and ugly, like she'd learned to do from the ward full of sick wolves. "Just tell me what you want. What Dagger wants."

There was a shuffle on the line, like he'd moved to a quieter room. "You need to get out," he said. His voice dropped to a whisper. "Look, they're gonna finish you. Dagger is going full fucking psycho. Word is he wants to kill everyone, but you most of all, because they think you're the one who took out Silas."

I could see her jaw lock, the muscle twitching in her cheek. She didn't say that she'd known Silas was dead, or that she was the one who put him down. She let Axel fill the silence with his own noise.

"You think Dagger gives a shit about you?" Parker asked, her voice rising. "He's the one who sent you to steal in the first place. Or did you forget that?"

"Don't put this on me," Axel snapped, but he sounded more scared than mad now. "I did what I had to do. It was either that or end up in the river. You know how they play, Parker. No one survives long unless they're useful. You gotta get out. I mean it."

She pressed the phone so hard into her ear I could see the shell of it going white. "What are they planning?" She said, low and urgent. "Is it tonight?"

Axel hesitated. Then: "They want to hit the compound at dawn. They think the pack's too weak to fight back. Dagger's got a demon backing him now, too. And fucking vampires, but who knows with those fuckers? All I know is, if you don't leave Iron Valor territory, Dagger's gonna string you up outside the club. For real. You need to go, Parker."

She let herself break, just a little. "Where would I even go, Axel? You already burned every bridge we had. You're with Greenbriar now, so I'm sure you don't give a fuck, but there's nothing left for me out there. Nothing." She choked on it, and I wondered how much of the desperation was acting and how much was real.

"I never wanted this," Axel said, and for a moment he sounded like a brother who cared, before the gambling, the debts. "But you picked the wrong side. You always do."

She almost laughed. "I picked my family, asshole. You're the one who left."

Axel was silent a long moment. "Doesn't matter. If you're not out by dawn, you're dead. Dagger's got a death list, and you're at the top. He's calling himself Alpha now, by the way. Silas is gone, and nobody's contesting it. That's just how it is."

"Fine," she said. "When I hang up, I'll be gone. You can tell Dagger you did your brotherly duty." She paused, then in a softer voice: "Stay safe, Axel. If you can."

He hung up without a word.

Parker stared at the phone, her thumb still hovering over the screen. I waited for her to break, or scream, or do anything that wasn't just sit there and vibrate with rage. Instead, she set the phone down, picked up a pen, and scribbled something on the edge of the notepad: Dagger. Dawn. Possible demon help. Maybe vamps.

"You okay?" I asked, knowing it was a stupid question.

She didn't look at me. "It worked. He bought every word."

"Of course he did. He's never not fallen for you." I tried to make her smile. She didn't.

She shoved the notepad across the table at me. "Dawn. That's hours, Eli. We need to tell Bronc."

"We will," I said. I wanted to reach out, to touch her hand, but her energy was kinetic, dangerous, already pulling away. She was already gone, racing ahead to the next move.

I watched her walk out of the room, the little black dog limping after her. For a second, I envied the simplicity of the animal: it wanted only to be near her, to protect her, even if it cost everything.

I closed my eyes, tried to savor the moment: we had the intel, the trap was set, and all that was left was to make it through the morning alive.

I opened them again, and the war room was empty, save for me and the cold blue light.

I didn't trust dawn any more than I trusted fate.

But I'd walk through hell with her, if that's what it took.

We drove to Bronc's place with the heater blasting and Parker's hands buried in Rocket's fur, the air between us thick with the residual cold of her call with Axel. Even Rocket—usually thrilled at any car ride—sat with his head on her thigh, ears flattened like he sensed the storm brewing at the edge of the horizon.

Bronc's cabin was a massive timber house with a large front porch that spanned its entirety, on the highest point of the compound. A large wrought-iron pendant light hung over the front door making the house feel welcoming and warm. The yard was already ringed with security lights, the front porch swept clean, the window glass dark as a tombstone. There were six cars in the drive and two bikes on the walk, all the good guys accounted for. I parked by the curb. The grass was stiff and brown; the soil rutted—a sign of winter.

Parker paused before the door. I reached for her hand, and she let me, just for a second, before she pulled away to knock. It was Bronc who opened, blue eyes clearer than I'd seen in days, the silver streaks in his hair looking almost staged in the porch light.

"Come on in," he said, voice pitched low to keep the house calm. "Everyone's waiting."

Inside: Bronc, Juliet, Savannah, Menace, Papa. The air reeked of coffee, lemon, and the wet wool scent of nervous wolf. The women clustered on the sofa, Juliet with a notepad, Savannah curled around a mug, Menace perched on the armrest looking less like a wolf king and more like a disgraced quarterback. Papa sat in the corner, silent, hands steepled over a crossword.

I led Parker to the big oak table in the kitchen, the conference spot for anything too dire for the war room. The wood had knife marks and rings from a thousand bottles. Bronc slid into his usual seat at the head, Juliet scooted in beside him, and the rest of us scattered like chess pieces. Parker stood for a moment, eyes flicking to the window, then leaned against the counter, arms crossed. She looked like a prisoner giving her own testimony.

"Tell 'em," I said.

She did, voice sharp and precise: "Axel says Dagger's new Alpha. Greenbriar will hit at dawn. They're hoping we're too weak to fight. Dagger's got demon backing, maybe more. They're going to kill everyone, but me most of all, because they think I killed Silas. He said I should run."

Menace exhaled. "Classic move. If you're on the list, Parker girl, they're going to be coming hard."

Bronc leaned in. "So, at dawn?"

"That's what Axel said. He didn't know if there was a countdown, but he made it sound like they'd be ready as soon as they saw an opening. I painted the grimmest picture I could. Told him you were on a vent."

Bronc looked at her and grinned.

Juliet put her pen down. "Do we think Maltraz will show himself? Or is he still just sending minions?"

Menace snorted. "Demon's a coward. He'll never risk Council eyes on him. He likes to work the shadows and let the wolves tear each other apart. If anything, he'll send his right hand to supervise. Adramal. But even that would be a tremendous risk to him."

I remembered the demon from the last time: his suit, his teeth, his eyes like ground obsidian. "He'll just be waiting for the call when it's done," I said. "Pussy that he is. He'll let Dagger and the other sick fucks do the dirty work."

Savannah looked up, lips tight. "Do they have witches? Or vamps?"

Papa said, "If they did, we'd know by now. They'd want credit for it. Vamps don't work with wolves unless it's a suicide mission. And with the witches—most of them remember what happened the last time the packs tried to get them involved."

Parker spoke up. "I think vamps *could* be involved. I remember seeing three at one of the meetings I was required to attend. They didn't speak, but there was no doubt they were vamps. Axel mentioned them in passing also, but he didn't sound certain."

Juliet frowned. "Should we tell Kazimir? I think he'd want to know if Otero had some involvement. Especially if it involved harm to Iron Valor."

Bronc agreed. He picked up his phone and scrolled, then slid it across the table to Juliet. "Call him on speaker."

Juliet did. The phone rang twice, then picked up.

"Dobryy vecher." Kazimir's accent was thick, barely filtered by the transatlantic lag. "You call again, so this must be about the war."

Juliet let him know it was her and filled him in, reading Parker's notes straight from the pad.

Kazimir listened without interruption. Then, "Dagger is desperate. He has nothing to lose. I send your padruga Lucia and two enforcers tonight. They watch the perimeter. If any vampires interfere, we eat them for you. For free."

I could hear Lucia in the background, laughing. "We like to see good wolf fight. It is entertainment for us."

Juliet said, "Thanks, Kaz. We owe you."

He laughed. "You owe me nothing unless you want to kill Otero for me. I hate that prick."

Juliet said she'd pass it on. Then, before she hung up, Kazimir dropped his voice to a hush.

"Tell Parker: if she survives, she is always welcome in Philadelphia. Our hackers are lonely." Then the line went dead.

Menace grinned. "See? We have friends everywhere. They come in damn handy in a fight."

Bronc turned his attention to Parker. "You did good. We have the intel. Now we make the plan."

We spent the next hour running down every option, every weak spot, every route in and out. Gunner and Arsenal would man the gate with heavy weapons. Doc and Maddie had already moved the civilians into the storm bunkers with quad leaders. Menace and I would sweep the perimeter at midnight and again before dawn, looking for anything that didn't smell like us. Papa would coordinate in the war room, running comms through the new secure relays Parker built from scratch in her bedroom while she was still healing.

Parker stayed on the edge of the conversation, taking notes, occasionally correcting someone, but never quite joining the circle. I wanted to pull her in, to remind her this was still her pack, but she seemed determined to keep one foot out the door.

The plan settled like cement: We'd let Greenbriar in. Lure them toward the compound, then hit the kill box. If Adramal or another demon showed, we'd try to draw him into the old meat locker on the property, then collapse the structure with C-4. Thankfully, our munitions were kept separate from the clubhouse, so the bomb hadn't come near them. If it had, the explosion would have taken out half of Dairyville.

Then, as if on cue, the front door opened and in swept Pearl, her silver hair glowing in the kitchen lights. She wore a yellow sweater, carried a tray loaded with sweet rolls and a thermos of coffee. Maddie followed, her eyes dark but alive, clutching two huge boxes of medical supplies.

"Brought reinforcements," Pearl announced, as if her entrance had been scripted. She set the tray down on the table and began pouring coffee for everyone. Maddie set the boxes down on the island.

"You planning on starting a field hospital?" Bronc asked, with a little smile cracking the granite of his face.

"We already did," Maddie replied. "Doc's setting up cots in the old shed. Anyone who can hold a gun is on guard. The rest are locked down, per your order."

Pearl smiled at Parker, her eyes warm but tired. "You holding up okay, sweetheart?"

Parker managed a nod. "Just ready to be done with this."

Pearl's look was all sympathy, but she didn't push.

We were halfway through another strategy run when a new car pulled up in the drive—a blacked-out Charger, engine idling like a panther. Bronc's son, Tyler, home from deployment. He walked in with the loose stride of a man who's spent too much time in desert heat: tall, lean, haircut so fresh it looked like it still itched. He nodded to Bronc, hugged Pearl, shook hands around the table.

Then he saw me and Parker. He hesitated. His eyes, blue like his father's, narrowed at the sight of us together. Maybe he'd heard the stories, maybe not. It didn't matter.

He sat at the table, took in the maps and printouts. "So it's war again," he said, as if reading the weather report.

Bronc nodded. "That's the long and short of it."

Tyler looked at Parker. "You're the one who killed Silas?"

She met his gaze, flat and even. "I am."

He grinned. "Cool." Then he poured himself a mug of coffee and started reviewing the plan.

The rest of the night passed in fragments: people coming and going, the house filling with the ghosts of past battles and future casualties. Parker slipped outside just after dark, and I followed, the wind sharp on my face.

She stood on the porch, staring at the sky, arms tight around her ribs. I leaned against the rail beside her.

"Everything ready?" I asked.

She shrugged. "It's never ready. But it's close."

We stood there, listening to the wind rattle the storm windows, until the world felt calm again.

I wanted to tell her it would be all right, but I didn't believe in that kind of lie. Instead, I took her hand, and she let me.

Back inside, the lights burned all night, and the house was a beacon in the prairie dark.

We were barely healed, but for the first time in weeks, I felt something close to hope. We had the fiercest pack in the South. Hell, maybe in the entire country. Greenbriar was about to get a taste of the pain Iron Valor delivered.

Menace's healer—a coven witch named Claudia, maybe forty, half-patched hair and a voice like a pack-a-day smoke—worked through the house with a box of vials and a notebook. She wore latex gloves, which was funny, since all the Iron Valor guys had immune systems that laughed at bacteria and normally bled out toxins like beer through a shot glass. But she was thorough, checking temps and pupils, making each of us swig something clear and stinging from a conical flask. It tasted like vodka with notes of gasoline and sweet basil, but whatever was in it, it did the job. By the time Claudia hit me, I was back to normal—more or less.

"You'll live," she said, pressing her thumb into my wrist until I flinched. "But if you see blue light again, call a doctor, not your local exorcist. That goes for all of you." Her accent was somewhere between rural Wisconsin and straight-up witch. She moved to the next patient—Juliet, who grumbled but choked down the tonic, then wiped her mouth on her sleeve and grinned at me like a hyena.

The Iron Valor guys filtered in and out throughout the afternoon and early evening. Gunner first, still favoring his left side, but with that crazy look in his eye that said he'd been waiting for an excuse to shoot someone all week. Arsenal next, carrying a duffel with at least three illegal rifles poking out the top. Then Doc, who nodded at Claudia. Clearly he respected her ability despite what he called "witchy shit." They ended up comparing notes and swapping recipes for ten minutes before Bronc smacked the table with the flat of his palm and called the war council to order.

The kitchen was already full, so they moved to the big front room. The table was gone, replaced with a plywood slab on sawhorses, covered in maps, printouts, and a tray of mostly eaten sandwiches. Bronc stood at the head, arms folded, shoulders broad enough to block the lamp behind him. When he started talking, everyone shut up.

"Here's the play," he said, voice steady as an anchor. "We assume Greenbriar will send its main column through the south road at dawn. They're going to try to draw out anyone who is still healthy enough to fight. They won't expect a full fighting force. We'll put Arsenal and Gunner on the south line, with the heavy stuff. Tyler and the new guys will cover the west and east. Everyone else is on fallback in the compound, or on quick-reaction. If you're not a fighter, you're in the bunker. No exceptions. By the time they get off their first volleys, they'll know they're fucked."

He looked around the room, letting the weight of it drop. "If anyone from Greenbriar makes it past the perimeter, we cut them down. No mercy. They want to end us; we'll show them what that means."

Arsenal grinned. "Copy that."

"Questions?" Bronc asked.

Juliet raised her hand, mock-innocent. "What about the demon? Or Parker's brother? What if they try to double back or sneak in from the north?"

Bronc nodded to me. "Wrecker and Parker are on that. They'll be running the cams, the drones, and if Axel shows, they get first shot."

I wanted to say I hoped Axel would just run, that maybe he'd finally grown the backbone to cut and bail, but I doubted it. In my heart, I hoped he'd catch a bullet early, save Parker from having to see it.

Tyler, who'd been silent up to now, spoke: "What about the women and kids?"

"They're already in the storm bunker," Bronc said. "Armed and ready if anyone tries to breach. Maddie and Doc took them down earlier, and Menace's healer, too."

The room buzzed with low talk—banter, old jokes, a little gallows humor. I caught Parker leaning in close to Maddie, the two of them laughing at something on a phone screen. The sound hit me right in the chest, the same spot that used to ache when I thought about my real family. The old one.

As the night went on, the house shifted from war council to barracks. Juliet, Pearl, and Maddie turned the living room into a patchwork of blankets, sleeping bags, and couch cushions, so everyone could crash in the open together. It was an old Iron Valor ritual: before the worst battles, everyone packed into the same room, so you could see the faces you'd die for or live for, all in one sweep of the eyes.

The air was thick with breath and hope and old, unspoken fear. Some of the younger guys started a poker game on the corner of the plywood slab, betting cigarettes and loose cash. Gunner and Arsenal took apart rifles on the floor, metal clicking like teeth in the quiet. Menace stood at the window, one eye on the road, the other on the night. Savannah drifted between him and the kitchen, always in his orbit, always ready. For a princess, she was as tough as they came.

I found a spot at the edge of the blankets, Parker curled against my side. Rocket wedged himself between us, snoring like a freight train. I ran my hand through her hair, found the spot behind her ear where the angel's mark still glowed faintly in the dark.

"You nervous?" I asked.

She shook her head. "Not as much as I should be."

"Good. You'll need that tomorrow."

She kissed my jaw, then burrowed closer. "If we get through this, I want to go away for a while," she whispered. "Like, the ocean. Or the mountains."

"Deal," I said. "Wherever you want."

The lights went low. The last sound before sleep was Pearl telling a dirty joke to Juliet, both of them cackling. I closed my eyes, the warmth of the room wrapping around me. Tomorrow, the nightmare might finally be over.

Or it might just be the beginning. But tonight, I had my pack, my girl, and a reason to live.

It was maybe more than I deserved. And certainly more than I thought I'd ever have.

CHAPTER 28

PARKER

The world after midnight is always stranger than the world before. The lines between possible and impossible blur. At 2:01 a.m., the sound of a twin-engine jet cut through the sleeping calm of Dairyville like an autopsy blade. The pack's private airstrip—just a flattened stripe on the plain, lit by two arc lamps and a dented pickup with its brights on—catered only to the very rich, or the very desperate. Tonight, I was sure, we'd get both.

Fifteen minutes later, Bronc blew through the door, bringing the night in with him and something colder still. Everyone on the floor was awake and alert at the new arrival. Lucia Kozlov looked like she always did. Black curls perfectly in place. Tonight piled on top of her head. Red lips, perfectly glossy, and big dark eyes lined with that cat eye look. The daughter of the eastern Vampire King had the kind of beauty that made you forget what species she was. Her bodysuit was black, seamless, except for the blood-red sports bra visible under the mesh panels, and on her feet were Louboutin tennis shoes—yes, apparently those existed, and yes, she wore them like they were as ordinary as flip-flops.

Lucia's entourage was three vampire men who could have doubled as nightclub bouncers or professional wrestlers. I didn't get a good look at their faces, only the moving bulk of muscle and the glossy sheen of their skin in the hallway light. They didn't try to sit at the kitchen table, just stood against the wall with the stillness that was more military than undead. Bronc gestured for Lucia to take his chair, the only one with an actual backrest and armrests, but she demurred with a little wave of her hand and a honeyed Russian, "Please, I like floor."

She meant it too. Lucia Kozlov, vampire royalty, settled cross-legged among a scatter of blankets and sleeping bags, smack between Gunner and Maddie, and accepted a mug of Bronc's burnt coffee like she'd done this a thousand times. Her legs folded perfectly. Her back never touched the wall.

She scanned the room as if cataloguing us for later, her attention sweeping the pack's tired, battered faces. She found Juliet, and something in Lucia's entire posture melted—her entire persona softened, sharpness replaced by a curve of genuine affection. She smiled at Juliet, a smile without teeth, and reached over to squeeze her arm.

I watched the interaction, trying to place the feeling in my chest. It wasn't jealousy, or even suspicion. It was just...otherness. Lucia was here to help, and you could see in the way her eyes slid past the rest of us that the only one who really existed to her was Juliet. The pack, for Lucia, was just a necessary background. Only Juliet was in focus.

Bronc used the opportunity to go over things again, wasting no time on the endless posturing and banter that usually accompanied supernatural guest arrivals. "We have a three-hour window. After that, we expect contact. Parker's mapped the routes, but we're assuming infiltration by at least two teams—one wolves, one other. Maltraz is backing them."

Lucia sipped her coffee, wrinkled her nose with the polite disgust of someone raised on finer things, then nodded. "We are ready. My men will patrol the northern edge of your territory. If the demon brings any vampires, we will know before they cross your line. We are very good at killing our own kind." She paused, letting that hang. "You have protocol for inviting us inside?"

Bronc nodded. "You're welcome here, all of you."

"We're happy to help," she said. She looked at me next, her eyes an uncanny violet in the fluorescent light. "You are hacker?"

I nodded. "I am."

"Good. We will need all your surveillance, if you have it. And your best weapons." She smiled again, this time a little wider, like she'd just received an especially clever Christmas present.

Wrecker tightened his arm around my waist, his muscles flexing. Rocket, our little ugly pooch, pressed against my shins, growling a low warning at the vampire men every time one of them exhaled too hard.

I watched Lucia as she watched Juliet, and I realized what I was actually seeing. Not just devotion, but adoration. I wondered if all vampires loved like that, or if it was just Lucia's curse. It made me shiver.

The rest of the meeting was logistics; the most boring kind of terror. Bronc walked Lucia through the security overlays and fallback points. She took it in with zero visible emotion, not even blinking at the mention of C-4 or thermal. Her men never moved, except to occasionally sync their phones with mine, eyes flicking over blueprints of the Iron Valor compound like they'd memorized the whole thing at a glance.

When Bronc was done, Lucia leaned in, lowered her voice to a register only wolves could hear. "We do not trust the demons," she said. "Their word is nothing. If you see the one called Adramal, do not try to kill him. Run. Call for us. He can only be killed by those who are not human, not wolf, not vampire."

Gunner snorted. "And what the hell is that supposed to mean?"

Lucia's lips twitched. "You have one already. She's sitting next to you. The other is sitting over there. She nodded toward Menace." He nodded at me.

Every eye in the room went to me. I stared back, caught between pride and nausea.

"I'm just a girl," I said.

Lucia laughed, a quick, genuine sound. "So was Pandora. So was Medea."

I didn't get the reference, and I wasn't about to ask. Instead, I pulled my knees up and circled my arms around them, resting my chin on the shelf they made. I looked at the circle of faces, some haggard, some hard, all of them lit by the same cheap LED and the blue haze from the kitchen clock.

I felt for the first time since my parents died that I was part of something worth protecting. Not because I was useful, or because someone would die if I failed, but because these people—my pack, my friends, my monstrous little dog—were all I had left. They were the only family that mattered.

Wrecker's hand found mine. His thumb traced the bones of my wrist. The mate bond hummed like a struck tuning fork. It was a lifeline, a wire through the darkness, and I clung to it.

The rest of the meeting blurred. Lucia exchanged numbers with me, then Juliet, her focus never wavering. The other vampires filed out, silent as falling snow. Bronc pulled Maddie aside for a whispered conversation, then turned her loose to relay instructions to the rest of the compound.

I curled back against Wrecker. Rocket worked himself deeper into the gap between us as if he was worried we might disappear. Around us, the rest of the pack sorted themselves out for a few hours' sleep.

Lucia curled herself into a ball on a thin black sleeping mat, her knees tucked up, hands folded under her head. She was the only one in the room who looked at peace.

I watched the entire scene—wolves, vampires, broken warriors, mates, settle into uneasy rest, and realized the thing twisting my stomach wasn't dread, or anger. It was belonging. I belonged here, with them.

My body ached with fatigue. The last thing I remember was the sound of Wrecker's breathing in my ear, the scratch of Rocket's claws on the hardwoods, and the faint throb of the mate bond lighting up my skin.

I let myself drift, hand curled protectively on my dog, the warmth of Wrecker at my back, and the knowledge that when this world ended, we'd end it together.

It was 4 a.m. when Wrecker shook me gently awake. Most of the house was dark, but the air vibrated with something more than caffeine or cold. I drank down a mug of black coffee, hands trembling with a little more than anticipation, then walked with him through the pre-dawn silence toward the main compound.

The snow had stopped, but the ground was covered, the ice creaking under our boots. Every light on the perimeter burned white and clean. I could smell gasoline from the generator house, and the faint, savory scent of the sausage biscuits Bronc insisted on as "breakfast of champions." I wasn't hungry. I was too wired.

I set up inside the war room. First, the comms panel: check, double-check, color-coded for Bronc's system. Then, the tablets—one for drone feeds, one for the security grid, one for remote patch-in to the backup servers that we'd stashed off-site. I lined them up like chess pieces on the large solid wood table. The tactile clicks of the keyboards, the soft beeps of systems coming online, were all the comfort I needed.

Pearl and Maddie arrived ten minutes later, Maddie still in pajama pants under her parka, Pearl in a butter-yellow sweater and the pearls that gave her name. Pearl's hair was pinned up, her makeup perfect, even at this hour. Maddie was all sleep-creased skin and wild hair, but her eyes were sharp as a hawk's.

"Showtime?" Pearl asked, taking the rolling chair at the monitor bank.

"Not quite," I said, "but close."

Maddie pulled her own seat up to the main comms desk, elbows on the table, waiting for instruction. She'd always been quick on the uptake, but she looked like she wanted to say something.

"You good?" I asked.

She nodded. "I'm." Then she took a deep breath. "Look, I never got to tell you that I think it was incredibly brave of you to run into this damn clubhouse thinking I was inside when you knew they were planning to blow it up. I know everything started because of the whole hacking thing." She looked down at her hands. "And I was mad at you at first. But when I heard about what your asshole brother had done to you. I thought about if someone had threatened Bronc, and what I'd do to save his life." Her eyes met mine. "I can't blame you for what you did. I'd probably have done the same thing. Your getting yourself blown to hell has nothing to do with my knowing what a good person you are."

I squeezed her arm. "I appreciate you saying that. I was still wrong in the way I'd handled things. I should have just come to Bronc. Hindsight and all. But we're here now, and maybe Iron Valor might get closure for what Greenbriar did to Emma Harding all those years ago."

She just nodded.

I started the system check: camera feeds, every quadrant. Gate 1—clear. Gate 2—clear. South fence, nothing. West approach, a tumbleweed drifted in the wind, but otherwise empty. I pinged each team leader by radio and got a quick status report in return.

Arsenal, up on the ridge: "Locked and loaded."

Gunner, covering the main gate: "Nothing but whiteout, boss."

Tyler, on the western perimeter: "Just the coyotes howling. Kinda pretty."

Each voice in my ear made the world a little more real, a little less like the nightmare of the past week.

Pearl, eyes never leaving the security monitors, said, "I heard Lucia's vamps had a run-in on the county road. Everything okay?"

"Yep. They shredded two Greenbriar scouts at the gas station just past the airport. Lucia says they're running clean now."

"Good," Pearl said. "Nothing ruins a plan like unexpected company."

Maddie yawned, then asked, "You nervous?"

I was, but I shook my head. "I'm good. I've seen what they're sending. It's nothing compared to what's in this room."

Maddie flashed a wolfy smile. "God, I love you, Parker."

"Save it for when we win," I said with a small smile.

I tapped the earbud, ran diagnostics, synced it to the primary channel. I tested the backup and then the private line that only reached Wrecker. He was already out in the sub-basement, prepping the remote explosives that were our last line of defense.

I checked the time: 5:00 a.m.

I ran the final systems check, hands flying over the keys. The muscle memory was perfect. I didn't have to think about it anymore; my body was wired for this.

Pearl watched me, eyes creased at the corners. "You're good at this, you know."

I shrugged. "I have to be. There's no one else."

She nodded, satisfied. "You ever think about what you'll do after?"

I blinked. The thought had never really occurred to me. "I don't know," I admitted. "Maybe get a real job. Maybe write a book about all of this."

Maddie snorted. "Better change the names."

Pearl smiled, then turned back to the monitor. "I'm glad you're with us, Parker."

I was too. But I couldn't say it out loud.

There was a beep: incoming alert. I snapped to it, eyes on the monitor, waiting for the first sign of motion.

Wrecker came back just then, his boots caked with mud and snow. He put a hand on my shoulder, and in that moment I felt the mate bond kick, a pulse of heat through the cold. He didn't say anything, just squeezed once, then let go.

"I'm ready," he said, voice so low only I could hear. "You?"

"Always," I said.

He nodded, then left again, heading to his assigned station outside the bunker.

The war room monitors glowed with promise or threat; every radio hummed with half a dozen voices. I could feel the tension in the air, electric and wild.

We were as ready as we'd ever be.

I sipped my coffee, let the caffeine burn a hole through the fear. My fingers hovered over the keys, waiting for the first sign of trouble.

And when it came, I'd be ready.

At 6:03 a.m., the first truck appeared on the southern feed. A U-Haul, the kind you'd rent to move your grandmother's couch, only this one had all the markings stripped, its windows painted over in flat-black. Two more trucks followed, then an old school bus with the roof cut low, its interior dark as a mausoleum. The lead vehicle crawled down the approach, twin beams panning the frozen road ahead. Nobody tried to be subtle.

I watched it all from the command seat, three screens aglow in a field of gray. My hands moved on autopilot: a finger flicked the drone cam to thermal, another dialed in the compound's perimeter grid, a third toggled the directional mics embedded along the main road. Pearl hovered behind me, a mug of tea cupped in both hands, her gaze soft but steady. Maddie chewed the end of a pencil, updating the call-in sheet as each contact hit the outer line.

"South quadrant," I said into the headset. "Three vehicles, two dozen bodies minimum. Arsenal, you got eyes?"

A second of static. Then Arsenal's voice: "Copy. Confirm three. Maybe more in the bus, but hard to see through the tints."

Gunner, a lazy drawl: "We're on the roof. Can take the tires anytime."

I shook my head, even though he couldn't see. "Hold for now. Let them stack up. I want a full house."

Pearl reached over, squeezed my wrist. "You're doing fine," she whispered.

I wished I believed her.

On the monitors, the lead truck braked hard, skidded in the frost, then rolled to a stop outside the front gate. The bus angled itself sideways, blocking the only clear exit. Five, six, ten wolves piled out of the U-Haul, each wearing the same dollar-store body armor and carrying a mix of handguns and rifles. I recognized Dagger first—his hair, his height, the way he barked orders and shoved the smaller men ahead. Rook followed, all muscle and dead-eyed focus, a wolf tank. Vex emerged last, her white-blond hair buzzed tight, face painted with black camo stripes. The rest were unknowns, but their posture was the same: tense, adrenal-ized, hungry.

Behind them, the bus doors hissed open. Out stepped the vampires, six in all, dressed in matching suits and gloves, hair slicked and faces sharp as knives. Their eyes scanned the terrain, slow and reptilian. I felt my skin crawl.

The last to arrive was the demon crew. I knew instantly. Even on the cameras, their silhouettes were wrong. Too tall, too thin, shadows pooling around their feet like oil. They stood apart from the others, unmoving. The biggest one—the leader, I guessed—wore a long coat and a smile that never reached his eyes.

They started up the road, slow and deliberate. I keyed the directional mic and listened in.

Dagger, loud and cocky: "Told you it'd be empty. They all bailed."

Vex: "Or they're waiting. Don't get cocky, D."

Dagger: "You calling me dumb?"

Vex: "No, I'm calling you dead if you don't pay attention."

They bickered, voices pitched low but mean. I let it play out, the background noise to the main event. Every so often, I'd catch Rook say "Quiet," and the rest would shut up for a beat. They were scared. Good.

As they reached the outer gate, I switched to the security cam at the entrance. The wolves fanned out, checking every angle. Dagger strutted up to the gate, rattled the chain, then grinned at the camera.

"Hey, Iron Valor! You in there?" he shouted, voice echoing.

I muted the audio. Maddie snickered. "What an asshole."

Pearl just shook her head. "They're almost cute, aren't they?"

I could have laughed, but my stomach was in knots. I punched up the map overlay, watching as dots representing the enemy moved into our kill zone. I called the next phase:

"Arsenal, Gunner: stand by for breach. Once they're all inside, we go hot."

Arsenal: "Roger that."

Gunner: "Waiting for your word, boss."

The vampires hung back, eyeing the demon crew and occasionally glancing up at the camera. One of them—tall, black hair, pretty in a way that was almost offensive—tilted his head and looked straight down the lens. I felt a little chill.

The demons never moved, not even when the wind picked up and started to peel the loose paint off the sign above the gate. They just watched.

Now the main pack of wolves, thirty or more, flooded out of the bus and formed up, all in loose clusters. Most were young. None looked like they wanted to be there.

And then I saw him. Axel. My twin, my blood, my first friend and last enemy. He wore a jacket two sizes too big, face gaunt and pale. His eyes, even at this distance, looked haunted.

He moved with the other wolves, slow and hesitant. He was near the back, head down. For a second, I thought he'd break ranks and run, but Rook barked something and Axel fell in line. My hands shook. I fought to keep my voice steady.

"Main force is thirty, maybe forty. Demons in the rear. Vampires at the tree line," I said into the mic.

Pearl put her hand on my shoulder. "You okay, Parker?"

I nodded. I wasn't, but I had to be.

The gate stood between them and the heart of Iron Valor. It was heavy steel, welded shut and wrapped in a logging chain. Dagger pulled out a bolt cutter, snapped the links like thread, and gestured the others through.

Now the trap was set. I keyed in the command: "On my mark, collapse the kill zone. Arsenal, Gunner, take high points. Juliet, you're up when they clear the second checkpoint."

Juliet's voice came back, calm and even: "Copy, standing by."

The tension was a living thing, crawling under my skin. On the feeds, the enemy poured into the open, spreading themselves thin, moving faster now, the anticipation bleeding into panic.

I watched Dagger and Vex argue at the edge of the compound. She pointed to the south tower, making a slicing motion across her throat. Dagger shook his head, then shoved her aside. Typical. The demon leader sauntered behind them, hands in his pockets, looking utterly unconcerned.

I scanned the faces, looking for a sign—any sign—that they knew what was about to happen. They didn't. Not a clue.

"Arsenal, Gunner: go," I said.

There was a flurry of motion on the roof cam, then the sharp pop of suppressed gunfire. The lead truck's tires exploded, the U-Haul sagging to the left. The wolves dove for cover. Vex rolled behind a boulder, cursing. Dagger hit the dirt, then started screaming at his men to return fire.

But there was nothing to shoot at. The compound was silent as a crypt.

I checked the drone: vampires and demons, still holding position, not even flinching. On the far end of the field, a lone figure moved through the shadows—Wrecker, running the side approach, setting charges at the fallback point.

I keyed the private channel. "You good?" I asked him.

"Perfect," he replied, voice a low rumble. "Just tell me when to blow it."

I glanced at the monitors. The kill zone was full. Every enemy was in the open, pinned down, with nowhere to run but forward or back.

I grinned. "Now."

Wrecker's voice: "With pleasure."

The charges lit the morning like lightning, a ripple of controlled fire running the length of the east wall. The ground trembled. Shards of rebar and debris ripped through the first rank of wolves. They scattered, howling, and the survivors fell straight into the crossfire from Arsenal and Gunner above.

It was chaos on the screen: bodies moving, some falling, some charging. Dagger and Vex regrouped, huddled with Rook behind the burning hulk of the U-Haul. I scanned the field for Axel, but he was gone, vanished into the mass of panic and blood.

In the war room, Pearl let out a sigh of relief. "Beautiful work, Parker."

Maddie high-fived me, her palm sweaty and shaking.

I took a breath, felt the mate bond hum in my chest. Wrecker's pulse, alive and sharp.

I watched the monitors as the enemy forces tried to pull back, only to find the way blocked. The vampires started moving in now, fangs bared and faces twisted in something like joy.

Dagger screamed at his men to hold, but the line broke almost immediately. The young wolves dropped their weapons and ran. Vex shot one of them in the back for cowardice.

I clicked over to the next phase. "Bronc, Juliet, you're up."

On the screen, Bronc, Juliet and their squad burst from the north wing, flanking the stragglers. Gunfire echoed. I felt every shot in my bones.

The demons? They didn't react. They just watched, smiling. I realized then that they weren't here to win. They were here to watch us suffer. It made my skin crawl.

In the chaos, I finally saw Axel running with three others, bleeding from the leg. He ducked behind the bus, eyes wild. For a moment, he looked right at the camera—at me. I didn't know what to feel. Rage, pity, love, grief. All of it.

I hit the general comm. "This is it, boys and girls. Bring it home."

The wolves of Iron Valor emerged from the hidden bunkers, weapons drawn, fangs bared. The fighting was close now, brutal and fast. Every second, Greenbriar's numbers thinned. My stomach twisted, but I kept calling the plays, kept the voices calm.

"North wing, you're clear. Juliet, take your group around to the south. Wrecker, close the east loop. Gunner, Arsenal, cover the stragglers."

The plan worked. It was merciless and efficient, and over in little more than an hour.

When it was done, the feed showed only bodies and broken vehicles, the ground slick with blood and burning rubber. The demons melted into the woods, gone. The vampires, all but one, lay dead or dying. Lucia and her men were relentless.

I slumped in the chair, every muscle shaking.

Pearl hugged me from behind, her arms warm and strong. "You did it," she said. "You did it, girl."

I watched the cameras, scanning for Axel. He was gone.

Wrecker called in, voice breathless: "You okay?"

"Yeah," I said. "You?"

Just then I saw movement from behind a barrier. Axel.

"Wrecker, behind you! Axel."

He turned in time to see my brother. I could hear Wrecker's voice crackle through my headset.

"Axel, if you want to live, put your gun down. It doesn't have to end like this."

Axel's head swung left and right as though he thought maybe there was someone coming to save him.

"How else is it supposed to end, man? We all gonna live happily ever after? My own fucking sister set us up, *again*."

Wrecker just shook his head. "You came here to help slaughter the pack who did everything for you and your sister when you lost your parents. That says way more about you than her."

Axel sneered. "Yeah, well, things worked out just great for me didn't they? If my life is shit, I think hers should be too. Here you go, Parker, cuz I know you're watching somewhere." He raised his gun to Wrecker's head.

At that moment, the world slowed to just the two of them. A shot rang out as a massive black wolf tackled Axel to the ground, ripping out his throat. My brother lay in a pool of blood, dead. Wrecker had been tackled to the ground. When he came back into camera view, he was standing with Menace by his side, and a very naked Bronc had joined them.

"WRECKER?"

I closed my eyes and waited for his voice.

"I'm here, Wren. I'm sorry." His voice was barely above a whisper.

"Don't be. I'm so glad Bronc and Menace were there."

It was over.

The world outside was silent, the sun rising over the smoldering remains of the last enemy who ever thought they could break us.

And I was still here.

Alive.

CHAPTER 29

WRECKER

Dawn cut through the kitchen window with the flat, expressionless light of a morgue. The clubhouse stank of blood and cordite and burnt plastic, and the HVAC system did nothing to cut the cold. I ran my hand down the side of my face, and it came back streaked with gray-black, which could have been soot or the dried remains of someone who used to have a name. The comms hissed low, waiting for the next alert, but no one had the energy to even hope for trouble.

We'd taken the field and held it. Our plan had worked perfectly. The bodies of Greenbriar's last line—Dagger, Vex, Rook—were still cooling by the compound gate, tangled in a pile of their own limbs like trash after a tornado. They'd tried to run, but Arsenal's shooting had cut them down before they'd made the first tree line. There was a weird symmetry in it, the three of them together, mouths open in the same shocked O, staring up at the gray morning like they couldn't believe it was over.

Inside, the war room, the air felt like relief. Every chair was taken, most by people who looked exhausted. Pearl was doling out food and whiskey, hugging every wolf who'd fought so bravely.

Maddie sat in the far corner, arms wrapped around her knees, head buried, rocking in time to her own heartbeat. Menace was up and moving, but every step looked like it was paid for in small, hard currency. He couldn't get to Savannah fast enough. Bronc had his arm around Juliet, who was the only one not drinking. She looked clear-eyed, bright, like the only person in the room still running on hope.

Parker took the comms table, headset clamped over her pink-highlighted hair, voice tight and clear as she ran the roll call. "Arsenal, status?"

A cough, then: "Still here. North ridge. It's quiet."

"Gunner?"

A pause. "South wall, present and accounted for. No movement since last sweep."

"Papa, check in."

Static. She waited.

"Papa, it's Parker. You copy?"

More static.

Juliet looked up, a tremor in her hands.

"Papa, come on. Respond."

I felt my gut twist. I set my coffee down and stood, pushing past a pair of patched-up prospects slumped in the hallway.

"Try again," Bronc said, voice soft.

"Papa, this is Parker. Please check in."

The silence went from annoying to terrifying.

I broke into a run, out the back door and into the yard. The snow had gone to slush, tinged red in patches where the wounded or the dying had crawled. I could see people gathering in the compound square, shoulders hunched and faces drawn. No one was talking. The sky had lightened to the color of old newsprint, and the first crows were already picking over the meat.

Pearl was there first, arms wrapped around her midsection, eyes scanning the horizon. Arsenal limped up, gun cradled in one arm. He didn't speak.

Menace emerged from the bunker, saw me, and shook his head. "He's not in there. He was supposed to be with Juliet in the east wing."

I keyed the mic on my jacket. "Parker, any location on Papa?"

A hesitation. "His GPS is down. The last ping was by the west perimeter two hours ago."

I jogged to the fence line, heart a snare drum. The path was churned mud, littered with shells and scorched by the fires from the last wave of fighting. The air tasted metallic, like coins held on the tongue. I ran to the first bend, then the next, scanning the ground for any sign of him.

A pair of prospects trailed behind me, but I barely registered them. I checked the drone feeds on my phone, fingers numb with cold. There was movement by the northwest sector—something big, collapsed near the tree line. I zoomed in, and my heart sank.

"Got him," I said. "Northwest edge, by the old cattle gate."

Arsenal and Menace followed, limping and cursing as we navigated the mess of downed fencing and debris. We rounded the last corner and saw him.

Big Papa was down, sprawled on his back, arms outstretched like he'd been nailed to a cross made of dirt and snow. The front of his shirt was black with blood, soaked through to the skin. There were bites on his arms, deep enough to show bone, and his face was battered, one eye swollen shut. He looked smaller than I remembered. For a man who'd once carried two full-grown wolves out of a burning house, he seemed impossibly diminished. Like someone had taken all that gentle, stubborn weight and wrung it dry.

Menace dropped to his knees, hands going to Papa's chest, pressing hard, desperate. "Hey, J.T. come on now, wake up."

Papa's eyes flickered. His mouth worked, trying to shape a word.

Arsenal stumbled forward, cradling Papa's head in his hands. He was crying, nose running, voice gone to mush. "Fuck. Fuck, don't do this, brother. Hold on, you big bastard. Just hold on."

Pearl and Parker arrived next, skidding to a stop. Pearl gasped, and I thought she might faint. Parker looked at me, then at Papa, then at her phone, like she could logic her way out of it.

Lucia, the vampire, materialized from the woods behind us. She wore a black coat with red piping and walked with the casual indifference of someone who'd seen this scene a thousand times. She knelt by Papa's side, and with a gentleness that belied her seeming indifference, placed two fingers to his throat.

"He is not dead," she said, glancing at the group. "But he is close."

Bronc and Juliet joined the circle, Bronc's breath coming ragged. He knelt beside him and took Papa's hand, the way you'd take the hand of a dying father. There was a moment where no one spoke, the only sound the distant caw of the birds and the low, painful sound that came from Bronc's chest.

Parker knelt, hands shaking. "Can you help him?" she asked Lucia.

Lucia shook her head. "The wound is not natural. Demon. It eats the soul before it kills the body."

Juliet knelt and took the other hand, murmuring a prayer in a fervent way I'd never heard before. Pearl just stared, tears streaming, unable to move or speak.

I looked at Menace and saw the ruin on his face. Even though Papa was the youngest of us, Menace had always looked up to him, saw him as a sort of moral center. Now the man was dying, and there was nothing any of us could do.

Menace pressed his forehead to Papa's, sobbing quietly. "Don't go," he whispered. "We still need you. I need you."

For a second, Papa's eyes fluttered open. He looked at each of us in turn, then tried to smile. The effect was more grimace than grin.

He tried to say something, but all that came out was a wet gurgle.

Arsenal bent low, whispered in his ear, "It's okay, brother. You can rest. We'll take it from here."

Papa's hand twitched, squeezed Bronc's once, then went slack.

The silence was total. For a moment, the world stopped.

Then, as if on cue, the wind picked up, and the crows started in, a hundred black shapes swirling over the tree line, hungry and merciless.

I closed Papa's eyes and stood, head spinning. I wanted to hit something, to destroy the world that had done this. Instead, I stared at my feet, felt the blood soaking into my boots, and waited for someone to say anything that would make this less pointless.

No one did.

We all knew the price of war. But it never got easier.

We were still standing around the body when the air changed. The wind stopped, and the world dropped a degree colder, like the sun had blinked out for just a second. Then, from nowhere, a voice—soft, maybe even amused—cut through the silence.

"You know, I'm spending an awful lot of time with Iron Valor lately."

Everyone turned. At the edge of us stood a man in faded jeans, white t-shirt, and a brown Carhartt jacket, hands jammed in his pockets like he'd just wandered over from the next ranch. His hair was wild and snow white; his face both too young and too old to read. If you weren't looking right at him, you'd swear he wasn't there at all.

Archon Seraphael. The fucking angel.

Nobody moved. Even the wind seemed to hold its breath.

He sauntered over; we stepped back automatically. He knelt at Papa's side and pressed a palm to his bloody chest, head cocked as if listening for a tune only he could hear.

"Demon work," he said, glancing up at Bronc. "Nasty stuff. Eats at the heart, the faith, the soul, all at once."

Lucia, all business, said, "Can you fix it?"

The angel smiled at her, then at the rest of us. "I can. But it's best if you step back. I've learned the hard way it's best not to be too close when I get rid of filth."

We scattered, circling up like kids on the edge of a fistfight.

Seraphael bent close, mouth right above Papa's ear. "Hey, friend," he said, voice gentle. "You're not done yet. Let's put you back together."

He placed both hands flat on Papa's chest, eyes closed. There was a sensation of pressure, like the air had thickened, then a faint blue glow—barely there, more sensation than light. Papa's whole body arched off the ground, every muscle straining. Then he jerked once, and something horrible poured from his mouth.

It was smoke, but not. Black and greasy, it spilled out, puddled on the snow, and began to sink into the earth. As it did, it made a sound—a voice, maybe, or the echo of a howl—low and furious. "No," it said, deep enough to rattle your teeth. "NO."

The last of it vanished into the earth. The glow faded. Papa flopped back, limp and still, but a blush of color returned to his cheeks. He took a deep, shuddering breath, eyes fluttered, then fell shut again.

Seraphael sat back on his heels, blowing out a sigh. "He'll need rest," he said. "A lot of it. But the demon's gone. He'll come out the other side quite a warrior, I think. Which is a good thing. He'll be needed."

Bronc gaped at him, the way a man might stare at the first sunrise after a long night. "Thank you," he managed, voice barely above a whisper.

The angel grinned. "You're welcome. I've sort of become the unofficial supernatural consultant for the Southern Territories it seems. I'll bill you later." Then he looked over everyone. "Menace." He nodded in his direction. "Parker, nice to see you free of those chains." He winked at her. Fucking winked at her!

She gaped at him as if she wanted to say something but thought better of it.

Nobody laughed, but it eased the spell just enough that people started breathing again.

Menace helped Papa up, cradling his huge head in his lap. "He's alive," Menace said, disbelief soaking every word. "Just like that. He's alive."

Arsenal knelt next, wiped Papa's face with a sleeve. The big man's eyes cracked open, glazed but conscious. "Always told you I was hard to kill," Papa mumbled; his smile filled with implants was beautiful to everyone.

Seraphael looked at Bronc. "Maltraz has it out for you. He'll try again. You need to be ready."

Bronc nodded, all the Alpha gravity restored. "We'll do our best. You have my word."

"Good." The angel patted Papa's shoulder, then rose, stretching like he'd just finished mowing a lawn. "I'd stay, but you don't need me for what comes next." He dusted off his jeans and flashed a grin at the group. "Take care of each other. That's always the answer, even if nobody likes to admit it." Then he winked at me, turned, and vanished. Just...gone.

Nobody spoke for a while. The air seemed thinner, the light a little less sharp.

I pulled Parker aside. "Can't believe we got him back," I said. "That he's alive."

She looked at the limp figure, at the blood that still pooled under his shoulder, and covered her mouth with her hand before speaking. "Seems to be a lot of that going around." She said through tears.

I pulled her in for a hug. She let me, just for a second, before pulling away.

We got to work then. The day passed in a haze of labor: moving the dead, patching wounds, burning the last of the enemy in three separate fires. The air stank of it for hours, the greasy black smoke stretching all the way to the highway. The kids stayed in the bunkers until the worst was over. Pearl and Juliet made rounds with soup and soft words, binding up the wounded. We'd gotten away with just injuries—mostly minor. The more serious ones were good with Doc's help and natural wolf healing.

Bronc set up a command post at the dining room table, calling in debts, letting the other packs know we'd won. He asked Rafe to reach out to Slade Stewart, the Western king, and let him know there was a compound in Clovis that possibly had women and children wolves with no Alpha. They were his problem now.

By sundown, the compound was as clean as it could get. The scars would take longer. But for the first time in a year, I felt like we'd see another Christmas, maybe two. Maybe a dozen more.

I sat on the porch with Parker, our little scrappy dog between us, and watched the last of the sun drag itself under the world.

"We made it," she said, leaning her head on my shoulder.

"Together," I replied.

I wrapped my arm around her and pulled her close. The cold bit at my skin, but for once, it felt okay.

Inside, someone played music—old country, the kind you'd hear at a truck stop at 2 a.m. It was perfect.

We sat in the dark, and for the first time in a long time, we'd earned this small, battered piece of peace. We didn't know how long it would last, but we'd take what we could get.

The snow hadn't let up, but the world was brighter, anyway. By Christmas morning, the field outside the compound was criss-crossed with the tracks of wolves, kids, dogs, and the half-buried footprints of yesterday's nightmares. I woke early to the sound of Rocket barking. The ugly little beast was already tracking breakfast from the kitchen. I dressed in the dark, muscles aching, scars from the last battle all but healed. It felt good to get out and walk the perimeter just to breathe the crisp morning air.

Parker found me by the barn, strolling out in jeans and boots, hair wild from sleep. She looked at the fields with a strange peace, as if every horror of the last year had been ground down into so much mulch and left to freeze.

"Today's the day," she said, voice soft.

"Yeah," I said. "The Run."

The Christmas Toy Run. Every year, Iron Valor MC delivered presents to every kid in the county, human or shifter or anything in between. Before, it was just a couple of pickup trucks and a box of wrapped toys. It's grown every year until this year; it was a caravan—every truck, bike, and SUV the pack could cobble together, all loaded to the gills.

Pearl was at the civic center, marshaling her army of helpers. We had followed Menace and Savannah who had just pulled up to the civic center with a trailer filled with toys that had been delivered from the Midwest packs. Gunner and Arsenal sorted the gifts by age and gender, though Gunner had to keep shooing the little ones from sneaking early looks. Even Bronc's son Tyler, who was still home, was on wrapping duty, cursing his own lack of skill while Juliet patted him on the back.

"Don't worry, love," she said, watching his mangled ribbon job. "The kids care more about what's inside."

Pearl had baked enough cookies to choke a linebacker, and Maddie kept the cocoa flowing until every surface was sticky with sugar. The entire pack was there—every survivor, every child. Even Papa made an appearance, swaddled in a blanket and with Pearl fussing over him like a prize heifer.

The run itself was chaos. We lined up the cars, kids shrieking as the first truck honked the signal. The MC officers led the pack,

Harleys screaming down the roads. I loved the feel of Parker pressed against my back. Down the county roads, out to the trailer parks, through every dusty neighborhood in Dairyville, we delivered. Some families came to the doors in pajamas, others in full Sunday best. Every house, every handoff, was a victory. I watched the faces of the kids, some wolf, some not, and felt something in my chest break and knit together at the same time.

Parker ran the tech side, cross-referencing addresses and names to make sure no one got missed. She even rigged a drone to follow the procession, streaming footage to the clubhouse where the smallest kids—too sick to travel—could watch the parade in real time.

By the time we got back, the sun was high, and the snow was turning to slush. Pearl's Christmas dinner was already underway, the smells of ham and turkey and every imaginable pie filling the hall. The new clubhouse, built bigger than the one we'd lost, was brighter, and somehow more alive. I'd never seen it so full.

We ate at long tables. Nobody had to dress up, but Parker wore a red sweater and the boots I got her before everything went to hell, and for the first time since we'd reconnected, she didn't seem haunted by anything. She even smiled—really smiled—when I handed her the present I'd been holding since the second time I snuck into her house. When I was her stalker.

She opened it at the table, eyes wide. It was a locket—silver, with a blue stone in the center. Inside was a picture of her family, the old one, and a new photo we'd taken at our house, a selfie of me, her, and Rocket. She traced the edge with her finger, mouth trembling.

"I love it," she said. "Thank you."

I shrugged suddenly feeling choked up. "You're welcome, little bird."

She kissed me, quick and hard, and the entire table erupted in hoots and whistles.

After dinner, Bronc stood at the head of the room and raised a glass. He waited for silence, which took a while.

"We've lost a lot this year," he said. "Too many. But we're still here. And we're family. So tonight, we honor the ones who didn't make it, and we count every single blessing we've got. Including," he paused, eyes glinting, "the new ones on the way."

There was a ripple of laughter. Juliet, blushing, took his hand and held it up.

"Juliet and I are expecting," Bronc said, pride rumbling in his voice. "So I figure it's time we do the thing right. Next month, we'll have an official claiming. You're all invited."

The room cheered, clinking glasses, someone howling from the back.

And maybe it was the whiskey, or the way the light hit Parker's eyes, but I felt something spark under my ribs. I stood, glass in hand, and banged it against the table for attention.

Bronc grinned. "Wrecker wants the floor."

I cleared my throat. "If he's getting official, then I want to do the same." I turned to Parker, who suddenly looked mortified and delighted at once.

"I know we're weird, and broken, and I've probably ruined every surprise you ever hoped for, but..." I knelt beside her, feeling every eye in the place. "I'd like to spend the rest of my life with you, little bird. I know I've already claimed you, and you've already claimed me, but I'd like to make it official with a ceremony. What do you say? Can we make it official? Will you take my name?"

The room went dead quiet.

She stared at me, eyes huge, lips trembling.

"Yes," she said. Not loud, but with so much certainty I thought I might die from it. "Yes, Eli Leonard. I will."

Somewhere, someone started clapping, and it turned into a roar.

Parker hauled me up and kissed me hard, her hands in my hair, and this time there was nothing but joy.

I looked out at the crowd—my pack, my people, my family—and felt the mate bond burn through me like a fuse, wild and bright and endless.

For the first time, I didn't dread the future. I wanted it.

I held her tight, and in that moment, it was all I needed.

After everything, after all the killing and losing and almost dying, I finally had something to live for.

It was her. It had always been her.

And this time, I wasn't letting go.

EPILOGUE

BIG PAPA

The best part about being the Iron Valor's chaplain was never the Sunday services, and it sure as hell wasn't handholding the half-drunk prospects through their first come-to-Jesus talk. It was these moments, right before "church" officially started, when all the club officers crowded into the conference room, each man carrying his own brand of quiet.

We met every Monday, rain or shine, in a room that was too clean to belong to a biker compound and too battered to ever pass for professional. The table had gouges and burn marks, and every chair was a different height—Wrecker had sawed an inch off Gunner's chair legs as a joke two months back, and nobody had bothered to fix it.

This morning, the whole place smelled like burnt coffee, and the ghost of last night's pulled pork. Sunlight cut stripes through the shades, landing square on Bronc's knuckles where he sat at the head, frowning into his third cup of black.

Juliet had arrived early and put out donuts. She lingered by the window, arms folded, profile sharp as a scythe. Her mate had finally claimed her in a way that didn't let her out of his sight, but she still liked to haunt the perimeter, like a wolf circling the herd. That woman had been to the pits of hell and came out the other side stronger than steel; a Luna we proudly would die for.

Next to me sat Gunner, slouched back so far his boots nearly propped against the table. He nursed his coffee with two hands, eyes half-lidded and chin speckled with stubble, cowboy hat low on his head. The big Texan's voice was slow and syrupy, but the brain behind it was sharper than most gave him credit for.

Wrecker, our newly named VP, paced at the back, restless as ever. He ran a thumb along the edge of his patch, occasionally pausing to glare at his phone. There was a rumor he slept with it under his pillow, and I'd yet to see him go five minutes without checking it.

Doc had arrived late, as always, sliding into his seat with a nod and a tired smile. The man looked like he belonged at a university, not a biker club, but he fit here better than most. He'd been up all night with a broken arm and a birth; he had the exhaustion to prove it. He adjusted his black-framed glasses when he sat.

Arsenal had arrived first, as always, and sat patiently nursing his coffee.

Bronc waited until the last chair creaked before he spoke.

"Let's get this started," he said, voice dry as gravel. "Anyone wanna open with a prayer?"

A few snickers circled the table. I raised my hand. "Lord, grant us the patience to deal with each other, the wisdom to out-think our enemies, and the humor to get through whatever the hell dad joke Gunner throws at us this morning."

Gunner grinned and tipped his hat to us. "Amen."

The laughter died quick. Bronc set his cup down and steepled his fingers, the blue in his eyes gone hard and cold. "Rafe's called a Council. It'll happen in a few days. He's not letting any grass grow under this one. It's priority one."

Juliet let out a low sigh, her gaze shifting to the floor. She hated the politics of the packs, but it was her burden now, same as Bronc's, especially when it came to our territory king.

"What's his angle?" Wrecker asked, arms crossed. "He hasn't called one in ages."

"To get to the bottom of the Greenbriar attempted massacre," Doc said, tapping a finger against the table. "He wants to see if he can make Maltraz and Otero squirm. And to make sure nobody tries to come back on us for wiping out Greenbriar."

Gunner shifted forward. "We handled Greenbriar by the old rules. They poisoned our water—killed seven of our own, including a damn child. They came at us. We mopped the floor. I assume nobody is questioning our response."

Bronc met Gunner's stare. "He's gonna make damn sure nobody gets the chance. He's using our situation as leverage."

Wrecker grunted. "King Rafe doesn't breathe unless he can profit from it. So who's he aiming at?"

"Look, we know there is no love lost between Rafe and the demons," Bronc answered. "It's about the same with that vampire prick. Rafe wants to lay the water attack at their feet and force a formal alliance among shifters. There's no taking out those factions, but maybe that can be weakened or something. Shit, I don't know why Rafe does what Rafe does. But he's our king, and we gotta believe he'll stand up for us. Plus, Menace may be the Midwest king, but he's our king too. If it's possible to make them pay for the attack, they had a hand in, I'm all for it."

There was a beat of silence. My wolf, usually calm, bristled with the memory of the attack on our compound: the first death had been quick, the rest less so. We buried the child ourselves. When it came to payback, Iron Valor hadn't left a single Greenbriar standing.

"He's not wrong about the demons," I said, remembering how they'd attacked me in that field. They'd literally killed me and possessed my body. "I'd like them to pay for what they did to me."

I said with a shiver, then continued. "And they're getting bolder. Maltraz is trying to carve a route across New Mexico, and the vamps run supplies for him."

Juliet's lips twisted. "Supplies. You mean human cargo."

I nodded. "And witches. They're abducting the solitary ones anywhere they can nab 'em. The ones with real power."

Doc slid his hands into his hoodie, knuckles white. "How do we get ahead of it?"

Bronc flicked his gaze at me. "You and Wrecker and Parker take point on the research. Every move Maltraz or Otero's made in the last twelve months, I want it on my desk after the ceremony. Gunner, you're in charge of security at the compound. Have Tyler help with double patrols, all hours. Juliet, you coordinate with Pearl—if there's a threat to the young or the elders, I want them safe before anyone else knows there's danger."

He ran through the rest of the assignments, his voice never raising, but every word hammered into our skulls. If he told us to jump, we'd ask how high on the way up.

Wrecker set his mug down. "This all means we need to pull off the mating ceremony without a hitch. If there's trouble, it'll happen while the pack's focused on the party."

Juliet smirked. "Typical. We can't even have a mating night without plotting murder."

Bronc's face softened, just a hair. "Three weeks. It's happening. Whether Rafe's Council goes to shit or not."

Pearl breezed in through the side door, carrying a tray of fresh biscuits and a carafe that steamed like a volcano. She wore pearls around her neck and a look that could shush a hurricane.

"Y'all look like you're about to start a funeral instead of a wedding," she said, setting the tray down. "Eat. I need the bridegroom and his Luna alive, not plotting world domination on empty stomachs."

"Thank you, Ma," Bronc said, meaning it.

Pearl poured coffee for everyone, topping off my cup, black the way I liked it. She eyed the rest of us. "So, have you picked a cake yet, or are you planning on serving Little Debbies to 200 hungry wolves?"

Juliet raised an eyebrow. "You think I'm eating cake with this morning sickness? Not a chance."

Pearl winked. "You could at least taste it. There's a new bakery on the square, open just this morning. Owner's adorable. But she's definitely not human. And she's not wolf, either."

Gunner perked up. "She single?"

Pearl shot him a glare. "That's not what you should be asking, young man. But yes. Single. Runs the place solo, and rumor is she bakes a cinnamon roll so good it's practically illegal."

Gunner grinned. "I'll volunteer to be taster."

"No, you won't," Juliet said. "You're on security. Big Papa, you go."

It took me a second to realize she had told *me* to go. I blinked. "Why me?"

"Because you're the only one with a palate. And you're the only person I trust not to sleep with the baker before we've even hired her," Juliet said, deadpan.

Even Bronc cracked a smile. "She's right. You're the best we've got."

I tried to protest, but Pearl just patted my arm. "It's settled. Go around noon, be nice to her, and don't scare her off. She's new to Dairyville and looks like she's been through hell. You, of all people, should understand that, son."

The room dissolved into laughter and groans. I finished my coffee and watched the others file out, each to their assignments, their burdens stitched into the backs of their jackets. Bronc lingered a moment, giving me that measured, piercing look.

He nodded once, then left, boots thudding down the hall. I could hear Juliet scolding Wrecker in the hallway for not bringing

Parker, Gunner's laughter booming, and Pearl's voice trailing after her son like a prayer.

I stared at my empty cup, then out the window, where the wind was already picking up dust from the canyon and sending it across the empty plains. There was a wedding to plan, and a Council to survive, and a whole world of uncertainty that could be waiting to tear us apart.

And apparently, I had a cake to order.

I pushed to my feet, grabbed my jacket, and headed for the door. It was a long walk across the compound to my bike, and I needed the air to clear my head. The wind tasted like dry grass and pine; the sky already sharpening to blue.

The last thing Pearl had said played in my head: Be nice to her. I was nice to everyone. It's who I was. Don't know why I felt like I wanted to be *not* nice to this girl.

I'd try. But if she put raisins in the cinnamon rolls, we'd definitely have problems.

I decided to reserve judgement just like I wanted people to do with me.

The sun was just starting to bake the streets when I made it into Dairyville proper. My bike rumbled under me, stubborn and loud and comforting. The main square was buzzing: the hardware store's lights flickering, drug store clerk propping the door with her hip, a couple of ranch hands sipping coffee from to-go cups on the courthouse steps.

The bakery was impossible to miss. The yellow paint didn't just stand out; it shouted. Looked like somebody had poured a can of daylight over the old facade. On either side, the buildings were more subdued—hardware store to the left, hair salon to the right, both painted a tasteful gray and navy. The bakery blazed in the middle like a beacon of warmth.

I parked at the curb, killed the engine, and took a breath. There was a sweetness in the air that hit me even outside, something rich and golden, like the memory of Sunday mornings our housekeeper baking delicious treats my mom was too busy to be bothered with. My stomach gave a hopeful twitch. So did my wolf the moment I stepped through the door.

The bell above the entrance announced me with a happy little jingle. The sound was so at odds with the world I came from that it almost made me shiver. I squared my shoulders like I was looking for a fight, and stepped inside, boots leaving a dust mark on the freshly mopped tile.

It was bright in here. Sunlight pooled on every surface, bouncing off lemon-painted walls and glass display cases. The counters gleamed. There were several small tables, each with mismatched chairs, and the smell—God, the smell—was a full-bodied gut punch: vanilla, caramelizing sugar, a sharp drift of citrus that made my teeth ache. I wasn't sure if it was the pastries or the beauty standing at the counter.

There she was, five feet five inches of delicious curves and softness. She stood, back straight, hands folded on the counter, waiting as I took her in. Even from here, I could see her subtle nervousness. Her skin was pale as fresh milk, hair a black river of silk falling over one shoulder. Her eyes, like two emeralds, sharp, and assessing.

I knew before she opened her mouth or even smiled that she wasn't human. It was in the stillness of her hands, in the unnatural green of her eyes, and in the way her presence pressed against my chest. My wolf bristled, then settled, as if recognizing some ancient rule.

"Mornin'," she said, with a voice soft as air. Southern, maybe Savannah or Atlanta, with a sweetness I didn't want to trust. "Can I help you?"

I tried not to let the military training take over. I kept my voice easy. "Depends. You the new owner?"

She tilted slightly. "That's what the deed says," she affirmed. I wondered if she was using magic on me right then. Her voice had a definite, natural, magical lilt. "I'm Aspen."

Aspen. It suited her. Delicate but tough, the kind of name you give something that survives bad winters.

"Big Papa," I said, offering the club nickname out of habit. "I'm with Iron Valor."

Her eyes darted to my jacket, to the patch. She didn't flinch, but something in her posture shifted. "I heard about y'all. From the hardware guy. He said your club runs most of the town."

I shrugged. "We don't run it. We just keep things quiet."

She smiled, a quick flash of white teeth. "That's what people say right before they admit they run things."

My lips twitched. I liked her for all of three seconds. Then I caught a glint of a large leather-bound book on a shelf behind the counter. A grimoire. The reminder that she was a witch. I stiffened, old habits coming back.

"You're a witch," I blurted.

She blinked hard as though she had misheard. "Excuse me?"

I nodded toward the shelf. "That's a grimoire. You can't deny it."

A flush crawled up her neck, but she held my stare. "So what if I am?"

"I just like to know what I'm eating," I said, deadpan.

The friendly atmosphere I'd been enjoying had gone frosty. She looked at her hands, then back up. "You're here for the cake tasting."

I wondered if she was clairvoyant as well. "Mind reader, also?"

She rolled her eyes at me. "Pearl called this morning. She said you'd be coming."

Of course. Pearl never left anything to chance.

She gestured to a table. Yep, the charming beauty was all business now. "Sit. Let me just hop on my broom and fly back to the kitchen to get your samples."

I just stared at her for a minute.

"It's called sarcasm. Geez." She called over her shoulder as she walked back to the kitchen, unaware that the luscious sway of her hips was almost as intriguing as her personality.

I picked the chair that put my back to the wall. Old habit, again. She disappeared into the kitchen, and for a moment I just sat there, breathing in the sugar and butter and watching sunlight creep across the floor.

She came back with a wooden tray, four slices of cake on clean white plates, each with a tiny fork stuck in the side.

"Carrot, chocolate, strawberry, and lemon."

I glanced at the slices. The carrot was topped with a smear of cream cheese icing so white it glowed. The chocolate was almost black, dusted with something golden. The lemon wasn't fancy but was iced with some kind of fluffy icing and had a creamy curd-type filling.

I tried the carrot first. It was good. Too sweet for my taste, but the texture was right, and the frosting had that tang people liked.

The chocolate was dense, and rich, and bitter in a way I respected. She watched my every move, her eyes anxious and curious at the same time.

The strawberry was fresh, moist and full of flavor. The icing creamy.

Then I tried the lemon. The moment I did, the world just about stopped.

The cake was light, so delicate I barely tasted it before it melted away. But the flavor—it was sun-warmed, sharp, so perfectly balanced it nearly made me angry. And that acid bite hit right in the jaw.

I set the fork down.

She waited, holding her breath.

"What did you put in this?" I asked, almost accusing.

Her brows pinched together. "Lemon. Sugar. Eggs. Butter. Little bit of buttermilk, maybe."

"No magic?"

Her face closed up. Now she just looked hurt. "I promise you mister, if I had any discernible magical abilities, I likely wouldn't even know how to bake. Now, do you like the damn cakes or not?"

I tried to read her, but all I saw was exhaustion, and wounds that ran about as deep as the scars I carried. I knew that look. I'd seen it in the mirror off and on for years.

"I'm not judging," I said, voice softer now. "Wolves and witches don't usually mix. Experience makes me a little skeptical."

She laughed a sarcastic laugh. "Really? I wasn't aware of the ancient history between wolves and witches." She looked away, then back at me. "Someone told me the Iron Valor Pack was different. That I might be safe if I were to move here alone. Maybe they were mistaken?"

Shit. She looked so small and vulnerable. "I didn't mean anything by that. Iron Valor judges people strictly on their merit." I told her.

"Maybe you could have given me that courtesy before you threw out accusations." She attempted to glare at me. Cutest thing ever.

She was right. I came in here with a chip on my shoulder ready to judge her. "Again, my apologies."

I looked down at the cake, then up at her again. "You ever bake for two hundred?"

She blinked. "Two hundred?"

"We're doing a mating ceremony in three weeks. Might be more like two-twenty if the vampires show."

Her jaw dropped, just enough to be funny. "Vampires?"

I nodded. "They're friends of ours. You'll know them when you see them. Pale, overdressed, allergic to small talk."

She grinned, but it faded quick. "Who's ceremony?"

"Our Alpha and Luna," I said. "Pretty big deal. We need something good."

She was quiet for a moment, then said, "I can do it."

I believed her.

There was a pause, long enough for the clock over the counter to tick three times. I tried to picture her in this place, alone at dawn, mixing batter and humming to herself. I wondered if it made her happy, why she was here alone.

"What's your story?" I asked.

She raised an eyebrow. "You mean, why is a witch baking cakes in the middle of wolf country?"

"Something like that."

She looked at her hands, then out the window. "My mom died. Before she did, for some reason she bought me this place. Said it'd be safer here than with my coven. She actually told me to run. So I ran."

"Sorry about your mom. Why would you need to run from your coven? Thought they are usually your family."

"Thanks." She didn't say anything for a long time, then, "My entire coven always said I wasn't much of a witch. Treated me like garbage. Never called me by my name, just 'dud.' I could never do what the others did. Never reached the point to where my magic manifested. But my mother, who was the most powerful witch in our coven next to the Wyrdmother, taught me how to bake. Don't know if she knew what the future held or what, but here I am."

The last word trembled, and I saw it for what it was: a plea not to push any further.

I cleared my throat. "We'll take the lemon. It's delicious."

She tried to hide her smile. "That's the first real compliment I've had since I can't remember."

Her reaction to the praise hit me in the balls. "Well, you should get used to it."

She hesitated, then said, "What's your actual name, Big Papa?"

I considered lying, then thought better of it. "Jonas. But everyone calls me JT, or just Rice."

She nodded. "Nice to meet you, Jonas."

I looked at her again, really looked, and the urge to run had faded. There was an edge to her. She wore the look of someone who'd been through her own hell and survived it, same as I did.

"I'll send payment through Pearl," I said, standing.

She followed me to the door. "I'll make a small sample cake by tomorrow. Prefer a style? I can do fancy, but I like it simple."

"Simple's better," I said. "And Aspen?"

"Yeah?"

"Keep the magic to yourself. Most folks in Dairyville are human, and they don't like what they can't explain."

She nodded, but there was a spark of defiant humor in her eyes. "If I ever figure out how to make my magic work, I'll be sure to keep it under my witch's hat."

I smiled, despite myself. "See you around."

As I stepped outside, the sunlight hit me like a slap. My wolf grumbled inside, annoyed at how I'd handled her, like I should've been softer or at least less of an ass. Because I truly was mostly a nice guy.

I turned back. She was in the window, hands pressed around a coffee mug, looking after me like she half expected I'd vanish.

My wolf growled, deep and low, a wordless warning. Then he said the word that I'd already had rolling around in my brain and had been trying desperately to dismiss:

"Mate."

I started my bike, the engine snarling, and took off down Main. The taste of cake was still on my tongue. The girl was still in my head. This was something I didn't need right now with everything else that was on my plate. How could I explain it? I didn't know any examples of wolf and witch mated couples. Was this even a thing? Maybe I just hadn't been laid in so damn long my dick was just confused by the first new gorgeous flesh it had seen in forever.

"*NO, MATE.*"

"Alright. Calm the fuck down. Her flesh *is* gorgeous. You just want to sink your teeth into her."

Great. Now I'm arguing with my wolf. Life just keeps getting better and better. That little witch said she had no ability to use magic, but she sure as shit put a spell on me.

THANKS FOR READING

If you've reached this page, you've survived the emotional whirlwind of Wrecker—and I need a moment to catch my breath right there with you. Writing this story was like holding my heart in my hands, raw and trembling, as I navigated the jagged edges of life, death, and the tenacity of the human spirit. Editing it? Well, let's just say my tear-stained manuscript (and my bewildered dog, who kept nudging tissues my way) could tell you tales.

This book was born from moments that left me breathless: the crushing weight of near-loss, the fragile triumph of beating death, and the quiet, aching beauty of resilience. And that epilogue... Oh, I can't wait for Big Papa to find his happy ending too.

I'm just so blessed and grateful that y'all love these characters as much as I do and enjoy reading their stories as much as I love writing them.

Thank you, from the depths of my ink-stained soul, for reading. For feeling. For staying.

With endless gratitude,

Dex

P.S. If you ever need to debrief after any of my books, find me on my socials: Facebook (www.facebook.com/dexhavenauthor) Instagram (@authordexhaven) or Tiktok (@authordexhaven), or haunt my website (dexhavenauthor.com) for autographed copies of my books and other merch.

ALSO BY DEX

I f you loved Wrecker and somehow missed the other books in the Wolves of Iron Valor MC series, you need to read them all! There will be seven when the series is completed.

And if you're a fan of romantasy, my first series is a fun tale of an orphan from Texas who realizes she's actually not so much from Texas as she is from an entirely different realm. She's tasked with saving the realm from destruction by a power-hungry goddess. Along the way she meets her mate, a dreamy shadow-wielding vampire king, as well as a host of other fabulous creatures, including dragons, of course. Read the completed hot and steamy Kingdoms of Eldoria series **Claiming Starlight, Starlight & Luna Rising, and Starlight & Fire**, where you'll meet Olivia and Cade as well as the Dragonia and group of wonderful friends and family she comes to know and love. You'll find yourself on the edge of your seat with the heart-stopping action and needing a fan to cool yourself off as the steam heats up between several couples.

My Thanks

Having people I trust read what I write and give me honest feedback and catch mistakes before the book goes to the masses is so damn helpful. I'm lucky to have a couple of ladies willing to do this for me. And they do it just because they love my books and more than that; they are just good people. I want them to know how much I appreciate it. **Denise Pruitt**, and **Patti Kapusta**, my heartfelt thanks to both of you.

www.ingramcontent.com/pod-product-compliance
Lightning Source LLC
Chambersburg PA
CBHW071202100726
47908CB00002B/487